# THE JEFFERSON LEGACY

# THE JEFFERSON LEGACY

## NICK THACKER

# WAIT!

Have you read the first book in this series, *The Enigma Strain*?

You can certainly enjoy this book even without having read *The Enigma Strain*, but if you'd like to start from the very beginning and follow along in order, you can get *The Enigma Strain* FREE:

Just visit the link here and sign up!

# THE ARYAN AGENDA

## HARVEY BENNETT THRILLERS, BOOK 6

Want to read the next part of the adventure?
Click here to check out *The Aryan Agenda*.

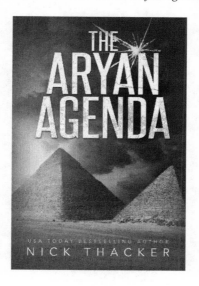

# ONE

**OCTOBER 11, 1809.**

*THERE'S NOT much time left.*

He *had* to make it. There was no other option, or the fate of the entire republic…

He didn't want to think about that. He shuddered, and not just because of the cool breeze of late fall that had descended upon the forested path.

Lucius kicked his horse's side urging it faster through the wind. The wind, it seemed, was his main antagonist tonight. Darkness had settled in hours ago, and yet even the darkness waned against the brisk wind, the two forces battling it out and making Lucius and his poor steed their pawn.

The moonlight from the waxing sliver wasn't much of an ally, offering nothing but thin wisps of light that were immediately consumed by the deeper shadows as he raced on.

Hohenwald was a mere four miles away, close enough he thought he could already smell the wood-burning stoves and ovens of late-night workmen and their families. It was an illusion, a smell burned into his mind from years of stoking a late-night blaze as the incantations began. It brought him back, to a time when this night was a mere speculation, nothing more than a dream and the barest of plans.

And yet he was still far enough that he knew the enemy was closer. They would reach the destination first, before he could alert their target. The target would be caught off guard, perhaps for the first time in a decade. Sleeping soundly, unassuming, the target would certainly be unable to rouse, fend off the attack, and eliminate the threat.

Lucius' orders still stood, however. He would ride.

He kicked his steed's sides again, but felt no increase in its speed. Instead of cursing, he sniffed a deep, sharp breath through his nostrils. The air hit the top of his palate and forced his eyes open. It was crisp, laced with the beautiful smell of pine and earth, yet it seemed to also carry the dismay of being too late. He was going too slow, and he wasn't going to make it in time. It wasn't the horse's fault, nor was it his own. The Society had sounded the alarm, yet it had taken over an hour to put a plan in place.

Over an hour for a plan that had *already* existed. This was the downside of government by committee, Lucius knew. This was the downside of not remaining lean and nimble. He had urged his leaders to make the call, and to do it with haste, but the time it had taken to gather and vote was going to be the difference between life and death.

It meant life or death for Lucius' target, certainly. Possibly for others, as well. Possibly for the nation itself.

Possibly for Lucius himself.

He gritted his teeth and dove forward over the final gentle crest that led into the village of Hohenwald. Nothing but a collection of small houses and a town square, the village wasn't even Lucius' destination. His target lay sleeping in an inn along the route to Hohenwald, just east of town. There the proprietor, Griner, operated the small establishment and sold whiskey to the Indians, whose land backed up to his property.

All of this had been in the report given to Lucius' leaders. They had mulled over it, and the greater mission, as if it had been the first time anyone had heard of such a thing. Lucius had stood by, calmly biding his time, until he knew they were running out of time. He couldn't understand why they were hesitant — didn't they understand that the fate of the nation was in their hands?

So he had set out, knowing that his target would be at Griner's Stand hours before he would arrive. Hours to wait, think, and ponder. Hours to wonder, and worry.

Hours to sleep, soundly or otherwise, until either Lucius or the enemy arrived, to seal the fate of the young nation once and for all.

# TWO

**OCTOBER 11, 1809.**

GRINER'S STAND was less than a half-mile away, and for the first time since Lucius had left, he could see it with his own eyes. No more speculation, no more running through the details in his mind's eye. He could see it, and he knew it was his final destination.

Griner's Stand sat on the edge of Indian territory, either by design — Griner himself was known as a high-quality moonshiner — or by accident. Perhaps Griner had hopes to use his proximity to argue against the Indians as the young nation continued to expand its own territory, or perhaps Griner was sympathetic to the native population.

None of that mattered to Lucius. His horse, beaten and sweaty, had slowed to a jog a quarter-mile ago and he hadn't tried to force it along. It had been a long, arduous journey, but the end was in sight.

The first of the matching cabins came into view to Lucius' left. The Natchez Trace that Lucius had been following descended downward again, heading toward a still out-of-sight river. The path wound around a few trees, admitting its inferiority to the age-old forest inhabitants.

The trees alone could attest to the age of this long stretch of road. They stood as silent sentinels for generations before even the game and wildlife used this intra-mountain route through the ridge. When the American Indians later explored and conquered the area, they assumed ownership of the route and further flattened it beneath their feet.

Today, Lucius had taken the same exact winding route through the forest, trusting the feet of previous generations to get him to his destination, and they had not let him down. The second of the right-angled cabins swung into view, separated by the narrow dog run between the buildings, and he could see the smaller kitchen building farther back on the land.

A lone horse had been tied to a post outside this second cabin, and Lucius knew it belonged to his target. The innkeeper maintained a small barn and a few horses elsewhere on the property, but there was no barn in Lucius' immediate view. The target must have arrived and tied up promptly, not bothering to house his mare for the night.

In his mind, the target was likely not concerned with bunking down tightly. The stay would be for less than a full night, coming in late and leaving early the next morning. Long enough to fulfill orders, and short enough that bedding down a horse for the night wasn't worth the trouble.

The horse neighed and scuffed in the distance. Lucius eyed it as he jogged his own horse in, trying to get a feel for the situation. He couldn't see much beyond the direct perimeter of the house; the Natchez wound down to the front of the first cabin and then back out through the trees, but it was hardly a large road. The weak moonlight did nothing to make the area feel more open, and Lucius suddenly felt himself strangely vulnerable.

He wanted to get inside, to stoke the fire in one of the cabins' chimneys, and take his boots off and rest. He wanted to throw his own steed's rope over the post and let it graze for the night while he slept, earning back the hours he'd spent with his eyes glued to the hard-packed dirt. He wanted to stretch out, his legs pulled back together for once in the past week, and just... be. He didn't want to play the role he had been playing for so long, since he had grown from a boy to a man to a man with a purpose.

But, like usual, he pushed those thoughts back down and ignored them. Self-discipline was a nasty habit, but it was a true habit. He had honed his perception of himself just as he had honed his perception of the world, and it had so far provided him with the edge he needed to ascend the ranks of his organization far faster than anyone his age.

Self-discipline was a virtue, he knew. Yet Lucius often felt it was a curse, burdening him with knowledge he didn't want to carry, with the lifestyle he never wanted to lead, and with the drive toward a goal he could never admit outside his closest circles.

He had led a life of depravity, of celibacy and singularity. A man intently focused on his sole purpose, never erring from the path of righteousness he knew would save the republic. He had bought it so long ago, when he was barely old enough to work the fields, but he wanted nothing more than to *not* have to work the fields.

He'd run away from home and joined the Society, promised by the leaders riches and importance the longer he committed to the cause.

Yet it hadn't been either the money or the status that he'd eventually committed to. He cared not for the social posterity or friendship circles he'd been brought into, and he certainly didn't want to be known for this or that in his local community, as others in the organization desired for themselves. And he didn't even care that to leave the organization, at his level, would mean death.

No, he hadn't stayed in the Society for any of those reasons. He had stayed because of a simple, unfortunate truth.

He had stayed because he *knew* the truth.

# THREE

**OCTOBER 11, 1809.**

LUCIUS FORCED HIS EYES OPEN again and guided his horse down the path that connected the Natchez Trace with Griner's cabins. It was a rocky, horrible trail, and he wondered if Griner had ever taken the time to maintain it. This was an estate likely devoid of slaves, so Lucius figured Griner or his wife would have been the ones to do it. Perhaps they had many visitors to keep them busy inside, or Griner's whiskey operation was doing far better than Lucius' report had indicated and they cared little for the integrity of their small estate.

Lucius made it to the tree line that marked off Griner's property and stopped. He sniffed the air again, an old trick a farm hand had taught him years ago. It didn't help much to know the smell of a place, but somehow sniffing the air forced his other senses to attention, ready to take in anything out of the ordinary.

He couldn't believe he was the only one here. He'd been *adamant* that there wouldn't be enough time, and his superiors had almost gotten angry with his argumentative tone. He had convinced himself that he was not going to be alone, or if he was, it would be because the enemy had beaten him here and the job was already finished.

There were no lights on to destroy the moonlight, and he could see clearly into the open area of Griner's Stand. The two cabins now dwarfed the circle of grass, but they were in turn dwarfed by the massive pines surrounding the property. He took in the details of the cabin. Nothing elaborate, just a simple utilitarian home with a replicate addition. Two matching buildings connected by a dog run, with a kitchen and barn behind. A small field, unplanted but tilled into rows. The barn, now in sight, barely larger than the cabins.

In all, a moderate estate for a family. Something that could provide a decent revenue stream if it were on a main route, like the Trace. It helped that it was known, both by locals and travelers. The Natchez Trace was one of the few routes that led from the North to the harbors and ports of faraway cities, and it was the only direct route.

Lucius had traveled along it before, but only once. His first impression had been somewhat of a disappointment. The underwhelming width of the trail made it difficult, if not impossible, to travel with more than a horse in some spots, and section of the route had been in such disrepair that he'd had to guide his horse through the trees to the side of the actual trail for a stretch.

Not to mention the banditry he'd encountered. He'd found two murdered bodies the first time, ditched along the side in a trench, their purses and good clothing removed and stolen. He'd felt disgusted and nearly carried on, ignoring the bodies, but dug the graves anyway and presided over the two funerals with the obligatory care and attention his organization had required.

Later on the route he'd come across a family — a man and woman and small child — who had been robbed and beaten. The child was near death, choking and coughing in the heavy winter air, and the father seemed nearly gone as well, but the mother had urged his help. He obliged, guiding them to a village he knew about to the west.

The Natchez was known for its villainous flair. Many vagabonds and castaways called the trail home, subsisting on the scraps they could take from more legitimate travelers. It was a nasty reality, and yet it still remained the quickest and most direct route, so it remained the most popular.

Lucius was about to advance onto the property when he sensed movement. Across from him, opposite side of the cabins. Not on the trail — whatever it was, they had come up behind the property and taken up a place like he had, watching. Waiting.

*Was it the enemy?*

He couldn't be sure. It could be an Indian, or it could be nothing more than an animal.

He crouched, knowing it was useless next to a horse that was utterly incapable of concealing itself. Lucius watched with well-trained eyes, timing the movements opposite himself.

The person — he was sure of it now — was watching as well, though he couldn't see their face. *Were they watching me, or were they watching the cabins?* They shifted on their feet once, tossing the cold off their body. That meant they didn't know they had been spotted.

Lucius reached into his belt for the knife he had packed, not wanting to retrieve the rifle from the horse's pack. It wasn't much of an offense, but if the enemy reached the front steps he knew he could throw it a good distance, likely sticking them in the back.

Not a clean attack, especially with the variable of the high winds, but it was all Lucius could hope for at the moment. He slid forward, inching along the ground on his knees, tightening his grip on the —

*Crack!*

The sound of a gunshot rang through the trees. He ducked instinctively, unsure where the blast had originated from. Lucius backed up a few inches, even rolling sideways slightly, but noticed that the horse hadn't moved. The gunshot hadn't fazed the animal, so Lucius was still in the clear.

*Then what had the shooter been aiming for?*

He squinted, trying to beg more moonlight into his eyes, but couldn't see anything beyond the darkened shadows of the enemy against his tree line and the outlines of the cabins themselves.

*Has it grown darker?*

Lucius waited, but didn't hear another shot. The enemy across from him hadn't moved. They both waited, a dark, silent standoff. Yet the shooter, a third person altogether, hadn't revealed themselves either.

He wondered if the target had woken upon hearing the shot. What were they thinking? Were they alarmed? Were they trying to defend themselves? Had the target been the one shooting? If so, at whom was the target shooting?

These questions plagued Lucius as he lay prone on the cold dirt, gripping his knife. He wanted to get the rifle, the weapon he knew would protect him from such a distance as this. Yet he didn't want to alert the enemy across the way that he was here, that he had arrived.

The enemy, however, started moving toward the house. Lucius gripped the knife tighter, watching the man's every step. He could tell it was a man's walk, the stretch of the legs and the careful yet forceful placement of each step. He was trying to be stealthy, to keep himself silent.

I was working. Lucius heard nothing as the man neared the porch of the second cabin. There was a door there, and the man stood in front of it, one hand on his side. On a pistol.

Lucius sat up, suddenly not caring about his being seen. The man on the porch didn't turn his head, but Lucius could almost feel the man gazing at him through his peripheral vision. He didn't move, and that fact terrified Lucius. He knew Lucius was there — Lucius had all but screamed his location when he'd sat up — but the man didn't care.

The man waited, and Lucius watched. *What is happening?*

Suddenly the door opened and a thin line of light spilled out onto the grassy land in front of the porch. A silhouette appeared — *the target?* — and pushed the door open more.

Still Lucius watched. He couldn't understand why the target — *his* target — would be conferring with the enemy. Especially after the gunshot, which *surely* originated from inside the cabin.

The man and the silhouette stood there a moment, as if deep in conversation, then Lucius saw the man outside the cabin nod. He stepped back, still facing the cabin, then turned fully and started toward the edge of the wood, where he'd come from. The silhouette pushed the door open farther and stepped out as well. In the briefest instant, in the faintest of light, Lucius could see who it was.

Or, rather, he could see who it *wasn't*.

The target was still inside, and this was a *second* enemy.

Lucius' blood ran cold, and he stood up and began to mount his horse as the second man walked the same path as the first and entered the woods.

# FOUR

THE AIR HELD THE CERTAIN emptiness and sharpness of near-winter, and Ben sucked it in like it was his last breath.

Harvey "Ben" Bennett had left his cabin half an hour before, shouting to whomever inside would listen that he needed some fresh air. The workers, with their unspoken hierarchy and silent back-and-forth orders he couldn't interpret had been smacking and banging hammers and driving screws all day, incessantly.

His fiancée, Juliette Richardson, had claimed busyness by working in the kitchen all morning and in the garden behind the cabin all afternoon. It was the waning months of summer, the last few weeks a garden was even possible in the remote Alaskan wilderness, and yet she had feigned interest in the project so believably the foreman on the job had turned to Ben to ask his input.

He hadn't *had* input, as usual. His 'input' was for everyone to leave him alone. To go home, wherever that was, and leave him and his perfect little cabin and his perfect little fiancée to their perfect little fall retreat.

He couldn't even remember what he'd told the foreman, but it had ended with something like, "I don't care, just do it."

A perfect way to give direction to a man paid by the hour.

He shook his head in frustration as he leveled off onto a trail he and Julie had pounded into the earth over months of hiking and exploring. They called this trail 'The East One,' because it was to the east of his property and they were both feeling uncreative at the time.

Harvey Bennett was a simple man, an ex-park ranger who enjoyed the wilderness, the wildlife, and the simple life of subsistence living. It was the absolute worst invasion of his ideal life to have a team of know-nothing contractors and hired help banging away on the cabin he'd called home for over two years.

Two years ago he'd found the listing, and not long after that he'd bought the place. Two years ago it was another man's property, now it was Ben's.

But to Ben it had existed forever as 'his' cabin, as if it had suddenly appeared one day in one piece, under the ownership of a Mr. Harvey Bennett, through a bank in Anchorage.

To Ben it was home, and to Ben it was perfect as it was.

Or, rather, as it *had been*.

The workers were trying to build an addition to the cabin, another set of three rooms, one of them larger than the current living room inside the cabin. Ben enjoyed the one-bedroom, 700-square-foot living space he and Julie had occupied together for the last year, but Julie had complained of not enough space. He had to admit, being a larger man himself, having a bit more room to stretch his legs would be nice, especially in the winter months.

But hiring a crew of men who had absolutely no idea what they were doing? Having them work from half-baked plans written up by what he assumed had been a kindergartner with an architectural degree? It seemed insane to Ben. He could do the work himself if they'd just trust him with a hammer.

And that, he figured, was the worst of it. He knew more than they did, and he'd know more than they all did, collectively, for a lifetime. He wanted to show them the tricks *he* knew, the things *he* had already tested that could save money.

But that was the rub. Ben wasn't in charge. He had signed away his little cabin — at least the 1,300 square feet that were in the process of being added — to a small company owned by a certain Mr. and Mrs. E. The company was 'small' in a sense that all of the major decisions were made by the proprietors, but it was very much *not* small in the sense of the capital it was able to put toward a renovation like the one taking place at Ben's.

This was one of the caveats of the deal he and Julie had made a few months ago. They had met with Mr and Mrs E, along with the rest of the new team that had been formed, in Colorado Springs after their return from Antarctica. Harvey, Julie, their friend Reggie, and Joshua Jefferson. Together they formed the Civilian Special Operations. The CSO, Mr. E had explained, was intended to 'bridge the gap' between the military and the civilian sector.

Chaired by each of them, as well as a member from each of the armed services, the goal was to provide a non-military solution to domestic and foreign problems that the United States might want solved. Problems that the military itself was unable to get involved in directly due to either political or resource reasons. Mr. E had not given them specific examples, but he had told them that the military heads of the CSO had envisioned a group that was not bound by the same rules of engagement, the same lines of funding, and the same prioritization of projects as the US military.

Ben had taken all of this to mean that Mr. E and his wife would be calling most of the shots, as he was the one who would be funding the group's endeavors. He would focus on the issues that were either not important to the government or had simply gone unnoticed. Ben wasn't exactly upset that the government wouldn't be strong-arming the group to take care of its interests first and foremost. He was an American, but he was an American who enjoyed his freedom — *including* freedom from overbearing government regulation.

So he was torn between enjoying this new chapter and trying to find the sanity and solace of being alone. When Julie had found him back at Yellowstone, he had spent his entire adult life as a ranger, opting for a life of solitude and simplicity.

Massive additions and gigantic work crews buzzing around his home were not his idea of simple and solitary.

He sighed, kicking a small rock off the path. The trail twisted around to the right, and he picked up his pace. He knew what was coming — a gentle slope to the left, over a few small boulders, and then a hop over a trickling feeder stream — and he was once again riveted back into the present.

Ben took the right turn and the immediate left bend with a fast jump in his step, realizing that the months of working out and training with his friend Reggie were starting to pay off. He had already lost twenty pounds, and he figured he had at least another twenty he could stand to shed. He wasn't interested in becoming a glistening hulk of a male specimen, but he had to admit Julie seemed a lot more interested in him lately. He could only assume it was related to the training regimen.

He barely let his feet hit each rock as he cleared the sloping path and landed on the other side of the stream. Ben's heart rate hadn't increased enough for this to be much of a workout, so he increased his pace again and started up the hill on the other side.

Reggie had taught him all about 'high-intensity interval training' and how it was supposed to be a great all-around strategy to working out, and that it could be used for just about any form of exercise. Ben decided to make this short walk a full-fledged workout, so he pulled out the humongous 'phablet' Julie had talked him into buying and opened a running app. He set his parameters and pressed the start button.

The ding seemed to ring through the trees and bounce back at him a thousand times, but all he needed to hear was the first one. He sprang into action and bolted upward over the last boulder on the hill. A narrow straightaway would be next, followed by another hill, this one a more shallow slope but a lot longer. Then he would be at the cabin once again.

It would be less than two minutes at this pace, but he knew it would be enough to get his heart rate up a dozen clicks. He breathed in another sharp early-fall breath, lifted his chin, and focused on his steps.

# FIVE

BEN HIT THE OPEN AREA behind the cabin and decided to keep going, heading out on the western trail for a bit. The western trail was longer, took a more circuitous route through the forest, but was flatter. It was a great running trail, even though Ben despised the idea of running.

Unless someone was chasing him, he preferred to stay in one place.

Today, however, he was feeling more inclined to work himself a bit harder. Maybe it was the season, maybe it was the thought of Reggie pushing him tomorrow at their next training session and Ben not being ready.

Or maybe it was just that Ben wanted to run away from all the insanity happening at his home.

He stopped, talking himself into a short break from his workout. He rested for a moment, letting his breath slip back into its normal rhythm.

He picked up the phone and pressed on the phone app, then scrolled through the numbers until he reached the one he wanted.

"Mr. E?" he asked.

"Speaking."

"I — sorry, it's Ben," he said, pausing.

"I know that, Mr. Bennett, these phones have Caller ID."

"Uh, right. Hey, so, I was thinking. This addition to the house. It's… it's a little…"

"Big?"

"Yes, exactly. It's big. Huge, in fact. I didn't really know what you had in mind, but this —"

"It is a bit larger than your existing infrastructure, I do admit," Mr. E said, "but I truly believe your mind will be changed when you see the completed renovation."

"I liked things the way they were," Ben said.

"Ah, yes, that is the Harvey Bennett I know. However, I assure you the renovation will be up to your *fine* standards."

Ben stopped. He looked around, taking in the pristine peace of the deep woods surrounding him. He wondered if this was really what his life had come to, arguing with a man he'd never met in person. It seemed like every other day the only peace he got was found in the massive stretch of trees and wilderness that separated him from normal civilization. He longed for nothing more than to take this walk every day, with Julie, not burdened by the pressures of his new job.

For the thousandth time in the last two months he wondered if he had made the right decision. Julie seemed enthralled by the idea of the CSO, but — as usual — Ben had been more reluctant.

"Your new role in the organization we are building is going to be a simple one, Mr. Bennett," the man said.

"Yeah, but it's one that I don't have control over."

"You can opt out of any of the assignments we will be giving you, Mr. Bennett. We told you that up front, and we told you that again in the contract."

"But Jules is always going to jump in headfirst. She's… you know…"

The man laughed. A weird, staccato thing that made Ben think the man on the other end of the phone had just pressed 'play' on a recording of a robot laughing. "Mrs. — I'm sorry —*Juliette* — is certainly a bull-headed woman, and one of great drive. But that is part of your attraction to her, is it not?"

"It's… I don't… yeah, I guess."

"And Juliette has assured me that you are more than willing to help us with our upcoming projects, no matter the nature of the assignment."

"She… said that?"

"Indeed. And as a matter of fact, we have one such assignment that might prove to be lucrative for the company. And for both of you. You called at an opportune time."

Ben had never in his life been attracted to money for money's sake, but the last few months seemed to have been working in him, changing him. He perked up, against his better judgement.

"What is the assignment?"

"Gareth and Joshua are returning from their engagement tomorrow, and they will deliver the assignment in person. They will receive the details tonight upon entering United States airspace once again, and I have scheduled them for a redirection to your estate immediately after they land."

"Geez, you aren't even going to let them hang out for an hour? Get a drink or anything?"

"Reggie will be flown by private jet to Anchorage, which will allow him ample time to rest and — if he so desires — engage in the debauchery you are implying. Joshua has an appointment in Anchorage that will cause him to be a bit later."

Ben started walking again, trying to piece things together. Over the last month, random workers had descended on his small and insignificant cabin in the wilderness, paid for and directed by a man he had never met in person to build out and finish an addition to the log home he had purchased two years ago. The same man had orchestrated the overthrowing and disbandment of a large corporation that had plagued Ben's life ever since he had been a park ranger at Yellowstone.

Now, the same man was bringing them all together for another mission.

# SIX

**OCTOBER 11, 1809.**

LUCIUS COULD HEAR THE GROANING as soon as he reached the porch. The 'porch,' really nothing more than a section of grass around the bottom step of the log cabin, was still damp with early dew and a late morning rainfall. He stepped up and entered the cabin.

The smell of a small fire, recently smothered, wafted to his nose, mixed with the smells of pine and leather. A glass of whiskey sat on a small rickety table on the opposite wall, and the bottle next to it. There was no label — probably a bit of Griner's moonshining work — but he could see through the deep amber of the bottle to see that it was half-empty.

Next to the table a pair of boots and a saddle sat on the bumpy floorboards, and beside that a packsaddle. A rifle leaned against the wall, nearly an exact replica of Lucius,' and beside that the wood-burning stove sat with its door open in the corner of the room. The corner adjacent to the wood-burning stove housed a small chair, on which was laid a few pistols, some ammunition, and a tomahawk. Next to the chair, on the floor, a spread of buffalo robes and bear skins. On the skins was Lucius' target.

The man lay still, barely breathing.

*But he* was *breathing.*

Lucius approached.

He watched, waiting for the man to see him. He wouldn't recognize Lucius, but he would know. He would understand what was happening, what was about to happen.

Lucius came to the chair and stood behind it — no need to put himself in any danger by underestimating the target — and looked down at the poor, dying man.

He would die, tonight. It wouldn't be long.

The target had a wound in his abdomen, and he was holding his side with his hands. The breaths were steadily pumping, but they were sporadic in their amounts of air. Sometimes heaving, sometimes pitiful, they came, one after the other, over and over again.

Lucius was mesmerized by the man's breathing. How it must feel, he thought, to be dying of such a wound. He'd always admired those who had died of a gunshot wound. A horrible, horrible thing to admire, yet his self-discipline had not yet been able to overcome that truth. He wanted to die like that, he knew. He wanted to be the one young children admired, long after he was gone.

This man, the one dying on the bed in a cabin he had been in only hours, would be admired long after he was gone. His life had ensured it, and his martyrdom would solidify it. There was nothing Lucius or anyone else could do to take that away.

There was, however, something the enemy could do to lessen the impact of the man's death, and Lucius feared they had already accomplished it.

For the first time in more than a day, Lucius spoke.

"Have they — have they asked you?"

The man's eyes opened. Not much, but enough. Lucius could see them, youthful in their nearly four decades of life, yet burdened with a massive weight.

*The weight of truth.*

He sputtered, a bit of blood pouring from his mouth.

Then he nodded.

"And I… and I have told them. As I always knew I would."

Lucius' head dropped, and the tears nearly fell from his eyes.

"No," he whispered. "It cannot be true. You — why would you have told them?"

The man on the bed heaved, the tempo of his breaths now growing more random.

He coughed, and — to a stunned Lucius — seemed to smile.

"I could not… I could not bear the thought… of my… work."

Lucius waited, trying to understand the man's sentence. *Was there more? What was this man trying to say?*

"The thought of your work?"

"The thought of my work becoming… used for…"

Lucius nodded.

Neither man spoke for a minute, Lucius' eyes widening every time the man on the bed breathed. He wondered each time if it would be his last.

Finally the man looked up at him.

"You will... not prevail..."

Lucius shook his head. "No, sir, you are mistaken. We *will* prevail. The nation will live on. It will be resilient, like its founders were so many years ago. We will find those who share your secret, and we will ensure they do not spread it further."

Another cough, another smile.

"It's too late," the man said.

"It's never too late."

"For me... it is too late. I am not a coward..."

"You will not be remembered as one."

"...but I am so strong."

Lucius gripped the handle of his knife once more. The man on the bed stirred again, reaching beneath his side, his hand covered in his own blood. On the bed beneath the man's torso, Lucius saw the glint of cold steel.

*I am unarmed but for this knife*, he realized.

The man looked up at Lucius through one open eye, his left hand wrapped around the pistol. He pulled it up, slowly. Meticulously. His hand was shaking.

Lucius withdrew the knife and held it out in front of him, making sure the man on the bed saw it and understood what it meant.

*You attack, I attack.*

It was a man's gesture, an intimate promise of respect and self-defense. He would allow this man to die with his pistol in hand, but if he turned the gun on Lucius...

The man pulled the gun to his own head, holding it there, shaking. Lucius dropped his hand to his side.

"...so hard... so hard to die..."

He pulled the trigger, and for the second time that night Lucius heard the blast but had no part in the battle. This time, at close range, Lucius nearly fell back at the deafening sound of the shot.

He recovered, gaining his balance once again, and strode toward the bed. A single, purposeful stride, bringing the knife up once again.

The man in the bed was writhing in agony, blood pouring from both his abdomen and his head. His hand, devoid of the gun, was seizing, shaking uncontrollably. His face was contorted in pain, his mouth flopping open and shut opposite the movement of his eyes.

Lucius squeezed his own eyes shut.

No man could live through this.

This, however, was no ordinary man. This man was a legend, a man among men, a hero to the young republic. He wouldn't go out without a fight.

"So… strong…"

Lucius could not believe the man was still alive, but alas, he lay writhing in the bed struggling with the invisible enemy he fought off to remain in this world and not travel silently to the next. Lucius was horrified, fascinated. In awe.

A great man lay before him, one he had come to kill. The target had been intercepted by Lucius' own enemy, and there would be much more work now if they hoped to keep the enemy from capitalizing on the secret. That his enemy had shot the target after they had stolen his secret was only a benefit to Lucius. The target must have known, and he must have prepared himself.

He must have realized it long ago, well before he had embarked on this trip. It was the only explanation. Why a man of his stature would lie still, four pistols, a tomahawk, and a rifle laying in his reach, would idly await his own assassination meant only one thing.

*He had known about it all along.*

He had not embarked on a journey to deliver his news to the leaders of the fledgling nation. He had not attempted a dangerous solo trip up the Natchez Trace out of a desire to protect the secret, to prevent the inevitable backlash that would ensue if such a secret reached the public's ears.

He had done it because he had finally understood that he had been betrayed. The man, the *dead* man, laying on the floor, all but bereft of his last breath, punctured in two places by the stinging precision of the bullets, had known his fate before he had even left Fort Pickering with his servants.

The servants would be sleeping in the barn, likely behind enough hay and wood and far enough from the scene to have heard the gunshots, or they would have already been at the cabin, checking in on their master.

Or, in a sick twist of fate, Lucius considered that perhaps the servants were in on the ruse as well, and had been ordered to stay inside the barn, no matter what they overheard. Their master, Lucius' target, may have told them just enough to convince them that his plan was far more important than his personal safety.

Whatever the details, Lucius knew the man in front of him was part of something much larger, much more sinister, than either of the men could have known.

# SEVEN

**OCTOBER 11, 1809.**

THE DOOR BEHIND HIM OPENED. A large, heavy log door
cut from the same trees as the surrounding structure. A woman
entered.

*Mrs. Griner.*

"Is… is everything okay?" she asked.

Lucius noticed that the woman did not look toward the bear skins
on the floor and the man lying on them. She kept her gaze fixed
straight ahead, on Lucius.

"Everything is…" he paused. Waited. For what, he didn't know.
"Yes, ma'am. Everything here is fine."

"I heard —"

"I understand you are concerned of the safety of your guest this
evening." He took a gentle, careful stride toward the door and the
waiting Mrs. Griner. "Thank you for your concern."

She frowned.

"Do not be alarmed. This man has been sick for many weeks.
Tonight he has decided to take his own life, and that is a perfectly
honorable task. I urge you to refrain from moving his body until the
morning. Can you do that?"

She nodded.

The man on the floor spoke. "So hard… to die…"

Lucius couldn't believe his ears, but he kept on, trying to make his
way to the exit.

"Good," he said, stepping still closer to the exit and Mrs. Griner's body in the doorway. "I will ask one favor of you, dearest hostess. Would you indulge me one request?"

Mrs. Griner nodded, hesitatingly. He read the fear in her eyes. Lucius forced his face to relax, his posture to soften. He imagined himself sinking down to her level, both literally and figuratively.

"Thank you," he said, his voice almost a whisper. "I was worried I would not be able to fulfill a dying man's last request."

At this, her face softened. *Just as I suspected,* he thought. *She has no understanding of who this man is, or why he is here.* The woman in front of him was decent, kind. She felt for the dying man, and now Lucius.

"You do know the nature of your guest's travels, no?"

Griner shook her head.

"Well, that is a shame. But you will — you certainly will. For now, would you be able to fetch us a pot of boiling water, and partake in a tea with me?"

"A tea?" she asked.

"Aye," Lucius said. "A strange request, I understand. Yet this was my friend's last wish. I believe it would be an honor to his legacy to enjoy his personal tea with a mutual friend."

"But… sir," she said. "I did not know the man."

"Nonsense," Lucius said. "He was a private man, and his deathbed is of your possession. As such, you have every much a right to share in his final wish as I."

She nodded, a look of concern on her face, but finally turned and left the room.

Five minutes later, Lucius heard her hastened footsteps on the wooden planks outside the room, then saw her enter.

"Perfect," he said. The woman was carrying two cups, one in each hand, and the steam of the heated water inside each was rising and flowing over her face.

Lucius nodded reverentially.

"Here," he said, walking to the satchel near his dying target's pile of weapons. "This is the tea."

He handed the leaves to Mrs. Griner, who began tearing them in half lengthwise after she had placed the steaming cups on a nearby table. He watched, feeling a wave of anxiety wash over him.

*This is the tea…* he had said it as if it were, in fact, nothing but a traditional English tea, brought here from the Old World and traded in one of the larger cities in the east. *This is the tea,* he thought again. *That would bring down a nation.*

He would do everything in his power to make sure that did not happen.

He placed the remainder of the tea leaves — a small sprig of preserved leaves still connected to their stem — into his pocket. It would be the only sprig his target was carrying. He knew the instructions that had been given to the man, and he knew that besides his ultimate betrayal, the man would have been true to his word.

He had made a career and built a life out of it.

Mrs. Grinder picked up the first of the cups, then handed it slowly to Lucius. Lucius nodded appreciatively, then reached for the cup. He waited for the woman to turn around once more, then he reached inside the cup.

The near-boiling water stung, but he gritted his teeth. He reached for the leaves at the bottom of the mug, both gripping the bottom of the hardened clay. He slid them sideways, then up. They poked through the top of the water, and he picked them out of the cup and crushed them in his hand.

With an awkward flourish, he turned his palm away from Mrs. Grinder just as she turned back around with her own cup in hand. His hand dropped in his pocket and he released the soggy leaves to join the others.

He raised his cup a bit, signifying the beginning of a toast.

She waited, and he stared, turning his head slightly sideways. There wasn't much time, but this moment had to be perfect. He had to be sure she drank the tea.

"This, this man here…" he paused with a flourish of his hand, "this man is the greatest American hero since General and President Washington himself."

He took a sip from the cup. The sting of the hot water was nothing next to the bitterness of the tea. The tannins in the leaves were pungent, acrid, and he hadn't even allowed them to steep for long enough to impart their medicinal tendencies.

He couldn't imagine how awful the woman's tea would taste.

"Hot," he said.

She nodded, then took another sip.

They continued in this way for another few minutes. Finally he reached the bottom of his cup, and she followed suit.

He watched her face. Looking for a sign of something. Anything.

Griner's eyes moved up, widened a bit, nearly imperceptibly.

*I am out of time,* he thought. Whether the drug had taken its effect, he didn't know. He didn't care — his job here was done.

He turned to leave the small cabin, hoping the servants were still asleep and the enemy was riding away, making a route to the capital. As he stepped over the threshold of the wooden building and onto the porch, looking out over the lands that were filled with the natives who had kept this secret for so long, he felt a pang of regret.

This woman would remember nothing the next morning, and for all he knew she would have concocted a story as potent as the tea itself in her deliriousness. She deserved to know, at least, the nature of his visit.

*Since she won't remember a thing tomorrow.*

"I thank you again for your hospitality this evening," he said. "This man is the governor to the entire Territory. His name is Meriwether Lewis, of the famed Lewis and Clark Expedition, and he has come here to die."

# EIGHT

"LOOK AT YOU, PRETENDING LIKE you're working hard!"

Ben looked at Reggie with the contempt of a man who had just had the food stolen out of his mouth. He stared back at Reggie, silent.

"Can't even deny it, can you?" Reggie asked.

Ben continued staring. "I... uh, no —"

Reggie's face broke into a gigantic smile, his eyes glistening with a fiery intensity. He felt amazing, even after a day of travel and an exhausting week.

"Don't get all starstruck, Bennett."

Ben's face flushed. "I'm not —"

Reggie held up a hand. "You know you wish you were free and aloof like me," he said. He glanced at Julie. "Not tied down to a little old lady and stuck in the backcountry."

Julie laughed. "Who you calling 'little old lady?'"

The reunion was taking place in the living room of Ben's cabin. He and Julie had been living there together for close to a year, but lately it seemed like a commune with the number of visitors passing through. Reggie knew Ben was somewhat of a recluse, and that the work on the house and the number of people coming in and out must be driving him crazy.

Still, Reggie was not one to pass up an opportunity to poke fun at his friend.

"I see you logged a cute little workout yesterday, Ben."

Ben shook his head, smiling. "You wish you could run it in that time."

Reggie's eyes widened at the challenge. "What was it? Four, five minutes?"

"Two and a half."

"I can do it in one-fifty."

At this, Ben laughed out loud. "Let's go, partner. Right now."

Reggie walked over and extended his hand, waiting for Ben to grab it. "Good to see you, too. I'm just making sure you're keeping it tight while I'm gone."

"Yeah, right. You just know you can't take me."

"Give me a nap and a beer and I'll do it with my eyes closed."

Reggie released, noticing that Ben held onto the handshake a few seconds longer than necessary, and then he backed away and looked around the small room.

The cabin was simple — the perfect description of a cabin, in his mind — but surprisingly well-appointed. He assumed bringing Julie in had forced Ben to up his decorating game a bit, or Julie herself had been in charge of it.

The couch was leather, worn, and absolutely perfect for sitting, sleeping, or just looking nice. Reggie had coveted the piece of furniture the moment he'd laid eyes on it, and he had yet to ask where they'd gotten it from.

The rest of the furniture in the living space was 'rustic,' a combination of wood and bronze, screwed or nailed together in a way that allowed the imperfections to shine through. Everything was new or seemed new, but it all had character that neither clashed nor took away from the rest of the room.

The only thing missing, in Reggie's mind, was a massive mounted deer or elk head on the wall. He hadn't done any hunting, but he knew Ben had and that the man would have had many trophies to display. He also knew Ben probably shied away from showing off anything he'd shot and killed — to Ben, it would have been disrespectful to the creature to put it forever on display.

Reggie and Ben had known each other since their explosive introduction to one another in Brazil. Reggie used to own land there, running an executive wilderness survival program and gun range, but the pressures put on small businesses — and a high-intensity race through the Amazon rainforest — had soured the appeal of the exotic locale.

Now he split his time between Alaska and the road, living with Ben and Julie when he wasn't traveling. He had grown to love the state as much as the couple he stayed with, and it didn't hurt that he was a fan of cold weather as well. Alaska had always been, in his mind, as exotic a place as Brazil, but there was something grounding about setting up a home and lifestyle in a new location. Brazil's appeal had been beautiful women and great weather, but the country's true colors inevitably began to shine through after some time, and his escapade through the rainforest with Ben and Julie had put the final nail in the coffin on his stay in Brazil.

Alaska, he knew, would eventually feel like home to him as well, for better or worse. The plan Mr. E had put in place involved Reggie living in one of the rooms on the new addition that was being added, allowing Reggie to have a comfortable place to crash after away missions and globe-trotting. He was looking forward to the arrangement, but he wondered how Ben and Julie felt about opening their home to a semi-permanent guest.

The next few months were going to be wild, with development on the cabin ramping up to a feverish pace and the news of the team's first assignment. Reggie had beat Joshua to the cabin, but Mr. E wanted both of them to be there to deliver the news to Ben and Julie.

Reggie figured that meant it was a perfect time for a bourbon.

"Come on, Ben. Let's get down to brass tacks. You got anything worth drinking in here, or have you not been into town since I left?"

"I haven't been into town since you left, but I *do* still have some decent stuff."

# NINE

**TWO DAYS AGO**

THE HAWK stretched his back, feeling it pop lightly in some spots. The tension of crouching, knees bent, for three hours had worn on him. Before that he had been lying prone, watching with one eye through the scope, for four hours.

And still before that he had hiked, alone and isolated, a circuitous route for recon through the back country near the small city toward the park where he now stood, perched on a rock at the edge of the municipal recreation center.

No one would see him; no one *could* see him. He wore black, covered in it from head to toe, a black ski cap and black boots, black garments in between. His face was black, his dark skin painted an even darker shade.

Still, he didn't like feeling exposed. He thrived on stealth, basked in it. He was The Hawk, after all. Standing on a rock in a city park was far from the battlefields he'd known in the years prior, but for now it *was* his battlefield.

The battle, however, was far simpler than the real battles he'd fought in. This one was nothing but a reconnaissance mission. His team would move in tomorrow morning, just before daybreak, and do the job. He would ensure the target was at home, tucked away in bed like everyone else on that street.

He'd discovered from experience that most of the 'thieving hours' — the time from about 2300 hours to about 0300 the next day, at least in residential neighborhoods, were best left to the thieves. Petty crime that flourished during the moon's highest hours were hours The

Hawk didn't want to be around. During those hours there were more police patrols, midnight-snackers watching out downstairs windows, and geriatric insomniacs moving around inside.

No, he preferred the time when most people were *actually* sleeping — about 0300 to 0500. Sure, there were early birds and a few corporate types who like to get in an early-morning jog, but statistically speaking there were far more people during that time doing what he needed them to be doing: *sleeping*.

It was going to be that way now, as well. He'd had someone on his team watch the street for the past few days. There was an odd-day jogger who arose and got started at 0515 Monday, Wednesday, and Friday, and there was one executive-looking fellow who drove to work at 0530, but other than that, the street was quiet. Even quieter the hour before.

Tomorrow morning — a few hours from now — would be one of those quiet mornings. The Hawk wanted to surveil the street from this spot himself, to verify the details and begin to formulate a plan. It was simple, but simplicity rarely meant easy. He knew that from experience, as well.

His team was good, the best he'd ever had, in fact, but he still preferred running the final check-through himself, personally. Their reports had so far been nothing but accurate, but The Hawk felt calmer about missions if he himself could lay eyes on the battlefield. He also liked to visualize the space as he planned, just to be sure there weren't unforeseen obstacles, like a broken-down vehicle that wasn't apparent on maps and satellite imagery.

Everything checked out so far, and he was happy about that. This would be a simple smash-and-grab, but they wouldn't even need to do any grabbing and hardly any smashing. He should have called the mission a 'sneak-and-place.'

He slid back down to the top of the rock. He'd watch for a few more minutes from here, then slide to the left off the side of the boulder and back onto the ground, and into the cover offered by the rock and the tree it sat next to. His rear was uncovered, as he was backed up to a sidewalk that ran the circumference of the park, but at this hour no one was likely to come by, and there were no direct lights illuminating this section of the park anyway.

The Hawk reached for the pack he'd slung at his feet and grabbed a protein bar from the front pouch. He'd already removed the loud, crackling wrapper before he left, so he simply reached into the plastic storage bag he'd placed them in and retrieved one. He had two more, one he planned to eat at 0200 and an extra, just in case.

There was a bottle of water on his hip, a canteen-style jug fastened to his belt using a custom carabiner assembly. He hated straps — they always found the worst possible times to get tangled — and he hated anything that fastened to him too tightly, for fear he wouldn't be able to get it removed quickly enough. The canteen was the perfect size and shape for holding enough drinking water for the mission, so he figured out a way to make it work.

Aside from the scope, his bag, the canteen, and a sidearm, he carried nothing other than the clothes on his back. This wasn't an away-mission, so there was little need for overdoing it. Still, his precaution and care with any work was part of what had given him the reputation and moniker 'The Hawk' in the first place, and it was a fitting title. His vehicle was parked at the other end of the municipal square and was loaded down with mission gear, including a small arsenal of weaponry. He wouldn't need it, but he hated the idea of being caught somewhere without it.

He ate the protein bar and took a few swigs of the water, then rolled his neck side to side to work out the kinks there. He was in great shape for his age, not young anymore but certainly far from old. He felt like he had the perfect balance between youthful energy and strength and the wisdom that only comes from experience.

He was good at what he did. The best, even. It was a small niche, but for that reason it paid well.

He would be paid well for this job, like he had been paid well for all of his jobs. His team liked him for that — he was able to find the best-paying jobs, and most were low-risk. He had plans to expand this year, to bring in a second team that would be able to provide more specific services to his clients.

*All in good time,* he told himself. The Hawk was a man of patience. Patience when it came to planning and executing a mission, patience when it came to running his business, and patience in life. *Good things come to those who wait.*

He had waited, all his life he had waited. This was an opportunity he had built for himself, and he had worked nonstop to create the network he'd needed to lay the foundation. Now, the client had found him, and he was ready. They'd come to him pleading — begging, even — for his help, and he was only too happy to oblige.

The payoff was the largest he'd ever had, and it was likely the largest he would ever have. It was a massive amount of money, and even if he failed the mission — he wouldn't fail the mission — his team had already been paid a quarter-million each, half a million for himself. It was enough to live on for years, in the right corner of the globe, but he had no plans to settle down and start spending money.

He had plans on making *more* money.

# TEN

JULIETTE RICHARDSON STEPPED BACK FROM the range top and wiped her brow. She looked down, smiled, and shook her head.

*I'm literally standing in a kitchen, wearing an apron, cooking dinner for men.* It was a hilarious thought to her mainly because her role in the cabin *rarely* involved cooking.

She and Ben had a great partnership. Neither of them bought into antiquated expectations of typical gender roles, so for each chore there was to do around the cabin — chopping wood, cleaning, dishes, laundry — one of them would tackle it when it became too annoying for them to bear.

For Julie, she hated piles of laundry stacked to the ceiling, so she did loads of it when it got out of hand. Ben enjoyed the catharsis of chopping wood, the rhythmic pounding at a chunk of log until it was split and sized, so that became his chore.

And Ben loved to cook — or rather, he loved to *try* to cook. Julie had to get used to his awkward choices of seasonings and over-salted dishes. He'd gotten better, especially after he began cooking for two, but she liked to joke that he had a ways to go before he was ready to open his own restaurant.

Still, he wasn't terrible. He could make a mean chili, and his way with fish and game was second to none, in her opinion. He enjoyed grilling most, but the winter months typically proved too unbelievably cold to do any grilling outside, so he had developed a proficiency with baked fish. Most nights they ate a meat and a vegetable or two, and they had recently begun to cut out their bread intake per Reggie's request.

She had lost weight as well, but not as much as Ben. Their workout regimens were different, designed personally for them, and hers was more of a diet change than an exercise change. She had always been active, running most mornings and sometimes hitting a yoga class after work at the CDC when she was there. She tried to eat well, but she had never really had a problem with her weight. Reggie — their assigned nutritionist — wanted her to focus on her food intake, specifically *what* she was eating and drinking, rather than try to burn more calories by exercising.

Ben, he'd told them, had the exact opposite problem. He ate well for a man in his mid-thirties, and even though he ate a lot it was a healthy balance of mostly protein and fat. He wasn't one to snack or go for ice cream after dinner, so Reggie turned his attention to burning more calories by building stamina and physique through a sort of home gym system he'd built.

Ben and Reggie, when they were both at the cabin, would spend an hour each morning running, working through bodyweight exercises, and rolling a huge tractor tire around on the open area behind the cabin. Julie knew Ben enjoyed the exertion and the rapidly increasing size of his biceps, but he never let Reggie know it. He would complain at every turn, whine about the next session, and tell Reggie to take his time before he came back for more training.

Julie watched all of it with a smirk. She knew Ben better than anyone now, and his games and feigned apathy at the workout regimen was a ploy. Ben had a knack for not letting anyone get too close, and this little form of acting out, she believed, was birthed from that same desire. Reggie had become a close friend to both of them, and they spent a lot of time together, so Ben had to make sure he didn't express his gratitude or act too friendly too often.

Reggie, for his part, seemed to love heckling Ben about it. Reggie, it turned out, seemed to have a bigger heart even than Ben's, and he had surprised Julie by just how much he cared for them. He took every opportunity to stay with them at the cabin when he wasn't on a mission or working elsewhere, and he always knew the right questions to ask to get them talking.

He loved to listen, and he was good at it. Julie hoped that Ben would pick up on some of that during their engagement.

She looked down at the ring he'd given her and twisted it around on her finger, a beautiful round cut diamond his mother had kept and passed along to him in her will. She'd died less than two years ago, and Julie and Ben had been the last people she'd seen on this planet. It was heartbreaking to watch Ben go through that, but she felt a special appreciation for the memory now that she was about to share the rest of her life with the man.

When he'd asked her to marry him, they had been on the floor of a secret research facility in the Antarctic, bullets flying above their heads. She remembered not knowing whether to smack him or smile at him.

She might have done both.

He had told her that he didn't have a ring, and that he would get her one. He had wanted to get her a traditional engagement ring, and then surprise her with the wedding band at their wedding — at a date still to be determined — but she'd told him to save his money. She wasn't much for jewelry, anyway. Any little thing would do, she'd told him.

His 'any little thing' had been a gorgeous, high-clarity, and *expensive* diamond wedding ring that his own mother had worn. Julie wasn't able to keep the tears from falling when he'd presented it to her in the cabin, shortly after their return from the southern hemisphere. He'd worked up a whole evening, too. His 'famous' chili on the stove, a cinnamon candle lit in the bedroom, and all the laundry cleared from the floors and dumped into the tiny laundry and washroom attached to the back of the cabin — she was always nervous that he'd ruin her clothes if he washed them, so having them piled in front of the washing machine, to her, was as good as having it completely done.

For all his stubbornness, all his imperfections, she loved him. He was brutish in some ways, large and bullish, but the most caring and sweet man she'd ever met in others. He always knew what to cook for dinner, it seemed, and he always was in tune to what she wanted to watch on television. He didn't always agree that they *should* watch it, but he knew.

He was kind, generous, and passionate for justice, which is how they'd met in the first place. He couldn't bear to see any wrongdoing go unpunished, even if that meant he'd get them both involved in something over their heads.

In a way, that's what he'd done again, but Julie had been every bit as responsible for it as he had. This new endeavor they were all embarking on together, the Civilian Special Operations, was just a formalized way of allowing Ben to fight injustice wherever they found it. Sure, they'd have to plan for it better than they were used to, and they'd have to communicate those plans with the rest of the team, including a representative member from each of the armed services, but it was still a perfect fit for them.

Or so she hoped.

In truth, she didn't really know *what* to think about it all. It seemed to be a great fit for their fledgling team, a group of people who had barely known one another but had come together to fight and overthrow an organization. They'd succeeded, and their new leader, Mr. E, had encouraged them all to join the new band of heroes he wanted to form. It had all happened so quickly, and Mr. E and his wife had jumped into renovating and expanding their tiny cabin in the backcountry of Alaska, and they still had yet to receive their first orders.

Tonight, she knew, that would change.

Reggie had returned from some sort of work he had been assigned to, somewhere, and the talk was — between her and Ben, at least — that he had their orders from Mr. E. They were just waiting for Joshua, who would be arriving at some point that evening.

Her smile turned slightly, a manifestation of the uncertainty she suddenly felt, but she continued cooking and cleaning the kitchen as the boys in the other room laughed and joked with one another.

# ELEVEN

"JOSHUA!" REGGIE YELLED.

BEN HADN'T heard anything, but he knew Reggie's hearing — and just about all his other senses — were profoundly adept. Better than Ben's for sure, except for perhaps Ben's taste.

When Ben had made his chili for Reggie and asked Reggie if he could tell what was in it, the best the man could pick out was 'some kind of chili spices?' between gargantuan bites of meat and beans.

Reggie and Ben started toward the front door, and Ben could now see the handle turning. He set his bourbon down on the end table near the couch, in preparation for a handshake.

The door opened fully and Ben saw Joshua's thin frame silhouetted in front of the fading afternoon light. Short-cropped hair in the style of most military grunts, yet a pair of eyes that spoke volumes more about his experiences than a haircut ever could. The man was close to Ben's age, but he had lived a hard life as a military man and then as the leader of a private mercenary force that provided security for the very company that Ben and Julie had taken down.

Draconis Industries had been Joshua's employer long before Ben had ever heard of the organization, yet their paths crossed in the Amazon rainforest earlier that year when Joshua had been ordered to seek out — and kill — Ben and his team. He'd ended up defecting from his own organization and joining the crew with Ben and the others, and together they'd gone to Antarctica to chase the last remaining leader and his final project.

Like Reggie, Ben had grown to admire Joshua, even though the man was quieter and more reserved. Ben himself was somewhat of a recluse, so it had taken the men awhile to get to know each other. He wasn't the personable, charismatic jokester that Reggie was, but Joshua had a strong will to be on the side of the good guys — a trait Ben required in his friends.

They'd all gotten along in Antarctica, and Joshua had even stepped into a role of the group's leader by the end of the trip, so Mr. E bestowed upon Joshua the official title. He was to lead the missions they were — apparently soon — going to be embarking on.

Joshua stepped up and into the cabin, glancing left and right to get a feel for the place. He'd been there a few times, but Ben assumed it was an old habit of careful reconnaissance for him to examine his surroundings thoroughly before entering a room. Ben smiled, and Joshua walked up to him.

They shook hands, Joshua grinning a bit from one side of his mouth. Reggie, next to Ben and next in line, was grinning from ear to ear and already laughing.

"You look like you need a drink, buddy," Reggie said.

"I'm good, but thank you," Joshua responded.

"Yeah, I figured," Reggie replied immediately. "But I'll get you one of these days."

Joshua nodded, then stepped into the kitchen to say hello to Julie. Reggie turned to Ben and brought his voice — and his smile — down. "He seems excited about something."

Ben frowned.

"It was a joke, Ben. He seems distraught."

"You have any idea why?"

"Probably thinking about our mission."

"You know the details, right?"

Reggie nodded.

"Then why aren't you distraught?"

Reggie laughed. "What's to be distraught about? I'm excited about this one. Going to a simple snatch-and-grab. Nothing to it."

# TWELVE

**TWO DAYS AGO**

"SIR, IT is done."

The words sounded like money to The Hawk. They *were* money.

He smiled, knowing the man on the other end of the phone couldn't see it.

"Fine," he said, his voice as steady and calm as ever. "Good work, tell the others to pack it in and head home. We've got another appointment."

"Affirmative, sir. Orders?"

"They will be emailed over. Check the secured account at 0700."

"Roger that, sir."

The Hawk hung up the call and placed the phone back in his pocket. He chewed the last bit of jerky and spat. *So far, so good.* He needed to call in this update, but he knew the client would have other priorities. This was a low-risk mission, and that meant it was relatively low-priority for the client.

He could call in the success later, right now he wanted to sleep.

The Hawk was a solitary man, alone in ways that would make other people crazy. He required the solitude, however, as it allowed him to focus on improving himself and his work. He could focus without distraction for as long as he liked, never needed to check in with the outside world.

To him, the outside world was just that — outside. It was distant, away from him, and he was detached from it. The everyday necessities most of his men required — debauchery, entertainment, pleasure — he despised. He had his ways of finding what he needed, when the urge struck, but the urge rarely struck. He had trained his mind and body to require little from the offers of the outside world, as the 'inside world' he'd built was far more fit for him.

Six years ago The Hawk had walked off the side of a mountain, a new and completely changed man. His mind had been cleared, thanks to his own willpower as well as some particularly uncomfortable 'external' motivations. He had been through trials, through hell and back, and he had emerged stronger than ever.

He had emerged stronger than *anyone else*.

He had completed the first part of his life as one man, and upon stepping off the mountain, he had begun the second.

He turned to the man standing at his side, a man he only knew by one name.

"Morrison, confirm the details. We can't have any loose ends."

"We never have any loose ends, sir," Morrison replied.

"And that is because we always check for them."

Morrison nodded and stepped away from The Hawk. He watched him for a few paces, his bear-like gait belying the man's true speed and cunning. Morrison was a perfect second, ruthless and dedicated as The Hawk, capable as a soldier, but missing the special ingredient that made a man a leader and not just a manager.

The Hawk preferred this arrangement. He wanted no man to question his authority, and he wanted no competition from his subordinates. Morrison wanted The Hawk to lead, and he would do whatever necessary to ensure The Hawk stayed in power.

It was an arrangement that pleased The Hawk, yet it had only been forged from years of less-than-ideal situations. He had built this team — small, yet agile — from nothing, working his way through the amateurs and the hotshots until he had retained only seven men.

Morrison had been one of the first recruits, and he was neither an amateur or a hotshot. He simply performed, asked for nothing in return besides his paycheck, and he didn't interfere in the affairs of the other men. He was, in a word, ideal. Out of the hundred or so men The Hawk had interviewed for the first batch of candidates, Morrison had struck him as both alarmingly adept and ruthlessly effective. A solid combination, but without much leadership ability, The Hawk knew Morrison would make a perfect second-in-command. A man who cared nothing for the gripes and complaints of his subordinates, but just wanted to get the job done.

It may have been overkill to put a man like Morrison in charge of the rest of the men, anyway. The Hawk ran a tight ship, personally interviewing and training the small army he was building. They responded to his leadership, and they responded to Morrison's drill-sergeant command. After all, they were all from one branch of service or another, no matter what country the recruits hailed from.

Most of the men on The Hawk's shortlist were American, but only because America was the nation he was born and raised in, and the country he knew best. Quite a few men made the list from South America and Eastern Europe, trained either in the jungles as mercenaries or in the war-torn climates that were constantly plagued with political strife.

He kept his 'army' small — at most twelve men, and as few as six when he was getting started — but his list of candidates, those who were interested in serving on his security team, was about two-hundred strong now. Men found him through word-of-mouth, mutual acquaintances, and recommendations. It wasn't a difficult sell, either — he paid better than anyone in the business, and his team was known for its high-stakes missions and exotic travels.

In short, it was a soldier's dream. Traveling the world, serving out justice where it was due, and returning home for a few months of well-funded peace and quiet.

He had started the company a few years ago and he was already considering expanding. He wasn't sure how he would do it, but there were more good men wanting to help out than he had room for — and he knew now that there were *plenty* more corporate clients around the world willing to pay his fee.

This mission was actually a rare thing for The Hawk: it was domestic. Most of his work was abroad, working to quell uprisings and prevent — or control — organized labor forces that got unruly with their corporate overlords. He had been in more than a few close scrapes, but it seemed the more challenging the mission was, the more intrigue and excitement his men felt. They wanted more action, and they told their friends.

The Hawk played this up as much as possible, and when the promise of real action, plenty of intrigue, and an amount of money that made him look twice came along, he knew that domestic or not, this was a mission for his team.

So Ravenshadow found itself temporarily headquartered in a Philadelphia warehouse district, working out of an old, abandoned building that had been part of a larger group that had once spanned the entire city block. Many of the warehouses surrounding the space were also abandoned, and those that were occupied wouldn't notice the goings-on of a few black-clad men that came went through a back alley.

A handful of his list of candidates lived within driving distance of Philadelphia, so he put those men on alert: Ravenshadow was engaged with a client, and additional help could be needed. Be ready, he'd told them.

The Hawk spun around and walked toward his vehicle. The worn 2007 Hyundai Santa Fe was a perfect urban vehicle — powerful enough to get through a barrier, small enough to outrun a threat, and normal enough to not warrant a second glance.

He'd lived out of a van at one point in his life, but he preferred the comfort of slightly more spacious accommodations so he'd traded in the van for a one bedroom efficiency and the midsize SUV. The home base allowed him the ability to have a place to return to after missions, but it also afforded him the ability to store more gear and equipment than he could have before. The SUV gave him a way to be mobile, to be able to move freely throughout the country without needing to fly often.

As he entered the vehicle and started the engine, his phone rang. He frowned, not expecting a call and not liking the fact that he'd gotten one. He checked the number and frowned deeper. *Especially not a call from* this *number.* He considered not answering; allow the phone to send the call to his default voicemail so he could check it later. The caller likely wouldn't appreciate the fact that he had ignored the call, knowing that the mission would be complete by now.

"What," he said gruffly, not bothering to lift the end of the word into a question.

"Is it — is it done?" the woman's voice asked. Her voice was frail, weak, as if on life support. He knew better, however. She was a professional just as he was — albeit a much different type of professional.

"It is."

He waited, not caring to fill the dead space with more sound, more useless questions. He didn't need to fill her in, that would come later with the report.

*Still…*

Until the contracted job had been completed, this woman owned his time. She owned *him.* That was the one downside of his job — his time was never his own. He was left to complete the job however he saw fit, and using whatever means that had been previously discussed, but while under contract he was expected to be available at any time.

"Okay. Okay, great. So — it's finished. I mean —"

"It is done. I will provide a report later today."

He could almost hear her nodding. She was nervous, but he didn't care about that. She was a professional, and she knew how to manipulate emotions. She had control of her own, as he did, so he knew she was playing a game.

He didn't play games. He wasn't *paid* to play games.

"Good. That's… good."

He hung up the phone, knowing there was nothing more that needed to be said. There hadn't been anything worth saying in the first place, and he had no new information than he'd had before the call.

*Except…*

Maybe there was *something*. Something in the way she'd spoken to him. Something deeper than even the false emotion she'd summoned.

He considered it for a moment, sitting silently in the driver's seat of the vehicle. Wondered what it would mean.

What if his employer was *actually* nervous?

# THIRTEEN

REGGIE WAS LOOKING AROUND THE cabin's small living room, frowning and pacing while he tilted his head sideways as he tried to place whatever it was he was looking for.

"Need something?" Ben asked.

Reggie looked up, then smiled. "Oh, sorry — I was just wondering if there was another TV around here, one we could move into the living room."

The only television Ben and Julie owned was in their bedroom, as the living room area was really not much more than a foyer that connected the two other rooms — the kitchen and small dining room and the master bedroom. Since Reggie stayed often, the living room couch served as his bed, folding and turning the already tiny space into almost unusable space.

Ben shook his head. "No, but did you think you'd find one just laying underneath a book or stuck behind an end table?"

Reggie laughed. "Never hurts to look, I guess."

"Sorry, we'll have to use the one in the bedroom."

"We can get cozy on the bed. You know, I could sit next to Julie —"

Ben held up a hand. "I'm going to stop you right there, buddy."

Reggie laughed even harder and started in toward the bedroom. "Come on, guys, I just sent Mr. E a text and told him we're all here."

"We're still doing the "Mr. E remote feed thing, huh?" Julie asked from the kitchen. "Seems like it'd just be easier to meet him in person one of these days."

"Seems like it," Joshua muttered. "I'm not sure what his deal is. He's even more of a recluse than Ben."

"Not even close," Julie said, nudging Ben's side. "Mr. E at least lives in a normal place. San Francisco or San Diego, something like that, right?"

Joshua nodded. "San Fran. Apparently has a mansion there."

The three of them followed Reggie into the bedroom. If the living room was small, the bedroom was positively cramped. The queen bed took up most of the central space, and a small end table that held a lamp sat in the corner, smashed between the bed and the wall. Julie enjoyed reading at night, and Ben hadn't been able to get her to switch to an electronic reading tablet. It was a source of pride to him that he had jumped to a Kindle, opting for a lighter and more portable way to read, while she was a dinosaur, clinging to her tried-and-true ways like a little old lady.

Reggie was already on the bed, his tall frame seated on the foot of the bed, his face no more than two feet from the television.

Joshua squeezed past him and chose to stand between the bed and the window on the side wall, and Ben and Julie took up a spot on the opposite side of the bed. Ben let Julie slide backwards and rest her head on his chest, and he sat up straighter to see over Reggie's shoulder.

Somehow Reggie had already turned on the 'smart' television, navigated through the menu system to a popular video streaming app that had come pre-installed, and opened up a window and was currently typing — painfully slowly, using the tiny remote control's navigation to select one character at a time — an address into a URL field.

"How'd you know how to do all that?" Ben asked.

He immediately felt sheepish. Julie twisted around and looked at him, and Joshua glanced over, a raised eyebrow cluing him in that this sort of technical finagling was apparently common knowledge.

"The question is," Reggie said, his eyes still glued to the television, "how do you *not* know? With a techie wife like yours?"

"She's not my wife. Not yet."

"Well, you'd better hurry up and lock her down," Reggie said. "Else I'll have to —"

"Whatever you're about to say sounds like it's going to be extremely flattering," Julie blurted out, "but I'm more than happy to be the tech genius in Ben's life. Makes me happy knowing he'll always need me."

"Like a toddler needs its mom," Reggie muttered.

"What was that?" Ben asked.

"We're ready to roll. Everyone can see?"

They all nodded, but Reggie wasn't looking at them. He'd typed in a long URL and pressed the main button on the remote, and after a few seconds a pixelated bust of Mr. E loaded onscreen.

"It'll improve as the connection solidifies," Julie said. "Maybe."

"As long as we can hear him, we should be fine," Joshua said. "He's not big on facial context clues."

The television's built-in speakers crackled to life. *'Good afternoon,'* the man's voice announced. *'I am glad you all are together. I hope your reunion is restful and enjoyable.'*

*Who talks like that?* Ben wondered. The man they'd come to call their benefactor and new boss had always seemed a bit off to Ben. Not in an uncomfortable way, but just somehow socially different than anyone he'd ever met.

And Ben knew he wasn't the perfect example of a socially gifted individual, so if he was able to pick up on Mr. E's odd mannerisms, they must have been pretty obvious.

*'I am assuming Gareth and Joshua have told you that we have a mission, as of yesterday morning.'*

Reggie, — Gareth Red — looked around to ensure that they were all tracking. Ben nodded at the screen, even though he knew the tiny webcam Reggie had placed next to the television was hardly high enough resolution for Mr. E to pick up the movement.

Mr. E insisted on calling each of them by their full names. 'Harvey,' 'Juliette,' and 'Gareth,' instead of their shortened nicknames. The first time they'd heard Mr. E use Reggie's real name they'd all looked around surprised, only to find Reggie grinning. During his military service as a sniper, apparently, his team had smashed his last name and first initial into the moniker they all now knew him by. 'Red, G,' became 'Reggie,' and the name stuck.

"We're all aware, thank you," Reggie said. "What's the mission?"

Ben knew Reggie had at least some of the details regarding their mission, but all he'd told Ben was something about a 'smash and grab.' It didn't sound terribly appealing to Ben, and it certainly didn't sound safe, but Reggie hadn't seemed concerned.

Of course, Reggie *rarely* seemed concerned. The only time he'd seen the man lose his characteristic grin and get serious was in Antarctica, when he'd gone ballistic and taken out a team of enemy guards nearly single-handedly.

*Unarmed.*

The moment had been etched into Ben's mind forever, and it had only increased the respect he had for his friend. Reggie was a cool, calm, and fun-loving guy who would go absolutely insane to protect his friends.

'The mission is really more of a reconnaissance. Information-gathering mostly, though there will be some investigative work.'

Ben frowned. "Seems simple."

Mr. E nodded. 'Indeed, it seems so. I hope it is, but I cannot help but feel there is more to the story than what we have been led to believe.'

"Okay, boss," Reggie said. "Tell them the story."

# FOURTEEN

JULIE PUSHED UP FROM BEN'S chest and sat up on the bed. She didn't worry about Ben's ability to see — he was a whole head taller than she was, even sitting down — and besides, the audio was more important than the video, as the feed's quality hadn't improved.

Rural satellite internet connectivity was about as reliable as that of any small-town coffee shop. Sure, it worked, but in a way that allowed for little more than checking email a couple times a day and streaming a YouTube video every now and then.

Mr. E had provided them with an upgrade through his communications company and satellite it owned, and it was nice to be able to browse faster and stream longer shows and movies, but the reliability was still sporadic, especially during the winter months during storms.

The plan, he'd said, was to eventually get them set up with a state-of-the-art array on top of the new addition to the cabin that would allow them higher speeds and connectivity — no matter the weather or time of year — that any city-dweller would rival.

Julie was excited for it, as her background and recent consulting gig was in IT, and she was good at it. But there was also a twinge of nostalgia, a small sliver of grief as she watched the reclusive, rustic cabin set in the middle of a gorgeous Alaska backdrop disappear and get replaced by a fully-modern, large, and likely corporate-feeling addition.

But it would still have the same beautiful backdrop she'd come to love.

Every day on her walks or runs she felt like she was moving through a computer's screensaver. The picturesque wilderness surrounding them was immaculate, and the cabin's tiny frame, always pumping out smoke from its tiny chimney, seemed like heaven to her.

She and Ben had no idea what the final addition would look like. Part of their acceptance of this new role with the newly formed Civilian Special Operations was to turn over a chunk of land adjacent to the cabin's current location for an addition that Mr. E and his wife would manage. There would be a small hallway connecting the two buildings, but other than the addition being two stories tall, neither of them had any idea what it would look like.

She focused again on the television as Mr. E began to speak. His words were chopped a bit as the small satellite dish on their roof worked to keep up, and after a few words the audio came in more smoothly.

'— her way — up… now. She will arrive in Anchorage early tomorrow morning, but I do not know when she will arrive at the cabin. I predict it will be early afternoon, but I do not have that update just yet.

'However, she will stay behind in the new addition to your cabin only for a few hours, to test some of the communications equipment I am installing. Assuming everything is in order there, that will give us two points of contact with you during your travel. Your travel documents are already being processed, and your final briefing will happen upon your arrival. Before all of that, let me get you all updated with the full situation.'

He paused, and Julie saw him sip from a bottle of water. He swallowed, closing his eyes, then continued.

'At roughly 3:15 am, two days ago, a small pawn shop in St. Louis was broken into. Nothing of note was stolen, even though the shop contained a total of nearly four-hundred thousand dollars worth of electronics, antiques, and furniture.'

"'Nothing of note?' What does that mean?" Ben asked.

'Well, there was one item, according to the shop's owner, that was found missing. She alerted the authorities the next morning about the break-in, but it took her a few hours to even notice that the item was gone.

'The piece was a small glass vial that contained some sort of mineral specimen, quantity and weight unknown, though she said it appeared to be silver. She had just purchased the vial — for what I believe to be a very generous price — from a local widow in St. Louis. It seems she was doing the widow a favor, as early reports state that the women knew each other and may have been friends.'

"May have been?" Joshua asked. His arms were crossed, and he had a slight frown and his chin was lifted. Julie observed him, trying to read his expression.

He hasn't heard this part of the story yet, she realized.

*'Yes, past tense,'* Mr. E replied. *'The widow, Gloria Rutherford Braxton, was found dead in her home yesterday.'*

Joshua's chin tilted back farther.

*'Local police have all but determined the cause of death to be accidental overdose on her prescription medications, and no one is claiming that the two events are related.'*

"No one but *you*," Reggie said.

*'Correct. I am curious as to the nature of this mineral. Why it was protected in a vial like a sliver of gold, and why it was the only item sought out in the theft. I am also curious as to how Ms. Braxton came to own this vial, and why she would feel the need to pawn it.'*

"Local police aren't doing anything about it?"

*'No, but their hands are tied, really. The break-in was an obvious attack, the place is in shambles, and the front windows are all broken. Braxton's house, on the other hand, shows no sign of breaking-and-entering. Not even anyone's else's fingerprints anywhere.'*

"So the two *would* seem unrelated."

"Probably on purpose," Ben said.

"*Obviously* on purpose," Julie added. "But I get it. Authorities have enough to deal with, and it's an unfortunate truth that if the evidence is stacked up to point to a suicide, and there's not really a scandalous reason to keep digging, they'll stop digging."

"True," Joshua and Reggie said almost in unison. Then Joshua sighed. "What was the price Braxton was paid for this little gem, if I may?"

*'Yes, of course. I said I believed it to be a generous price. Apparently the proprietor of the establishment, Ms. Monique Delacroix, paid Braxton, in cash, the sum of $18,000 in exchange for the mineral.'*

Julie coughed. If she had been drinking or eating anything at the time, she would have choked on it.

"You — you've got to be *kidding* me," she said. "*$18,000?* That's… absurd. Even if it was gold in there, or diamonds."

*'As I said, I believe the transaction to be partly related to their relationship. Perhaps Ms. Braxton had fallen on hard times — why else would she have felt the need to pawn something sentimental like this? And why would the price be so high? I believe there was, at least partly, a desire for both women to feel as though there was a real transaction, so Ms. Braxton didn't simply receive charity from the pawn shop owner.'*

"Where is Delacroix now?"

*'She left on a business trip to Australia late last night. A massive conference in Sydney about antiquities and pricing structures for rarities dealers.'*

"Sounds like a bucket of fun," Reggie said.

*'I want to find this woman and offer our protection,'* Mr. E said. *'She may be targeted next, for her knowledge about the vial and its contents. If the two cases are related, there is a strong possibility the attackers will want to silence anyone with any information about this.'*

"Yeah, good call," Joshua said.

"So we're going to Australia?" Reggie asked. Julie could see the excitement on his face.

*'No, you are not. I will be sending Mrs. E to Australia to collect Ms. Delacroix and bring her back after she confirms that our communications equipment is in place and online, so I can access it remotely. When they return, I can offer Ms. Delacroix safe haven, at least until we know she is in no danger.'*

Reggie looked bummed, but he shook it off and smiled again. "Well, we can't find the bad guys here, I guess. So that means we're off on a grand adventure once again. Where to then? Someplace exotic?"

*'No. Philadelphia.'*

# FIFTEEN

"GROSS. REALLY?"

ONSCREEN, MR. E nodded. *'Indeed. Specifically to the American Philosophical Society. There is a museum in the original building.'*

"The original building of what?"

*'The original building of the same society, built by Benjamin Franklin to meet with the society he helped to form. Today it is a museum that sits near Independence Hall in the old historic district. The museum is really a revolving collection of items of its own archives and those of visiting exhibits, all of which are part of American history.'*

"So what are we going for?" Ben asked.

*'I want you to speak with a curator of the museum. The curator is a friend of one of the military representatives on our board. He told the curator that the CSO would be perfect for this type of work.'*

"Talking to a crotchety old museum guy?"

*'Speaking with the* female *curator about a recent theft of one of their items.'*

Julie's ears perked up. She was starting to see a link in the chain of events Mr. E had described. She straightened her back, pressing forward on the bed.

*'The curator believes that one of the Society's prized collections has been raided and one of the possessions has been stolen.'*

"I — I don't get it," Joshua said, interrupting. "She doesn't know it's been stolen?"

Mr. E shook his head. *'Well, actually, it's a bit more nuanced than that. The item in question is a journal. A leather-bound book, about the size of a large index card. The curator was very explicit in her description of the artifact, which tells me that she has a very intimate knowledge of the item, and has perhaps handled it personally.*

*'Yet she was also hesitant in her description, as if its mere existence is, well…'*

"Secret," Ben said.

*'Correct. She was only convinced to speak to me about it because of her relationship with and trust in our board member. She wanted to be clear that this topic is — how did she put it — 'rather touchy' with the Society. Apparently they have not ever disclosed their ownership of this journal.'*

Julie nodded. She now understood what the man was trying to say. A prized possession, owned by one of the oldest clubs in America, had gone missing, and they couldn't talk about it openly because, well, no one knew they had it.

She raised her hand, then felt silly, so she lowered it and started asking her question.

"Still, it seems like if they just said, 'hey, we're sorry, we messed up. We've had this other journal for a while now, but it just turned up missing; can you help us find it' they would be fine. What am I missing?"

*'Well,'* Mr. E began, *'this journal is one that no one knew existed in the first place. She was clear that there are very few people in the organization who knew about it at all, and outside of the organization — no one.*

*'And it would be a major embarrassment, and perhaps a major legal snafu for the Society, if it was discovered they had been hiding a journal like this. All of the other journals and notes from this collection are well-documented, protected, and public knowledge.'*

"Wait… 'other journals?' What collection?"

Mr. E cleared his throat. *'My understanding is that this journal was part of the original Lewis and Clark Expedition Records, and was written by Lewis' hand himself. It was kept secret from all the rest, and even his partner, Captain William Clark, did not have knowledge of the journal or its contents.'*

"And now it's gone missing," Julie said. "Fascinating."

Joshua's arms were still crossed. "E, when we spoke earlier, you told me that this mission would be 'quite simple.' Yet you don't even have a suspect, and we're supposed to fly to Pennsylvania — *all* of us — and just meet with this curator?"

Reggie nodded. "Right, why all of us? And how are these three things — the 'suicide' of old lady Braxton, the break-in at Delacroix' place, and this 'missing journal' related?"

*'For one simple reason — the chronological chain of events. The first thing, the break-in at the pawn shop, led to the second — the death of Widow Braxton. And I only learned of those first two events because of the*

third *thing — the missing journal and the personal request of one of our board members on the CSO to look into it.*

*'It turns out our curator at the APS told me one other thing, and this was the clue that led us to believe it was a break-in, and not just a case of a misplaced notebook. The museum was in perfect order upon her arrival. She inspected the first floor for its daily opening procedure, then headed down into the basement to repeat the process before she could open the facility to the public.*

*'In the basement, she noticed a single chest had been disturbed — not where the journal was kept, mind you — but she noticed it because it had been slid back into place and in doing so had upset the fine layer of dust that had fallen to the floor over time. She happened to notice that the dust was streaked and marked through where the heavy chest had been rotated.*

*'When she opened the chest, she saw the locked wooden box with a glass top where the Society had stored an old exhibit. About a foot by eighteen inches, and about eight or nine inches deep, the heavy case is segmented to separate multiple small artifacts found within it, and the glass top allows visitors to see through into the case.'*

Julie had seen such a box before. When she was a child, her parents had gotten her a similar case to fill with plants and stones she found during what they had called Julie's 'scientific phase.' She remembered walking through her yard and surrounding fields, picking up and turning stones over in her hands, and finding specimens of flowers and sticks that looked interesting, then carrying them back home to put on display in her tiny museum.

"Let me guess," Reggie said. "Something was missing from the case?"

*'Something was missing,'* Mr. E continued. *'She noticed that the lock — a simple mechanism on the front side of the case — was still engaged, meaning it had been picked or opened with the key, then closed afterward. Considering she was the only key holder, she assumed it was a simple procedure to unlock it with a paperclip or something of the sort.*

*'Anyway, she saw immediately that the contents had been disturbed. She opened it and browsed through the inside until she came to an empty slot. The case had been full, each section housing some small item or artifact, so it was an oddity indeed that there was nothing in this slot.'*

"That's how she knew it was a break-in," Julie whispered.

*'Correct. The item that was missing was nothing of note, she thought, but it been taken nonetheless. As she described it to me, I took notes, and ran a quick search for some of the terms she used. It turned out that this break-in shared a remarkably similar trait with the break-in at Ms. Delacroix' shop.'*

"A little glass vial?" Ben asked.

'Yes, Harvey. A small glass tube, filled with a single sliver of stone, speckled with a quartz-like sediment that sparkled and shone in the light. She was unsure as to the specific name of this stone, and the museum had no detailed records of how they came to acquire it, but when she opened the case and read her reference sheet of its contents, she realized that this single, small vial of stone — as well as Lewis' journal — had been stolen.'

# SIXTEEN

BEN SAT CLUTCHING TWO THINGS inside the tiny Cessna. His left hand was squeezing Julie's right, with a white-knuckled grip that probably would have crushed her had she not already expected such treatment.

His right hand clutched a flask that Reggie had passed him just before takeoff, full of some sort of cheap whiskey that was only barely better than the feeling of helplessness and lack of control he was experiencing.

Ben hated flying, more than he hated anything else. He didn't like to travel in general, especially when he was already in a spot he liked. Whether it was the couch in his living room or the cabin in Alaska, he didn't want to get up to walk to the fridge or take a vacation to a beach paradise.

He was already in a place he liked to be in, so why would he want to change that?

Julie had pressed him on a few times, and the best answer he could come up with was 'I just like things the way they are, especially if they're good.'

She seemed mildly satisfied with that answer, so he doubled down on it and used it as an excuse whenever she mentioned traveling for fun.

Flying was the worst way to travel, he thought. Sure, it was faster than just about anything else, and it was an efficient way to move around the world, but it was against the laws of physics. A giant metal tube full of explosive liquid shouldn't be able to float through the air.

Not to mention they floated through the air at thousands of feet of elevation and at hundreds of miles an hour.

Above the *hard* ground.

He hated it, and the best therapy he could find was squeezing Julie's hand to death and taking a long, slow sip of something that burned.

The whiskey did, in fact, burn. It had to have been no more than ten dollars for whatever bottle this terrible moonshine had come from, but he wasn't about to complain. Or talk at all.

Not until they were 'safely' up in the sky, breaking the laws of physics and the sense of acceleration had given way to the calm, steady, vibration of the plane's engines.

Of course, that calmness may not set in at all — there were flying in a peashooter of a plane. A human-sized matchbox, crammed together like sardines, and flying through a terribly windy season in Alaska.

He squeezed his eyes shut and waited for things to settle down.

"Ben!" Julie yelled.

He hated that she'd yelled — it probably meant they were all about to die, and he would rather have just been surprised about it — but he also knew that yelling inside the plane was the only way to get someone else to hear you. Even if they were sitting right next to you.

He opened one eye and saw Julie staring up at him.

"What?" he yelled back.

"How you doing?"

He shook his head. *What kind of stupid question is that?* he thought. *She knows how I'm doing.*

To underline his point, he forced back another shot of the fiery liquid sewage Reggie called whiskey.

The shot burned, and he coughed.

He saw Reggie smile from the cockpit. He wondered how the man had seen him — or heard him cough — but he knew Reggie was laughing at him.

Reggie was a decent pilot and had put in a lot of hours since their hair-raising experiences in Antarctica and the Amazon, and he was getting better at not terrifying Ben while they flew.

If Ben was honest, he had to admit that Reggie was a *fine* pilot, it was just Ben's own insecurities that caused him anxiety when they flew.

Still, he wondered if they always flew around in these tiny planes because the others were in on some prank against Ben, or if they were in fact more economical in some way.

He looked up at the cockpit again and noticed that Reggie was staring at him. Reggie shouted something, but Ben couldn't even hear a single word. He shook his head.

"What?" he yelled.

"— the flask —"

*Did he just ask for the flask?*

Ben thought he must have misheard the man. He shook his head again, and mouthed the words *I can't understand you.*

Reggie smiled, then pointed at the flask in Ben's hand.

"You can't be serious," Ben yelled. He wasn't sure if Reggie had heard him, but more importantly, he noticed Reggie *still* hadn't turned back around to see where they were flying.

The man charged with getting them safely to their destination was trying to talk Ben into giving him a drink from his flask.

He looked around. Julie and Joshua had a straight-laced expression on their faces. Their lips were a thin line, their eyes were on Reggie. For Joshua, Ben figured this was normal behavior.

He stared at Julie, eyeing her closely, until she burst into laughter.

"Don't worry, Ben," she yelled. "He's just messing with you."

Even Joshua began to laugh, and Reggie finally turned back around to pilot their aircraft. Ben smiled, but there nothing genuine behind the smile. Julie winked at him.

He lifted the flask and poured another shot into his mouth.

*This is going to be a long flight.*

# SEVENTEEN

THE FLIGHT WASN'T ACTUALLY VERY LONG — they landed in Anchorage to switch planes, then took a connecting flight to Seattle, then over to O'Hare International, then finally landed in Philadelphia.

Twelve hours later.

Ben was exhausted. He was surprised that their first plane, the Cessna, had been the most room he'd had during all four of their flights. The 737 they'd done the last two legs on offered little more than a straight-backed chair and hardly enough room for even his knees.

He was cramped, tired, irritable, and ready for dinner.

Reggie, on the other hand, seemed to be the exact opposite. When they landed in Philadelphia, Reggie bounced up and out of his seat, chipper and ready for the next adventure.

Ben scowled at him.

"What's the problem, big guy?" Reggie asked. "Couldn't get enough of a cat nap?"

"Couldn't get *any* nap," Ben replied. "And I'm hungry."

Joshua appeared behind Ben and Julie as they walked up into the airport. "We'll stop on the way for something quick. Hopefully enough to fill us up until dinner."

"Wait," Ben asked. "When's dinner?"

"Whenever we're finished talked to the curator at the APS."

Ben sighed. "We're not even checking into a hotel first? Just jumping right into work?"

Julie and Reggie exchanged glances, then she turned to Ben and looked up at him. "What — what were you reading on the flights?"

He shrugged. "I don't know, whatever was on my Kindle. Part of a novel. Wasn't any good. I could do better. I fell asleep after a page or two."

Julie and Reggie smiled, while Joshua looked confused.

"While you were dozing off, pal, the rest of us *were* already 'jumping into work.' We've been reading through the briefs and backgrounds Mrs. E sent over to prepare for the trip."

Ben's mouth opened and closed, but couldn't think of anything to say.

"Don't worry — we'll fill you in on the way to the American Philosophical Society headquarters downtown. Just stay awake long enough to let it sink in."

Ben nodded. He hated feeling like he was behind the ball, but he *really* hated being left out of this group's activities. He felt like he was considered the weakest link on the team, and moments like this didn't help things.

They walked along through the airport until they came to baggage claim, and Joshua and Reggie posted up near their plane's baggage drop while Julie and Ben waited back a few paces, against the wall.

Julie grabbed his arm and linked hers within his. She stepped up onto her tiptoes so she was able to whisper directly into his ear.

"Don't worry," she said. "They're nerds. They like that sort of stuff, but I'm more into the strong silent types."

"Yeah, but — "

"And I made sure you and I got a room together where we're staying," she continued, a coy smile on her face. "So whenever we're done talking to this museum lady, I'm hoping we can steal away and do some 'catching up' on the brief information."

Ben smiled. "Yeah, I need a little extra time to get through all the information," he said.

She winked at him. "We'll go slow."

# EIGHTEEN

REGGIE KNEW BEN AND JULIE were hoping to get to the hotel and relax a bit, but they had work to do. He had always been a man unable to focus on anything else than the task at hand when he had a job to do, and he had that in common with their team lead, Joshua Jefferson.

It had taken some time for Reggie to come to like Joshua, as the man had first introduced himself to the in the Amazon rainforest by ordering his men to kill them. After betraying his own men and killing his own brother, Joshua Jefferson had tried to convince Reggie's group of his apparent side-change.

Reggie allowed it, but he kept a close eye on the man for the rest of the trip. Only after successfully completing their mission did he start to trust Joshua more, and it had taken months for Reggie to fully understand and accept the emotional turmoil his new friend had undergone.

Now, the two men were inseparable mirror images of one another. They shared a common background in weapons knowledge, organizational strategy, and training, even though Joshua had never served in the military. They shared a passion for well-planned and perfectly executed missions, and both men were adamant about putting in more than their share of the workload.

However, their personalities could not have been more different. Reggie was an outgoing, talkative loudmouth who enjoyed fun and practical jokes, while Joshua kept to himself and preferred talking only when asked a question, and even then answering with few words.

Reggie liked Joshua, but he was constantly reminded of how different the two men were.

They made a great team — Reggie's wit and ability to adapt in sticky situations, and Joshua's leadership calm and resiliency. Reggie wasn't upset when Mr. E had appointed Joshua the group's de facto leader on missions, as he knew Joshua was the proper man for the job.

They were sharing a room as well, adjacent to Ben and Julie's, yet he knew they would be spending little time inside. The brief had explained that Ben and Julie would be staying in Philadelphia and working with the curator of the American Philosophical Museum to provide information to Reggie and Joshua, who would be moving around and searching for the missing journal and vial.

Before anyone could check into the hotel, however, Reggie needed to eat and get to the museum. They had taken a mid-sized SUV from the airport, and Julie had offered to drive. Reggie sat shotgun and navigated, while Joshua worked through the briefs once more and Ben slept.

"How much longer?" Joshua asked from the back seat.

"We're stopping at a fast-food joint first," Reggie answered. "Then about twenty minutes, depending on traffic."

"Fast food?" Julie asked. "Seems like there ought to be somewhere a little better to eat."

"Maybe better, but not faster," Reggie said. "I want to get started, see what this gal knows about this little journal and why it's so important."

"I second that," Joshua said. "What's Ben want?"

"Food," Julie said. "Just food. Doesn't matter what kind or how cheap. I guess I'm the one outnumbered."

They decided on a drive-through taco stand just off their route, but Julie parked in the lot so they could get out and stretch their legs. They walked to the window to order, then brought the food back to the car.

"Last time we were all together on a project like this we had some better food options," Ben said. "How come we can't do this at The Broadmoor again?"

Before the team had left for Antarctica months ago, they had all met at The Broadmoor, a world-famous resort and hotel in Colorado. Mr. E had presented to them via video feed in one of the beautiful ballrooms and asked for their help on the project.

"Gotta admit this is a bit of downgrade," Reggie added. "But at least the food's paid for."

Reggie got back into the car and took a bite of his first taco. A spot of sauce dripped down the corner of his mouth, but he was too focused on the amazing flavor to notice. "Never mind," he said. "This food's better."

"I second that again," Joshua said.

Julie drove on, heading south on 4th street after exiting the highway. As she turned onto Walnut and then 5th street, heading up into the historic downtown district of Philadelphia, the centuries-old Philosophical Hall and a block away Independence Hall came into view.

The building consumed Reggie's focus. He had a love for history, and while visiting Philadelphia hadn't initially struck him as someplace 'exotic,' he was excited to be surrounded by buildings and works of art created by a brand-new nation. Benjamin Franklin had been a father of this city, and many others had walked its streets long before they were even paved.

Independence Hall's beautiful steeple jutted out and pierced the skyline, its square white facade that housed the bell tower moving upward until it met with the cylindrical top section. The clock on the front side of the steeple was not in view, but he could make out the very top point of the building from their location.

The red-brick Georgian-style landmark served as the main attraction of the Independence National Historic Park, and had been completed in 1753. Reggie had read a little about its renovations and reconstructions over the years, but he had never seen the building in real life. Modern-day architecture had surpassed what the architects of the Founding Fathers' era could accomplish, so the skyline of Philadelphia now included plenty of buildings and monuments that stretched taller than the Hall, but to Reggie he could see the building as it had been intended, so many years ago.

He pictured the horses and carts that traversed the much narrower streets, the ruts of hundreds of cart wheels catching remnants of rainwater and mud and sending it downhill. Men and women dressed in the best colonial fashion had to offer, heading to the state house for business or government affairs. Children playing on the streets and running through the crowds, racing to beat their brothers and sisters home.

Reggie smiled, watching the scene unfold in front of his eyes while the real-life present took place outside the car's windshield. He felt the urge of nostalgia, pulling him toward the simpler life of colonial America.

But as he felt it, he knew it wasn't accurate. Colonial America was certainly not an easier time, nor simpler. There may have been fewer people, but history had done a great job painting a blurry-edged picture of what life was like back then. Reggie knew that each of those people had been faced with situations that he had never considered.

He had been under attack and in real danger before in his life, but when his mission was finished he always got to come home to a heated or air-conditioned home, with the comforts of the modern day.

Perhaps the nostalgia he was feeling was one of the reasons he loved visiting and staying with Ben and Julie. He enjoyed the straightforward appeal of the cabin, the ease of life, and the lack of distractions. However, he had been amazed at the number of chores and tasks needed to keep the cabin up to a livable standard. Aside from chopping wood every morning, there was the initial felling and hauling of the trees, the hunting and trap setting — if they hadn't been into town in a few days — and the maintenance on the cabin, including chinking and sealing.

And that was just the outside.

Reggie glanced back at Ben, dozing in the backseat. He once again felt a sense of pride for his friend. Ben was a living juxtaposition — seeming lazy and outwardly antisocial, yet the hardest worker, most resilient man, and one of the best friends Reggie had ever had.

And they'd still only known each other for about a year.

He smiled, catching Julie's eye as she turned into the parking lot of their destination.

"Watching him sleep?" she asked.

He nodded, the grin growing wider on his face.

"He's easy to love in this state," she said.

"I feel like a dad watching his kid," Reggie said.

"Tell him when he wakes up and see what he thinks of that."

From the back seat Joshua chuckled.

Reggie turned away from Ben, who'd now opened his mouth and begun snoring quietly, and looked the other direction. Out his window he could see the final destination of this leg of the journey, Philosophical Hall.

"Home of the American Philosophical Society, founded by none other than Benjamin Franklin," Joshua said.

"Finished in 1789," Reggie added.

"Amazing," Julie said. "It's hard to believe this stuff's been here this long. All the *history* in there. It's overwhelming, really."

Ben snored loudly and then woke up. "We… we here?"

"We're here," Julie answered.

"How long will this take? And when's dinner?"

"You *literally* had food half an hour ago," Reggie said. "You can't wait a few hours?"

"A few *hours*? That's when dinner is?" He paused, getting ready to get out of the car, and added. "I hate traveling with you guys."

# NINETEEN

THE BUILDING WAS, TO BEN, a mansion. Even though no one lived there, the building was too small to seem like a full-fledged museum but much too large to act as a simple meeting place for any society.

He wondered if that's why the Society had rented out its space to a local university, the city, and various other organizations during the years of its existence. Perhaps the American Philosophical Society was large enough to need a meeting hall, but never quite large enough to require all the space it had built.

Still, the building was well-appointed and beautifully adorned. The entranceway held the air and superiority of the history it contained within, and the walls and ceiling seemed to bulge with the knowledge of the men who had met within its confines. Ben observed everything he could as they walked into the main foyer and down a hallway to the left.

They walked in silence, each of the others in Ben's group apparently as deep in thought and reverence as he. Reggie, he noticed, seemed particularly fascinated as he walked. He nearly bounded around, poking and prodding at the air in front of artifacts and paintings that hung on the walls, all but touching them with a pointed finger. He whispered to himself, no doubt caught up in a sense of awe and wonder. There were plenty of such artifacts and things on stands and side tables along the walls, but Ben noticed nothing that seemed like a museum — no large, open rooms, no signs, nothing. It actually felt more like a small office building, he realized.

"You going to be okay, buddy?" Ben asked.

Reggie turned, his eyes darting around. Finally he realized who had spoken to him, and his gaze focused on Ben as he nodded quickly. "Yeah, yeah, I'm okay," he said. "It's just… it's all so… I mean can you *believe* there were people here *two-hundred years ago?*"

Joshua and Julie laughed, but Reggie's question was answered by another voice.

"It is particularly *miraculous*, is it not?"

Ben tried to see where the faraway voice had come from, but there was no one in the hall. He searched, finally seeing a foot appear in a doorway about twenty paces away at the end of the hall. The foot was followed by a leg, then a woman's body.

A woman's *amazing* body.

Ben tried not to notice the appearance of the woman who had just spoken and stepped out into the hall, but it was impossible not to. She was short, shorter than Julie, and had a tightly wrapped bun that pulled most of her hair up and onto the back part of her head. Unlike other buns Ben had seen on women, this one wasn't too tight — it allowed a few strands of the woman's golden-brown hair to bounce back down and land on the back of her neck, and one longer strand had been tucked into the space behind her left ear.

She had a pair of black plastic-rimmed glasses on her nose, and the small, upturned nose itself seemed to be providing most of the support for the frames. Her face was petite, young even, and her small mouth was upturned slightly in the makings of a smile.

Of all the attraction the woman's face held, however, it was not her *face* that Ben had noticed first, nor was it her face that beckoned for his continued attention.

The woman was wearing a skirt that bounced around her knees and a loose, white blouse that was of a thin, nearly see-through material. It all would have been nearly provocative had Julie or any other woman been wearing it, but the woman in front of them now somehow made it seem like a perfectly conservative, albeit very flattering, outfit.

Julie elbowed him in the side and he blinked a few times and looked down at her.

"Wha —?"

"She asked you a *question*, Harvey," Julie said. Her expression gave him the impression that she did not seem pleased.

He looked at the the women approaching him. The others — Joshua, Reggie, and Julie, had parted and were allowing her to walk directly up to him.

"You must be Mr. Bennett," she said, extending a hand.

Ben frowned, then looked again at Julie.

"We had a quick video chat in the car," Julie said, answering his silent question. "You were asleep, but we all made some quick introductions and made sure we had the directions to this place correct.

Ben felt sheepish, but he shook her hand anyway. She had a firm grip, even though her hands were about half the size of his.

"Nice — nice to meet you," he mustered. He subconsciously pulled himself straighter and sucked in his gut a bit. He hoped his hair wasn't still disheveled from his short nap in the car.

She grinned, a cute, shy thing that completely contradicted the intensity and seriousness in her eyes. For a moment it seemed he was looking at two people — the youthful, innocent woman whom he had first seen in the hallway, and the professional, experienced woman who could see through him and into his soul.

He took an involuntary step back.

# TWENTY

THERE WAS A CERTAIN TENSION in the air as Julie and the others stood in the hallway, watching the woman approach. Julie knew the other men would be ogling the young-looking curator, enjoying her petite, well-dressed yet slightly disheveled appearance.

The woman, even as she gripped Ben's hand and shook it, seemed to be constantly trying to catch her balance. Not in a way that made it look as though she had been drinking, but in a way that seemed delicate and klutzy.

And yet Julie could see right through her. There was nothing 'delicate' or 'klutzy' about this woman. Their brief had explained the woman's background, and though it had only included a few sentences about her education, it was enough to immediately make Julie feel defensive about her own schooling.

The woman, Daris Johansson, had earned her undergraduate degree in American history at the University of Texas, but then she'd gone on to receive *two* masters degrees — one in anthropology and another in Native American history — and finally a doctorate in something related to history that Julie couldn't even pronounce.

Julie herself had been a great student, graduating magna cum laude from the University of Ohio, but then deciding against a graduate degree in computer science because of a job offer right out of college — with the Centers for Disease Control.

She had taken the job, moved around the country, and generally had a successful career.

But the woman in front of her now, squeezing her fiancés hand, wasn't just a great student. Daris Johansson had cashed in her phenomenal track record as a student into a lucrative position at the American Philosophical Society. The APS paid well, but Mrs. Johansson, according to the brief Julie and the others had been supplied with, was not just on the APS' payroll.

And she wasn't *just* a museum curator and glorified tour guide.

Julie cleared her throat, and Daris released Ben's hand. She looked over, surprised.

"Hi," Julie said. "I know we talked on the phone, but I'm Julie."

"Juliette Richardson, yes," Daris said. "How are you?"

"I — I'm okay," Julie said. "You know, I could use a glass of water, though."

Ben's face was flush with embarrassment, as apparently he had just realized how long the handshake with the cute museum worker had lasted, but Reggie had a humongous grin plastered across his face.

Joshua, for his part, was completely oblivious to the tension in the hallway and just stared, stone faced, at Daris.

"Yes, right. Well, let's get back to my office — right this way — and I'll get us a pitcher of water. You've all had quite the trip, I presume."

Julie nodded, too fast and too awkward. She stopped her head abruptly, likely also too fast and too awkwardly. *Dammit.* She was acting like an idiot, and for what? *Ben's the most loyal man I've ever met,* she told herself.

Still, she watched Ben's eyes as they walked down the hall. To his credit, they were dead-center on the back wall they were walking toward.

She sidled up next to Ben and casually slipped her elbow around his. She pulled him closer, feeling his strong arm and shoulder bump against hers. Julie suddenly felt goofy; she felt like she was in middle school all over again, minus the pimples.

"You okay?" she asked.

He frowned, looking down at her. "Uh, yeah. What do you mean? Just a little hungry."

She smiled, turning back to the walk and watching as the tiny Daris turned — danced — on a heel and her small, perfect little body maneuvered into the corner office at the end of the hall.

She sighed, following Ben inside.

# TWENTY-ONE

THE OFFICE WAS SPARSE, A surprising revelation for Julie. She had expected shelves of books, artifacts from dig sites from expeditions the woman had been on, and scores of research papers and journals stacked in piles on her desk.

Instead, the office seemed to have been taken directly from a furniture catalog and turned into real life. A matching desk and chairs set filled most of the small room, while a long, low bookshelf cut of the same wood as the desk and chairs spanned the wall on Julie's left. The bookshelf wasn't filled, either. A few sections held collections of textbooks and other books, while the majority of the piece was empty or housed a kitschy object from the same furniture magazine.

The office was nice, well-decorated even in its plainness. Julie could tell the woman cared little for fancy adornments, and probably had only purchased those she had out of respect for any visitors she had. As much as she tried to deny it, Julie felt herself intrigued by this woman.

"Welcome," the woman said. "Come in, have a seat."

Julie and Reggie sat in the two leather chairs in front of Daris' desk, while Ben and Joshua sat in a small couch against one wall. Joshua leaned in, his elbows on his knees, expectantly.

"Thank you for meeting us," Joshua said. "Are you okay?"

She frowned, then smiled and nodded. "Yes — yes, I am, thank you. Really, it was nothing. I didn't even notice the pieces were missing until I came in for my shift. So it didn't happen on my watch."

Julie examined Daris' expression as she recounted her story. She'd probably said it to confirm that she was, in fact, okay — she wasn't even there when the break-in had happened — but Julie it came across as overconfidence, as if the woman was trying to prove to them all that the theft hadn't been her fault.

"Of course," Joshua said. "But you noticed the journal missing first?"

She nodded again. "Yes. I opened up and then began walking the floor. It's a habit I have — I am a geek about this stuff, after all — and I saw that the case it was in had completely disappeared."

"You didn't have the journal on display?"

"No, I didn't. It's not... *known* to the outside world that we even have it. Or that it even exists. So it's always been in a case, locked up, and kept inside the vault."

"The *vault*?" Reggie asked.

"Well, it's just a room, really. We don't have very high security here, as it's not at the same level museum as something like the Smithsonian or the Louvre. Usually the patrons of our library are fascinated specifically with early American history. You sort of need to be a history buff to truly enjoy this place, and you certainly need to have a strong desire to dig around and do some research to understand all of the things we have here."

Reggie grinned, holding it long enough to ensure that Daris saw it. "*I'm* a history buff," he said. Julie even thought he saw the man wink.

"Anyway," Joshua said, shooting Reggie a glance. "The vault — or the room you call the 'vault.' Where is it?"

"It's right off the main meeting hall," she said, as if they were all already intimately familiar with the building's layout. "Just a closet, really. But it's where we keep all of the items that aren't currently on display, if they're not lent out to another museum."

"And this room was locked?"

"Yes. It's always locked."

"How did you notice the room had been entered then, if the room was locked when you came in for your shift?"

She nodded, seeming to have anticipated this question. "It's part of my walk through. I check everything — the hallways, the main floor, and the vault. Just a habit, but I go through each room and just..."

Her cheeks turned a slight shade of red as her voice trailed off. Her eyes sank, her gaze falling to the desk.

Reggie leaned forward. "What's up? You just... what?"

"Sorry," she said quickly." I apologize. "It's just that... it's a weird routine, I admit. But I just like to *be around* those items. It's an amazing collection, actually. So much history that has gone unnoticed for so many years..."

Julie suddenly felt sad for this woman. Obviously educated, obviously very beautiful, she wondered how Daris had come to be the curator at a place so… *underwhelming*. It was true what Daris was saying about the place — there was a *lot* of history in this building, but the general public didn't know, or even care, about it. It wasn't the architecturally alluring building of Independence Hall, and it wasn't the storied internationally popular attraction of the Smithsonian in Washington, D.C.

But Daris was here, and she seemed utterly fascinated by her job and caught up in the importance of it all, even if she was the only one who felt that importance.

Julie smiled. She understood, to a small degree. Julie herself was passionate about certain things that made no sense to anyone — the elegance and beauty of perfect syntax and simplicity in server code, for example, or the logical chain of adoption in a new disease her old employer, the CDC, was studying.

Things the general public cared little about, but impacted their daily lives more than they knew.

*Could that be what's happening here?* she wondered. *Is there something hidden under the surface of this organization that makes all of this more important?*

"Daris," Julie said.

Daris' head snapped up and her attention burned a hole through her head.

"Y — yes?"

"What's going on here?"

"I'm sorry, Miss Richardson," Daris said. "I'm not sure what you mean."

"A journal that *no one* — in your words — knew about was stolen, as well as what sounds like the most insignificant artifact in human history. An artifact that wasn't even important enough to live in the vault with the other out-of-rotation things. This one was in the basement."

"Correct —"

"But *someone* knew they were there. Someone knew *exactly* where to look, and how to get into both the vault and the basement."

Julie sat back, suddenly realizing her questioning had escalated from confusion to interrogation. She considered apologizing, but thought better of it.

"Again, correct."

They sat there a moment, Daris on one side of her power desk, and the four of them on the other.

Julie broke the ice. "Your story doesn't add up."

Daris' cheeks burned even redder. "My *story* is not at all fiction. I'm telling you *exactly* —"

"Perhaps," Julie said. "But you're leaving something out. Something *crucial*."

The tension in the room ratcheted up a few notches, and Julie felt like she was swimming in it. It was thick, bold, and obvious.

No one spoke. Reggie looked around, his eyes wide.

Julie couldn't tell if the others were on her side or upset that she'd even opened her mouth. But she was right.

She knew it.

# TWENTY-TWO

*DAMMIT, JULIE,* REGGIE THOUGHT. *YOU had to go and clam her up.*

Reggie was sitting in the leather chair in front of Daris' desk, still surprised at how comfortable it felt. He was *also* surprised at how forward Julie had just gotten with her, and he was afraid it would end the conversation.

He knew something was fishy as soon as they'd entered the office. Decorated with furniture that looked like it had all been purchased at the same time, from the same store, and placed around the office in exactly the same way as the picture on the outside of the box it all came in, Reggie got the immediate feeling of strangeness.

He would have been able to ignore the feeling, however, and write it off as a personality quirk. Some people, especially reclusive types who like to work in museums, aren't as savvy when it comes to inter-personal skills. It would have made sense, and he would have simply thought of it all as a characteristic that made him like her more.

But her clothes contradicted that feeling. They screamed trendi-ness, from her hair down to her shoes, and they were certainly out of place in downtown Philadelphia.

The woman in front of them now wasn't who she said she was, and Reggie had already planned his attack — how he'd get her to confess and tell them what was *really* going on.

But Julie had ruined all of that. She'd opened her big mouth and called out the 'curator' for lying to them, or at least withholding infor-mation. Now it was almost guaranteed Daris wouldn't talk to them anymore, and they'd have to figure out another way to —

"You're right," Daris said. She sighed, a short, huffy thing that seemed genuine to Reggie. "You're right. I've left some things out."

Reggie's eyebrow danced up. *This is a twist,* he thought. He looked at Julie and caught sight of the very end of a smug smile.

"First, I'm not the curator here."

Reggie waited. Ben and Joshua, sitting behind him on the couch, also waited silently.

"My name is Daris, but I do not work at the APS. Or, rather, I do not work at the *museum*."

"Where do you work?" Joshua said.

"Well, I work here," she answered. "But there's no museum here."

"Wait, what?" Julie asked.

"It moved, a long time ago. The Society needed a place to have larger meetings, so we purchased a building nearby — the Benjamin Franklin Hall. We moved the library and meeting hall there. This building —" she held up an open hand and flourished it around the room — "is just smaller offices, a small conference room. Nothing else here."

"Okay, so you were in the *other* building and noticed the stuff missing. So what?"

"Well, *I* didn't notice it missing. Like I said, I'm not a curator. I just work here."

"So you've got someone you're covering for."

She paused. "Yes, something like that."

"Fine," Joshua said. "We'll let that slide for now, but go on. This *other* person noticed the journal and the rock missing, and told you about it?"

"Right. They called it in, and I told them to tell no one else about it until I could figure out the next move."

"You told someone in the military. They passed it on to our benefactor."

"Yes," she continued, "but I specifically told them I was handling it."

"Why tell them in the first place?"

Another pause, this one longer.

"Listen, Daris. It really is important that we're on the same team here. And that means we need to know what you know."

She swallowed. "I understand. It's just… all of this is happening so fast. I never thought it would…"

"Never thought *what*?" Julie asked.

"Never thought it would happen at all," she replied. "At least not in my lifetime."

Reggie looked at the faces of everyone else in the room. Aside from

Julie, they were all masters of their poker faces. Ben, Joshua, and Daris all had a blank, expressionless silence written on their faces.

Reggie felt the tide turning in their argument, but he turned back to the woman seated across from him and drilled into her with his gaze.

*This is it,* he thought. *The moment of truth.*

"Daris," he said, calmly. "*What* are you afraid is happening?"

She swallowed again, then a third time. She sat back in her chair, sinking into it a bit and getting even smaller. Then she turned her focus back to Reggie and laid her hands out on the desk, palms up.

"We call it… *The Shift.*"

# TWENTY-THREE

*OKAY, NOW I KNOW THIS woman's crazy,* Ben thought. For a lady who had played a role as a museum curator well, he had been surprised to hear she wasn't exactly who she'd said she was. She was well-dressed, working in a decent office, and telling them a story that they'd all — as far as Ben could tell — believed.

Now she was admitting to Reggie that there was a *bit* more to the story than she'd initially let on. She wasn't the simple, lowly museum curator of an all-but-forgotten monument of American history.

Ben stared her down. He didn't like people who used lies and deceit to get what they wanted. Then again, what *did* she want?

"What the hell is *The Shift?*" Reggie asked.

Julie and Joshua nodded, but Ben continued staring at her. He watched her face, studying it. He had already decided that it was a nice face — nothing compared to her tiny, petite body — but it was a decent enough face. Pretty, slightly upturned nose, small features. All of it together made for a very beautiful human.

But she was holding back information from them, and that didn't sit well with him. It made her less attractive to Ben. Her face showed no sign of regret, however, aside from the very slightest of tics: the left side of her mouth popped up and down just a bit every few seconds, as if she was deep in thought and trying to work through her response.

*Or work through the response she was* supposed *to give them.*

She'd already played her hand, at least the part of it about *what* she was worried about. Ben figured she might as well explain the rest of it, too.

"It's…"

A loud *crash* sounded from outside the room. It echoed into the hallway, but Ben thought it might have even come from outside the building entirely. It was quiet in a distant sort of way, but also intense, as if glass and drywall and brick had suddenly — and violently — just been disrupted.

"Everyone get down," Joshua said. His voice was calm, as always, and he sounded more annoyed than surprised.

Ben dropped to a knee, moving over slightly to make sure Julie knew he was next to her. She nodded at him, also coming to rest on her left knee. Both of them swiveled and looked out the door.

Ben saw out of the corner of his eye an odd movement — Daris flicked her eyes left, then right, and then back to the door. Only then did she crouch down as well. Her eyes stayed riveted on the open door that led to the hallway.

*She's waiting for something.*

*Making sure* we're *waiting, too.*

Ben's mind immediately filled with possible scenarios. He knew Reggie and Joshua would have been better equipped to decipher the odd behavior Daris had just portrayed, but he wasn't sure if they'd seen it.

Reggie and Joshua were already whispering to each other in the corner of the room, Reggie pointing at his eyes with two fingers of his left hand while pointing out the door with the other.

Ben knew they weren't armed with much more than a sidearm, so whatever defensive ruse Reggie had cooked up was going to be a crapshoot.

And if he was right about Daris…

*Time to go with my gut instinct.*

He poked Julie in the side.

She frowned, smacking away his hand. "Not n —"

"Hey," he whispered. He hoped even in a whisper she could pick up on his tone. He wasn't trying to fool around.

She looked at him, barely moving her head.

*Good,* he thought. *Keep it subtle.*

"We need to get ready to bail," he whispered, trying to keep the words smooth and slow, yet indecipherable by anyone more than a foot away. "There's a window behind us. You think —"

He noticed the gentle rise of Daris' arm, the easy, casual pace her shoulder lifted. Her eyes were on the door, but her focus was on the desk. Specifically, a drawer that she was sliding open.

Ben would have missed the nearly inaudible scraping sound if he hadn't been intently focused on what she was doing. Dari's shoulder dropped again, and then he heard it.

*Click.*

The gun came up from beneath the top of the desk, already aimed and pointed directly at Julie.

He didn't even take the time to yell. He threw his arm sideways, knowing it was a large enough appendage that it would be possible to knock Julie out with it. He hit her, hard, and she flew backwards, a small gasp leaving her mouth.

The pistol fired, the deafening roar of the bullet only reaching Ben's ears long after the lead had landed.

Thankfully it hadn't landed in Julie. She was on the floor of the office, spread-eagled, and the bullet had sunk into one of the books on the shelf behind her head, only inches above it.

Ben took in a deep breath, hoping to speed along the adrenaline rush he knew was close by, but he was already moving. He lunged over the desk, flying headfirst directly at Daris and aiming at her head. His large body was going to be his weapon, and he hoped that Daris was as weak as she was small.

He never got the chance to find out. If Daris was lacking in the height and weight department, she was certainly not lacking in nimbleness.

She ducked and fell to the side into a perfectly executed roll, her shoulder barely scraping the rug beneath her desk as she easily side-stepped Ben's attack. Ben hit the back wall, saw stars, and then fell into a heap behind the desk. His feet landed on the office chair Daris had previously been sitting in.

Daris followed through her juke and came up on one knee, pointing her pistol at Ben while she breathed through a small 'O' she'd turned her lips into. She steadied her aim...

*Crack!*

Another gunshot rang out in the room, then another. Ben barely heard the third shot as his ears were already ringing after the first one, but he was able to swivel around and see who had fired.

It hadn't been Reggie *or* Joshua. Instead, a man was standing in the doorway. Larger than Ben, his skin a deep shade of brown, with a thin goatee surrounding his mouth.

The barrel of his pistol was aimed at Daris, but when Ben looked back at her she was nowhere to be found.

Reggie had his own pistol aimed at the new intruder, but the man hadn't moved from the doorway and hadn't changed the direction he was aiming. Slowly, deliberately, the man lowered his weapon. He stared at the spot Daris had been crouched in only moments ago, his eyes fixed in a permanent scowl.

Ben didn't move, didn't speak. An inch difference in the man's aim would put Ben's head in the sights of the pistol. He stared, glowering back at the huge black man, but he didn't move a muscle.

# TWENTY-FOUR

"WHERE IS SHE?" THE MAN asked.

"Who?"

Ben flicked his eyes over to Reggie, who'd spoken from the corner of the room, his gun still fixed on the man in the doorway. Joshua had his weapon in his hand, holding it with his finger ready to pull the trigger but pointing it toward the floor.

"Where is *Daris?*"

"She — she was right there," Julie said. "Right next to Ben. Only a second ago. You *had* to see her —"

"I *did* see her," the man said. "I *shot* at her. But she's not *here* anymore, is she?"

Julie shook her head.

Ben stood up, arms out to his side. The gun followed him, until the man was aiming directly at Ben's head. He held his hands open, trying to convince the man that he was no threat.

"Talk to me," Ben said. "I can tell you what you need to know."

"Okay, *fine*. Where the hell'd she go?"

"She went... into the floor."

Ben wasn't sure if the truth was going to get him shot or earn him a friend. The man was obviously not here to kill them, but he also wasn't afraid of getting shot himself. Reggie was aiming directly at him, and Joshua was ready with a loaded pistol as well, and the man hardly seemed to notice.

"Into the floor? Where?"

Ben shrugged. "Right where she was standing, I guess. Probably a trapdoor or something."

"A *trapdoor*. You've got to be kidding me. What is this, a middle-school play?"

Ben shrugged again, then nodded. "She planned all of this out. I saw her, right after you exploded your way in — by the way, thanks for not blowing up *this* room instead — anyway, I saw her eyes. She was *waiting* for you. She looked at all of us, like she was waiting for us to get into position or something. Calculating it all."

The man's tongue hit the inside of his cheek, and his eye squinted closed. He was deep in thought, and Ben wondered if he was trying to decide if he was telling the truth or trying to figure out what Ben's statement meant.

Finally he spoke, dropping his pistol. "Move over. We need to find that door."

Ben slid over so the huge man could search the room. He wasn't about to let his guard down, and he also wasn't going to start helping him.

"Who are you, by the way?" Joshua asked.

The man knelt to the floor and started feeling around the edges of a square piece of wood flooring. It was the door, but it was flush with the rest of the room and wouldn't open by applying pressure to the top of it.

"Derrick," he answered, gruffly.

"Derrick *who*?"

"That is the *who*," he said. "Roger Derrick, FBI."

"You guys are just coming out and announcing that now?"

He stopped what he was doing and looked up. "No, but you're already involved in a federal investigation, obviously on to the same lead we're following, and it wouldn't convince anyone of anything if I said, 'I work for the government,' now would it?"

Reggie grinned. "You and I are going to be friends."

Derrick squinted an eye in his direction. "I *highly* doubt that."

"Why, you don't have friends?"

"That's right. I don't have friends. Now, if you don't mind, we need to find out how to get this door opened."

Ben and Joshua walked to the opposite side of the desk, while Reggie and Julie started looking around the room. Ben figured since Daris hadn't moved from her position behind the desk until she had walked onto the movable platform, the button or activation switch for the door would be somewhere on her desk.

He was right. Just inside the top drawer, impossible to find unless you knew it was there, was a small brass button. He pushed it and Derrick yelped and rolled out of the way as the door fell open.

He scowled at Ben, but then jumped over the opening and slid smoothly down through the floor. Ben rushed over and looked down. "You okay?" he asked.

"Yeah. She's got a nice little landing pad down here, but she's long gone."

Ben waited until Derrick was out of the way and then he too jumped down the trapdoor and found himself in the basement of the American Philosophical Society building.

Julie, Reggie, and Joshua followed behind, but he was already taking a look around the room with Roger Derrick. Stacks of books, rows of filing cabinets, and shelves floor-to-ceiling on two walls. It seemed like exactly what he imagined the basement of a museum would look like.

Except that the 'curator' of this 'musuem' wasn't at all who she'd claimed to be.

Ben turned to Derrick. "Where'd she go? There aren't any other doors here except the one at the top of the stairs over in the corner, but we would have noticed her leaving — she would have had to walk right by us."

"Keep your eyes open," Derrick said. "There's got to be something on one of the walls. Maybe a door or a crawl space or something."

"*Or* she's a *real* magician and just *disappeared*," Reggie said, his voice dripping with sarcasm.

"Do you folks always act so nonchalant? Where I'm from, this is a serious mission."

Ben saw Joshua frown. He walked over and reached out a hand. "Joshua Jefferson. We're with —"

"I know," Derrick said, interjecting. "I read all about it on the flight over. 'Civilian Special Operations.' Cute. You have any sort of leader, or are you hippies about your organizational structure as well?"

Ben wasn't sure if he was more offended by the man's abrupt interruption and dismissal of them all or the fact that he'd called Ben a hippie.

"You're talking to him," Joshua said. "What about you? You guys still operate as teams, or are you the new guy in the office who got assigned to babysitting duty?"

The two men, both clearly experienced professionals in the art of espionage and battlefield tactics, stared each other down for a few seconds.

Or more precisely, Derrick stared *Joshua* down — he was a full head taller than everyone in the room but Ben.

Finally Derrick's face split into a wide grin. "Come on, man, I'm just *Joshing* you."

Joshua didn't smile.

"Fine," Derrick said. "Tough crowd. Whatever. Anyway —" he turned to the rest of Ben's group who had inadvertently gathered around the two men as if they were about ready to spar. " — Sorry we got off on the wrong foot. In the world I come from, things are… a bit more *sterile*. It's good to loosen up a little."

Julie smiled, a genuine, beautiful specimen, the one that Ben had fallen in love with nearly a year ago.

"Like I said, my name's Roger Derrick, and I *am* with the FBI. No, I don't have a team on this one, though I've still got an office I report to, which means I can probably call in a few favors as I see fit."

"So be nice to you?" Reggie asked.

Derrick ignored the joke. "I was sent out to just take a peek at the operation here and keep an eye on things."

Julie spoke up from next to Ben. "*What* operation?"

"Well… yours."

They all looked around for a few more seconds until Reggie actually raised his hand, a goofy expression on his face. "So, this would, you know, go a lot quicker if you would just *tell* us what the hell you're after. If it's our hot librarian chick, she's probably called an Uber and is halfway to Boston by now."

Derrick nodded. "Right. Sorry, yes, I'm here to observe *your* operation. I was sent by my boss to look in on things."

"Your boss wouldn't happen to be friends with Mr. E, would he?"

"*Your* boss? No. But through a mutual acquaintance, yes."

"So Mutual Acquaintance heard from your boss — who heard from Daris — that there was a break-in in her precious museum? And Mutual Acquaintance then passed it on to Mr. E, who's been trying to start up a 'Civilian Special Operations' team to look into these exact sort of things?"

Derrick listened to Reggie's explanation, nodding along. "Yes, actually. So since this is considered pretty low-level, there isn't an action team in place. It's just me."

"What exactly are you supposed to do, then?" Julie asked.

"Watch, observe, and report back to my superiors whether or not I think this group — *your* group — is worth investing in."

"You mean if this group is a *threat* to national security," Reggie said.

"Well, that's part of it, yes. That's at one end of the spectrum, but 'giving you a lot of money' is at the other end."

"Seems like it'd be a conflict of interest to have the FBI involved with a civilian team that's also working with the US military," Joshua said.

"Why?" Derrick asked. "We're all on the same team."

"Are we?" Reggie asked.

Derrick's nostrils flared, but he didn't get upset. He paused, searching for the right words. Finally, he dropped his head and then brought it up again and met Reggie's hard gaze. "I'll be the first to admit that my organization hasn't always appeared to have the best interests of our nation in mind, but I *assure* you, I do."

"You have the nation's best interests in mind, or just those of your employer?"

"I'm a hard worker, and I do the job right," Derrick said. "And I'm not going to apologize for that. But I'm an American. I signed up for this job, with you all. I *wanted* to be here."

"Why?"

Ben suddenly felt like the conversation had turned into an interrogation that he was on the wrong side of. He held up a hand, timidly at first, then with more conviction. "Wait," he said. "This guy's on our team. I believe him, at least for now. But no one's getting their job done if we're just standing around in the basement talking. There's time for that later."

Reggie nodded. "Yeah," Reggie said. "He's right." He turned to Derrick. "Where to now, then? You have any idea where she went?"

Derrick nodded. "Yeah, I do. New York City."

"Wait, really? New York?"

Derrick nodded again. "Yep. She's catching a train in an hour, and then she's got a date early tomorrow morning, in New York. Times Square."

"Who's the date with?" Julie asked.

Derrick took a deep breath. "Patricia Gonzales. She's scheduled to appear on live television first thing tomorrow morning. Good Morning America."

# TWENTY-FIVE

"HAWK, WE'VE JUST GOT A report," Morrison said.

They were standing on opposite sides of the large gym, yet The Hawk heard his second-in-command's voice perfectly, thanks to the wireless communications systems they both wore.

"Tell me," The Hawk said.

"She's no longer at the APS, sir," Morrison said. "Ran out via a basement door, and we don't have a track on her."

"Well *get* a track on her. That should have been done already."

"Yes, sir."

The Hawk shook his head, then turned back to the rest of the room. It was a gymnasium, empty in the center except for a single chair. The windows, small rectangular things that hung right at the top edge of the building, had all been blacked out. The two doors into the facility were at opposite sides of the room, one locked and blocked off with a thick braid of chain around the handle. The Hawk stood at this door, the very edge of his own private realm.

He watched as half his team, the three men currently working inside, performed their various duties. Morrison had begun walking to the center of the room to capture the attention of two of the men and give the order to find their employer and place some tracking gear on her person and her vehicle.

The Hawk touched his ear once again and began talking. "Morrison," he said.

"Sir?" Morrison stopped short near the center of the room.

"What happened? Why did she bail?"

"Unclear sir, but it appears there were others on the premises. She could have been spooked and then left via the trapdoor in the office."

The Hawk frowned. "Not our men?"

He saw Morrison shake his head even before he heard the answer. "No, sir. Jenkins and Velacruz hadn't even entered the APS building when they saw her emerge from the basement into the parking lot and then into her vehicle."

The Hawk sucked in a breath. "And *why* did they not tail her?"

"They did, sir. But they watched the building for another minute to ensure there was no one inside."

"They cleared?"

Morrison hesitated. "…no, sir. They watched from outside. Then they decided to follow her."

"But by then it was already too late, wasn't it?"

"Yes, apparently it was, sir. They said she was headed in the direction of the airport, but they lost her about three blocks from the APS."

The Hawk nearly cursed, but caught himself. He would have to punish them, but that could wait. Better, he could have Morrison himself do it. He walked over to Morrison, standing next to the chair in the middle of the room, and the two men working.

"Morrison, why was she in a hurry to leave the APS? We had agreed upon a schedule that would allow us the correct amount of time for each party."

"Yes, sir, we had. We don't know, sir. Maybe there was someone else involved? A third party?"

"What third party?"

"Maybe that agent that's been snooping around?"

"She knows about the FBI, Morrison. She wouldn't have been spooked by them."

"Him."

"Excuse me?"

"Him — just one, sir. The FBI doesn't even have a team on this on. They've just sent in one of their agents to scope things out."

The Hawk frowned. This, too, was new information. The FBI *never* sent in just one person at a time. Agents worked in pairs sometimes, but more often teams of four, covering a city block or watching a house or tailing a target by 'leapfrogging' and following. Two of agents would hang back, providing support and staying out of view as much as possible, while the other two agents would move in.

He'd had a few encounters with FBI-types, and he'd never seen one working alone.

*Curious.*

He filed the information away, making a mental note to revisit it at a later time, or to let his subconscious work on it until something clicked.

"What else, Morrison?"

"Sir?"

"What *else?* She knew about the FBI, she knew they were watching her, because I told her that. So she'd have no reason to be spooked by them. What other information do we have on this?"

The Hawk could tell Morrison wanted to shrug, to squirm away and move to the other side of the room. He wasn't trying to grill the man, either, but this was important.

*This was crucial.*

The Hawk refused to be played by more than one side. He operated under the expectation that the enemy was *always* trying to play him, as that was the game.

But it was another thing entirely when a *client* was trying to play him. If he was getting the run-around from his employer somehow — if she was trying to pit him against the other side so she could extract some sort of benefit from the situation, there would be hell to pay. This was part of the reason he hated American contracts — there was always more of a bureaucratic slant to the work. Someone needed protecting, but it was typically protection from a political enemy, not necessarily a physical one.

He specialized in the *physical* enemies. The ones who could be hunted.

The ones who could be shot.

Simple, foolproof two-sided warfare. Drug lords running up against a larger empire. A group of small companies fighting an oligarchy. Bankers working to keep their position at the top of a countries' fiscal food chain safe.

It didn't matter which side hired him, but he certainly preferred to keep the playing field as simple as possible.

Americans never saw it this way. They *thrived* in the convoluted grounds of political trench warfare. They wanted *confusion,* because confusion could be monetized.

He shook his head and smiled, already considering what he might have to do if his boss was playing him against someone else. He raised his eyebrows, focusing again on Morrison.

"We — we don't have any, sir. As I said, it's speculation, but there could have been a third party involved, besides the FBI."

"And if there is?"

Morrison looked blank for a moment, and The Hawk could almost feel the fear inside him. Finally, Morrison recovered. "Then we'll find them, sir."

The Hawk nodded and spun around. "Do it fast. We don't have time."

# TWENTY-SIX

REGGIE STARED AT ROGER DERRICK while he spoke. He wasn't sure if he trusted this guy yet, but everything he was saying seemed to add up, and seemed to make sense.

*And I've already been proven right about someone once today,* he thought, thinking about Daris, the secretive runaway curator-turned-illusionist. He smiled as he recalled the way she'd just simply *disappeared* into the floor. He hadn't seen a trick like that since his high school's stage production of *The Phantom of the Opera.*

He wondered if she'd had the trapdoor installed just for that moment, or if it had once been used as an access hatch for the basement.

Reggie's ears perked up as he heard mention of the trapdoor.

"...apparently had it installed shortly after the real APS moved in," Derrick said.

"The *real* APS?" Ben asked. "I thought this building was home to the real APS back in Benjamin Franklin's day?"

"That was the *Junto,* Julie answered. It wasn't the APS until later."

Ben frowned, staring at her.

"What? I read the brief," she said, shrugging.

Derrick smiled. "She's correct. But even then, when this building was designated by the American Philosophical Society, it was used for meetings and gatherings of the group, when the office and library needs were still small. The bulk of the Society's usage moved from here to the Benjamin Franklin Hall, nearby, later on."

"So what's this '*real*' APS, then?" Reggie asked. He stepped up closer to Derrick, who was still encircled by the group in the center of the basement. As Reggie waited for the answer, he looked around the room once again, trying to take it all in.

Trying to find something he'd missed.

He wasn't sure what it was, as he'd scanned the dimly lit basement a thousand times already, but something was nagging at him. He wasn't even sure if there *was* something he'd missed, but still...

*That feeling.*

Reggie had learned long ago to trust his gut in these situations. Heightened state of awareness, adrenaline pumping, on edge, waiting for something to snap.

The man in front of him now wasn't going to snap. The man reminded Reggie of Joshua, actually. Darker skin and a foot taller, but he had the same calm, collected demeanor. Reggie had the impression that if he hadn't barged into a room full of strangers who were now surrounding him and forcing him to talk, Derrick would be as quiet a man as Joshua.

So there was still something else... something in his subconscious urging him to analyze, just as he'd been trained.

*What is it?*

He looked around once again as Derrick delved into the history of the APS. Reggie had read the brief, but as a history buff he also knew much of the story already anyway. Benjamin Franklin and a handful of close Philadelphia friends started a group for thinking, discussing, and discourse, called *The Junto,* then through numerous years and iterations it became the original *American Philosophical Society.*

He made a mental note to check in with the story once it had come full-circle and Derrick explained what he'd meant when he'd told them of the *"real"* APS, and started walking toward the shelves along the side of the room.

The shelves were industrial-strength, the type of structure fit for an auto shop or a distribution warehouse. As such, they seemed out of place here in a relatively small basement. The floor plan didn't support such massive shelves, and yet they were mostly full.

He stood beneath the first set of floor-to-ceiling shelves, admiring them. Each shelf was filled with office boxes, plastic tote containers, and some canvas bags.

*Looks like a museum.*

He peered into the first cardboard office box. Boxes, folders, and some canvas bags with tagged ends. Pretty much exactly what Reggie would have expected if they were in a museum.

Then it hit him.

*This isn't a museum.*

Derrick looked at him, their eyes meeting. He knew Reggie had put it together. How could he be so dense? Daris had literally just told them upstairs: *'this isn't a museum.'*

*So why does everything down here look like it belongs in a museum?* He was standing in a basement with a trapdoor entrance, an exit via the stairs as well as one they hadn't yet found, and he was surrounded by rows of shelves that would fit perfectly in the warehouse basement storage of the Louvre.

"It's not a museum," Reggie said.

Julie frowned, and Ben rolled his eyes.

"I know — Daris already told us that, but think about it. Why does it look *exactly* like a museum down here, *if it's not a museum?*"

"It's just storage, possibly for —"

Reggie walked over to the box he'd peered into. "Look," he said, holding up the first thing he grabbed. A clasp folder, filled with something bulky. He opened it and showed the others. "A fossil." He grabbed the next folder and opened it. "Another one. Interesting."

He returned the item and moved to the next box on the shelf. He pulled out a canvas bag, complete with the tag and label. Another fossil, this one larger and seemingly taken from the leg of a large animal.

"Everything down here belongs in a museum," Reggie finally said. "Why would everything look like it came from a museum if it's *not* a museum?"

"Like I said," Julie said, "it could just be storage. Maybe these items are part of a collection, and they're just being kept down here for —"

"It's not storage for a museum," Derrick said.

All eyes turned to him, still looming in the center of the room.

He continued. "It's not a museum, *per se,* but rather the private collection of the American Philosophical Society."

"But there's nothing on display," Julie said. "No way to see this stuff. Why would they want to hide it all?"

Reggie realized Julie had just answered her own question. *The APS wants to hide this stuff because, well, they think it needs to be hidden.*

Derrick once again met his gaze. Reggie walked back over to the group and stared back at the huge man. "This junk room is really where that journal was kept, wasn't it? The journal that Daris says is Meriwether Lewis' own private journal from the expedition, and the one she said had been 'locked in the vault?'"

"She said that? There's no vault here. Sounds like she was giving you the runaround."

"Sounds like it. And so all the rest of this stuff is junk they — the

APS — wanted to hide, presumably for the same reason they've been hiding the Lewis journal all these years."

Again, Derrick nodded. Reggie looked around at the others quickly before adding, "and I don't suppose you want to elaborate on any of that?"

He raised an eyebrow. "Honestly, I'm not really sure why they've been hiding it all these years myself. I started investigating Daris on assignment, after she began working on the book she just released. I've known that she was APS for a while, and my office likes to keep tabs on people with the sort of influence she has."

Julie frowned. "What sort of influence? And what book?"

"Actually, that's why she will be on Good Morning America tomorrow morning," Derrick said. "She's a pretty big hitter in the realm of political blogging. Just released a book called *The Jefferson Legacy.*"

"'Political blogging,'" Reggie said. "Sounds fun."

Derrick shrugged. "Apparently there's a lot of money in this stuff, and not just through advertising revenue. Her platform has thousands of supporters, and quite a few contributors as well. It's been enough for her not to have to have another job."

"So she's definitely not a museum curator," Ben said.

Derrick shook his head and laughed. "No, she is certainly not a museum curator."

"Still," Joshua said, "I don't understand why this is all such a big deal. Why would she reach out to our boss to ask for help? Especially if she was just going to set us up, try to kill us, then disappear in a cloud of smoke?"

Reggie noticed Ben was staring at the space between two of the great shelves. He suddenly walked over and started feeling along the edges, near the sides of the shelves.

"What are you doing?" Reggie asked.

"She didn't disappear into a cloud of smoke, actually," Ben said. "She fell down the trapdoor, came down here, and then disappeared into... *this.*"

As he spoke the last few words he pushed on the wall with both hands and it fell away, swinging into a dark, rectangular hallway. The doorway had been cut into the wall of the basement and then covered in the same drywall and paint as the rest of the room, creating the effect of an 'invisible' door.

Ben stepped into the space revealed behind the door and Reggie saw that there was only enough room there for the door to swing open before the passageway ascended up a small set of stairs. Ben climbed the first two stairs then pushed up on a set of cellar doors. A sharp sting of daylight cut through the newly formed crack between the doors.

He dropped the door and stepped back into the room.

"Looks like it goes up and out to the parking lot," he said. When he realized everyone was staring at him, he continued. "It was impossible to see," he said, "except that there's a faint line of dust along the top edge, where the door would have sucked in as it opened. Those old boxes near it on the shelves must be pretty dusty."

Reggie followed Ben's finger as he pointed at the line. It was just as Ben said — nearly impossible to see, and yet now that he was focusing on the spot it was impossible to miss.

"Wow," he said. "Great catch."

"Well we *didn't* catch her," Joshua said.

"Doesn't matter now," Roger Derrick said. "We know where she'll be tomorrow morning, so we can just be ready to grab her after the show."

"Why go through all this trouble?" Joshua asked again. "A building that's not really a museum, a trapdoor in an office she bought in a catalog, a hidden doorway? It all seems so… elusive."

"She's certainly got a flair for the dramatic," he said. "But the trapdoor and hidden cellar exit were probably here long before she was, probably something added during one of the many construction phases on this old building. And I honestly don't know what her motives are. She's been playing both sides of this thing since I've been watching her. Bringing you guys in here, telling you some of the story, then trying to shoot you. If I had to guess I'd say she wasn't expecting anyone to come snooping around. Not you, and not me."

"But then why would she tell someone else about the missing journal, and the missing artifact?" Julie asked.

Reggie hadn't wanted to reveal that part of their story yet, as he still wasn't sure how this Roger Derrick fellow fit in to it all. They didn't have a lot of cards to play, so if it were up to him, he'd rather keep most of them close to his chest.

If Derrick was in fact FBI, he would be well-connected and well-resourced, which meant they were probably in good hands. But there were still downsides. Derrick wouldn't be playing by the same rules, for starters, and he'd likely try to use his position to place himself in charge of the operation.

But if Derrick *wasn't* FBI, what was he? Why was he interested in Daris, the non-museum they were in, and finding this journal?

Derrick began to answer Julie's question. "Well, she's involved with the APS, just as she said she was. My guess is that she needed some help, so she asked another member. That member was the man who told your boss about the situation."

Reggie's eyebrows rose in unison. *Now we're getting somewhere*, he thought. "Okay, that makes a little more sense. So she didn't *want* us here — we came anyway, and she had to act quickly to make sure it didn't seem too far-fetched. The office furniture, the story, everything."

"Right," Derrick said. "She didn't do a great job of it, either, but she's still a step ahead of us."

"So we need to find that journal," Joshua said.

"And I need to find that woman," Derrick added.

"Sounds like we've got ourselves a working partnership, then," Reggie said. "You got someplace we can talk? Maybe somewhere a little less… dingy?"

Derrick smiled again, then walked over to the hidden door and toward the cellar stairs. Before he stepped out and into the small antechamber and onto the stairs, he turned back to the group. "I've got three rooms at the Rittenhouse. Will that work?"

# TWENTY-SEVEN

ALASTAIR JENKINS AND RENE VELACRUZ were brought into the gymnasium. As always, The Hawk stood at the far end, watching. Morrison met with the two men and their escorts — two more of The Hawk's men — and led them to the center of the room.

"There's only one chair, sir," Morrison said into his throat mic.

"I can count, Morrison," The Hawk replied. "Put Jenkins in the chair. He's the newest to our team."

Morrison nodded, then waited for Jenkins and his man to pass him, and he grabbed Jenkins' arm and pulled him toward the center of the room. Alastair Jenkins was a Scotch-American, raised on the East Coast in some small town that might as well have been Boston, for as much as the kid talked about Boston.

The Hawk hadn't taken a liking to him yet, which usually meant one thing: he was no good as a soldier or he was no good as an ally. This kid offered nothing The Hawk didn't already have, and he had no significant skills or networks his other men lacked. He was worthless as an ally, therefore, and he needed considerable training before The Hawk would view him as a worthy soldier.

He had, therefore, been placed on recon duty. An important, yet highly mundane, responsibility. He'd paired Rene Velacruz, his second-youngest member of the team, with him. The pair should have made a decent reconnaissance team, but apparently that was not the case.

Now The Hawk would be forced to make an example out of them. The young men had applied for the position at The Hawk's security company, promising that they were worthy of the enlistment. His initial interviews and tests were passed easily by the two men, but the final test — the *field* test, as he called it — was now underway.

The Hawk had learned long ago that training a man in the ways of war was impossible. You simply had to place them in a live-fire mission and see how they did. Their ability to adapt, to grow, to learn — these were skills far more important than how straight they could shoot or how large a man they could tackle.

So the final test was straightforward: join the company on a mission, and a vote would be cast at the end of the excursion. If they passed, they were in. If they failed…

Well, by his measure, they had both just failed. Miserably.

To leave not only their main contact *and* boss unwatched — allowing her to escape without a tail — *and* to fail to determine the reason she had fled two hours earlier than their initial plan was worse than treason to The Hawk.

They had botched a simple, no-skill-needed reconnaissance mission, and they had been stupid enough to return to the gym afterward.

He strolled to the center of the room. Jenkins was wide-eyed, but Velacruz appeared to have no knowledge of the fact that he had failed his mission.

"Sit down, Jenkins," he said. The Hawk watched as Morrison roughly pushed him down into the metal folding armchair, a thin built-in pad the only cushion provided.

Jenkins' wide-eyed gaze eventually found The Hawk's, and the boss smiled. "Welcome, Jenkins. Are you ready?"

Jenkins frowned, his eyes still falling out of his head. "Y — yes sir. Sir, it was an accident. We didn't —"

"Save it, Jenkins," Morrison said. "It's too late for that."

"But sir, I just want to —"

"I understand, Jenkins," The Hawk said. "I really do. But there's a lesson here, for all of us. It's important, and you're an integral part of that lesson."

Jenkins gulped.

"Are you ready?"

Jenkins forced a nod.

"Great. Morrison?"

Morrison and the two other men stepped forward and began fastening Jenkins' arms to the chair using zip ties.

"Sir, please —"

Morrison slugged Jenkins across the chin.

"Knock it off, Morrison. There will be plenty of time for that."

"He was mouthing off, sir."

"And you know how I treat people who mouth off, right?"

Morrison nodded. To his amusement, The Hawk noticed that Jenkins nodded as well.

"So because I don't appreciate people who mouth off, I'm going to allow *you* to interrogate Jenkins."

Morrison grinned, a sinister expression that involved his crooked nose bouncing up and down on his face, while his eyes sat unmoving in their hollowed-out chasms, dark and empty.

Jenkins swallowed again. The two other men stepped back and one of them returned to Velacruz' side. Around the room, other men looked up from their stations and began watching the scene unfold in the center of the gym floor.

The Hawk backed up, motioning for Morrison to take his place. Morrison's grin grew, and he stepped up to the spot just in front of Jenkins' chair, right next to where Velacruz was standing with his guard. Morrison cracked his neck, then his hands, then his back. The Hawk watched, knowing Morrison was going to enjoy this. Unfortunately Morrison was a simple man, needing nothing more than some entertainment — of the macabre variety as well as the sexual — and food and board to be happy. The Hawk reflected on his own habits, and silently praised the fact that he had all but removed the desires of common men and requisite emotions that plagued them from his life. He was still human, but he was as close to a perfect specimen as he'd ever seen.

Morrison licked his lips then began barking orders. "Bring the drug over here, Rogers. Richardson, get me the fans and set them up next to him."

Both men, from opposite sides of the massive room, sprang into action. A third man, Ashleigh, joined Emerson and helped with the large box fans. They ran to the wall, checking that their respective fans were still plugged in, then jogged to the center of the room and set them up around Jenkins' chair, angling them so their blast pointed upward, toward the ceiling of the gymnasium.

"Do we need the fans, sir?" Morrison asked. "The serum is probably a more —"

"The serum is fine, but it is expensive. We only have a few vials left from the prototyping lab. We'll use the traditional method."

"Of course, sir." Morrison turned back to the center of the room and helped the men set up the fans around Jenkins.

It was crude, using the 'traditional' method, but what The Hawk had said was true: there was not enough of the prototyped liquid version of the drug to be used on something so trivial as punishment. The traditional method would bring out a lesser reaction, but it would have far stronger side effects.

Another reason he'd opted for the traditional method.

# TWENTY-EIGHT

JULIE WASN'T SURE IF SHE was more impressed with the hotel
or with Ben's face as they walked through the lobby. The Rittenhouse,
Philadelphia's premier accommodations, was absolutely immaculate.
Rich, boutique, and flourished but not garish, Julie was in awe of the
luscious space. She gazed longingly at the massive ferns that poked at
the ceiling, rising out of huge concrete pillars that started on the floor
and ended in bulbous pots. An older couple dined just beneath one of
the pots, at a table that seemed to have been smelted from a single
block of gold, in large high-back armchairs that would have been
equally at home in the living room of a queen.

Just beyond the tables and plants was a wall of floor-to-ceiling
arched doorways, their glass doors revealing a picturesque dining patio
and garden just beyond. More guests talked and laughed as they ate
and drank, many of them holding and swirling wineglasses.

"This is nice," she whispered.

Ben nodded, eyes wide.

"It might be even nicer than The Broadmoor," she added.

He nodded again.

They'd stayed a couple nights at the Colorado Springs hotel and
resort a few months ago, before and after their trip to Antarctica. It
was the first time they'd met as a team, complete with Mr. E talking to
them through a television feed in one of the hotel's great ballrooms.

"It's an historic hotel," Reggie said. "I've never been here, but I've
always wanted to. It's fantastic — look at that!"

Julie followed the man's pointing finger the other direction, toward
the entrance to a bar. The bar was also perfectly appointed, designed to

match the decor and tone of the rest of the hotel, without distracting attention away from the beauty of the place.

"That's a beautiful sight," Ben said. "You buying?"

"First one's on me," Derrick said. "Then you're on your own. My per diem is enough to get me a cheeseburger at dinner most of the time."

Reggie laughed, then turned to Joshua. "I'm not sure we discussed per diem for *our* team, did we boss?"

"Drinks are on you," Joshua said, his characteristically dry voice not conceding to the joke. "And keep it reasonable. We're on the clock."

Reggie grinned again and pulled Ben over to the bar. "We'll bring it up to your room," he called out over his shoulder.

After the two men left, Julie looked again at Derrick. "Why three rooms?" she asked. "You're by yourself, right?"

Derrick nodded. "We always buy up a block of three rooms. I stay in the middle one, the other two are open."

"For safety?"

"Something like that. Used to set up surveillance crews in at least one of them, but that's a long-gone tradition. Still, it's nice in case I need to beef up the team last minute. And it's not so bad to never have any screaming kids or crying babies next to me."

Joshua and Julie nodded back at him. "Works for us," Joshua said.

"Good. We won't be staying long anyway, since we're just here to chat and figure out how we might be able to help each other. But the offer's open if you need a place to crash when this is all over. I can swing three nights after the mission's officially 'closed.'"

"Wow," Julie said. "I didn't realize the Bureau was so flush with cash."

"It's not," he said. "That's why I'm here alone."

Derrick was clearly done discussing it, and he turned and started toward the elevator. Out of the corner of her eye she saw Ben and Reggie walking over, a glass each in their hands.

She slowed and waited for them to catch up. Joshua was holding the elevator open, and Derrick had already stepped inside.

On Derrick's floor they all waited for the large man to maneuver out of the back of the elevator car and out toward his room. He walked purposefully toward the other end of the hallway, then stopped outside one of the rooms.

"This is me. I've got keys for the other rooms inside, if we decide to stay the night."

"I thought you said we wouldn't be here that long?" Julie asked.

"Well, as I was thinking about it more, I figured we'd want to watch the broadcast tomorrow morning," he answered, "and I realized I can just call in a favor and have her information tracked, so if she gets on a plane tomorrow we'll know about it. Besides, we're not going to surprise her by showing up on set. She'll have thought about that already and will have a plan in place, so our best bet is to lay low until we know where she's headed, then move in on her after we've made a plan."

No one argued, so Derrick unlocked the room and swung the door open.

Julie stepped inside and for the second time in an hour gasped aloud. The room was every bit as nice as the rooms at The Broadmoor, but these were even more spacious.

A full-sized couch sat in front of a huge flat-screen television, and two of the same high-back armchairs sat across from each other, forming with the couch three sides of a square around a small, long coffee table.

She walked through the main entranceway and saw a massive bathroom on her left and a sitting room on her right. A wall-sized mirror above the counter in the sitting room gave the impression that the room was even larger than it appeared. A walk-in closet had a folding door open, and she could see Derrick's suitcase and three pairs of shoes neatly placed inside.

Around the corner in the main room was the bed — an oak behemoth that rose four feet off the floor and was mounded with pillows of all shapes and sizes.

"I'm not married," Derrick said, "and I believe that's partly because I've heard women like these throw pillows. Drives me nuts. I wouldn't be able to handle it."

Reggie laughed, then fell into the couch with his drink.

Julie noticed that Ben's drink — whiskey, with an ice cube in it — was more than halfway gone already.

"You folks hungry?" Derrick asked. "Room service here is fantastic, and the menu's about as thick as my wrist."

He pointed to the end table near Reggie, and Reggie scooped up the book and started flipping through it.

"Let's order some food — my treat — and then we can talk a bit more about Daris, and her involvement in the APS."

# TWENTY-NINE

THE PILE OF FOOD THAT sat on Ben's plate — or *plates* — was far larger than he'd expected. He hadn't had a lot of experience with room service in fancy hotels, but what little he did had led him to believe that ordering from that menu meant he'd get a little food but a *big* bill.

Since there wouldn't be a bill that he'd have to pay, he went all out, rationalizing that it wasn't Derrick, after all, who'd have to pay for it, but the US government.

*Actually* I'm *paying for it,* he thought. *My tax dollars at work.*

He had ordered a steak, medium-rare, and a fully loaded baked potato. Assuming the steak would be one of those 7-oz. value options added to the menu solely to make people *feel* like they'd gotten the 'elegant dining' experience, he'd decided to also order a lobster tail and a side of fries.

The steak, however, was easily a 16-oz. hunk of meat. It was perfectly cooked, with a juicy, warm interior and a thin but delicious brown crust around it. The fries took up their own plate, and the lobster and baked potato another.

The others stared at him with the same faces they'd worn when he'd ordered the food.

"What?" he asked, innocently. "I told you I was hungry. I figured we could share the fries."

Julie laughed. "You guys go ahead — see what happens when you try to grab one of his fries."

Ben frowned at her but cut another bite of steak and shoved it into his mouth.

Derrick stood up in front of them, between the coffee table and television.

"Okay," he said. "We're here, we're eating, we know each other. Now let's talk about how we might go about finding this woman. We know she'll be in New York tomorrow, but after that? No idea."

"Well the first question to ask is, 'what does she *want*?'" Joshua said. "I got the strong feeling she *wanted* to kill us all earlier today, as soon as you crashed in and her ruse was up. But she fled, so I'm assuming that was just because she couldn't think of anything better to do, and she wasn't looking for a firefight."

"Right," Derrick said. "She didn't *want* to kill you until she realized she'd lost control of the situation. She's going to be able to regroup now, though, since she'll have time between now and tomorrow morning's appearance, and presumably after that on the plane to wherever she's going."

"Okay," Julie said. "That makes sense, but I'm still a little shaky on the details relating her to the APS. Is she a member? Or was she just using their building?"

Derrick started pacing. "No, actually. Her involvement with the APS goes much deeper than just membership. She's a legacy — someone whose parents or grandparents were in the club. In her case, both. She comes from a long line of APS members."

"So she's grown up in it," Reggie said.

"Yes, but when she reached adulthood she wanted more than just membership — she wanted to *run* it."

"Like, president or something?"

"Exactly like president. For the past eight years, Daris has been the president of the American Philosophical Society."

"Wow," Ben said. "Sounds like a pretty prestigious job."

Reggie grinned, but Julie and Joshua remained stoic.

"Actually, it is," Derrick said. "Akin to leading something like the Masons — most of what they do is secret, out of the public's eye, and they've got plenty of members in high places."

"Like the guy who ratted her out to Mr. E., our benefactor."

"Right. Military, comes from a rich family, a leader in his own right."

"And he's a member of the APS? This 'secret' version of the APS?" Julie asked.

Derrick nodded. "Just like plenty of other military brats, some even higher-ranking than him. And Daris is the president over all of them."

"What does that mean, though?" Joshua asked. "Even if they are like the Masons, what does the group actually *do?* Besides do secret chants and weird rituals?"

"Well, historically nothing," Derrick replied. "As you already know, they were founded based on Ben Franklin's original idea of a 'group for the advancement of intelligent thought,' so it was supposed to be more of a safe place for conceptual discourse than a group of action.

"But there was a schism shortly after it became the American Philosophical Society, and the members found themselves split, either on one side or the other."

"A split in beliefs?"

"Yes, sort of. A split about what the group was supposed to *be*, and what it was supposed to *do*. Members who believed in the 'old way,' the 'Franklinites,' wanted nothing more than a place where they could share and discuss new ideas and old wisdom.

"But the 'new way' crowd wanted *more* — they wanted to discover new things by *doing* things. They felt called to action, to actually take part in the new nation's political system, actively and openly."

"So they didn't agree," Reggie said. "Sounds like modern politics."

"Well, sure," Derrick said. "But remember, these guys have always had a 'closed door' policy. Everything they'd ever discussed was meant for their ears only. That means there were secrets — just like with Freemasons — that the APS charged itself with protecting."

Reggie stood up, putting down his food to start pacing as well. "Ah, I see. So 'old way'-ers wanted to keep the secrets, but the 'new way'-ers wanted to reveal it all. Scandals and skeletons."

"Exactly," Derrick said. "There were — are — things the APS wants to keep to itself, like the fact that this journal of Lewis' was something he'd written. But the other faction wanted to release it to the public, to let them know what it said."

Ben sat for another moment, thinking hard. His steak was nearly finished and the lobster and baked potato were already gone, but he hadn't even begun on the fries. He reached for a few of them, smashed them into some ketchup, and held them up to his mouth.

"Wait," he said, just before he'd taken a bite. "That means *Daris* is on one side of this, and the guy who told Mr. E is on the *other*. But she didn't know that, right? Or else she would never have told him."

Derrick nodded. "Yes, that is my interpretation of the situation as well. There are some who keep their leanings private, just like in the political sphere. This man must have been more of an old-school guy, but Daris guessed he was safely on her side."

"And why all the fuss with these 'sides,' anyway?" Ben asked. "Who cares? It's not like they're threatening national security or anything."

Derrick cocked an eyebrow.

"Wait — *really?* They *are* a threat? How is that even possible? Aren't there only a few members in the organization?"

"There are a handful of governing members, just as Franklin and his Junto designed it, but ever since the split between ideals, each side has been heavily recruiting."

"So… like a hundred people?" Reggie asked.

"*Thousands,*" Derrick answered. "Many of them from the branches of the armed forces. Young grunts, but also — like I said — some higher-level career types."

"The military is involved in a secret organization?"

"Don't be naive," Derrick said. "The military is its own fraternity, but in some ways the military hasn't been around as long as the Junto and the APS. Some of the folks in the military might have wanted something a little different than the flavor of 'faternity' the military provided, and the APS may have offered that."

"But then why haven't we heard of it?" Joshua asked.

"You're not looking for it. You've heard of the Masons because they get all the press. All the books written about them. All the fiction and movies that come out that need a scapegoat or a secret organization that's pulling strings behind the scenes — Masons get that reputation. But there hasn't ever been a need for *another* group, so the media ignores the APS. But go to a library, or start Googling, and there's plenty of information right there."

"Hmm," Julie said. "Makes sense. So there's a split between these two factions, and each side has been building its ranks, trying to get people who believe in their side of it all. But *what* are they arguing about, specifically? What's Daris trying to prove?"

Derrick eyed Ben for a long moment, and Ben wondered if he'd somehow missed a question directed at him. Finally, Derrick started toward the table and stopped, then answered.

"That's what she's talking about tomorrow on Good Morning America. Why don't we all try to relax a bit more, get some sleep, and then watch it here tomorrow morning?"

# THIRTY

JENKINS GROANED. THE HAWK WATCHED. Morrison smiled.

"Morrison, step back from the cloud; you're too close."

"The smoke is going straight up, sir," Morrison said. "There's no —"

"It's not worth it, Morrison," The Hawk barked. "Get back."

The Hawk watched as Morrison backed two steps away. Two *small* steps. Morrison had always known how to push his buttons, and if he wasn't a brutally efficient soldier that consistently brought out the best in his men, he might have been inclined to introduce Morrison to the chair instead.

But right now it was Jenkins' turn.

Morrison waited another minute. The man holding Velacruz in place stepped back from the thick cloud of acrid smoke, both their eyes widened. Velacruz took an involuntary step backwards, but ran into the barrel of the man's rifle.

"Jenkins," Morrison began. "You have taken the vows of service to this organization, given a mission, and you have been found wanting."

Jenkins' nodded, his head lolling left and right, as if on a swivel.

"And for that, your punishment shall ensue."

Jenkins hadn't stopped nodding. "Y — yes sir, Morrison. Sir."

"Do you wish to recount your mistakes?"

Again, a nod. Jenkins' head seemed as if it were about to fall off his neck. His eyes opened and closed, the smoke surrounding his entire body now. The fans had been placed strategically, turned on low, so they would blow the smoke up into a single column, directly at the swamp cooler air filter fans on the ceiling, which would funnel the smoke safely out of the building.

This 'traditional' method was still modernized; for one, the traditionalists who'd discovered the method had no fans or electricity, and therefore they had simply smoked the chemical inside a handmade pipe.

The Hawk had been tweaking the method a bit, according to Daris' orders. He wanted a way to use the smoke without needing to cut into the small cache of the next-generation version of the drug. The intravenous supply was still in testing, but The Hawk knew it worked. The side-effects had been lessened somewhat, but otherwise the drug was the same chemical as what Jenkins was inhaling now.

And unfortunately for Jenkins, the side effects of the inhaled version would be *far* more potent with this much smoke.

Jenkins started talking, mumbling. "I… I can… we tried — but then we…"

Morrison and the other men laughed, their chuckles reaching The Hawk's ears. The Hawk, however, wasn't amused. Watching a man get punished was nothing to laugh at.

It was leadership, and leadership wasn't always fun.

He sighed, knowing the strength of his team in the short-term would be diminished.

*But in the long-term…*

He would find new recruits, he always had. They had already lined up in droves; they were already on his list of candidates. They were well-trained soldiers who were either disgruntled or underpaid, or both. Most of them had already begged to be a part of his tiny elite team, knowing it was a unit of men so perfectly adept at killing they would do almost anything to be a part of it.

And they knew the perks — the pay, the travel benefits, the stretches of non-deployment time that allowed them the financial means to do almost whatever they wanted. It was like being in the Army, without as many rules, no government oversight, and only the parts they enjoyed.

It was a perfect fit for the type of men The Hawk needed. He knew it would take all of five minutes to call up five or six of these men on his list and have them ready to go in a few hours. They wouldn't immediately fill Velacruz' and Jenkins' shoes, but they would give him more breathing room with this current assignment. They would, ideally, also help him get closer to accomplishing the task at hand without losing any more members of his unit.

His three-month training program had so far successfully weeded out those who weren't completely serious about the team, leaving him with the current lineup of candidates, and from those he had chosen his 'working unit,' the men he had on payroll. Jenkins and Velacruz would be missed, but such was the nature of perfection.

Jenkins was mumbling to himself, slowly growing more agitated as he tried to reconcile the fact that his mouth was not doing what his mind was telling him to do.

The Hawk remembered those feelings. He knew all too well how the debilitating effects of the drug made him woozy, drunk. A feeling of helplessness had washed over him, and that part alone made him swear to never be under its influence again. It was enough to know what it could do to other people; he regretted that he had tried it on himself. He had done it upon Daris' request, agreeing that he should understand what the drug was capable of from a firsthand standpoint.

He had likened it to training programs that required its participants to undergo gassing, to experience what it would be like to be hit with a stream of pepper spray.

But this drug was worse.

He watched as Jenkins' faculties deteriorated. With the newer serum, this part would be a temporary — albeit stronger — phase. Jenkins could still move slightly, a feeling similar to having all of one's limbs asleep. But everything would be feeling heavy, and would cause pain to force into action. The internal switch that governed one's voluntary function would start to malfunction, and Jenkins would be unable to control his movements.

His head fell forward, and The Hawk stepped a few feet closer, intrigued.

Velacruz was standing just outside the perimeter of the fans, the smoke column narrowly missing him. But he could see Jenkins, and The Hawk could only imagine what his second-newest recruit was thinking.

Morrison stepped forward again, and The Hawk could hear him through his comm system, his voice low and controlled. *'Jenkins,'* he said, *'please draw your sidearm.'*

Jenkins responded immediately, the pain he was feeling now manifesting on his face. His lips curled downward, his eyes pleading to Morrison to make it stop.

*'Thank you, Jenkins. Please raise the weapon and disable the safety.'*

Again, Jenkins complied.

*'Thank you again, Jenkins. Now, please turn the weapon and place the end of the barrel on the side of your head.'*

The Hawk grimaced, surprised at Morrison's ruthlessness. *Apparently Jenkins would* not *have to deal with the side effects.*

He sighed again. *The price of leadership.*

Through his comm, he heard Morrison give the kid his final order. *'Thank you, Jenkins. I'm sorry your recruitment did not work out. Please pull the trigger.'*

# THIRTY-ONE

AS A BOY, YOUNG HARVEY and his kid brother, ten years his junior, would spend their summers traveling with their parents around to different national parks. They visited Glacier, Yellowstone, and Yosemite, and stayed in dozens of campsites and state parks to and from each. Many of the smaller sites kept swimming pools that looked barely safe enough to swim in, and his parents would have preferred their boys to jump into a nearby pond instead.

It was impossible to keep Ben and his brother Zachary out of the water, however, and Ben's love for soaking and splashing grew as he did. On rare occasion a cheap hotel offered a better deal than a campsite, and his family would share a room together for the night. On such nights, when there was a hot tub on the premises, Ben would race his brother through the halls to find it and jump in.

In his adult years Ben began to prefer more 'soaking' to 'splashing,' and he considered a soak in a hot tub a well-deserved treat whenever he got the chance. As of yet he hadn't asked anyone — even Julie — about the plans for the remodel and addition to his small cabin, and if there would be room for a hot tub. He made a mental note to ask the builder when they returned if there was money in the budget to get him a nice tub on the porch.

Ben slid into the hot water after dropping his room key and shirt onto the floor, then brought his drink up to his lips as he waited for Julie to join him. He closed his eyes and leaned back, sighing.

The steam rose around him, immediately and thoroughly relaxing him, and he let his feet and legs rise to just below the surface as the jets and bubbles turned on, their fifteen-minute cycle starting.

"You look like you're having a good time," Julie's voice called out from the doorway of the bathroom.

Ben had been shocked and dismayed to discover the Rittenhouse didn't have a hot tub on the premises, but he regrouped and set his sights on the next-best thing: the jacuzzi tub in his and Julie's bathroom.

She walked in, her eyebrow rising off her forehead.

"What?" he asked.

"At least you kept your swim trunks on."

"Out of respect," he said, grinning. "But there's enough room in here for you."

She scoffed. "Yeah, you wish. I need to get in there to actually *clean*, not just soak the dirt back in like you. You're hogging it all up — when will you be done?"

Ben let his eyes roll up to meet Julie's. "Depends. What's on the agenda next?"

She dodged the question and moved to the mirror stretching along two walls of the bathroom. She started checking her makeup, then her teeth.

"Well, enjoy yourself."

He closed his eyes again, smiling. "I've had worse days."

"Well soak it up," she said. "Tomorrow's a different day."

He sat up a bit and opened his eyes. "What's that supposed to mean?" he asked. "You think we're heading into something rough?"

She made a face, then looked back to him through the reflection in the mirror. "Well I don't know, it's just that Mr. E and this new guy, Derrick, seem awfully serious about catching up with Daris."

"Do they?" Ben asked. "I mean, Derrick didn't seem terribly interested in chasing after her once we got down to the basement. And E doesn't get riled up about anything. Why would he care about some nut-job conspiracy theorist?"

"That's true," Julie said. "But Derrick took the time to bring us in, like he really wants our help. If he's FBI, like he says he is, he's working alone and could use a team."

"He could use some *pawns*, you mean."

"Whatever we are to him, he's not the enemy."

"No one is," Ben said. "That's the thing. Daris tried to shoot at you — but it seemed like it was out of primal fear or something. Like she was looking around trying to figure what had happened, and that gun happened to be in her hand so she used it."

"Yeah," Julie said. "I guess. She's definitely strange, but she doesn't seem like a killer."

"So that brings me back to my point. *Who* is the enemy? Daris is crazy, but she's running a pseudo-secret philosophical organization, not the US Army. How dangerous can she possibly be?"

Julie shook her head. "That's why it seems weird that Roger Derrick would just show up, claiming he's been watching her for some time, and that only now were those artifacts and the journal stolen."

Ben slipped back down beneath the surface of the water so his broad shoulders could relax, and he found he had to put his feet up on the wall on the opposite side of the bathtub. He stretched, feeling the tension of flying for hours on end, cramped into a corner seat, wearing off. The drink next to him looked even colder and more inviting than it had a moment ago, so he downed it and placed the heavy glass back on the rim of the tub.

For a moment he considered asking Julie to order another drink, but decided against it. He was settled, at ease, and he was enjoying the time with Julie. In the craziness of the last few months and the many visitors and builders they'd had up to the cabin, he and Julie hadn't had much time to be alone together.

He shifted, trying to get comfortable, then noticed Julie looking at him.

"What?" he asked. "You think of something else?"

She shook her head once again. "No," she said. "Not related to the mission, anyway. I'm just thinking about you."

"Me?"

"You look hot in there. Your workouts have been working."

He brushed off the compliment. "'Bout time they started to do anything for me. I feel like I've been busting my butt for Reggie just to almost keep up with him, and I've got nothing to show for it."

"Well," Julie said, stepping up to the edge of the tub. She reached a hand up and began undoing the buttons on her shirt. "Let me remind you of who you're *really* busting your butt for."

# THIRTY-TWO

JULIE TOUSLED HER HAIR AND waited for it fall down into place. 'Into place,' in her hair's case, meant 'haphazardly falling around her shoulders.' It didn't look bad, but it was far from the elegant 'purposeful' look she was going for. Her hair, deep brown and kept to just below shoulder-length, had always been an annoyance to her.

Ben loved it, but she knew that he was obligated to tell her that. Her classmates at school told her that as well, but she knew they were just playing the role of competitive girlfriend and trying to befriend her.

She sprayed a bit more of the product into it, remembering her mother teaching her how to treat it so many years ago. Her hair was the only thing that hadn't changed since then. She styled it as she always had: straight, flipped up just a touch at the bottom, and slipped her bangs sideways and clipped them down.

Examining herself in the mirror for the hundredth time that morning, she wondered if Ben was awake yet. He liked his sleep, and after last night she knew he'd be reveling in it as long as possible. The combination of fun, traveling, and a perfect bed made up with a couple selections from the hotel's 'pillow menu' would be enough to allow Ben to sleep well into the next day, but they had work to do.

"Ben," she called out, moving now to her eyelashes. "You up?"

An affirmative-sounding groan echoed into the bathroom, and she focused in on her eyes. She was a simple woman, girlish face with a well-kept body, but she wasn't proud. She knew she was beautiful, but it never went to her head. She was happy with her appearance —

minus her hair, of course — and refused to let vanity get in the way of the natural beauty she'd been given.

Not a knockout, but certainly better-than-average, Juliette Richardson had always had an easy time with boys. Growing up she'd had her fair share of boyfriends, but none had been serious. She'd realized early on that they were into something besides her brilliant mind and knack for computers.

The funny thing was, Ben initially struck Julie as exactly the sort of man she'd dated — and dumped — numerous times before. Brawny, muscular, and somewhat oafish, at first she'd written him off as a reclusive bear of a man with daddy issues. She'd been right about the daddy issues, and mostly right about the reclusiveness of Harvey, but after their chance encounter at Yellowstone National Park, they were forced together for a time, and only then did Julie recognize something in him she liked.

In fact, she'd *really* liked it. Ben's personality was raw, open, and transparent. He said what was on his mind, but usually only after prodded. He was quiet, sure, but that didn't mean he wasn't thinking, processing. Julie recognized in Ben an intelligence that burned deep — different from her bookish technical knowledge and hands-on experience in IT, but very much useful. Ben had a resiliency to him that made her proud. On more than one occasion, that resiliency had saved her life, and the lives of everyone else on their team.

She fell in love with him at some point during their escapades after their first meeting at Yellowstone, and they'd moved in together into Ben's cabin in Alaska shortly after that. He was funny, strong-willed, and had a heart larger than himself, and they made a good team. They'd had their difficulties, but they were nothing remarkable. Both were stubborn, but it meant that they were each too stubborn to walk away from a fight, and they inevitably worked things out quickly.

"Ben," she called again. "Seriously. Show starts in five. You ready?"

Another groan, this one longer and more pronounced.

*Man loves his sleep,* she thought. Ben could out-drink, out-eat, and out-sleep just about anyone she knew, and she often wondered if he thought there was some secret competition he was competing in.

She walked out of the bathroom after twenty minutes of getting ready. She'd set her alarm early enough to give her time to herself to think and get ready. She wasn't sure what the day would bring, but a few minutes in the morning did wonders for her confidence.

He rolled over, apparently sensing that she was there. His large, brown eyes danced up and down her body, and she frowned back at him.

He pulled himself up to a sitting position on the bed, then rubbed his eyes. "Damn, you look hot this morning. How do you girls do that? Roll out of bed looking great?"

"I don't look great," she joked back, "but I stand next to you most of the time, so it just *looks* like I look great." She started back to the bathroom to finish the last bit of preparation — looking once again at her hair and wishing it was different. "Come on, you're out of time."

# THIRTY-THREE

BEN STROLLED INTO DERRICK'S HOTEL room next door thirty seconds later, but already the last one to arrive. Julie's shocked expression told him that she was either impressed with how quickly he'd gotten out of bed and dressed, or that he was bleeding from his face. He hadn't bothered to check.

She walked over and started fixing his hair, but he swatted her hand away. "Stop it, Mom," he said.

She made a *tsk* sound and resumed her position behind the couch, facing the TV.

"Good thing *you're* not the one on TV this morning, pal," Reggie said from the couch. "You look like you had a rough night."

"I bet I had a better night than you," Ben shot back. "How was spooning with Joshua?"

Joshua and Reggie had bunked together the previous night — they hadn't planned to stay at the hotel, and the place was full. Every room booked, they were forced to sleep in the room next on the opposite side of Derrick's, sharing the king bed.

"Like sleeping next to a fish on a dock," Reggie replied. He made a smacking motion with his hand, alternating it palm-up and palm-down on his other arm, miming the look of a fish flopping back-and-forth as it gasped for air.

"At least I don't snore like you," Joshua said.

"How would you know?"

"Good morning, Ben," Derrick said, interrupting the jostling between the three men. "Hope you had a decent night's sleep. GMA is about to start, but there's breakfast over there if you want any."

Ben looked over to the desk set next to Derrick's bed and found a veritable feast spread out on the top of it. A pile of scrambled eggs, toast, and a ramekin of jam sat on one side, while a stack of pancakes and a bowl of syrup next to another ramekin of butter sat on the other. He walked over, noticing a slight spring in his step. Food made him happy, and he liked being happy.

"Don't overeat," Joshua said. "Keep it light, protein and a bit of toast."

"Thanks again, Mom," Ben said.

"Seriously," Joshua continued. "Sounds like we might have a bit of hiking to do."

"Hiking? Here? In downtown Philadelphia?"

Joshua shook his head. "No, we'd have to fly to get there."

"What? Where? Flying?" Ben looked back at the rest of the group. "I wasn't *that* late, and you've already had a whole meeting without me? When are you going to bring me up to speed?"

Julie opened her mouth to answer, but the television unmuted and a woman's voice sprang out from the tinny speakers.

*'Good Morning, America,'* she started. *'My name is Patricia Gonzales, and we have a special guest with us here today. But first, let's catch you up on everything you missed!'*

The bouncy, exaggerated joy the woman wore made her act seem even more faked, but Ben knew that was all part of the show. Reality television had stopped being anything close to actual reality about five minutes into its life, and he had little hope for the rest of the programming on most channels. He and Julie didn't even have cable at the cabin; aside from the egregiously expensive cost of rural cable service, they simply didn't spend enough time in front of the television to justify having it. They watched streaming shows every now and then, downloading them to a tablet or phone when they were in town at a coffee shop, then playing them before bed.

So it was all the more jarring to see the false happiness of thousands of Americans standing behind the woman and her cast members, everyone smiling and jumping and shouting and generally looking like giant marionette puppets that had been painted more terrifying than any clown.

They watched on in silence for a few minutes, until the first commercial break.

"When does Daris come on?" Julie asked.

"No idea," Derrick responded. "But probably toward the end. Makes everyone wait for it, so they can show ads to you until then."

Ben ate, choosing to sit in the armchair right next to Joshua's out of spite, knowing Joshua was watching. He'd piled most of the eggs onto the plate, right on top of two of the pancakes and a piece of toast, then drizzled syrup over the entire monstrosity. He took three bites, each bigger than the last, and finally gulped down the whole mess at once.

Julie and Joshua looked away, horrified, while Reggie grinned.

"Anyone have coffee?" Ben asked.

"Right over there," Julie said, pointing to the table above the mini fridge set up in an alcove near the entranceway.

Ben started to stand, but Reggie laughed and rose to his feet. "No, buddy, let me get it for you. These guys are watching you eat, and I think they like the show."

Joshua made a disgusted face and turned back to the television. Derrick, to his credit, hadn't even looked over at Ben.

The commercials ended and the woman was back, this time joined by a man to her left and Daris to her right. They were in the studio now, sitting in three chairs that looked about as comfortable as broken glass. The man shifted once, getting comfortable, and the woman crossed her legs beneath the chair. Daris sat straight up in her chair, her feet flat on the ground.

"God, she looks so uncomfortable. Completely different than yesterday."

"Some people are cut out for TV, some aren't, I guess," Joshua said.

*'Welcome back,'* the woman began. *'We're glad you're with us this morning, and we are* so *glad our guest is with us as well. This is my friend, Daris Johansson. She is a museum curator and author, and she has recently completed a* wonderful *book called 'The Jefferson Legacy.'*

"Does anyone buy that crap?" Ben said between mouthfuls of food. "A museum curator? Really?"

"Well anyone can be an author these days," Reggie said. "Maybe they think everyone will think the same about museum curators."

*'Daris, you've written numerous articles and pieces before, but now you've released an entire book. Why did you decide to publish a book?'*

Daris sat up even straighter somehow, her back now almost at the front of the chair. *'Well, I decided that my message needed to get out to the masses. I want everyone to know what really happened back then, and a book is the perfect way to do that.'*

*'Of course,'* the woman replied, barely giving Daris enough time to breathe after she'd answered. *'And what a fine book it is. Can you tell us, briefly, what it's about?'*

*'Well it's about Thomas Jefferson, and his legacy.'*

The studio audience burst into laughter, and the hostess and the host next to her laughed as well. Daris looked frightened, then blushed, apparently not understanding what was so funny.

'Of course,' the man said, jumping in. He leaned closer to Daris as if about to reveal a secret. *'And I feel that most people have* no idea *what Jefferson's legacy really is. Or, for that matter, what he was really like. Would you say that's true?'*

*'Yes, absolutely. Jefferson was known as a great president, and a founder of our nation. But he also had a dark side.'*

*'A dark side? Really? What do you mean by that?'* the woman asked.

*'Well, for one, Jefferson was a slaveowner.'*

The man and woman onscreen shook their heads, solemnly, as if this was not only the first time either of them had ever heard such an accusation but also something that was completely unique for the time.

"This is trash," Ben said. "Everyone knows that."

"It's American television," Derrick said. "Don't rush off and assume anyone knows *anything.*"

*'But that's not all,'* Daris said. *'Jefferson also stole money from the Spanish to pay for the Louisiana Territory.'*

*'You mean the Louisiana Purchase?'* the man asked, once again acting shocked. *'That Jefferson bought from Napoleon for pennies on the dollar?'*

*'Yes, one and the same,'* Daris said. *'He used Spanish gold, taken from shipwrecks, and paid for the territory with that money.'*

# THIRTY-FOUR

'BUT IT'S WELL-DOCUMENTED THAT Jefferson had the approval of Congress to make the purchase. Why would he need to purchase the Territory using anything other than the money that was in Congress' coffers?'

Derrick was shaking his head, fuming. "She's lying, through her teeth."

"...American television," Reggie said. "What'd you expect?"

"Integrity, intelligence, good acting? At least one of those."

'Jefferson did use some of Congress' money — after all, it was considered good for the young nation. Doubling their land with one simple purchase? And for that price.... But still, he did it because he could. He had Spanish money, and it didn't cost him a thing, so he used it.'

'Still, Daris, it does seem a bit far-fetched. Why not hold onto the money? Why not save it, let it grow in value, or —'

'You don't understand,' Daris said, this time nearly jumping out of her chair and standing up. 'Jefferson used the money to taunt the Spanish — and the rest of the world. He wanted them to know he had it, that he had more of it. By using some of it to purchase the Territory from Napolean, he got their attention. He told them America wasn't something to mess with, that he had access to things no one else on Earth had access to.'

'Are you saying he —'

For the second time, Daris interrupted the woman. She didn't seem terribly excited about it, but she stopped talking and allowed the on-air interruption once again.

'Yes, I am saying that. It's all in my book. Jefferson had access to

119

*Spanish* treasure *that had been found by someone Jefferson trusted, and he held it privately, in the Office of the President. But it wasn't just treasure — it was extremely valuable to the Spanish for other reasons, namely that they had been looking for this treasure for some time.'*

*'Since the year 1715?'*

Daris looked proud that the man knew the details of her book, and she turned and addressed him directly.

*'Exactly. The Spanish Treasure Fleet of 1715, departing from Cuba, ran into a hurricane somewhere around the Florida coast. All eleven ships were lost.'*

*'But they found the fleet, right? The shipwrecks?'*

On screen, Daris shook her head. *'No, in fact. They haven't found any of the ships. Every now and then, reports of Spanish gold washing up on the coast come up in treasure hunting circles, but nothing noteworthy.'*

The woman next to Daris jumped back in. *'But you're implying that the fleet has* already *been found, correct? By Jefferson?'*

Daris laughed, and it was obvious she was now purposefully trying to make Patricia Gonzales look silly. *'Well, not by Jefferson himself, of course. But someone he employed.'*

*'And who was that?'*

*'We don't know, but at some point the Spanish gold and silver, identified as the same treasure that was on board one of the ships, began to appear around the world, placed back into circulation by Jefferson himself, upon paying for the Louisiana Territory.'*

The man smiled, a genuine, if naive, smile, as if he were discussing the universe with a toddler. *'Well, that's quite a yarn you've strung there, Daris. Thank you for discussing it with us, and of course — you all can read more about Daris' theory in her book, The —'*

*'It's not a theory,'* Daris said, interrupting yet again. *'It's based in hard evidence, evidence I've seen with my own two —'*

The screen cut to black for brief moment, then a commercial — its volume gained hard up and taking everyone in the room by surprise — jolted from the television.

"Wow," Reggie said.

"Wow is right," Julie replied. "That was probably the most awkward thing I've ever seen."

"I didn't know they just cut to commercial like that," Joshua said. "I figured they'd, you know, ask her stop or something."

"They put her segment there," Derrick said, "right before a commercial break, so they could get away with it if they had to. They're probably still listening to her rant on the set, and no one there has a clue they're not live anymore."

Ben's eyebrows rose. "Man, that was awful. It's like she walked into a trap. Why would she do that?"

"She's maneuvering," Derrick said. "It's about the treasure, I know that now. She believes it exists, and she intends to find it. Now she'll have support."

"Support? I can't possibly see how. She just went and got herself absolutely *hammered* on live TV," Joshua said, shaking his head. "They made a laughingstock out of her."

Derrick stepped in front of them, blocking their view of the television. "If Daris Johansson is anything, it's cunning. She's whip-smart, and you'd be best off acknowledging that. She's thought this through, played all the angles, and — while it may be hard to believe — I'd bet this was absolutely best decision for her to make. To get the American people to feel sorry for her, to feel like she had something great to say, but never got to say it because of the media or whatever."

"She's studied this, orchestrated it all, and she's now conducting. Acting it out, whatever her plan is. Going on television was all part of it, and she's undoubtedly been working on getting her little show just right for quite some time, now."

Julie stood up and walked toward the pot of coffee. "Yeah, well she pulled it off well, then. I feel sorry for her."

"Don't," Derrick said, harshly. "She's a professional, and she's got more tricks up her sleeve."

"How'd she even land that deal, anyway?" she asked. "Hawking her book on *Good Morning America*? She must have friends in high places."

"She does, like I said last night. She's well-connected, and she's leading an organization — at least half of one — that wants her message to succeed."

Ben stood up and walked over to where Julie was standing. He took the pot from Julie's hands and began pouring them both another cup of coffee. He wore a slight frown, a physical expression signifying the deep thought he was engaged in. He liked puzzles, but this woman was one that seemed unsolvable. He couldn't figure out why the leader of an organization — a *secret* organization, for that matter — would *publicly* announce her book and her whack-job theory.

"Why tell the world? Why does she need their support?" Ben asked.

Derrick shrugged. "Could be as simple as transparency. She might want to have plausible deniability in case things go south for her. If someone ends up killed, she can claim her GMA appearance as proof that she was always on the right side, aligned with the public's interest."

Joshua cut in. "And she'll probably have support out in the field, too. You know, if she needs to look for that journal she lost, she can now show up to any museum on the planet and get let in, probably even get a staff of researchers working for her immediately."

"Right, that makes sense," Ben said. "But still, her story's completely bogus, right?"

He looked around the room. Julie was next to him, looking back at Ben, but the others were all staring off in different directions. It meant they either thought Daris was lying about it all, or that they were considering that she may have been telling the truth.

"I think she's lying," Derrick said. "I *know* she's lying, and I said that already. She's morphing facts to fit her conspiracy theory. She *wants* Jefferson to be guilty, because it supports her claim in her book. And it makes her more powerful in the APS."

"But it *could* be true, right?" Julie asked. "I mean conceptually. It could have some *basis* in reality?"

"All conspiracy theories have at least *some* basis in reality," Derrick said. "But hers is one that's been half-baked since it was put in the oven. Jefferson wasn't without his flaws, to be sure, but stealing Spanish treasure and then giving it to Napoleon and then covering it all up wasn't one of them."

Reggie cocked his head sideways and stared at Derrick. Derrick saw Reggie, but neither man spoke for a moment. Ben watched on, knowing that Reggie had just realized something important.

Reggie frowned, then looked at the floor, then back at Derrick. "Why do you care about all this, Derrick? What's in it for you?"

Derrick opened and closed his mouth once. "What do you mean? I'm FBI. This is my job. And I —"

"I get it," Reggie said, holding up a hand. "And you want to do a good job, you're a patriot, we know. But why care *this* much? You've obviously done your research, and you know your history. I've met a few of you bureau types, and you're the first one I've come across who seems so invested in his job he's done a bunch of *proactive* research."

"You trying to say we don't normally —"

"I'm not trying to say anything," Reggie said. "And I like you, so let's get that straight. I just feel like you've got more to say and you're not saying it. Only time I've seen FBI or any of the other acronyms get this worked up about something was when there was a *very clear* threat. And Daris, while a bit loopy and not an actress, doesn't seem to be much of a threat."

He looked at Julie and smirked. "But I guess if Ben was any slower, she'd have been a pretty big threat to *you*."

Ben nodded. "Yeah, we were talking about that. She didn't seem to know what was happening. Like she let things get out of control, so she tried to fire at Julie."

"Could be," Derrick said. "But again, I'm warning you not to underestimate her. She may have planned and orchestrated every move at the APS building, and she might be getting ready to make her next move as we speak."

"Don't change the subject, Derrick," Joshua said. "Reggie thinks you're holding back from us, and I've learned to trust the hell out of his gut when he gets a notion. But I get it. You're not sure if you can trust *us*. That's fair, but it needs to stop. If we weren't who we said we were, you'd already know that. FBI and all, right?"

Derrick nodded.

"So if you're *really* FBI, you'd have no reason *not* to trust us, which means you can start by telling us the truth now, or don't, and then we'll know you're not who *you* say you are."

Reggie seemed confused for a moment, and Ben didn't blame him, but Derrick straightened and sighed.

He spoke. "I am FBI, I assure you of that. You're welcome to call in to my boss, but it won't do much good. We're pretty good at pretending we're *not* Bureau, so there's going to be a lot of legwork needed in order to back up my claim."

"Fair enough," Reggie said. "But why are you working alone? I thought you boys never worked alone."

"It's pretty rare, admittedly. But the answer — to all your questions, I believe — is that this was a sort of passion project for me. I'm doing this on my time, mostly. My boss thinks it's a waste of time, for the exact same reasons you do. 'Daris isn't a threat,' 'the APS is a hoax,' you name it, I've heard it."

"Yet you're here."

"And yet I'm here. I believe in what I'm trying to prevent, and Daris knows the clock's ticking. I just need to find her —"

"Why? What are you trying to prevent?"

"I thought you said she told you that already," Derrick responded. "I thought she told you yesterday she was trying to prevent The Shift?"

# THIRTY-FIVE

"THE SHIFT. THERE IT IS AGAIN," Reggie said. He was pacing the carpet between the chairs and couch and the bed, and he was looking down at his feet, trying to place them in the same spot each time he passed over a section.

"The Shift is just what we use to describe the change in power from the old way to the new way. It's never happened, and my job — my *charge* — is to prevent it.

"*'We?'*" Ben asked. "Are you trying to say you're —"

"Yes," Derrick said. "I'm sorry I didn't tell you sooner, but it seemed more important to make sure you understood the nature of the situation first, so you wouldn't immediately discount what I have to say.

"For most of my adult life, I've been a member of the American Philosophical Society, working hard to prevent the exact thing Daris Johansson, our president, is trying to accomplish."

"The Shift."

"Exactly," Derrick said. "The shift in power from the group that supports the integrity of the nation's history to the group that wants to prove Daris right."

"So we're stuck between a crazy lady who can't act and a guy who's FBI but also part of the same crazy organization that's big enough to maintain membership but not big enough for anyone else to know about it?"

Derrick looked back at Reggie. "Yeah, something like that. And I'd really appreciate your help."

"Finding Daris?" Ben asked.

"Finding Daris, and then proving that she's out of line. That Jefferson used money — American money only — to purchase Louisiana."

"But again, why does it matter?" Julie asked. "I mean no disrespect, but we're not a part of your organization, and it doesn't seem like she's harming anyone."

Derrick stuck up an index finger. "That's the part I haven't told you. She fired at you, Juliette, and — thankfully — missed. But it's not the first time she's attempted harm, and it won't be the last. In fact, she's killed before."

"Daris?" Ben asked. "The little librarian who couldn't react fast enough to get off a shot?"

"Yes, Ms. Johansson might not be a dead shot, but I assure you she has other… talents. I've been on her case for two years, and I've got a body count about fifty people long."

"All thanks to Daris?"

"All because of Daris, either indirectly or directly."

"So whatever she's trying to accomplish, she's willing to kill for."

Derrick nodded. "As well as her half of the organization. The 'New APS,' as they call it. They're willing to do whatever it takes to smear Jefferson, prove they're right, and then —"

Derrick cut himself off as his head flicked sideways at the noise.

"What was that?" Joshua asked.

"Sounded like a door getting thrown open," Reggie said. "A door *close to us*. Derrick, you got any way to defend us?"

Reggie had left his 9mm handgun next door, and he wasn't sure if Joshua was armed. He figured Ben and Julie weren't either, as neither of them had any sort of concealed holster with them and they weren't carrying in a pocket or belt.

Derrick nodded, then pointed. "I've got two more pieces. The Glock is for me, and I've got a Taurus and an S&W. All nines."

Reggie and Joshua dashed off to load up, and Derrick started barking orders to Ben and Julie. "You two, heads down and eyes up. We don't need any civilians getting —"

"I'm in this, and you can use the extra hand," Ben said. "I'd recommend coming up with a better plan for the two of us than, 'heads down,' or you're going to have to put up with whatever *I* come up with."

"I'm with him," Julie said. "This isn't our first rodeo."

"Fine," Derrick said. "Your funeral. But the weapons are for us." He motioned to Reggie and Joshua.

Reggie ripped open a duffel bag and rummaged around in in until he found the case for the Taurus. He opened it and began loading the first magazine into it, placing the second in a back pocket.

Joshua tossed the Glock to Derrick, who caught it, then the magazine, and all three of the men began working their weapons and testing them out.

"Ben, why don't you post up in the bathroom?" Reggie said. Derrick shot him a glance, but he ignored it. He'd seen Ben in action, and a pissed-off Harvey Bennett was a thing of beauty. *Just wind him up and point him in the right direction*, he'd told Joshua once. "Get Julie in the closet across the hall, but you're last out of the gates, okay? We don't need any casualties today."

He locked eyes with Ben, and the two comrades shared a moment of understanding. *Take care of Julie, and we'll take care of you.* Julie was a renegade, a solid fighter, with a scrappy and spunky attitude that flourished in high-stakes situations like this, but Reggie knew she still wasn't a trained soldier like him and Joshua. Ben wasn't either, but Ben had something no one else he'd ever met had.

Pure, unbridled fury combined with an absolutely massive frame. Ben was like a freight train: it took some time to get up to speed, but once it was moving it was nearly impossible to stop. If Joshua was the quarterback of the group, Ben was the linebacker.

Reggie, for his part, wasn't sure where exactly he fit. He was a soldier, an ex-Army sniper who had been trained as well as any special forces operative, and what was missing from his training he'd later made up on his own time, through teaching and directing a survival training program from his Brazilian home on the edge of the rainforest.

They'd met there, Reggie and Julie and Ben coming together to track down a group of mercenaries led by Joshua, who had been the face of the enemy they were after. Joshua realized later that he was on the wrong side and promptly adjusted for it, gaining the trust of Reggie and the others.

They were a great team together, but it was hard to say exactly why. They hadn't been trained together and they had barely known each other for half a year, yet they had so far been brutally effective. Mr. E and his wife had done a fine job bringing them together and corralling their individual skill sets into a cohesive whole.

Ben nodded, and stepped behind Julie to lead her to the hallway. She didn't argue, knowing that unarmed she wasn't likely going to be able to put up much of a fight against any intruder.

"It's time," Derrick said. "Hurry it up, Bennett."

Reggie watched as Ben spun around and ran to the bathroom

across the short hallway from Julie's closet. He closed the door, but Reggie didn't hear it lock.

The walls were thick, and the hotel was well-built, but he could hear the faintest sound of heavy footsteps — more than one set — on the floor in the next room, as well as some low voices. The footsteps moved around the room more, checking in each of the smaller closets and bathroom, then they started toward the main door once again.

He didn't hear the door close, and he no longer could hear the footsteps or voices.

A few seconds passed, and Reggie gripped the handle of the Taurus a bit tighter. He forced himself to relax, to wait for the right moment and not anticipate the shot. With small arms such as the 9mm, he knew aiming across a room, even one as small as a hotel room, was going to be a chore. Their door would form a natural choke point, forcing their attackers into a small confined space and therefore only allowing one or two of them to enter at a time, and Reggie hoped that with three guns pointed at them at least one of them would land a shot.

He tested the give of the trigger, waiting.

He heard a click. The sound of a room key sliding into the lock and and disengaging the magnetic catch. He watched the hallway, unable to see all the way to the door from this angle. The lock clicked once again, and he heard the handle being turned and the door slowly pushing open.

Then the door flew sideways, the shadows and lights mixing from the hallway and spilling into the room. He gripped the pistol and waited.

Derrick shouted, but Reggie couldn't understand what he'd said. He raised the Taurus to eye-level and prepared to fire.

The first man barreled into the room, running at full-tilt toward Derrick. Derrick fired two shots in quick succession, the first glancing off the man and landing wide of the mark.

The second round hit, but the man's momentum kept him in motion and he collided with Derrick before he could release a third shot. Reggie had waited too long, and now his target and Derrick had congealed into a large, writhing mass. He swung his pistol around again and toward the doorway.

*Crack!*

A shot rang out through the closed space, and Reggie fell sideways. The man who'd fired on him had missed, but it was a close miss. Reggie felt the sting of the bullet's hot arc sear through his shoulder, and he brought the handgun up once again.

Another shot rang out, this time from Joshua's Smith & Wesson.

The man fell, and Joshua hit him again. He stirred, and Reggie didn't think he was dead. He hoped, however, that the man was injured enough to be out of the fight for a while.

A third man was at the doorway, and Reggie dared a stretch around the couch to get a better look. Three gunshots rang out from the hallway, the first landing dangerously close to Reggie's head. He ducked back behind the relative safety of the couch and looked back at Joshua.

Joshua was shaking his head and shrugging, as confused as Reggie.

"You get a look at them?" Joshua asked.

"Just barely, right before they took a few potshots at my head. Nothing memorable, though. Just a big guy, standing, black clothes."

"Mercenary?"

"Sure," Reggie said. "No idea. Doesn't matter. They're shooting at me, so I'm going to kill them."

Joshua nodded.

Just then, the glass window behind Reggie smashed into a thousand pieces and his mind shifted into slow-motion. He rolled sideways, knowing he only had a foot or so space before he'd bump up against the couch.

It turned out to be the wrong move.

A person flew through the window, right on top of Reggie, and he felt the air leave his lungs. He groaned, trying to shift his weapon to his other hand. A foot landed on his hand, crushing it, and kicked the gun away. Another stomp and he felt his nose crack, a gush of blood following shortly.

Out of the corner of his eye he saw Derrick still wrestling with the first attacker.

*No help there.*

He shifted his gaze just a bit and saw Joshua aiming his pistol at the man standing on top of Reggie. Reggie closed his eyes and waited for the shot to ring out, but it never did.

Instead, another window broke, this one right behind Joshua. Joshua jumped, but he was a moment too late. Another person sailed through the smashed glass, feet-first, sending Joshua flying.

*Shit.*

The man who had previously been just outside the hotel room in the hallway and had fired at Reggie walked in, his swagger confident and his gaze on Reggie.

"Gareth Red," the man said. "I never thought I'd find you here."

For a moment Reggie — Gareth Red — was stunned. He wasn't sure how this man knew who he was.

Then it hit him.

# THIRTY-SIX

"YOU SON OF A —"

"SAVE it, *Reggie*. Isn't that what we called you, back then? What kind of a welcome is that, anyway? Aren't you glad to see your old commander?"

Reggie considered spitting on the floor in front of The Hawk, but he refused to even acknowledge his disgust for the mercenary.

*Still, a well-worded note of encouragement couldn't hurt anything.*

"You washed-up piece of —"

"Again with that mouth of yours," the man said, cutting him off. He nodded over his shoulder and two more men stepped into the room. They stopped to help the man Joshua had hit, who appeared to have just been dazed when the bullet hit and lodged in his body armor. The two new men helped him to his feet, and then turned back to their leader who was standing in the center of the room.

Reggie didn't recognize them, but he didn't need to. He knew their leader, so he knew what they were now up against.

"Ravenshadow," Reggie said. "You guys are still around, then? Last I heard you were taking potshots at foreign ambassadors."

Derrick and his attacker had reached a stalemate, with Derrick held tight in a half-nelson standing in front of the man who'd ran in and tackled him.

"What's Ravenshadow?" Derrick asked, his voice strained.

"It's a security company," Joshua said. He, like Reggie, was prone on the floor, his weapon lost, a man standing over him with an assault rifle pointed down at him. "They specialize in less-than-reputable corporate clients, and they'll do just about anything for a buck."

"We *specialize* in ensuring our clients' safety," the man said. "And yes, we're still around. Thanks for asking. And it's a pleasure to finally meet you, Joshua Jefferson. I'm surprised that *you're* surprised we're here. You're leading this little mission, aren't you?"

Joshua glowered.

"My recommendation? Leader to leader? You need to operate with a *bit* more stealth. You know how *easy* it was for my men to figure out who you were and where you were located?"

Joshua's face didn't reveal anything, but Reggie was a bit surprised that the man knew Joshua.

"Who the hell are you?" Joshua asked. "I mean, besides Ravenshadow."

"I'm in charge of protecting and securing Ms. Johansson's assets, domestic and abroad. My name is Vicente Garza."

"*Captain* Vicente Garza," Reggie added.

"You know him?" Derrick asked.

"I served with him. He was a good soldier, and a decent leader. Sometimes they fall hard though, you know?"

Garza walked over to Reggie and knelt down, pressing the barrel of a sidearm against his temple. "You've always had a way with words, *Mr.* Red. I heard you were out as well — ran off with some girl and then started a survival company?"

"Something like that, asshole."

"But you lost both, no? Now you're doing pretty much the same *I'm* doing, but for *far* less pay, I'm sure."

"I'm nothing like you, Garza. I still have integrity."

Garza threw his head back and laughed. He stood, then walked over to where Derrick was standing and stared up at the large man.

"You must be the government grunt they sent in. Nothing much to see here, huh? Just a scared little lady with a secret? Find the secret and call it in, no sense sending more than one?"

Derrick clenched his jaw.

"That's the trouble with you — all of you. You head into situations *far* understaffed. It's the US government, for crying out loud, you can *literally* print money whenever you want. Why can't you figure out how to print some, then use it to hire more guys?"

Garza stared at Derrick for another few seconds, then turned back and headed toward the center of the room, right in the middle of the couch and set of chairs. He turned to address Joshua and Reggie.

"Okay, boys. Introductions have been made. It's time we get back to headquarters. I have a scheduled call with Ms. Johansson this afternoon, and I'm *dying* to tell her how simple it was to take care of this little issue."

He nodded again at the two new soldiers who'd walked into the room and they started forward.

Just then the bathroom door ripped open, and Reggie could hear the heavy footsteps. He couldn't see the bathroom from his position on the floor, but he knew what was happening.

*No, Ben. No.*

He silently willed Ben to stop, to turn around and hide in the bathroom once again, but he knew Ben too well. He also knew the others had heard the same thing and were better prepared for the attack.

Reggie caught sight of Ben's thick legs pumping up and down as he closed the distance between the bathroom door and the first soldier on the right. He heard the snapping sound of the contact, then both sets of legs lifting off the ground.

*Dammit, Ben.*

They landed loudly on the chair next to Garza's position and tumbled over it. Reggie could see them now, wrestling just like Derrick and the first soldier had minutes ago. They fought for a few more seconds before Garza smiled and stepped over to Ben.

He held the gun up and out, and Ben stopped moving.

"Save it, boy," Garza said. "I'd hate to kill you so easily."

Ben muttered a profane response under his breath.

"You're a feisty one, aren't you? You must be Harvey. Tell me, Harvey, did Mr. Red tell you anything about me?"

Ben glanced at Reggie. His face was red, flush with anger, and there was a welling bruise around his left eye. He shook his head, once.

"Good. It will be all the better to have him catch you up on our endeavors together. Your friend, Reggie, has some history lessons for you all."

The man who'd wrestled with Ben pushed Ben off of him and stood, brushing off his pants. He raised his own pistol and held it at Ben's back. Reggie watched, trying to get a measure of the men in the room. On a better day, with better weapons and better preparations, it would have been a fair fight.

But a fair fight in Reggie's world was unacceptable. A fair fight meant some of them — some of *his* men — would be hit. Probably killed. A fair fight, with equally balanced teams, meant there would be some casualties.

It was a mistake for Ben to rush out of the bathroom, especially unarmed. Ben knew it, and everyone else knew it. The fact that Ben wasn't bleeding out on the floor of the hotel room right now was a lucky thing.

"Mr. Bennett, I have been looking forward to meeting your FBI friend here for some time. I've even prepared a special welcome for him, back at our facility."

Reggie stared at Ben, who was staring at The Hawk. Garza was smiling, a small, thin sliver of evil.

*No.*

"But now that I know *you're* here, I know that your *girlfriend...* sorry — fiancée, correct? — is here as well."

Ben's nostrils flared, his cheekbones grinding into each other over and over again.

*No,* Reggie thought. He squeezed his eyes shut. *Please, no.*

"Where is she? I would *very much* like to meet her."

# THIRTY-SEVEN

UNFORTUNATELY, JULIE COULD HEAR EVERY word of the transaction taking place outside her closet in the main hotel room. She was panicked, but she was able to force her breaths into steady, long increments.

*Inhale, exhale.*

She focused on the breaths, but the voices just on the other side of the door terrified her. She heard Reggie, apparently recognizing the man — The Hawk — who'd come for them. The man and his team was working for Daris, apparently, as some sort of security team.

But rather than security, Daris had hired them to find Julie's group? It didn't add up. If they were after Roger Derrick, they would have simply taken him and left the rest of them alone.

The Hawk told Joshua a little about the company, and still she focused on her breaths.

*Inhale, exhale.*

She waited, her heartbeat growing louder with each thump. She had control of her breathing, but there was nothing she could do about her heart.

Julie looked around the closet, hoping there was something there she might be able to use as a weapon. Through the light streaming through the crack between the two doors, she peered around the small, L-shaped room. Derrick's shoes were on a shoe stand, a belt hanging from one of the wooden hangers. If he had a suitcase with him, it wasn't in the closet.

A shoehorn hung from a small leather string that had been wound through a hole in its top, and in the opposite corner, an ironing board hung on the wall.

*No iron.*

The iron, she figured, would be in the bathroom, hidden in a small cabinet near the sink. The board itself could be useable as a crude weapon, but she had neither the strength nor the space to swing it wide enough and hard enough to do much damage.

Julie couldn't easily justify the belt or the shoes as a weapon, either. What would she do? Throw the shoes at the first man to enter and try to choke the other?

Still, she felt she had to do *something*. She had to prepare. She had to —

The bathroom door crashed open, and she heard Ben's footsteps thumping down on the floor as he barreled out of his hiding place. A fight ensued, but it was quiet, and she could barely hear the sounds of the grunting men as they wrestled.

She tried to peek through the crack in the doors, but the angle was wrong. All she could see was directly in front of her, the opposite wall and the coffee stand just around the corner near it.

Then the sounds stopped, and she sucked in a breath.

*Who won?*

Then the man's voice, the one named Garza.

He spoke to Ben, Ben cursed, and Garza kept talking.

*Inhale, exhale.*

She forced the breaths, one after the other, until she felt her head wobbling and she had to stop. She was in full panic mode now, knowing that she would soon be discovered. *There was no way out.*

She wasn't a trained soldier. Before she'd met Ben, she'd only fired a weapon a few times as a girl and twice as an adult. Her job at the Centers for Disease Control, leading a now-defunct group called Biological Threat Resistance, was a glorified desk job, and there was no weapons training for CDC personnel that she knew of.

She wasn't a fighter, with her hands, feet, or anything else. She'd been fascinated by the idea of mixed-martial arts warriors she'd seen, and had even asked Ben if he had any interest in ever learning some of the throws and holds of Brazilian jujitsu. He'd shrugged it off, claiming that it wasn't helpful for attack as much as defense, and that she should instead look into something like Krav Maga.

And yet here she was, in a closet, about to be discovered.

Garza's voice cut through her subconscious. "Where is she? I would *very much* like to meet her."

She wanted to scream, but she remained silent. She wanted to faint, but she stood strong. She wanted to fight back, but she held fast.

Waiting.

Footsteps, into the bathroom.

More, from another man, into the area in front of the closet. A flash of darkness as the man passed directly in front of the closet.

She sniffed, darting sideways, hoping he hadn't seen her.

*He's going to check anyway*, she knew.

He checked anyway.

The man yanked the doors open, blinding Julie with the brightness of the hotel room, and she blinked a few times in response.

He had his hands on her now, deeply gritted old things that felt worn and hardened. They were prying, grasping, trying to get a hold on her without his having to step into the closet.

She wasn't going to allow it, but she still breathed and kept silent. She swatted his hands away, again and again, until he walked into the closet and pressed his huge, sweat-smelling body up against hers and grasped her wrists, pulling them hard down to her sides.

Then, at that moment, she screamed.

She couldn't hold it in any longer.

Ben screamed in response, something vulgar, but she wasn't paying attention to it.

The man was smiling, looking down at her with a strange expression on his face. He looked dirty, like the perfect match for his gritty hands, but all she could see in any detail were his eyes. His ugly, white eyes. They were slits in his head, barely open, contradicting his smile.

His nose hung to the left, longer than it should have been, and showing off far too many peaks and scars than one nose should host. She was revolted, disgusted, but more than that, she was *terrified*.

She screamed again, but he pulled her arms down harder, forcing her straight up against the wall, and then he pushed himself onto her, leaning in close to her ear.

Then he whispered. "I'm going to be ready, whenever The Hawk is done with you."

She swallowed, nearly vomiting, but her desire to faint won out. She fell forward, her wrists still locked in his hands, and the man swung her left arm behind her back. He let her continue forward, stepping out of her way, and Julie felt him wrench her right wrist up and onto the area between her shoulder blades.

It hurt, and she let out a sharp sigh. The man laughed, a guttural grunting sound that made her sick all over again, and he pushed her out of the closet. Her left wrist hung behind her back, held in place by his large, leathery hand, and her right wrist was pinned up on her back by his other hand. She had no choice but to lean forward at the waist to relieve some of the pressure.

In this way, she walked out of the closet. Ben was the first person she saw.

She cried, unable to speak.

He glared, likely dumbstruck as well.

Then she saw the rest of them — Reggie, Derrick, Joshua — all stunned into silence at the end of guns, each weapon held by a man dressed similarly to Julie's captor.

"Wh — why?" she stammered. "What are you going to do?"

The man who stood in the middle of the room, pointing a gun at Ben, turned to her and smiled. His lips were thin, and his eyes gave her the impression that he wasn't truly happy about anything. "Hello, Juliette. I hope you've enjoyed the accommodations here. We have another place we'd like to take you, now, so say goodbye to your friends."

The man holding her pushed her upper body farther down, bending her forward even more at the waist. She grunted in pain, but tried to hold her head up.

"Jules," Reggie said. "Stay calm. We'll come for you. I promise."

She wasn't sure if she was angry or terrified, or both. Or neither. She didn't know *what* she thought.

Reggie's expression was pained, and Joshua was clearly upset. His eyes were hard, as they always were, but he seemed to be looking through her. Studying her, as if trying to decipher how she'd hold up.

And then she saw Ben.

Still staring up at her, his eyes lost in some trance. There were tears in them, and he wasn't trying to hide them. She cried more, not sure what she could possibly say.

"Ben," she finally muttered. The man swung her around so she was face-to-face with him. "Ben, I —"

The Hawk turned and began walking out of the room, and the others backed away from their posts a few steps, still pointing their weapons at the group. One of the men gathered the handguns from Derrick's bag that had been dropped on the floor and collected them, carrying them out of the room.

Finally, in a leapfrogged way, the soldiers took turns moving backwards toward the door, guarding their teammates methodically, anticipating any movement from Julie's group.

Julie's man had her side pushed up against the wall, and he held her there as they walked out of the room and into the hallway. The Hawk was waiting there with handcuffs, and he placed one shackle around her right wrist.

He leaned down and spoke to her, making sure she was looking at him. "Juliette, I am only going to tell you this once," he said. "If you try to run, we will simply make the proceedings later much more difficult for you. If you try to scream, I will have my men walk back into that room and put a bullet through each of your teammate's heads.

"And if you attempt to call out to anyone, or try to explain what's happening, I will personally drown your fiancé in the bathtub, while you watch."

She swallowed.

"Do you understand?"

She nodded.

He leaned back up and had one of his men walk around with badges, handing one to each of the soldiers. Only then did she realize what their plan was — on the back of the man's shirt as he passed, printed in large, gold block letters, was a single word:

*SWAT.*

They were attempting to extract Julie right out from under the hotel's watchful eye, likely with a story already in place. They would be able to proceed uninhibited, right out the back door and into a vehicle and onto the Philadelphia streets.

The door closed behind them. Garza turned and nodded, and they started off down the hall. A room opened on her left side, near the elevator, and an elderly woman's face popped out from the open doorway.

The Hawk held up his badge. "Ma'am, everything's under control. We're sorry for the inconvenience, but everything should be back to normal shortly."

She saw him force a smile in the woman's direction, and then she disappeared back into the safety of her room. Julie wanted to scream.

"Don't forget what I told you, Juliette," Garza said. "The length of your stay with us is directly related to how cooperative you are with my men."

Her shoulders sagged, and her head dropped. Still, her stubborn internal strength forced her to put her feet forward, one step at a time.

*Inhale. Exhale.*

# THIRTY-EIGHT

"BEN — *BEN!*" REGGIE YELLED. "ARE you okay?"

Ben was looking around the room, dazed. He felt tired, worn, exhausted even. A strange thing to feel, considering he hadn't worked out or run or fought or done anything warranting feeling tired.

"Ben — "

He shot a glance toward Reggie.

"Ben, I —"

"Save it, Red," Ben said. Reggie's chin rose just a bit, but he kept his gaze on Ben.

Ben understood what was happening now. Julie had been taken, *his* Julie, and Reggie was trying to make sure he was okay.

But he wasn't okay. He hadn't been okay with any of this, even before they'd landed in Philadelphia. It wasn't the flights, it wasn't the car travel, and it wasn't even Daris herself.

It was something else — something he *knew* the others felt as well. This whole mess had been started as a simple sleuthing project, something Mr. E wanted them to 'check in on,' to use his words. He'd thought it might be something more serious than a simple murder and two related break-ins and thefts, but he hadn't said what.

Ben also thought it sounded suspiciously simple. He had been prepared for more, for Daris to fight back the way she had, and even for something like an FBI agent to walk in on them and suddenly ask them to be part of his team.

But what Ben *hadn't* been prepared for — what *none of them* had been prepared for — was what was happening now. Julie was gone, they had just been left in a hotel room without weapons, and none of them had any idea what to do next.

In a situation like this, Ben's first reaction was to start hunting. To begin tracking down the men who'd done this and start walking deliberately in the direction he thought they'd gone. He had done it before in the Amazon rainforest, and he had done it in Antarctica.

*Find the threat, eliminate the threat.* There was no red tape, no budget meeting, no planning session. He wanted to just *start moving*. He wanted to find them, and he wanted to kill them.

The others did as well, but they would prefer to plan it out first.

Ben's conscious mind knew the stupidity and risks of barging out the door and just walking aimlessly until he had a lead, but his emotions were currently winning the battle.

He stood up, looked at each of the other three men, one at a time, then started toward the door.

"Ben," Reggie said again. "What are you doing? Where are you going?"

"I'm going to find her, Reggie. It's not that hard to understand."

Joshua walked up behind him. "Harvey, it's not a good idea. You have no idea where you're —"

"Neither do you!" Ben yelled, whirling around to face them. "Neither do you. Do you?"

Neither man spoke.

"That's what I thought. So *tell me* why I shouldn't just *start*? Why shouldn't I just start moving and figure it out from there? It's always worked for me in the past. Why not now?"

He started to turn around again but Reggie stopped him.

"Ben, please. Think about it."

Ben's head dropped, and a tear fell from his left eye and landed on his boot. He didn't care about hiding it, and he knew they wouldn't care he was crying. He sniffed.

"It's — I could have... I should —"

"Ben, come on. There's *nothing* you could have done. They got her, and we're going to get her back. I promised her that already, and I'm promising you that now."

"But what are they going to *do* to her?" Ben asked. "You saw the way that guy was looking at her, like she was a side of beef or something. Reggie, I *have to get her back.*"

"And we will, man. Just come back in here and let's plan it out."

Ben stood there, silently, for a half a minute. Then he turned, slowly, and walked to the center of the room. Stood where The Hawk — Vicente Garza — had stood. He walked over to the closet, where Julie had been hiding.

*Where I should have been, protecting her,* he thought.

He shook his head, anger now mixing with the tears. He clenched his fists and turned back to the room.

Derrick, Reggie, and Joshua were standing around the chairs, all watching him. Waiting for him.

"What do you want from me?" Ben asked. "I'm useless. You've got the United States backing you, and you all have training and experience. I'm just a fatass park ranger who's out of work."

Reggie shook his head. "No, Ben. You're wrong. That's all I'm going to say about that. Get over here and let's figure out how to get Julie back."

He walked over, sat down, and stared at Reggie. He had nothing to offer, nothing to say. He would sit there, as long as they forced him to, and he would wait. He'd nod along, shake his head, whatever they wanted from him.

Eventually, when they decided it had been long enough and they had the right direction, he would start moving, start looking for her.

Then, when it was time, he would fight.

He would kill them all.

# THIRTY-NINE

THERE WASN'T A LOT REGGIE could think about at the moment. Normally his mind raced, ready to throw in a detail or an idea or a thought. But now, in this moment, his mind was empty.

He wanted to find Julie more than anything, but he knew he would find Garza and his men as well. He would find them, and he would kill them.

*If Ben doesn't kill them first.*

Reggie had seen Ben do amazing things, things normal men couldn't dream of, and things his own soldiers had trouble performing. Ben's mind may not be filled with facts and brilliant revelations, but he was an animal when it came to brutal physical effectiveness.

Reggie needed that now, and Joshua needed both of them. They needed Joshua too, but Ben was the key to it all. He was the one they had to worry about, the one who was closest to the edge.

He'd seen it before, in the line of duty. Men would fall, and others would notice. They'd let it affect them, in a way that affected them more than it affected everyone else. They'd get attached to it, hold on to it, and it would hold them down.

Ben was close to being held down. Julie was gone, and he was in shock. He was a strong man, but this was something no one but Reggie himself had gone through. Joshua Jefferson had lost his father earlier this year, but to Joshua, the man had been gone for far longer.

Reggie knew how Ben felt right now, and he knew there was little he could do to help. No words would comfort him, and no false promises would hold him over. Ben was a man of action, so the only thing Reggie could do was invite Ben in and put him to work.

"We're going to need to know everything," Reggie said, looking at the FBI agent sitting across from him.

Derrick nodded. "I know, but not here. The police will be here in a few minutes, the SWAT team in another few. Those windows out, the gunshots? The hotel staff is probably already corralling everyone off of our floor."

Reggie nodded. "Which means we've got a few minutes to get out of here unseen. Can we take the stairs?"

"Probably — that'd be my preferred option. Let's head out; if we get separated, we'll meet up behind the hotel. There's a yogurt shop on 20th street that shares an alley with the Rittenhouse. Get there and wait for the rest of us."

Reggie nodded in compliance, then waited for Joshua and Ben to stand up.

Derrick hung back, rummaging through his bags. Reggie knew he would want to try as much as possible to leave the room as empty as he could. Not possible, but at least Derrick could retrieve anything that might point back to him.

The man would have booked the set of rooms under a pseudonym, which would put the hotel and SWAT teams behind a few precious hours. By the time they traced the rooms back to the FBI — if they did — the FBI would have commenced their damage-control mode: preparing their press statements and cover stories, effectively getting Roger Derrick off the hook.

Whether Derrick would take flack back at the main office, Reggie couldn't know. He imagined the man's boss wouldn't be terribly excited that a small reconnaissance and intelligence gathering mission like this one had blown up.

But that wasn't Reggie's problem. Derrick had probably anticipated this, or at least something like this. He was, after all, FBI.

*At least he says he's FBI.*

Reggie hadn't yet decided if he believed the man or not. So far the guy seemed to be on their side, on the level. He was playing his cards slowly, but he was playing them nonetheless. Reggie knew the FBI folk to be a finicky bunch, secretive and slow to dish out information. For that, Derrick fit the bill.

They jogged to the end of the hallway and found the door to the staircase. Swinging it open, Ben held it and waited for the other two men to pass through. Reggie glanced back at the room and was surprised to see their new FBI friend already making his way out into the hallway. He held a large case in one hand — likely the gun case he'd had earlier — and a smaller briefcase in the other.

"Right behind you," Derrick shouted. "I'll catch up."

Reggie nodded and turned to the stairway. Joshua was already making his way down, descending to the street level.

Reggie's mind suddenly flashed back to the last time they were together making their way down a staircase. Antarctica, earlier that year, a small Chinese army and an equal number of enemy station guards all trying to shoot them down. They'd escaped — narrowly — and lived to tell about it.

But Julie had been with them then.

He hoped Ben wasn't thinking similar thoughts.

As he reached the next level down, Derrick reached the flight above him. The large man swung the door back closed again, the loud slam of it echoing throughout the metal and concrete stairwell.

"Keep moving," Derrick said. "I thought I heard the elevator door opening right before I got in here."

# FORTY

JUST AS DERRICK HAD PROMISED, the yogurt shop sat on the corner of 20th Street and Locust Street, a narrow little storefront that backed up against a few other shops that all shared a common landlord.

Reggie wasn't a huge fan of yogurt, especially since the 'yogurt craze' had erupted in America. To him it seemed more of a thing designed for stay-at-home moms and hip high schoolers than an actual dessert. When he got ice cream, it was far from soft-serve: mounds of rocky road piled high with M&Ms and drizzled with hot caramel.

The thought brought a smile to his face. He'd have to check if there was a *real* ice cream shop nearby, if they had the time after this mess was over.

"Reggie, you good?" Ben's voice reached Reggie's ears and brought him back. The yogurt shop's trendy decor and bright lights were jarring, juxtaposing a false sense of hope on top of their dim reality.

He nodded. "Yeah, Ben, I'm good. How are you holding up?"

Ben shrugged.

"Yeah, I feel you."

"Okay," Joshua said, cutting in. "We're all here. Let's get some chairs into a circle and I'll set up Derrick's iPad with a call back to Mr. E."

Reggie and Derrick immediately started arranging the chairs in the empty shop, and the shopkeeper — a small, Asian man — seemed to sense that the men weren't here for yogurt. He wiped down a countertop, then disappeared into the back of the store. The group all sat, a single chair in the center of a circle. Reggie rotated his chair around and sat in it backwards.

"Before we call Mr. E," Ben said, "let's figure out who you really are."

Derrick frowned. "Me?"

"You're FBI?"

"I really am."

"Why have you been holding things back from us then?" Ben asked.

Reggie smiled. "Because he's *FBI*, Ben. That's what they do."

Derrick didn't seem to appreciate the joke, and he quickly began explaining. "I have not been holding anything back from you for any reason other than this: I had a feeling Daris had hired a security crew, and I wanted to make sure you were not in danger, or that you weren't her security crew."

"Thanks for that," Joshua said. "I understand where you're coming from, but we're in this now. Together."

"Right," Derrick said, leaning forward and working out a kink in his neck. "What do you want to know?"

"Where are they taking Julie?" Ben asked, jumping in.

Derrick shook his head. "I don't know. I have no information on this group that Daris hired, or where they're headquartered. It could be here in town, or it could be anywhere. You knew their leader, The Hawk?"

Reggie nodded. "Yeah, but I don't know him anymore. Your guess is as good as mine as to where they're keeping her."

Ben shifted to address Derrick. "Well have your grunts start looking. Don't you have technology for that?"

"We don't have the technology or resources for that. No offense, Harvey — it's not like we're dealing with the kidnapping of a president, here."

"Then have a team sent out!" Ben snapped. "You've got to be able to do *something*."

Derrick held up a hand, looking around the shop to see if anyone else had appeared. The shopkeeper was still absent, likely holed up in a back office watching their conversation on a security monitor. "I know how you feel, Harvey, believe me. But still, I can't make this investigation about something it's not."

"What's that supposed to mean?"

Reggie saw Ben's eyes flash around the circle of chairs to the other men. He was trying to piece it together, just like Reggie had. Joshua knew, and Reggie knew as well.

Joshua spoke next. "Ben, it means the FBI is only interested in their case. Julie's now a part of that case, but she's not the *most important* part."

Ben looked shocked, and hurt. "But she's *gone*, and you're telling me —"

"I'm telling you we'll find her," Reggie said. "But it's going to be on our own, or it's going to be with Derrick's help."

"And the only way Derrick's going to help us — the only way he *can* help us — is if he's working the case."

Reggie looked at Derrick to confirm, and Derrick nodded solemnly.

"I can't say it's ideal, Ben," Derrick said. "But it is what it is. I need to protect whatever it is Daris is after *first*, and only then can I help you out."

"Then we'll do it on our own," Ben said, preparing to stand. "Just like you said. 'We do it with or without this FBI guy,' right? So let's do it without him."

"Not that easy, Ben," Joshua said.

"Yeah? Why? Why is it *never* that easy?"

"Because whatever Daris is after is something she was willing to have her security force take Julie for. Meaning she's planning to use Julie as a bargaining chip somehow."

"Or as a way to get us to do something for her," Reggie added.

"Julie's a part of the same thing everyone's after," Derrick said.

"So we help Derrick, we find Julie. We all work together on this one."

Ben nodded. "I understand, but I still don't *understand*. What are we after?"

Reggie wasn't sure of the answer to that question, and he knew Joshua wasn't sure, either. Whatever it was it was worth killing — or kidnapping — for, and that made it something that was very likely a valuable prize.

"Well," Derrick said. "Do you remember what Daris said on GMA this morning?"

"About Jefferson? That he used money that wasn't his?"

"Correct. Specifically that he used money that wasn't his *or* the nation's. Money he found from a Spanish treasure fleet that sank in 1715."

"You think this is about *gold?*"

"I think it's about *proof*. Proof that there *was* gold, and that it was used to purchase the Louisiana Territory."

He looked at all of them in turn, then slowly, deliberately, sat up and leaned forward.

"But that's not *really* what this is about. The gold is what she's saying this is, to generate goodwill and to win over any of the silent majority who might want to join her side."

Reggie leaned in, pushing his backwards chair up onto the back two legs.

"I think Daris has already found something, and she's been following the trail left by Lewis in his secret journal to find more of it."

"More of what?"

Derrick paused, sucking his lips together, and Reggie knew he was silently debating whether or not he should play this final card he had in his pocket. Finally he leaned in a bit as well, nearly touching foreheads with Reggie.

"Have you ever heard of the plant, *Borrachero?*"

# FORTY-ONE

"BORA-*WHAT*?" BEN ASKED.

"BORRACHERO," Derrick said. "A plant, native to Columbia. It's very common there, grows just about everywhere."

"And Daris found some growing on the Lewis and Clark trail?"

Derrick shook his head. "No — well, not really. But I believe she's found something like it. Another strain, maybe of the same genus, but definitely with similar properties."

Ben's heart sank. "And what, exactly, are these 'properties?'"

"Well, have you ever heard of the date-rape drug?"

Ben nodded. "Yeah, the pill they slip into your drink at parties... and then you wake up the next day. No idea what happened the night before."

"Right," Derrick said. "But it's a bit more complicated than that."

"Of course it is."

"'Date-rape' drugs are really a whole *class* of chemicals, from alcohol to the more powerful barbiturates. They're really just a classification of things that cause those effects. Have a high-enough dosage of Ambien, actually, and you're out."

The men sitting around Derrick nodded.

"Well those drugs are all baby versions of the mother chemical of all date-rape drug chemicals, scopolamine. It's used in extremely small doses as Hyoscine in things like sleep medicine and motion sickness medicine, like the patch you wear which releases the scopolamine slowly on a set schedule."

"So this Borrachero plant has scopolamine in it?" Joshua asked.

"It does, but in *far* higher concentrations than what's considered safe. In the past few years, reports have been coming out of Columbia that scopolamine-laced items like business cards, gas pumps, and ATM machines have been incapacitating people."

"But not killing them?" Ben asked.

"Not always. Not usually, actually. The drug has been used by gangs and organized warfare to control their targets. The person wakes up, doesn't remember a thing."

Ben swallowed, thinking about Julie. He wanted to ask, but couldn't.

Reggie asked. "You think Daris' team has this stuff?"

"It's not hard to get," Derrick said, nodding. "I'm almost positive she's got a team of scientists working on it. Like I said, it's readily available thanks to the hardy plant that produces it. It can be grown just about anywhere, and it's cheap."

"But we already *have* 'date-rape drugs,'" Reggie said, making air-quotes around the words. "Even if this stuff is more powerful than what we've already got, how is it a national security threat?"

"Well, first of all, I don't think you understand the amount of scopolamine that it takes to have an effect. As little as half a milligram will knock someone out, and any more than that will take their memory away."

"Woah," Reggie said. "So a few more milligrams would kill someone."

"Absolutely, and it has. The bad guys down in Columbia have been using somewhere between 2 and 5 milligrams to not only render their victims helpless, but in a *conscious state* at the same time. They can then give them commands, and the person will execute them without argument."

Ben's nostrils flared, and he gritted his teeth. "And they don't remember it the next day."

"And they don't remember it the next day," Derrick said. "Last big case I heard about was in Bogota. A woman had her newborn baby boy stolen from her, right out of her arms. She was found three days later, muttering to herself and walking on the highway, topless."

Ben's eyes widened. "You've got to be kidding me…"

"Wish I was. They're calling it a 'zombie drug.' In those concentrations, if it doesn't kill, it *really* messes you up."

"No shit," Reggie said, muttering under his breath. "Wow."

"So I think Daris has stumbled onto something important, something that the Spanish themselves wanted to keep secret."

"Something the Spanish *wanted*," Joshua said.

"Exactly. They wanted it so bad they sent eleven ships to retrieve it.

They loaded up the ships with gold and silver, and other treasures, but also some of those *borrachero* plant, to take it all back to Spain."

"The Spanish Treasure Fleet of 1715," Ben said.

"Right again. They wanted to use it as a weapon, no doubt, to see if they could refine it, perfect it. Maybe figure out how many different ways they could deploy it. It would have been one of the world's first — and most effective — chemical weapons."

"An entire population under its spell, doing whatever you told it to," Joshua said.

"If you were in proximity to them, and could command them all, sure," Derrick said. "But even as a one-off chemical agent, one that could be deployed in teas, smoked like tobacco, or brushed onto someone's skin from a piece of paper."

Ben shook his head. "Daris wants to use it on Julie."

"No, Ben," Derrick said, touching Ben's shoulder. "We don't know that. And there's no reason to suspect that she would. But I *do* believe that's really what Daris is looking for — a cache of this stuff that whoever found the Spanish fleet brought back to Jefferson, who promptly wanted it hidden, and sent Meriwether Lewis to hide away."

"Fine," Ben said. "But I'm not convinced that Julie's safe from it. She's certainly not *safe* at all, for that matter. So let's figure out how to find her."

# FORTY-TWO

MISTAKES HAD BEEN MADE, THERE was no doubt about that. But they still had the girl, the pretty little lady who seemed to be just feisty enough to make it worthwhile.

The Hawk had planned on grabbing the FBI agent. He'd wanted to bring him back to the gym, string him up in the chair, and get what he could from him. It would take time to make the big man fall, but when they were done with him he'd be every bit as willing to serve The Hawk as the rest of his men.

He was now two men down, but that was already being remedied. He had ordered Joseph Mikel, one of his longest-serving men, to work on finding the replacements for Velacruz and Jenkins, whose bodies were currently being disposed of.

He'd decided after he'd left the hotel with Juliette that a perfect test for the men next in line to join his team would be to eliminate the remainder of the threat to his client. He originally hadn't wanted to take out the rest of the FBI man's team, as he wasn't sure what sort of mess that might cause him, but after weighing his options, and realizing that Julie would be more than enough of a bargaining chip with his boss if he needed one, he decided to send in more men to finish the job.

Mikel's call had lasted no more than thirty seconds; the man he'd called had been in the area for two weeks, hoping for an appointment to The Hawk's team. He told them where Julie's group had been staying, and how long they had been there.

The man had confirmed with Mikel that he was ready for the job, and he confirmed that he would contact the other five men The Hawk wanted to test. It would be a test of their abilities, but it was also a test of their leadership. Mikel gave The Hawk the thumbs-up sign from the side of the gym, letting him know the deed had been done, and the group of men would be ready within the hour.

He placed his attention back on the center of the gym.

The girl might not know as much as the FBI agent, but she would provide much more entertainment for the rest of his men when it was done. Maybe he'd even allow them some well-deserved entertainment *before* they were done with the interrogation. Perhaps even he himself might need some entertainment. Since he had all but removed such temptation from his life, he needed little of the opposite sex to keep him company, but when he did it was not a challenge to find someone willing.

Vicente Garza knew he was a good-looking man, at least better than average. He had black hair, cut short but not in a negligent sort of way. He kept it a bit longer in the front, as he liked the Roman-esque way it hung down over his forehead, tiny little strips of hair that gave him a George Clooney-type look.

His face was surprisingly pockmark free, especially considering his past and his history as a soldier. He'd been in plenty of live-fire missions, and many more clandestine operations that had hardened and weathered him over the years.

But he was a more powerful man from it, and he felt his look showed it. He had the look of a man with experience, with passion, and the look of a man with confidence. Not a swagger, like Morrison's overconfident attitude often appeared, but one of quiet confidence that the other men respected and responded to.

This woman, Juliette Richardson, would come to respect and respond to it as well. She would be difficult at first, pushing back when the time for questions came, but she would eventually crack.

*They always did.*

Either from the drug or from the fear of it, they always cracked.

He eyed her from the side of the gym, from the blocked door where he liked to stand as the rest of his men worked. It was his perch, his standing throne, where he could direct and dictate what needed to be done. He could call out an order or talk directly to another man in the room using the personal comm system they each wore. It was efficient, effective, and it kept things moving toward their goals.

The woman was at the opposite door, the door Morrison was standing in front of. He switched to Morrison's channel and gave the man instructions.

"Bring her in, Morrison. Let's see if she's going to be willing to cooperate."

"I'll make *sure* she's willing to cooperate, sir."

"Just bring her in. Don't do anything rash, like you did back in the hotel room."

Garza knew his second-in-command had roughed her up a bit, likely out of the man's own frustration. Morrison may have been a good soldier, but he was horrible with the opposite sex. He'd seen how Morrison treated them on more than one occasion, and on more than one occasion he'd had to pull the man away from the girl he was 'treating.'

The Hawk watched as Morrison and another of his men dragged Juliette through the open gym floor and forced her into the chair. She had a tight expression on her face, devoid of emotion. She wasn't scared, or angry, or confused. She just *was*.

He allowed a slight grin to cross over his face as she stared at him. *They always start out like this,* he thought. *Triumphant, as if they'd already beaten him.*

He wasn't surprised at her response to the men tying her to the chair. She sat, calmly, watching him. Staring at him. She knew he was in charge, and he *wanted* her to know.

He stared back.

She would keep that face as long as she could, but it wouldn't last forever.

Eventually, his men would wipe that face clean and force her to wear a new one. A face that *definitely* showed her fear, her confusion, and her pain.

It was a beautiful face, and he'd be sure to have his men keep that face beautiful.

"Morrison," he said.

"Sir?"

"Let them finish, and then have the men take a break."

"But sir, we're ready to begin —"

"They deserve a break, Morrison. She's not going anywhere, and I want to make sure she knows that."

Morrison looked from Juliette to him, then back again.

"Yes, sir. You got it."

The Hawk crossed his arms, watching as his men finished tying the woman's arms and legs to the chair. Finally, after the zip ties were all in place, they ran a rope around her neck and tightened it to the base of the chair's back, ensuring that she had enough slack to breathe.

He thought he saw a slight gasp escape her lips when they tied her neck, and he wondered if she'd crack much sooner than he'd expected. But she closed her mouth again, raised her chin a bit, and continued staring.

*Good, Juliette. Good.*

She was now hog-tied to the chair, unable to lean forward without choking herself, and unable to move any of her appendages. It had proven to be an effective and inexpensive way to hold a prisoner, and it was portable as well. He'd been able to hold many prisoners this way for years, no matter what third-world country or hellhole he found himself in.

But here, in this makeshift gymnasium, with his men keeping a tight watch and nowhere for her to run, the chair was hardly needed just to keep the prisoner in one place.

The chair was overkill for restraint purposes alone, and The Hawk knew it.

The chair was designed to extract *psychological* effects from his prisoners, and it had never failed him.

# FORTY-THREE

*'IT DOES SEEM AS THOUGH this has escalated quite a bit,'* Mr. E said. His face glowed from the screen of the iPad Joshua had placed on the chair in the middle of their circle. Reggie and Ben had slid their chairs over closer to Derrick's and Joshua's, so they could all see the screen.

"'Escalated quite a bit?'" Ben asked, nearly yelling. "You've got to be — Julie's *gone.* That's all you have to offer?"

Reggie felt the tension in the room start to rise. They had called in to Mr. E, just as they had planned, and so far they had told their benefactor everything that had transpired.

*'No,'* E said. *'Hopefully I have more to offer than that. My wife has contacted me as well, just an hour ago. She is with the pawn shop owner, and they are both safe. But there has been a development.'*

Reggie's eyebrows rose.

*'It appears the woman my wife went to find knows more than I initially thought.'*

"Like what?"

*'I believe she is part of the American Philosophical Society, for starters.'*

Reggie considered this a moment. The pawn shop owner who had flown to Australia to — ostensibly — attend a conference related to running a pawn shop, was part of the APS.

"I wonder if the woman who was murdered — Delacroix? — was also APS," Joshua said.

Mr. E's image nodded on the iPad's screen. *'That is what I believe as well. It makes sense that the two women would be willing to trade the item in question for such a high price in that case. Yet it doesn't tell us what the item* was, *and my wife was unable to find anything in that regard.'*

"I might be able to help with that," Derrick said, stepping forward so Mr. E could see his face. "My name is Roger Derrick, and I'm with the FBI."

*'Alone?'*

"Unfortunately, yes. At least for the time being. But after today, I might be able to talk them into sending out a team."

*'I do hope, for your safety and for Julie's, that is true,'* Mr. E said. *'But thank you for your protection and help thus far.'*

Derrick nodded. "It's a passion project, really. Something I've been tracking down for years when the time permits. We're close, now. I can feel it. And if your team is willing, I'd like them to —"

*'Say no more,'* Mr. E said. *'My team is at your disposal. I understand the situation has grown more dire, and that Julie's safety is now on the line. But helping you will help her, and vice versa.'*

Derrick nodded again, then looked around the room, as if asking for their final permission.

Reggie gave him a stern look, but nodded. "This project of ours has gotten a little out of hand," he said. "But we're here to help. Give us your word you'll help us find Julie when this is all over."

"Of course," Derrick said. "As I said, following this trail of Daris' will bring us closer to Julie. They're looking for the same thing, and they wanted her for a bargaining chip."

Reggie watched as Ben's face darkened, his jawline becoming exaggerated as he clenched his teeth together. Reggie had been there before, had felt that feeling.

*Total loss. Helplessness.*

It wasn't a feeling he had ever welcomed, and it wasn't a feeling he'd ever been able to overcome. He had trained his entire life to remove that feeling from his persona, to completely deny his mind the ability to feel it.

Ben was feeling it now, and he would be feeling it for some time.

But Reggie also knew that he'd be more alert, his mind in a state of heightened clarity, for the next few hours. Tomorrow he'd be dull, the throbbing sharpness of the pain he was feeling today pushed back to a constant tension. He would still be present, but he would be slipping away quickly.

It was important, if they wanted Ben's help, to get him moving today. Keep him moving, keep him awake and talking, if possible. He would rail against any support or encouragement, but he would be on a high-adrenaline kick.

Reggie and Joshua needed to point him in the right direction and let him run before he started to crash.

Ben finally nodded, agreeing with the rest of them. He stood up, walking into the iPad camera's view. "We need to get moving, then. We're wasting time."

"Ben," Joshua said. "That's why we called this meeting, remember? We don't know *where* to go. That's why we need to find the journal."

Derrick sniffed quickly and looked away.

Reggie turned to him and stared.

"I — sorry, I didn't mention this before…"

Reggie spoke through his teeth. "*What* did you not mention before?"

"We have — I mean *I* have — the journal."

Joshua let out a sigh, and Reggie's eyes closed. He clenched his fists.

"I wasn't sure if I could trust you before, and I didn't know why you were at the APS headquarters. I was watching Daris, and I was told I could move in whenever I felt comfortable with the situation, so I moved in quickly when I knew she wasn't alone in there. I didn't want things to get out of hand."

"Well they *did* get out of hand, pal," Reggie said. "Do you trust us, *now*?"

Derrick nodded. "I do. I'm sorry, I wasn't going to keep it from you the entire time. I just had to make sure we were all fighting for the same side."

"I'm fighting for Julie. That's it. You get us closer to Julie, I guess that means we're on the same side."

Joshua's hardened stare drilled into the larger, thicker Roger Derrick. Reggie had seen that stare before, and he knew it had weakened far stronger men than Derrick.

"Where'd you get the journal?"

Derrick looked at each man, then the iPad screen. Mr. E was staring back, stoic, his face an unmoving mask. If the video was frozen, they wouldn't have been able to tell.

"I took it from the APS facility. *I* was the one who stole it from Daris."

# FORTY-FOUR

BEN WATCHED THE LARGE MAN'S expression. He seemed to be telling the truth, but Ben had been wrong before. He wanted to trust this man, wanted to believe him. He knew the story made sense, and he knew he might have done the same thing if he were in Derrick's shoes.

But Julie was out there, and this man was willing to play ball with them. On their team. For now, at least, their interests were aligned.

*But what happens when our interests are no longer aligned?* Ben thought. *Will he still play ball?*

"Why?" Ben asked. "Why take it?"

"I told you, this has been a pet project of mine for some time. I've been following Daris, and her rise to power within the organization. When I found out about the journal a month ago, I knew it would be something worth getting my hands on"

"Because the journal seemed like an important piece of her struggle for power?"

Derrick nodded. "It did, and it is. It's crucial to her campaign."

"How?"

"It's the map, Harvey. It has everything inside that she needs to find her treasure."

"How do you know?"

"Because it's been kept secret from the rest of the organization — and the rest of the world — at large. It's something *no one* wanted to talk about, and only about seven living people at any given time in history has known about. Something that's going to be important. It's going to have the treasure map in there."

"Then why hasn't she found it yet?"

"She only found out about the journal recently, when it was bequeathed to her from the previous president. It's part of the tradition, passed down from generation to generation, all the way back to Benjamin Franklin. There are more secrets, too — some small, some large, some deadly. They pass them down to keep them inside the organization, but they only pass them along to the leadership in the group. Not all the members know everything. So she only recently got her hands on this thing, but she's anxious to figure out where it leads. Why no one else wanted to go searching for the treasure it's concealing is anyone's guess, but I'd say it's because no one really thinks it's what she says it is. More of a relic, a cool piece of history. But a treasure map? Hiding a conspiracy that goes all the way back to Jefferson and Lewis? I'm not sure anyone else believed it."

"So the APS *is* a lot more like the Freemasons," Joshua said.

"In that way, yes," Derrick said. "But since its inception, the organization was meant for good, meant to keep the young nation in check, by providing the country's leadership with ideas and solutions to problems."

"The original idea behind Ben Franklin's Junto."

"Exactly. He was a patriot, as were the other members. It was always that way, and it still is. But there are obviously different sides to the same story, and Daris' story — the one she's telling herself — is that the APS needs to have a stronger handle on US politics, more control overall in the nation, and she's willing to kill to get it."

Reggie nodded, and Ben listened silently. He took in the words, fitting them against the description of Daris Derrick had given them previously, against the woman he'd met in the office at the APS, and the woman he'd seen on TV.

She was manipulative, he'd seen that personally. But that meant she was clever, too, able to work different angles at once. Able to work different *people* at once.

Suddenly it hit him.

"You're APS, aren't you?" he asked.

Derrick looked at him, and he felt Reggie and Joshua's eyes on him as well. He couldn't see the iPad screen, he had a feeling Mr. E had leaned in to the camera, trying to hear better what Derrick would say next.

"You're APS, and that's why you stole the journal. You're against Daris and her side, and you want to make sure she doesn't get what she wants."

Derrick chewed on nothing, his jaw tightening and loosening.

"Say it," Ben said. "Tell us the truth."

Finally, Derrick spoke. "Yes," he said. "I am. I'm part of the American Philosophical Society. The Old World side. I want to protect the integrity of the nation I love. I want what's best for its people, and I want what's best for me."

"You're part of the leadership?"

"Sort of. I'm next in line to take their place. Not president, but one of the governing members. I'm close with them, though. I know what they're vying for, and I know what they're up against."

"Mercenaries willing to kill anyone and everyone who's against Daris?"

"Something like that, yeah," Derrick said.

"Well." Reggie said. "That's that. It's making a lot more sense now."

Joshua frowned. "Are you not FBI?"

"No, I am. But it's just like I said earlier. This is a pet project of mine, one I barely have any resources for. I had to beg for this assignment, since it's pretty low-priority up there. I'm actually on vacation right now, and my boss nearly had a heart attack when he found out I'm working. Most of what I've put in I've done on my own time, with my own money. I don't have the benefit of an entire team of guys helping out with the research and organization of it all for this assignment, so it's pretty much whatever I can pull together."

"And now we're here, which is why you want our help."

"Not want," Derrick said. "*Need.* I really do need your help. Even if you don't believe this crap, Daris is willing to sacrifice *anything* — and any*one* — to get her way. She'll *make up* a story if that's what it takes. She has to be stopped."

"She's got Julie," Ben said. "So she's going to be stopped. You have my word on that."

Derrick stood up, walked around the iPad sitting on the chair in the middle of the room, and stretched out a hand. Ben took it, squeezed, and felt the crushing strength of Roger Derrick return his own grasp.

"Thank you, all of you. I wish I could repay you, but —"

"Help us get Julie," Joshua said. "That's payment enough."

"You got it."

Reggie sat back down after the round of handshakes, then looked over at Derrick once more.

"Great. Now, about that journal. Can we see —"

A loud *crash* sounded to Ben's left, and the window shattered. Pieces of glass fell inward, the tiny sparks of crystal bouncing and flying up again as they hit the hard laminate floor.

# FORTY-FIVE

BEN FELL SIDEWAYS, INSTINCTIVELY TRYING to dodge the shards of sharp glass. He had barely heard the first gunshot, but the second and third sounded — far away, but obviously aimed toward him.

"Shit!" Reggie yelled. "What is that?"

"Someone's shooting at us," Ben responded, from his position on the floor. "Again."

Derrick crab-walked backwards toward the yogurt shop's counter, sliding his briefcase and hard case along next to him as he went. Reggie and Joshua followed suit. None of them were armed, as The Hawk's team had taken their weapons. Ben wondered if Derrick had another sidearm in his case and was trying to get to cover to get it loaded and ready.

"They're back? Why didn't they kill us the first time?"

Ben reached the counter just as the owner of the shop, the small Asian man, came running up to the front of the store.

"Get down!" Joshua yelled. "Now!"

The man, wide-eyed and trembling, dove to the floor, a grunt escaping his lips as a torrent of gunfire erupted over his head.

"Not sure if they're the same group or not," Derrick said. "These guys don't seem as careful. The Hawk's guys had our room key and everything, remember?"

"Well, careful or not, these guys are shooting a lot more," Reggie said. "And this is downtown Philadelphia, for crying out loud. They can't possibly think they're going to get away with it."

Ben had his hands over his head, helpless to defend their position.

He realized that they *all* were helpless, and he could see on Derrick's face that he knew it, as well.

"We need to get out of here, guys," Derrick said. "They're not going to stop shooting until we're all dead. And I doubt they'll run out ammunition before that."

"Back of the store," the Asian man said. "Back of the store, exit door."

"Back of the store, exit door," Reggie repeated. "Sounds good to me."

Ben pushed up into a squat, waiting for Joshua to order them to the back door. The bullets, temporarily, had stopped flying.

*Which means they're coming closer, to get a better shot.*

"What are you waiting for?" Joshua asked. "You heard the man — back door."

Ben didn't need to be told twice, and he started shuffling toward the back door of the shop, on his hands and knees. It was uncomfortable, and the brownish-tiled floor of the back-counter area was sticky with old, crusty yogurt spills and other unknowable brown stains.

He felt a wave of revulsion wash over him, but he pushed it down and continued on.

*This is disgusting*, he thought. *But I guess it's better than getting shot.*

"I wonder if this floor's ever been cleaned," Reggie said from right behind Ben.

Two more gunshots rang out, and one clattered loudly into a large metal bowl on a shelf above Ben's head. The bowl went sailing through the air, landing near a sink overflowing with dirty dishes and silverware.

"Screw this," Reggie said, rising to his feet and jumping over Ben. "If I'm going to be shot, I'll be on my feet."

Ben was about to ignore him when he realized Reggie had already made it through the small kitchen area to the door at the back of the long, narrow storefront. He followed Reggie's lead, rising to his feet and running the rest of the way.

Reggie was fiddling with the door, which was thankfully out of a direct line-of-sight to the front of the store, when Joshua and Derrick arrived.

"Is it locked?" Derrick asked. "Can you just kick it in?"

"No, and no," Reggie said. "It's just old. Stuck somehow, and —" he grunted as the handle finally gave way. "There."

He pushed the bar inward and down and the door flew open. The bright sunlight of the afternoon spilled in and blinded Ben, but he followed Reggie out anyway, stepping down the two steps that led into the alley they'd run in from a few minutes earlier.

His eyes needed a moment to adjust, so he looked down at the ground and blinked a few times, then lifted them up again.

And saw that they were all standing in the alley, face-to-face with three well-armed men.

All pointing guns toward them.

# FORTY-SIX

THE GUY WITH THE CROOKED nose, Morrison, tried to help the other two men bind Julie to the chair. He had pulled her into the large, open gymnasium, pushed her into the chair, and was now trying to offer help.

His way of 'helping,' however, was to reach in and grab at her arms and legs and simply… feel.

It was disgusting, and Julie felt the lump in her throat that she had to force back down whenever he'd come near. The man was sick, perverted, and obviously lacking for female contact. It didn't help that the man looked horrendous.

His craggy face and crooked nose nearly brushed against her own face as he dove in once again to 'check' that she was sitting back in the chair as far as she could.

He reached down, patted at her thigh, squeezing just a bit, then moved up to her waist. He sighed a little, only causing her more disgust, then pushed back. His knobby fingers pressed hard and she felt her gut give way, her inability to move out of his reach causing her to feel suddenly claustrophobic.

She wanted to scream, but she refused. That would allow him to win, and he would know it.

Instead, she stared. Straight across the room at the man who had taken her, Vicente Garza, The Hawk. He was staring back at her, the slightest grin of satisfaction on his face. She reeled, wanting to lash out and punch the pervert feeling her up, destroy the two men using zip ties to hold her to the chair, and then run at The Hawk and rip his head off.

But she couldn't. She wasn't a fighter, and she wasn't armed. She had no choice but to comply, to wait it out, to just sit there and let them do whatever it was they were going to do. It wouldn't help her to fight, but it would give them pleasure.

So she refused.

Instead, she stared.

Morrison had his hand just under her breast, and he was pushing it slowly upwards.

*Do it and die, bastard,* she thought. Then she realized that, no matter what this man did or didn't do, he was already dead. "I'll kill you myself," she whispered.

Morrison stopped and looked down at her. "What was that, girl?"

She shook her head. *I will remove your head from the rest of your body.*

She thought to herself a solid thirty-second-long string of obscenities directed at the man.

He continued his groping, inching ever closer to her breast. She continued staring, dead ahead at the man responsible for all of this.

'*Morrison,*' a voice said. She listened, realizing it was a small in-ear communications speaker Morrison was wearing. The man at the other end of the room had spoken to his subordinate.

Julie stared.

Morrison removed his hand, stepped back, then continued talking to The Hawk.

"Sir?"

She could no longer hear The Hawk's voice in the man's ear, but Morrison suddenly seemed upset.

"But sir, we're ready to begin —"

The Hawk cut him off, as across the gym floor his mouth had started moving before Morrison had finished.

Morrison looked from Juliette to his boss, then back again.

"Yes, sir. You got it."

Julie trembled, the moment of disgust finally over.

But she trembled again at the thought of what might lay ahead. The Hawk smiled at her from across the room, then crossed his arms.

Suddenly she felt her head being pulled backwards. A rope was placed over her neck, then pulled taut. Her eyes grew wide and she gasped.

*No, please no,* she willed. *Not like this.*

A moment later the rope loosened slightly, and she sucked in a deep breath. They weren't choking her, but simply tying her neck to the chair. It was an effective method, one she knew would be impossible to escape from. Her arms and legs were bound to the chair using zip ties in multiple spots, and now her neck was held back as well, preventing her from even moving her head forward to see her restraints.

She could handle being tied up. She wasn't afraid of the bindings, nor of the noose around her neck. She hardened her gaze once again and stared down the room at The Hawk.

*I'm going to beat you,* she thought. *And you're going to pay for this.*

The two men and Morrison finished their work and stomped off, out of sight somewhere behind her. The Hawk, too, started walking. He headed directly toward her, staring her down the entire time.

*Here we go,* she thought. *This is the moment I find out what this is all about.*

He watched her watching him, neither of their faces breaking. Her eyes were steady on his, not willing to sacrifice even that small amount of control to the man.

He must have known it, because just before he reached the chair he stopped, looked down at her, and smiled.

A genuine, true smile, as if what was happening in this room was the best possible thing he could think of, and that Julie was nothing more than a sideshow attraction that he was pleased with.

She felt shaken, suddenly vulnerable. She realized what had happened, the moments of absolute terror and agony she had so far successfully kept inside now tumbling out of her. She shivered, but she felt the strength of the bindings on her arms and legs.

She gasped again, this time the air entering her lungs in a staggered, frightened way. She sniffed, knowing that the tears were coming next.

Still, Vicente Garza looked down at her. His head was cocked sideways slightly, just a man standing over a prize. Intrigued by his prey, waiting for it to try to make a move.

She had no moves to make, and they both knew it.

The tears started to fall, even though she had begged them not to. She wanted Ben, she wanted him to be here to destroy this man and all the rest of his men.

And yet he still didn't speak.

Finally, after a full minute of his staring down into her, he lifted his head back up and started walking the direction his men had gone.

She was terrified, in pain, and now she was confused.

*What is happening?*

She heard his footsteps, hollow on the hardwood floor, the heels of his boots clacking over the worn surface, echoing around the concrete walls and steel roof of the facility.

And then the click and creaking sound of a door swinging open.

A moment passed, and the reverse of that sound — the whoosh of a large door closing, then the sound of a lock being turned — reached her ears.

She gasped again. She wasn't sure if this was better or worse.

The lights suddenly went off. All around her, darkness.

She couldn't see a thing, as the windows at the top edge of the walls around the room had been plastered over and allowed no light through. Julie was bathed in pure darkness, tied into a sitting position on a chair.

She hadn't been afraid of the dark at any point in her life until this moment. The fear was consuming her almost as quickly as the darkness. The Hawk and his men were no longer here, and she had no idea where they had gone or when they might return.

Or if Morrison might return... alone.

A gentle breeze from the closing door reached her chair, chilling her. She realized then that she was cold, too, just slightly cold.

She shook again, trembling freely now, crying and unable to curl up or even put her head down.

She closed her eyes, but it looked exactly the same.

# FORTY-SEVEN

"WHAT'S OUR MOVE, BOSS?" REGGIE asked, his hands already on his head. Ben knew this wasn't the man's first time at gunpoint — it wasn't his, either — but Reggie somehow kept that calm, almost humored attitude about it whenever he was under pressure.

And right now, baking in the sunlight and being held at gunpoint by three random strangers, Ben knew Reggie felt the pressure.

Joshua's jaw tightened, and Ben could almost see him processing their debacle. Finally, after a few more tense seconds, he spoke. "I don't know, Reggie. Seems like this is a bit of a surprise to all of us. Who are you assholes?"

The three men who were pointing their weapons — a handgun and two small subcompact machine guns — glanced around.

*They don't know who's in charge,* Ben realized. *They were hired to kill us, or bring us in, but they're not sure which of them is supposed to speak.*

The man in front of Ben flicked his eyes left and right, then back at Ben. He was the one holding the handgun, a huge .45 caliber that he held with both hands.

*He knows how to use that weapon,* Ben thought. *Even if he's not sure who's in charge.*

"You guys aren't going to talk, are you?" Reggie said. "You could at least tell us which one of you *we're* supposed to talk to."

"Don't talk, and you won't have to worry about it," the man in the center said. He was wearing a black t-shirt, sunglasses, and his neck was about as wide as his head. Not someone Ben wanted to mess with.

Reggie, apparently, *did* want to mess with him.

"How about this?" Reggie asked, his hands still above his head and his characteristic smile plastered across his face. "You tell me who you're working for, and I won't shove that shitty pair of sunglasses up your —"

"What my friend *means* to say," Derrick said, "is that you seem confused. We're confused as well, since we were literally *just* attacked."

"The Hawk," the man said. "That's who we're working for. Now shut the hell up, and follow me to the SUV over there."

The man on the far left of the line turned and pointed at a red SUV, a huge Escalade, parked near the alley's entrance.

"The Hawk just left," Derrick said. "He didn't think we were worth killing then. I doubt he thinks we're worth killing now."

"You're not worth killing. But he wants to talk to you some more, so go ahead and get in the car. Or I can help you, your call."

"Look," Derrick said. "I'm FBI, and your boss can verify that information. I'm positive you don't want the FBI messing around in your business, or bringing you in for —"

The man raised the gun up and directly into Derrick's face.

Reggie took a step forward and Ben heard the snapping sound of three weapons rise to attention. "Woah," he said. "Easy there, buddy. I'm just trying to get a good look at you."

"You make me wait until the other three guys are here and I *promise* you it's not going to be as painless as this," the man said.

Ben couldn't help it. He flicked his eyes to the end of the alley, trying to see if there was any weight to the man's claim. *Six against four, but right now it was only three-vs-four.* Decent odds, he figured, but his side wasn't armed.

He didn't like the odds, but he liked them even less if there were, in fact, three more men coming. But the man probably was telling the truth — these three seemed leaderless, and Ben and his group had been shot at from the *other* side of the yogurt shop.

It was very likely there were three men on their way to the back alley now, and one of them was leading this ragtag group.

Reggie looked at Ben, and Ben felt the man trying to read his thoughts. He did his best to help his friend. *Let's give it a shot,* Ben thought. *Please, let's just give it a shot. Julie's out there —*

Reggie was out of Ben's line-of-sight before he could finish the sentence in his mind. He stumbled backward, trying to figure out what had happened.

Reggie had fallen almost all the way to the ground, then popped back up *inside* the man's gun circle, coming up right in front of the man's face. His fist was ready, and he applied a perfectly timed uppercut to the man's chin, while grabbing for his gun with his free hand.

Ben recovered, then twisted quickly to dodge the flurry of bullets he knew was coming.

But the barrage never came. The other two men turned to Reggie and began to aim. They brought their weapons up to eye level, losing their nonchalant swagger and suddenly looking like *very* capable soldiers.

Ben reacted on instinct, diving forward to take out the man now closest to him. The man's back was toward him, allowing Ben to crush his forehead and shoulders into the man's lower back, crunching him forward and into the man Reggie had attacked.

Joshua, for his part, had ducked and rolled toward the man on the left, then come up and kicked at his groin. His kick landed, but it didn't seem to have enough power behind it to incapacitate the man. Joshua followed up with a trip, and the enemy fell, the two men now grappling for a solid hold on the other.

Ben reached for his man's head, grabbing a handful of the man's hair, and he smashed it as hard as he could onto the asphalt. The man seemed to anticipate the attack and had tightened his neck, as Ben was unable to get his head lifted high enough off the ground to do much damage. He groaned with the impact, a spattering of blood spraying to the side, but Ben knew it was far from enough of an impact to do enough.

He tried again, working his other hand in front of the man's head, on his forehead, then pulling up hard and fast, and pushing down with all his weight behind it. This time Ben heard — and felt — the cracking of the man's skull. He thought he could feel the man struggling beneath him, so he tried again.

And again.

"Ben!" Reggie shouted. "Let's go — now!"

Reggie sounded pissed, but even his scream wasn't enough to dislodge Ben from the enemy he'd felled. He felt Reggie and Joshua pulling up on his arms, gripping him beneath his armpits, literally ripping him off the man. Derrick was standing by, a shocked expression on his face.

"Enough, Ben," Joshua said. "Not here, not now."

A gunshot from a silenced pistol ricocheted off the brick wall of the building behind the yogurt shop, and another fell into the side of a dumpster. Ben realized what had happened — the three men they had attacked were being joined by the rest of their team — and he suddenly found his feet. It was about a hundred paces to the end of the alley, but the men bearing down on them were closing the distance, fast.

"I — I'm sorry," he said. "I didn't…"

"It's fine, Ben," Reggie said, still pulling his arm up and into the safety of the yogurt shop. "You just — you just need to plan that crap out better."

"Plan what?" Ben asked. "My temper?"

"Yeah," all three men said in unison.

They ran into the back kitchen, finding the Asian man still cowering behind the counter, now moved over into the corner, close to a walk-in freezer.

"Get in the freezer," Reggie said as they passed. "Please. It's for your own safety."

The shopkeeper nodded, then stood. He pulled open the door and ran inside, the heavy metal door falling shut with a deep thud.

Ben and Reggie watched the man retreat into the freezer while Joshua scoped out the front of the store. Derrick ran for the iPad they had left in the front of the store, scooping it up and placing it into his briefcase.

"Okay," Joshua said. "Looks like it's clear. But they're going to be running around the corner, or through the store, in a few seconds. So let's move."

"Where?" Ben asked.

Joshua shrugged. "Doesn't matter right now, really. Just stay together. How about that crowd of people over there?"

Sure enough, a crowd of young-looking people were crossing the street, the intersection of cars and trucks stopped behind their respective lights. In every direction, buildings towered above them, their roofs far above their heads. None of the surrounding buildings were as tall as the Rittenhouse, which dominated the immediate vicinity, but it gave the feeling that Ben was constricted, forced into a tiny box in the midst of larger boxes.

He had never been one for cities, especially downtown areas. Julie had a thing for perusing downtown streets, and she had pulled him along on numerous occasions, dragging him up and down tiny streets and between buildings, looking for that perfect cafe or coffee shop. She had even said she'd enjoy living in one of the tiny bungalows up above, their porch view of the bustling street below.

He tried as much as possible to steer her thinking away from such a fantasy, as he wasn't sure how he'd manage if she forced him to live in such a place. There were apartments just like that across the street from them now, above a corner dry cleaners the yogurt shop was facing.

"Even if they're fine shooting innocent bystanders, we'll be better

protected in that group, and they might have a hard time finding us."
Joshua was already moving, running out the open door. Ben, Reggie,
and Derrick hustled to keep up.

When Ben hit the street, he squinted, waiting for the line of
rounds he knew would be flying toward his back. But none came, and
he picked up speed and made it through the maze of cars and onto the
opposite corner, right where the group of young men and women were
standing. The group was about college-aged, an even mix of men and
women, and they all seemed as stunned as Ben felt. But, to their credit,
they didn't move.

"Stay below them," Joshua said, his voice commanding but calm.
"Don't poke your head up at all, we don't need them seeing us and
firing into us."

"Shouldn't we *not* be using people as human shields?" Derrick
asked.

Two of the boys closest to Ben shot him a glance, backing away
a bit.

"We're not," Joshua said. "We're just hiding. Whenever we get a
chance, we're ducking into this — *now!*" Joshua yelled the order right
as he started off, darting out of the group of people and into the corner
shop. Ben tried to move quickly, but he was the slowest of the men and
made it into the store a full two seconds after the rest of them.

He whirled around, finding the group, then turned and looked out
the front window, toward the yogurt shop. He could see their attackers, five men altogether, walking slowly up the street and toward the
front of the yogurt shop.

"You think anyone heard the gunshots?" Reggie asked.

"If they had, this intersection would be a madhouse right now,"
Derrick said. "Discharging a weapon in an urban area is the fastest way
to absolute chaos and rioting, so I think we'd know if anyone heard
the shots."

"And there's one less bad guy now," Reggie said. "Thanks to Ben."

"Sorry about that," Ben said. "I… it was just…"

Reggie placed a hand on Ben's shoulder. "Nothing to apologize for,
man, I was just trying to get your attention."

Ben nodded, and they turned to look at their surroundings. They
were standing in the dry cleaning shop. A counter stretched the entire
length of the tiny space, and a single wiry chair sat in the corner next
to an overly ambitious fake plant. There was hardly any room to
maneuver around the other men standing inside, and most disheart-
ening of all, there was only one entrance.

"We're stuck in here," Ben said. "If they decide to look in the
buildings nearby, they'll see us immediately."

"There's probably an exit in the back, just like in the yogurt shop," Reggie said. "These places are tiny, but they usually have a back-alley entrance for loading and unloading equipment."

"Well let's see if we can find it," Derrick said. "I don't like being stuck in here any longer than we absolutely have to."

The four men moved to the section of counter that lifted up and allowed for access to the back of the store, and Joshua led them through. A woman walked into the back-counter area and stopped, a startled look on her face.

"I — I'm sorry," she stammered. "Can I help you?"

"We're just passing through, ma'am," Joshua said. "Sorry to be an inconvenience."

"But you can't just —"

"FBI, ma'am," Derrick said, whipping out a wallet and shield identification.

Her eyes widened even further, but she stepped to the side. "It's — it's to the left, all the way back. The exit, I mean."

Derrick nodded, and they hustled through rows of long, curving racks of clothing, some covered in plastic and other rows waiting their turn to be cleaned. The cramped space created a sort of maze, and the door at the exit of the building was hardly a straight shot. They ducked and twisted around the clothing racks until Joshua found the illuminated exit sign and pushed the door open.

Ben found himself in another alleyway, but this time they were alone. They checked both directions, finding no one but casual tourists and businessmen and women walking up and down the city streets to their left.

"Looks like we're in the clear, for now," Joshua said.

"We're probably heading right back into it, soon as we figure out where to go," Reggie said.

"I can help with that," Derrick said. "I've been able to make a little headway into the first part of the journal."

"Yeah?" Ben asked. "Where is this little excursion taking us first?"

Derrick looked around at each of them in turn. "I hope you boys like to fly."

# FORTY-EIGHT

BEN WATCHED AS DERRICK REACHED for the suitcase he'd brought with. He retrieved another gun safe, one nearly identical to one of the smaller ones Reggie had given Ben and Julie earlier that year. Thumbprint-detecting, large enough to hold a weapon and a few magazines, and hardy enough to take a beating.

But there wasn't a handgun inside the safe; instead, Derrick unlocked the case and pulled out a small, worn leather journal. It looked like a Moleskin journal, palm-sized, with a tiny ribbon hanging from the bottom.

The journal was brown, and the cover cracked and faded. The ribbon was torn, the dangling part nearly completely worn off, and Derrick handled the piece as gently as possible. The first pages of the journal still held their rectangular shape, but the fraying edges of some of the remainder of the pages had torn and crumpled back, creating small peaks and valleys on the long edge of the closed journal. He brought it back over and placed it on the same chair the iPad had been on during their call with Mr. E.

"That thing looks like it's held up well after 200 years," Reggie remarked.

"And not to mention the beating it took *during* the expedition," Derrick said. "It's been wrapped in butcher paper and cellophane, tightly enough to keep the air out, then stored in a case under more plastic and paper."

"Since Lewis finished it?"

"Since he finished it and tried to give it to Thomas Jefferson," Derrick replied. "Jefferson, remember, hired Lewis — who then requested Clark as his equal for the expedition — to find and map a passage to the Pacific, and through the newly acquired territory."

"…that was purchased with Spanish gold," Ben said.

"Purportedly, if you believe Daris."

"And you don't believe her."

Derrick shook his head. "I don't. I *can't*. It's just too…"

"Far-fetched?" Reggie asked.

"Well, no. Not necessarily. I mean, the Spanish Treasure Fleet of 1715 *did* sink — thanks to a hurricane off the coast of Florida — and there have been reports of gold and silver washing up onshore ever since. And the Louisiana Purchase took place with Napolean and Jefferson, with some debatably *suspicious* considerations, and finally —" he paused for effect — "our nation has had a long history of back-stabbing and conspiracy, as well as needing to continue building the purse to fund its imperialistic tendencies."

Ben listened, nodding along. He wasn't sure how much of this he believed — history was more Reggie's bent — but it all sounded reasonable. He couldn't remember how many times something he'd learned in school as *absolute, concrete fact* had been overturned by later evidence, new discovery, or a simple rewrite of known history from someone besides the victor.

He thought of grade school and learning about the color of the sky, remembering that his teachers had not only taught, but truly *believed,* that it was blue because it reflected the ocean's color on the surface of the globe.

A strange thing, then, when his family had traveled through the Great Plains region of the country and the sky was still blue, like the ocean, yet there was a noticeable lack of ocean nearby and an abundance of green, rolling cornfields and yellow plains.

It had been a decade later when he'd learned the truth. Something about diffuse-something-or-other, and the length of light waves that reached the earth and his eye. He couldn't remember the details — another common feature of US public education — but he knew three things: one, the sky was blue; two, it didn't matter much why, and three, his teachers weren't the end-all authorities on everything they taught.

It also meant that knowledge was different than wisdom. He thought of the old adage, 'knowledge is knowing that a tomato is a fruit; wisdom is knowing not to put it in a fruit salad.'

Tomatoes and fruit salads aside, Ben knew knowledge changed as, well, knowledge changed. The facts he'd grown up with weren't 'facts,' per se, but 'things that we believe now, barring further evidence to the contrary.' He appreciated the scientific community's embrace of the idea that a 'theory' was not called a theory because it was a guess, but the opposite: a theory was considered the best explanation a group could come up with, and it hadn't yet been disproven. They were intelligent, yet willing to admit that life was ever-changing, and knew information and new ways of looking at old information was always on the horizon.

He tried to maintain this outlook on life, yet his stubbornness often got the best of him. He was a simple man, willing to accept new things but not actively seeking them out. He liked what he liked, and that was that. Not much of a quote, but Julie liked to remind him of those exact words when she cooked something new or dragged him to a new restaurant he'd never been to.

Now, listening to Roger Derrick explain his point of view on the history of early America, he had to admit it sounded far-fetched, yet plausible. But why was it far-fetched? Was it just that he'd grown up in a world that specifically believed something else? Had it been engrained in him at a young age to believe that the United States was the 'good guy,' entering every situation as the faultless police officer, offering truth and reason to the rest of the world?

He wanted to know the answer.

He wanted to find Julie, but there was a nagging inside his mind as well, something not based on emotion but on reason. He wanted to know, likely only because the question had been raised.

Reggie, too, seemed intrigued. His friend was leaning forward, the beginning of a grin on his face, as he listened to Derrick speak.

"So Jefferson could have needed something else — something over and above what Congress was willing to offer — to entice Napolean to sell. Something that could be used against the Spanish later, or something that could be used *for* the Spanish. He didn't care, as Spain was hardly the threat the British were in that territory, but he knew that what he had was valuable."

"Sounds like you *do* believe this theory," Joshua said. If any of them were unmoved by Derrick's monologue, it was Joshua. Ever the die-hard, he rarely allowed emotion to get in the way of the job. His job, now, was to stop Daris and find Julie. Ben appreciated that, but he also knew that the more they understood of Derrick's and Daris' beliefs, the better chance they had to get ahead of them.

"No," Derrick said. "I don't. I'm merely pointing out how it could be *plausible*. It's not a far-fetched theory, like aliens built Stonehenge, or anything like that. It's based in historic fact, and there would have been strong motives for it."

"So what *are* you saying, then?" Joshua asked.

"I'm saying that it's not too far-fetched. It's just too… *convenient.*

For all these pieces to simply fall into place that way — for Jefferson to have his hands on the Spanish treasure, Lewis to be willing to jump into a dangerous, life-threatening expedition, and the young nation in need of a 'secret' purse. It just seems too convenient for it to be true."

"And yet Jefferson *did* come out the victor, and he *did* send Lewis to the Pacific and back, and the nation *was* able to afford whatever it was they wanted, up until they were simply able to print more money whenever they needed it."

Derrick nodded. "Right. Still…"

"Look, we're with you, man. We've already told you that. Maybe what we find is nothing. Maybe we find a miraculous treasure and we all get rich. The point is, we're in it until the end now, until we find Julie."

Ben agreed. "Until we find Julie."

Derrick looked at him.

"I'm in," Ben said. "But when we get Julie, we're out."

Reggie looked at him. "I thought we agreed —"

"We did," Ben said. "And I stand by that agreement, that we look for Daris' treasure, or somehow disprove that it exists, and then we find Julie. But if we find Julie *first*, I'm taking her home. We're done then. Got it?"

Reggie sighed, then looked at Derrick.

"It's okay," Derrick said. "I get it." He turned to Ben. "I appreciate that, Harvey. Thank you. I'll take whatever help I can get. And I truly believe that if we *are* able to beat Daris and her team to their destination, we'll find Julie shortly after. She was taken because of me and my search, and I am in your debt for that."

Ben nodded, solemnly. He had made the mistake of buying into Derrick's story, of starting to feel excited about it all. The mystery, the history, the treasure calling out to them.

He shook that feeling away. Julie was out there, scared and alone, and probably being —

That, too, was a painful thought. He clenched his fists and reminded himself of what he would do to the men — and woman — who had taken her.

*They will pay,* he thought. *They will pay with their lives.*

He didn't know how, or when, but he would find them.

# FORTY-NINE

"I CAN'T BELIEVE YOU WERE going to make me fly here on a commercial airliner," Reggie said, stretching out his legs. "I thought you guys had expense accounts."

Derrick smiled. "We do, they just don't cover our expenses. Thanks for this, by the way."

The group of four men were in a chartered jet, flying cross-country with a heading that would bring them to Portland International Airport in seven and a half hours. Joshua had called Mr. E and explained their situation, that they had been shot at and were now on the run from more of the Ravenshadow men, and that they needed — quickly — to get to Oregon.

Within an hour they had reached the private charter section of the Philadelphia airport and were rising to their cruising altitude.

While the accommodations were far better than a commercial jet or a tiny pond hopper, Ben was feeling stress and anxiety more than he had in the past year. Julie was gone, presumably still in Philadelphia, and he had wanted to stay back with her. Mr. E and the other men had talked him out of it, as he wouldn't be able to find her — or retrieve her — on his own, anyway. And, they had argued, he was an integral part of the team.

He agreed that staying behind would only cause him more grief and strife, and it would give the group one less head to use for problem-solving. He'd reluctantly boarded the jet, sat down and strapped in, and white-knuckled the armrests during takeoff.

Now that they had leveled out at their cruising altitude, he turned on his phone's screen and poked around to the brief the others had read. He had meant to give it a skim, but the concise, simple explanations quickly pulled him in. He read, the others busy with a discussion about how best to acquire weapons when they landed. The current talk was inquiring about an FBI safe house in Oregon, having Derrick borrow the amount of handguns and ammunition they'd need without raising too many red flags at the same time.

Mr. E had arranged for a vehicle for them, and they planned on driving south to the safe house immediately after landing, which wasn't terribly far off the route to their *next* location: Fort Clatsop, the western camp of the Lewis and Clark expedition, now a national historic monument near Astoria, Oregon.

They were seated in their chairs, across the aisle from Ben, but Derrick's chair an aisle up had been swiveled around so he was facing Reggie and Joshua. Between them they had set up a small folding end table that Joshua had found in a storage closet near the back of the plane, and on top of this Roger Derrick had placed the item he'd removed from his briefcase. Ben stood and walked over to the other aisle, trying to get a better view of the tiny booklet Derrick had placed on the table.

Derrick then retrieved a set of tweezers from a bag he'd taken from his pocket, and a set of cheater glasses that now hung off the end of his nose. Ben had pegged the man at somewhere between 40 and 45 years old, old enough to justify the barely graying head of hair he wore, yet young enough that a pair of glasses seemed unnecessary.

But when Derrick open the cover of the journal Ben immediately understood why the glasses were needed. The handwritten text was scrawled, haphazardly and at an angle diagonally, on the first page.

*Meriwether Lewis, Captain.*

Derrick, thankfully, read aloud the line scrawled below the monogram. "The diary describing and recording the events and sights of the Expedition, intended for T. Jefferson."

"This was meant *only* for Jefferson?" Reggie asked. "Was that the case with the other journals?"

"No," Derrick said. "The rest in the journal collection all begin with his name alone, then simply jump into the details, but it's assumed they were always meant to be 'public records,' of sorts. Meant for the rest of the world to read and study. He draws pictures, writes essays on birds and wildlife, and describes in minute detail the plants and scenes they came across on their expedition."

"That sounds like a pretty impressive body of work," Joshua said. "We read about some of that in the brief."

Ben nodded, now able to agree with Joshua's statement. He had been impressed when he'd seen how much writing the Lewis and Clark expedition team had done during their cross-country trek and back.

"It was," Derrick said, a look of reverence on his face. "It was unbelievably impressive. The man would write 2,000-word-long essays *after* traveling 20 miles a day, hunting and fishing for — and cooking — their food. He was insanely productive, and his body of work remains a reliable guide to the high country to this day."

"Wow," Reggie said.

"Wow is right." He paused, taking care to flip the next page as carefully as possible. "This man was, among other things, an American hero. There were songs written about him, and the entire nation knew his name and his story."

The page fell, a slight crackle as it landed on the open cover, and Ben could see the first page of text — the same scrawled, nearly illegible handwriting filled the page. The paper was yellowed, but still sturdy enough to provide a decent backdrop to the writing itself.

Derrick continued his explanation. "He starts in December 1805, toward the end of their expedition and after they'd reached the Pacific and started home."

"So whatever the journal was meant for wasn't something he thought about until they were headed home?"

"Well," Derrick explained. "Perhaps. Or it's simply that his 'secret' mission wasn't supposed to begin until he'd accomplished his other goals: finding the Pacific, establishing some sort of trading agreement between America and the Plains Indians, and not dying."

"So he accomplished those things, *then* he starts the journal?" Ben asked.

"Correct," Derrick said, nodding. "He waits to start it until they're well on their way back home. But this first page is right in the middle of things, at Fort Clatsop, in present-day Oregon, where they wintered during the last month of 1805 and the early months of 1806."

"Outside of Astoria?" Joshua asked. "I've been there. I mean, I never saw the fort, but I remember seeing a sign for it once."

"One and the same," Derrick said. "They built the fort in December of 1805, hoping to get it in place before winter hit. It was rainy and miserable, but they finished it and moved in mid-December. It's been renovated and rebuilt by the National Parks Service since then."

"And Lewis started his *secret* journal then."

"Correct. He began writing Christmas night, 1805, after exchanging gifts."

"Why start then?"

Derrick shrugged. "That's part of the mystery, since he never addresses it. There's one single journal entry on Christmas Eve, then the journal skips ahead to March, the day they leave Fort Clatsop. But after the inscription, the journal simply begins, as if it's something he's been doing all along. It was quite a feat, too, as he still maintained his writing schedule in the *other* journals — the public journals."

"Where he'd write thousands of words a day?"

"Yes, or at least something. He had essays on plants, animals, and Indians they encountered along the way, and he collected, catalogued, and documented innumerable species of wildlife as well."

"Busy guy."

"Well, he didn't have a cell phone to distract him," Reggie said. "But yeah, that's impressive."

"It's damn impressive. Almost unbelievable. And Clark did this as well, to ensure they would always have multiple points of view, or overlap with other men's journals that would provide the most accurate analysis."

"It's amazing they even made it back," Joshua said. "I read in the brief that it was insane they hadn't been killed or scalped by a tribe."

"It is miraculous," Derrick said. "Yet they pulled it off. A remarkable journey, which is part of the reason why they are still celebrated today."

Derrick stopped and looked down at the journal in front of him, and Ben felt the weight of it, the moment of reverence. He respected that, and waited until Derrick was ready.

Finally Derrick turned the next page and began reading.

"Christmas Eve, 1805. We are weary, yet spirits are high. Men are unsure what tomorrow might bring, yet optimism rings true. They cannot fear what they do not know, and yet what I know I do not either fear."

Ben crossed his arms. "That's a cryptic way to start a journal."

"To say the least," Reggie said. "Man, that's weird. Are his other journals written like that?"

Derrick shook his head. "No, not at all. He's mostly straightforward, pretty to-the-point. After all, the journals were meant to be fact-based, just observations on what he saw, with little pontificating and speculation."

"Clearly he's not writing field notes anymore," Joshua said.

"So it would seem," Derrick said. "That's why I believe Daris was so into this journal."

"She's read it then?"

"She's probably got copies of each individual page, both hand-copied and scanned. I assume she's pored over them personally, and has probably even reached out to members of the academic community to enlist their help. Subtly, of course, and without mentioning what the scans were from."

"Yeah," Reggie said. "That's what I would do."

"Well, that *is* what we're going to do," Derrick replied. Everyone looked at him. "We're heading to Oregon, but we're not going to Fort Clatsop. We're going to meet up with the world's leading expert on Lewis and Clark. She's spent her life studying their trip, and she turned her home into a Lewis and Clark museum that she built herself after her husband left her."

"She's the world's *leading expert?*" Reggie asked.

Derrick cleared his throat. "Well... according to her."

Reggie chuckled. "Great. I'll bet she's really easy to talk to, as well. Husband left her, lives alone in a museum, weird obsession for Lewis and Clark. No social awkwardness or anything, right?"

Derrick frowned, then addressed Reggie directly. "Well, she's not without her quirks. Says she's a descendant of Sacagawea, actually."

"Even better. What's her name? Maybe we can do a little research before we land."

Derrick shook his head. "Well, she doesn't *do* Internet stuff, which is part of the reason no one knows about her little museum. But I know everything you need to know about her."

Ben noticed Joshua beginning to grin, and he felt he knew where this was going.

"Why's that?" Reggie asked.

"Because she's my grandmother. Cornelia Derrick."

Reggie groaned, and Joshua's grin turned into a full-on smile.

# FIFTY

IN THE LAST DAY, BEN had travelled cross-country twice. He'd been beaten and shot at, and Julie had been taken from him. He was pissed, cranky, and tired. The flight, as comfortable as it was, offered little reprieve. They had decided to try to get some rest, and then start in again on the journal when they woke up.

During the flight he'd tossed and turned in the airplane seat, and as the pilot's 'announcer voice,' declaring their descent, broke into his fitful sleep and woke them up, he realized that he was now sore, on top of everything else.

He groaned and put his seat back up.

"You too, brother?" Reggie asked, rubbing his eyes and blinking heavily.

"Slept like a rock," Ben said. "Falling off a cliff."

"And landing on a bed of nails," Joshua added. "Are we here already?"

"I guess so," Ben said. "Unfortunately. But every hour we spend sleeping, Julie spends…"

"Don't think like that, buddy," Reggie said. "We're getting her back. I promised you that."

Ben nodded. *It doesn't matter what you promise,* he thought. *I'm getting her back either way.*

Roger Derrick seemed to be the only man on board, save for the pilot himself, who wasn't upset. "We ready to roll?" he asked. "Clock's ticking."

"Can't go anywhere until this bird lands, big guy," Reggie said.

"No, but we can plan our next move. I'd guess we've got about a half-hour before we're on the ground and taxied in. That's a half-hour of planning."

"I thought the plan was, 'talk to your weird grandmother,'" Reggie said.

Derrick scowled at him.

"Sorry. I meant, 'talk to your *completely normal and well-balanced* grandmother.'"

"It is," Derrick said. "But... she might not be able to give us much more than we've already got."

"I thought you said she was the 'world's leading expert,'" Ben said.

"I did... but also that she was the *self-declared* leading expert, remember? It's been a few years since we've talked about this stuff, and she's been having... health issues."

"Sorry to hear that, pal," Reggie said.

Derrick shook it off. "Thank you. It's fine, really. Amnesia, probably an early form of Alzheimer's, but she's closing in on ninety, so I can't really complain. Sort of comes with the territory."

For a brief moment Ben remembered his mother, Diana Torres. She had taken back her maiden name a few years after his father had passed, and Ben had always assumed it was mostly because she couldn't forgive her son for her husband's death. She hadn't struggled with Alzheimer's, but she did have memory lapses frequently, even though she had been employed and maintained a healthy, active lifestyle up until the end.

*The end that I caused*, Ben thought. He had met Juliette due to a virus scare at Yellowstone, where he was working, and he had sent his mother, a chemical analyst, a sample of the strain.

Within a week, she was gone.

The hole in his heart was typically more than filled by Julie's presence, but since Julie was now gone as well...

"Anyway," Derrick said. "I'm just worried she'll spout the same stuff she's always talked about. That there's 'something out there, but it's been hidden to protect us.' It's always some form of that rumor. But when I press her on it, she clams up, like it's her duty to keep the secret."

Reggie nodded. "Does she know about the journal?"

Derrick looked at him. "No, I guess that might change things."

"If she really believes this stuff, and she's been *almost* talking about it with you, I'd bet she opens right up when you plop that old dusty book in front of her face."

"Yeah," Derrick said. "You're probably right. Still, I think it's best if we work through our next move, see if we can't figure out where this journal's trying to point us to."

He opened the journal once again and flipped to the page after the initial inscription, then started reading.

"Mar 23. Toward the Cottonwoods, where the unique three lay."

He looked up.

"That's it?" Reggie asked. "On page one? Just a sentence?"

Derrick smiled. "Why do you think we haven't been able to figure out whatever it is that's been hidden?"

"Because it's all gibberish," Reggie said. "It means nothing, like you suspected. It's just a madman's scribbling."

Derrick shook his head. "No, I can't believe that. *Logically* it makes sense that there's no 'great conspiracy,' that Daris is on a fanatical treasure hunt for nothing, but like I told you before, I think there's *something* at the other end. I think Lewis *did* hide something, even if it's just a few plants — albeit a few plants with the power to render someone inert for a few days."

"So it's all code?" Ben asked. "He was writing a coded message to Jefferson?"

"Well that much is clear," Derrick said. "He needed to get a message to Jefferson, so he wrote it down. But *what* he was trying to tell him is very unclear. It's not a code, per se, as it's written in plain English. There are numerous spelling mistakes, but that was normal for all of the men who kept a journal during the expedition."

"So where are these Cottonwoods?" Ben asked.

"We have no idea," Derrick said. "There are Cottonwood trees *everywhere* in this side of the world."

"Well then, where were they on March 23, 1806? Fort Clatsop, right?"

He shook his head. "No — I mean, yes, they were at the fort in Oregon, getting ready to leave. But I've scoured that area, numerous times. It's a tourist trap now, and even the surrounding area is well-traveled. If anything was there, it would have been found by now."

Joshua rubbed his chin, thinking.

Ben frowned. "*Unique* Cottonwoods. Three of them. Yeah, he's right. Those are everywhere, and we're supposed to find just *three* of them."

"Wait —" Reggie said. "You're only on the *first clue?*"

Derrick sighed, then looked up from the journal and adjusted his cheater glasses. "Well, yes — we have yet to determine what the first clue means — but the other clues aren't nearly as cryptic. I don't think."

Joshua stood up and started pacing. "Okay, then. How many clues are there?"

"Three."

Joshua stopped. "*Three?* There are only *three?* What kind of treasure hunt is this?"

Derrick nodded. "Just three. And like I said, I'm not sure it *is* a treasure hunt, as much as Daris wants to believe it is. And the second one seems pretty self-explanatory, as if Lewis couldn't come up with something clever to write. He may have been a great naturalist and surveyor, and certainly a capable leader of men, but a treasure map creator he was not." He smiled, then flipped the page with the pair of tweezers and let it fall gently onto the first two. "Inside the Cave of Shadows."

"Inside the Cave of Shadows," Reggie said. "Got it. So you've looked for this 'Cave of Shadows' place already?"

"As much as we could, yes," Derrick said. "It's a long trail, and there were plenty of places they could have found a cave."

"So there's nothing called 'Cave of Shadows' today?"

Derrick shook his head.

"What about the third clue?"

"Within the silver lies the gold."

"Within the — *seriously?*" Reggie asked. "*That's* Lewis' final clue?"

"I told you it was cryptic. He wasn't much for flowery prose, and I'd bet he wasn't super creative about his code. He needed something utilitarian, pragmatic — something he could write down that would effectively hide the treasure from anyone casually looking for it. Only someone with enough knowledge of the expedition, like Jefferson himself, could decipher it. And it's a linear progression, as well. There's no sense looking for answers to the second and third clue until the first one is solved.

"That's why we're going to visit my grandmother. She can help us."

"Great," Reggie said, rubbing his eyes again. He yawned. "Not only did I not get enough sleep, but now we've got no better ideas than to visit your grandmother."

"She knows her stuff," Derrick said. "You'll see."

"I can't wait to meet her," Reggie said.

# FIFTY-ONE

REGGIE FELT TORN. ON ONE hand, he had never in his life met someone so eccentric, so downright *odd*. The woman in front of him seemed to be a mix between French-Cajun and Jamaican, with hair that she wore high on her head, a la Marge Simpson. Bits and pieces of odds and ends she had obviously found on trips during her long life were stuffed into it, and Reggie couldn't help but stare.

It had been three hours since they'd landed in Astoria, collected weapons from the FBI safe house Derrick had brought them to, and then driven to Derrick's grandmother's small house-museum. He wondered if he was just delirious, suffering from a lack of sleep, and the woman in front of him now was nothing more than a normal, well-balanced, Oregonian.

*Three combs, two chopsticks, about a hundred beads, and — what is that? Is that a fake bird?* He kept looking at Joshua and Ben to see if they had noticed the woman's larger-than-life hair and personality, and if they were affected by it, but both men seemed to be better than he at holding their emotions inside.

But on the other hand, Roger Derrick's mother, Cornelia Derrick, was one of the best cooks he'd ever had the pleasure of meeting. Her food would have put a Cajun restaurant's jambalaya to shame, and he wasn't kidding. He'd tried *hundreds* of Cajun dishes, straight off the bayou and in other places around the world, and hers was the best.

"Living close to the water, my dear," she'd told him with her thick, chopped accent. "You get the best seafood in the world up here, but no one knows that." The words lilted from one to the next, rising and falling but stopped short just as one syllable ended and the next began.

"Well," Reggie said, trying to talk without losing the mouthful of food. "This is absolutely phenomenal. I — I can't even tell you —"

"I hear that from my boy," she said, nudging Derrick. "But I always say he's just humoring me."

Derrick shook his head. "I've tried to tell my grandmother to open a restaurant, but she won't listen. Says she's too busy."

"I have to water the plants," she explained. "They can't water themselves, now, can they?"

As Reggie finished his first bowl of jambalaya, even before he could drink the spicy broth, Cornelia had plopped another scoopful in front of him.

"Eat," she said. "My boy tells me you have an adventure."

"I didn't say that," Derrick said. "I told you we're looking for something."

"And if you came here, it means you are looking for something related to the Expedition."

Reggie smiled. "Now, why would you think that, ma'am?"

She frowned. "Don't you be calling me 'ma'am,' boy. Cornelia is the name my Mama gave me, and it should be good enough for you."

Reggie nodded, his smile growing. The woman reminded him in some ways of his own grandmother, now long passed. Growing up, visiting 'Meemaw' was a special treat — they could eat whatever they wanted, whenever they wanted it, and there was no one there to tell them to stop. As long as he and his siblings behaved and minded their manners, Meemaw was their best friend.

But if they *didn't* behave…

Reggie shuddered at the thought.

"Sorry, yes ma — Cornelia. Thank you again for hosting us. As Der — *Roger* said, we *are* looking for something. He says you're familiar with the, uh, *Expedition*."

"Familiar?"

The small woman with huge hair turned and glared at Derrick with an expression that, if not for the woman's miniature stature, would have frightened Reggie. Derrick burst out laughing.

"Sorry, Grandma. I *did* tell them you were the best at it, but —"

"I *am* the best," she said, turning to stare down the other three men at the table. "I know *everything* about the Lewis and Clark Expedition. Now, start telling me what it is you're looking for while I get you all more food."

Reggie watched his two partners. Joshua's eyes were bugging out, and his half-finished bowl sat in front of him, neither the man nor the bowl wanting more food. Ben, as his polar opposite, sat with his elbows on the table, a spoon in one hand and a napkin in the other, anxiously awaiting more of the soup. Reggie laughed, half-expecting Ben to begin licking his lips.

"Well, Ms. — well, Cornelia," Joshua said. "We're looking for a treasure. One we think Meriwether Lewis may have taken with him on the trail."

"Ah, yes," the old woman said. "The Jefferson Treasure."

"You — you know about it?" Joshua asked.

"I told you, I know *everything* about the Expedition. And it is said that it was hidden to protect us all, you know. I wouldn't go looking for something like that."

Derrick rolled his eyes. "Where is it, then, Grandma?"

She looked at each of them, one eye nearly closed and examining each of them in turn. Like it was a test, and she was the student. "I don't know," she huffed. "But I do know everything *else*."

Reggie smiled. He liked this woman, and not just because of her food. Everything together — the juxtaposition of the woman's personality and look with her cooking abilities, her take-no-crap attitude, and her graciousness as a host, letting the four of them in her house without so much as a question.

"Well, Grandma," Derrick said. "Did you know about *this*?"

He reached into his briefcase and retrieved the small, leather-bound journal and placed it in front of him on the table.

She looked at the journal, studying it, then finally reached for it. Derrick caught her small, frail wrist and held out his pair of tweezers. "Here, use these."

She took the tweezers and opened the cover to the first page. Reggie and the others waited until she'd finished reading. She looked up, eyes wide, her mouth open slightly.

"Wh — where did you get this, my boy?" she asked. And then, after a moment, "is it *real*?"

"It's real, Grandma. It's really his handwriting. I checked that out first, and the leather is old enough to be from the time period."

She cocked an eyebrow, waiting for him to answer her *first* question.

"I — I borrowed it," he said. "From the Society."

"You *borrowed* —" she huffed, then threw her hands into the air, exasperated. "You *borrowed* this? You *stole* this, my boy! You *took* it, from the Society itself. You know what this means for —"

She stopped, hunching her shoulders a bit and dropping her head.

"It's okay," Derrick said. "They know. They know everything."

"They know you're part of the Society?"

"They do, and they know I'm FBI as well."

"Is that how you got the journal?" she asked.

He nodded, not revealing whether it was his APS ties or his FBI career that led to his involvement with the journal.

"Well, this is… this is simply…" she reached for her forehead. "I need a glass of water." Cornelia Derrick pushed back from the table and started to stand.

"Here, Grandma," Derrick said. "Let me get that for you. You keep reading. We need to figure out what this little book is trying to tell us, and we need to do it fast."

Reggie glanced at Ben, but his face revealed nothing. It was a race against time, now, and Julie's life was on the line. It was no longer simply about a journal, and a man's fight against a power-hungry woman.

"I saw that friend of yours on the TV this morning," she said.

"Who?" Derrick asked.

"You know who. That cute woman, from the organization."

Reggie looked at Derrick, waiting for some confirmation.

"Grandma, she's not my friend. She's the new president of the APS, and I've talked to her before a few times. That's it."

Cornelius' smile hinted at more. "Well, she's cute. That's all I'm saying."

For the first time since they'd met, Reggie looked at Derrick's hand, and remembered his earlier comment about not being married. *No wedding ring.* He wondered about the man's personal life, whether or not he dated often, and what history he had with women.

*Hopefully not women like Daris Johansson.*

"Not interested, Grandma. Can we get back to the journal?"

"You're afraid of her, aren't you?" Derrick's grandmother suddenly blurted out.

Reggie felt the tension in the room ratchet up. He looked left and right, waiting.

"What do you mean?"

"I mean what I just said. You're *afraid* of that woman."

"Why would I be afraid?"

"Because of the Shift."

# FIFTY-TWO

*THE SHIFT*, BEN THOUGHT. *THERE it is again.*

"You know about that?" he asked.

"I know *everything* about the Expedition," was the woman's immediate response.

"But the Shift is part of the American Philosophical Society, wasn't it? That didn't really have much to do with the Lewis and Clark expedition. Or did I miss something in the brief?"

Derrick chuckled, and his grandmother started giggling.

"Okay," Reggie said from next to Ben. "What are we missing?"

"Well, nothing," Derrick said. "Except that the two are *intimately* related. Sure, the APS predates the expedition, and the expedition was just a one-off trip, but it was the APS that backed the trip."

"Wait, really?" Joshua asked. "I didn't know that. I thought it was Thomas Jefferson who backed the trip."

Cornelia straightened up in her chair, her eye twinkling. Ben got the impression he was back in school, a hapless victim forced to inhale information from a zealous teacher.

But, he had to admit, this story was intriguing. He wanted to know more, and he wanted to find Julie.

"The American Philosophical Society paid for much of the expedition *because* Thomas Jefferson paid for the expedition."

"Jefferson was a member of the APS?"

"He was," Derrick said. "He became a member of the Society a few years after it was revived. Benjamin Franklin's Junto, the precursor to the Society, sort of died off for a few years and was then refreshed when it merged with a group called the American Society for Promoting Useful Knowledge."

"ASPUK?" Reggie asked, pronouncing the acronym. "Yeah, no wonder they changed the name."

Derrick walked back over with his grandmother's glass of water. Ben watched as the woman drank it in one gulp, her wiry hands hiding a strength he knew was there, one earned from years of life. She might be an octogenarian, but the woman was as full of life as ever.

Her cooking alone proved that.

Ben looked around her small kitchen and dining room while he waited for her to finish her glass of water. Memorabilia filled every table, shelf, and corner of the room, and pictures hung from every wall, sometimes so crowded the frames' edges touched other pictures and paintings.

Everything was Lewis and Clark related, but there was a special emphasis on the most famous *woman* of the expedition, Sacagawea. The Indian bride was certainly the most important person in the house, and her busts and portraits filled corners and walls all around the house.

Apparently Cornelia Derrick was related somehow to the famous squaw, which would explain the emphasis on her side of the story in Cornelia's 'museum house.'

The room they were in was probably the least-decorated room, and likely because it had never been meant for tourists. The dining room was for family, just as it had been at his own grandmother's home. He had never met his father's father, and his mother's parents had died when he was young, so his paternal grandmother became 'Grandma,' the one and only.

He had fond memories of her home in North Carolina, on a small split-level acreage with two goats in the backyard. He and his brother, Zachary, would feed the goats whatever they found in the yard, testing the rumors they'd heard that goats would eat anything — and testing the fuse of Grandma's temper.

He smiled, unable to help but feel comforted by the thought. She was still alive, but his mother had moved her to a nursing home two years ago, and he had only visited once. He made a mental note to bring Julie there and have his two family members meet.

The happiness quickly turned back to dread, a sinking feeling in his stomach, when he thought of Julie. He wanted — *needed* — her back, and sitting here enjoying the company and the comfort food was only making it worse. Julie was out there, alone, scared. She needed him to find her, and though she was a strong woman, he knew her strength, like anyone else's would eventually run dry.

"Well," Cornelia said. "I guess you're waiting for me to tell the rest. Very well."

Derrick sat back down after asking the others if they needed anything else. They shook their heads and Cornelia Derrick continued the explanation.

"So Mr. Jefferson became a long-standing member of the APS, and he was always interested in expanding his — and others' — knowledge. He had a fascination with just about everything, a fact that probably had quite a bit to do with his eventual run as President."

"Of the United States," Reggie said, clarifying.

"No, though his love of learning didn't hurt his chances there, either," she said. "I was talking about the APS."

"Jefferson was *President* of the APS?" Joshua asked.

"March 3, 1797," Derrick said. "And a day later he became Vice President of the United States of America."

"And the entire time he continued pursuing knowledge, just as the organization had been founded for. He pushed ideas, wrote papers, and strove to bring together the greatest minds of the early nation. He worked on an early expedition to the West, led by a botanist named Andre Michaux, but the trip fell through.

"So in 1803, Jefferson tried again, inviting the APS to help back a trip led by the young Meriwether Lewis, of whom Jefferson was fully supportive. The trip was funded, plans were made, and off they went."

Ben shook his head. "So Jefferson *was* intimately involved."

"Remarkable, isn't it?" Derrick asked. "Almost seems too perfect."

His grandmother cracked a sly grin. "Nothing fits too perfectly when the pieces have been designed to fit perfectly."

"I guess not," Joshua said. "So the Shift, then, is the power changing hands. And this 'treasure' we're after is something that Daris — the current leader of the organization — needs in order to make it happen."

"Perhaps it is," Cornelia said. "But you won't find it."

Ben frowned. "Why not? We have the journal. The clues just need to be followed, and —"

"The *clues* will take you there, but the *clues* point to something that cannot be found."

"Why do you say that?"

"Because this treasure, this thing so powerful that it can 'shift' the power from one side to the other, cannot be held in one's hands. It cannot be stolen, traded, or discovered."

"Grandma," Derrick said. "That's not helpful. We have to find it, before —"

"It *is* helpful, my boy," Cornelia said. "Those are words from Mr. Jefferson himself."

Ben froze.

Next to him, Reggie stopped as well. Joshua cleared his throat and spoke. "You — you have reason to believe Jefferson said the treasure wasn't real?"

"No," she said. "I have an actual *letter* from him saying the treasure is not real."

# FIFTY-THREE

REGGIE WAS APPALLED, ALBEIT IN a very good way. This woman was just as he'd hoped — a little crazy, a great cook, and *actually* as knowledgeable as Derrick had implied. He had wondered about it, on the plane ride, figuring Derrick was talking her up, biased since she was family.

But she seemed to be the real deal. The decor in the tiny house was real, the memorabilia he walked past when he needed to use the restroom was real, and the pictures on the wall each had a story — a story researched and documented by the woman herself and then printed on a tiny card stapled to each frame.

She knew her Lewis and Clark, that was certain. She knew about the Shift, and the APS, and just about everything else they were talking to her about. Now, she was apparently going to tell them about a secret letter none of them had any knowledge about.

"This letter," Derrick said. "No one else knows about it?"

She shook her head as she waddled back to the table, a three-ring binder beneath her arm. "No," she said. "How would they? It was passed down through families close to the president, but it was kept hidden inside a box for years. My great-uncle discovered it in a closet."

"Wow," Joshua said.

"Wow is right, my boy," she said. She hefted the binder up and onto the table, allowing it to fall next to Lewis' journal. "Open it up," she commanded.

Derrick opened the half-inch binder and Reggie was surprised to see the thing was full of clear plastic page separators, each containing a single piece of paper. Some were scraps, while others were full-sized rectangular pages. None of the yellowed strips were large enough to fill their plastic containers.

"Toward the back, my boy. It's one of the bigger sheets, and there's a tab sticking out from the side."

"You — you just *have* this here?" Reggie asked. "It seems like it belongs in a —" he stopped himself.

"This *is* a museum," she said, smiling. "The *best* Lewis and Clark museum in all the world."

"I would have to agree with that," Joshua said. "This place is amazing. You've got all sorts of relics here, and I could spend a day walking through and looking at it all."

"You could spend a *lifetime* here, my boy," she said, her smile growing wider. "I did." She pointed a scrawny finger toward a long, narrow stick hanging on the wall above a tiny fireplace. "You know what that is?" she asked.

Everyone shook their head.

"It's an oar, or what was left of it," she said. "From one of the expedition's pirogues. A narrow canoe sort of thing, real goofy looking. But that's the real thing. Can't find that anywhere else in the world."

Reggie was impressed, and he said so. "I love it, Cornelia. It's a great collection. Thank you for sharing it with us."

"Well, of course! My boy Roger has been snooping around this whole place his entire life, it's about time he comes and asks me for help finding something. Stop — right there."

She reached down and placed her pointer finger on the page Derrick had just flipped to. The paper was less yellowed than the others, but there were tears along the two fold lines that crossed the paper. Remnants of a wax seal sat on the top and middle of the back of the page, visible through the thin parchment.

"Dearest M. Lewis," she said, reading the letter, "I am much obliged to your happiness for your agreement in participating, although I cannot express to you my worry for your safety."

Reggie noticed that the woman's eyes were closed. *She's reciting this from memory.*

"I anticipate much success for your journey, and I am overwhelmed with gratitude toward yourself and Mr. Clark. May your mind and eyes be filled with passion for the discoveries you shall behold. My — to be able to accompany you!"

Cornelia 'read' the letter with her own passion, stressing certain words and almost singing at other times. She was in her element, and Reggie felt the excitement and exuberance of history coming to life. This was the sort of history he loved — the stories, told by men and women who had a passion for them, and knew them inside and out.

He smiled as she continued.

"…among your prescribed duties, I ask one final favor, and one that is not to be shared with anyone. This expedition is, as it has been recorded, meant for the discovery of the new lands I have purchased for this nation. But it is also meant for something else, something greater.

"It is meant for the discovery of a hiding place, and your discreet markings leading to its final resting place. I have in my possession something that must be hidden, though it needs not be destroyed. This 'thing' of which I write will be described to you upon our final meeting before you embark, so as not to entertain any unwarranted attention.

"…this thing, so powerful that it can shift the power from one side to the other, cannot be held in one's hands. It cannot be stolen, traded, or discovered. It is already possessed, and it has never been traded. It has already been discovered, and must not ever be again."

She took in a deep breath with her nose, her eyes still closed and a satisfied smile still on her lips. Reggie felt the old woman's appreciation of the past.

*And what a past it was,* he thought. *This is proof that Jefferson was trying to hide something. Proof that he sent Meriwether Lewis across an unknown land to hide his secret, and proof that —*

"Daris was right," Derrick said, speaking aloud Reggie's thought. "She was right all along." He shook his head, his lips a thin line.

"Don't worry about it," Joshua said. "It doesn't mean anything. She's right, she's not right — it doesn't make a difference. We still need to beat her to whatever it is she's after."

"The plant?" Ben asked.

Cornelia perked up. "What plant, my boy?"

Reggie looked at Derrick to see if he was trying to give Ben any unspoken signals. Maybe he didn't want to reveal their hand, or perhaps Cornelia wouldn't approve of their mission.

She turned to her grandson. "Do you mean the Borrachero?"

Reggie's eyes widened. "You — you know about that, too?"

At this, she threw her head all the way back and laughed, a truly infectious laughter that made Reggie's smile grow wider than it had in the past year.

"You are no better than Roger," she said, her voice broken through tears of laughter. "When will you learn? I know *everything* there is to know about the Expedition."

"Except *where* this plant — the treasure — really is," Derrick said.

"Well, there is no *treasure*, my boy. I've told you that before."

"But you just read us the letter —"

"I just read you *a* letter, and it is real. From Thomas Jefferson himself to his young protege, Meriwether Lewis. And he is as cryptic as ever, I'll admit. It would appear that he is hiding something, trying to sell the intrigue he captures with his words. But as I have explained before, there is nothing out there but false hopes and lies."

"Explain."

She sighed. "Long ago, when Jefferson first had Meriwether hide this 'treasure,' there may well have been something worth dying for. But let's say it's this plant, the 'Borrachero,' from South America. This plant would have survived for how long out of the ground? Maybe a week? A month?"

"But it made it to the Spanish Fleet, didn't it? How long was that journey?"

"Perhaps not long enough that the plant would perish. Perhaps the chemicals in the plant made it all the way to Jefferson himself, as the legend has it. But that was over two-hundred years ago — what plants can live that long?"

Ben nodded. "Makes sense. But maybe it was re-planted. Stuck in the ground somewhere on the Lewis and Clark trail where it could survive and thrive."

Cornelia smiled at Ben. "Yes, that may have worked. But don't you think we'd have heard about it before? This plant that can turn people into zombies? This is America, my boy. That trail has been walked and traveled ever since that expedition, and there are cities along its rivers. Anything they wanted to hide on the trail has long since been found."

Joshua stood up and started pacing. "Yeah, you're right. Anything obviously hidden on the trail would have been found already, but — maybe, I'm just guessing here — what if it wasn't on the trail?"

"What do you mean?" Reggie asked. "What if the treasure is somewhere *off* the Lewis and Clark trail?"

"Well, yeah," Joshua said. "Why would you hide something that's meant to stay hidden on a trail that you know will be traveled by thousands of people after you're gone?"

"But she's right," Reggie said. "Anything organic would be nothing but dust by now. There'd be no sense trying to hide something like a plant, or a flower, and they would have known that. Heck, I'd bet half the specimens Lewis and Clark sent back to Washington were decomposed upon their arrival."

"Even if they'd preserved them?"

"They wouldn't have been able to preserve a massive amount of anything, and if Jefferson's treasure really is some sort of plant like this Borrachero thing, he wouldn't have gone through the trouble of hiding it unless there was a lot of it."

Reggie looked around at the others in the group. He could feel that they were all starting to agree, and that was dangerous. To agree in a situation meant they weren't thinking outside the box. They weren't solving the problem creatively, just tossing around the obvious reasons for 'why it can't be done.' It was a treasure hunter's fallacy, the greatest threat to the profession. 'Experts' told them something was impossible, and after a lifetime of failed expeditions, you started to believe them.

But Reggie wanted the truth more than he wanted the treasure. The treasure may be a lie, but the truth was out there.

"So maybe it wasn't a plant," he said. "Maybe it's as simple as Derrick thought originally: just an empty box, meant to throw people off, or to buy time. It would make sense politically, for that time."

"But it wouldn't make sense to Jefferson," Ben said. "Everything these two have told us about the man says that he wouldn't waste time — and money — on something as frivolous as that."

"So what about Daris' idea she shared on TV?" Reggie asked. "That it *is* Spanish silver and gold, mined from South America and taken by the conquistadors?"

"Silver doesn't decompose," Ben said.

"No, and if you had enough of it, it'd be worth hiding," Derrick said. "And sending it with Lewis and Clark would have been a brilliant move — get it out of sight, away from the leaders of the new nation, and hidden in the land you now own. Land that's not inhabited by many people."

Cornelia's eyes twinkled again as she listened. "See, *now* you are thinking like a treasure hunter. Of course — why *would* you hide it on the trail?"

"Because that's the only way to know where to find it," Reggie said.

"Unless you have the *map*," she quickly replied. "And it seems as though my boy Roger does, in fact, have the map."

"But we don't know where it's pointing. We have no idea how to read it."

"Let's see it again," she said, nudging up to the dining room table. Reggie leaned in closer and watched as Derrick flipped the page to the first clue. He read it aloud.

# FIFTY-FOUR

"CHRISTMAS EVE, 1805. WE ARE weary, yet spirits are high. Men are unsure what tomorrow might bring, yet optimism rings true. They cannot fear what they do not know, and yet what I know I do not either fear."

Cornelia Derrick's thin, white eyebrows rose and fell as her grandson read the first inscription. Her giant mound of hair bobbed up and down like a buoy as she nodded. When he'd finished, she looked up.

"That's Fort Clatsop, just down the road. Are you planning on visiting the park?"

Derrick shook his head. "No, Grandma. I don't think it's going to give us anything we don't already have."

"I would agree," she said. "I've been there about forty times, and I've hiked the entire area, including —" she lowered her head and grinned — "the off-limits areas."

Derrick chuckled. "As you've said before. No, I don't think there's anything there besides tourists and souvenirs."

"There wouldn't be," she said. "If Lewis was to hide something, the last place I imagine it would be is inside — or near — a fort they'd wintered in. The dangers of the other men finding it would be too great, and the obviousness of the hiding spot would be, well, disappointing."

"True. So it's not at Clatsop," Joshua said. Then, facing Cornelia, he added, "if it's real."

She smiled. "I can believe what I want, and you can believe what you want. What's important to me is that you *believe* what you believe, and don't let anyone take that away from you."

Derrick smiled again, placing his hand on his grandmother's. "Thank you. Let's say you *did* believe. Where do you think we should start looking?"

"Well, you've got the treasure map right there in front of you, my boy. What's the next page say?"

Derrick read it aloud after he'd turned the page. "Mar 23. Toward the Cottonwoods, where the unique three lay."

"That's it?" she asked.

"That's what I said," Reggie said. "Seems like a lousy clue."

Cornelia wore a sly expression on her face, and her eyes darted toward the three-ring binder sitting nearby on the table.

"What is it?" Reggie asked. "I know that look — you know something we don't?"

"I do," she said, reaching for the binder, which was still open to the Jefferson letter. "I still haven't read the *back* of the letter to you."

"Wait — there's a back?" Derrick asked. "Why didn't you — why didn't you say anything?"

"I like the thrill of it all, my boy," she said. "Now stop yammering and help me with this."

She slid the binder toward Derrick and he flipped the page protector over. From across the table Reggie could see a postscript inscription on the top of the page. He was intrigued, but he kept silent and waited impatiently for Derrick to read it.

"P.S.: please inform me of your chosen locations for the objects which I will bestow upon you upon our next meeting. I wish you to record the location and approximate bearing of your decided caches, accurate to a measure that may be followed successfully by later explorers."

Derrick blinked a few times, then read the last sentence Jefferson had written on the back of the letter. "I trust this information will be kept between only this house and yourself."

Ben sat back. "Wow, so Jefferson explicitly asked Lewis to write down the locations of these *caches,* keep them secret, and tell no one but Jefferson? Ms. — Cornelia — I'm sorry, but how can you not believe there's a treasure?"

She laughed at this. "You see, my boy, there was always a question in my mind. Always. But I never had this journal in front of me. I never had any information that made me believe there was, in fact, a treasure, and I came to the conclusion long ago that this letter was not from Jefferson, but nothing more than a hoax."

"But now, with the journal?"

"It does present an intriguing possibility," she said. "All of the other journals have been catalogued and well-documented. They have been translated, reviewed, and placed in order of chronological creation. There are no holes, no gaps in time, that would allow anyone else to insert the idea that there is a treasure — a missing journal."

"Makes sense," Joshua said. "And that's how the APS has kept *this* journal secret for so long. Still, you admitted yourself that there not only *wasn't* a treasure, but that it's nowhere near Fort Clatsop. But the next clue just about *forces* it to be nearby."

"Really?" she asked. "How's that?"

"It's about Fort Clatsop, the day they left at the beginning of spring, 1806."

Derrick nodded along, then read the next page. "March 23. Toward the Cottonwoods, where the unique three lay."

She frowned, looking over the tiny journal page as her grandson read. Ben hadn't been sure until that moment how well the old lady's vision had held up over time, but he was now. She could apparently read every word of the chicken scratch without even leaning forward more than a few inches.

"You didn't read it correctly," she said. "You read '*March*,' but it says '*Mar.*' Mar, period."

"Right. A shortened form of *March*, correct?" Derrick asked.

"No, not in this case."

Ben stared at the woman. *What was she about to reveal?*

"Remember, Lewis was not the best speller. None of the men were, and we have had to go back and translate into proper English much of the entries they wrote. They were inconsistent with their spelling and descriptions as well. But this word, *Mar.*, is likely spelled correctly, but inconsistent with what we know of the current vernacular."

"You mean it's not meant to be *March* at all?"

"Correct. The word *Mar.* in this case, if you're asking me, is actually *Marias.*"

Ben looked at Reggie and Joshua, the excitement building within him. He knew what it meant, and he was surprised that he hadn't considered it already. When he realized that the other three men around him were still in the dark, he spoke up. "Marias? As in Maria's River?"

"Yes," she said. "Maria's — named by Lewis for his neice — is a very important river to the Lewis and Clark expedition."

"It's a river in Montana," Ben said. "In Blackfeet Indian territory. It's a ways north of Yellowstone, and I fished it a few times back in the day."

"That is right," she said. "And it's important because it's the location of the 'Marias Expedition' Lewis led with a small group of men on their way *back* from the Pacific."

"An expedition within an expedition," Derrick said. "Seems fitting."

"It's perfect," she said. "Lewis and Clark actually split up in early July of 1806, in order to 'cover more land,' as the history books describe. They each took some men and went their separate ways, Lewis traveling north and Clark south. Lewis cut across Montana to intersect the Marias River, where he spent a couple weeks in mid to late July. He was, purportedly, there to determine whether or not the river flowed as far north as the 50th parallel, which would have increased the amount of American land the Louisiana Purchase had given Jefferson."

"It *is* perfect," Ben said. "It fits, it fits everything perfectly. The Marias starts right in the mountains, way up in the Rockies. If you wanted to hide something…"

"Then that's where I'd hide it," Cornelia declared. "Take as few men as possible, run up to a far-off point that hasn't been fully explored, and then leave clues that can be interpreted only if you're looking in the right place."

"And I can't believe I didn't realize it before," Ben said. Everyone turned to look at him, waiting. "The clue — it's talking about the 'three cottonwoods,' right? The three *unique* cottonwoods?"

"Yeah," Reggie said. "You know which three Lewis was talking about?"

"I do," Ben said. "It's been right in front of me the whole time. I worked at Yellowstone, so I should have known it. I read a book about Rocky Mountain plants earlier this year, and —"

Reggie burst out laughing. "You read a book about *plants?*"

"It talked about animals a little too," Ben said. "The point is, there are different types of Cottonwood tree. *Three* distinct species."

Cornelia started nodding along, her eyes twinkling again.

"Those three types all live around the United States, but they *only* all grow in the same geographic location… in *Montana.*"

"An astute realization," Cornelia said. "I remember reading in one of the Lewis and Clark biographies that even Meriwether Lewis came to the same realization. He wrote in one of the journals that all three species grew together in those foothills of the mountains, unlike anywhere else."

"That's brilliant," Joshua said. "That's exactly it. So somewhere on the Marias River, in the foothills, is where the first clue's pointing to."

"Wait a minute," Derrick said. "What about the *23*? It says right here, *Mar. 23*. If 'Mar' means 'Marias,' then what does the '23' mean, if not 'March 23?'"

"It's the location," Reggie said. "23… miles?"

"23 miles from the Marias?"

Cornelia shrugged. "Could be. Lewis and his men camped between 20 and 30 miles from the foot of the mountains," Cornelia said. "It is written they were in Blackfeet Indian country, the mountains visible in the distance."

"So they were on the Marias, camping out, about 23 miles from the mountains." Ben sighed out of relief. "That narrows it down. If this is accurate, and there really is something out there, I'd say we start at the Marias River. Yeah?"

Nods all around. Cornelia's smile lit the room. "You boys have been good to me," she said. "I won't forget that. I don't drink, but my late husband left some sort of booze behind, and it's been sitting in the cabinet for twenty years. I don't know if this stuff goes bad, but do any of you want some Scotch?"

Ben caught Reggie's eye as the woman spoke. He almost laughed out loud. Reggie, thankfully, spoke up. "You — you have *Scotch* that's over twenty years old? Yeah, I'd be interested in a taste."

"Yes, and it was twenty-five years old to begin with. I'm not going to do anything with it. Why don't you just take it?"

# FIFTY-FIVE

IT HAD BEEN ALMOST A day, as far as she could tell. Julie's legs and feet were numb, and her hands were close behind. She'd been sitting in the exact same position, unable to move an inch, for hours. The blackness of the gymnasium had crept into her, chilling her, and even her breathing felt slow and out of sync with the rest of her body, as if she was listening in on someone else breathing.

The breaths couldn't be coming from her.

There was no way…

She yelped, and suddenly felt a hand over her mouth.

*It* wasn't *my breathing I was hearing,* she realized. Horrified, she blinked rapidly, trying in vain to force her eyes to add more light to the room. Instead, nothing but more blackness.

She was panicking, and it was going to take its toll on her. Whatever was about to happen, she needed strength. Willpower. Panicking sapped that from her, and she did her best to calm her breathing, but…

The stench of sweat and flesh filled her lungs, and she gagged. She could taste the hand, the hard, cracked leathery hand of a soldier.

*The* soldier. The one who'd tried to grope her and touch her earlier. Morrison.

"Hello, little lady," he whispered, his voice somehow more disgusting than his hand. She gagged again, nearly choking on her tongue for fear that she might let it touch the man's palm.

She didn't speak — she *couldn't* speak. His hand was tight on her open mouth, easily covering it and preventing her from speaking. She nearly couldn't breathe, either, as the top of his monstrous hand was smashed next to her nostrils.

Still, she forced a breath, then another. And another. Slowly she beat the fear back into submission. The disgust, the anger — those would stay. But the fear had no place here, not now. This man wanted one thing, and that was nothing to fear.

She could fear the man in charge, Morrison's boss, the man they called The Hawk. *What was his name again? Vincent?* Something 'Garza,' she knew. She could fear him — he was an organized, purposeful man, with a plan that involved tying her to a chair in the middle of an abandoned gymnasium, where screaming wouldn't be heard, and men like Morrison could sneak up on her in the dark, and…

She feared The Hawk, but she wouldn't fear Morrison. This man was a rat, a scourge, the kind of bottom-feeder every organization had in spades. The Hawk probably knew it, too, but he would allow Morrison his little games as long as the man delivered results.

"I said, *hello, little lady,*" Morrison said again.

She squinted in the dark, trying to glare at him. "What do you want?"

A chuckle.

"Oh, I think you know *exactly* what I want."

Julie felt another hand on her thigh. He squeezed, tightly. It hurt.

"Stop and I won't kill you," she said. Her voice didn't crack, and she was proud for that. *No telling when I'll lose it,* she thought.

Another laugh, louder this time. "*Kill* me? You? Right now?"

"No," she said. "Not now. Maybe not even here. But I *will* kill you, unless you let go of my leg."

There was a pause, as if the man was considering her bargain. Then her mouth was free, the cold air flowing onto her face and chilling the area where the man's sweaty hand had just been.

Then the hand went to her *other* leg.

"You mean, let go of *these* legs?"

She thrust sideways with her torso, trying to dislodge the man and throw his hands off of her, but it only served to send a sharp pain through her left side. She yelped in pain, then screamed.

"You think anyone's going to hear you?" Morrison snapped. "Actually, they'll hear you. Every one of them. They're right out there."

If he was pointing, Julie couldn't see it.

"But they won't come in. We were ordered not to. But my boss — The Hawk, I think you've met — and I have a bit of a *special* arrangement."

"Touch me and die, asshole," she whispered, through gritted teeth. "I'm warning you. I will rip your head from your body."

His hands slid up, slowly. "I'm going to take my time with you, little lady. We got off to a bad start, right down the street at that hotel. You remember that? Just you and me, in the closet. Hard to forget, I'd bet."

Julie turned her head sideways, a slight gasp escaping her lips. *Stop*, she willed herself. *Don't give him the satisfaction.*

"You know I don't like that he made us tie you up so well. I like it when you're able to move around a bit, make it interesting. Wouldn't you agree?"

Julie felt a tear fall from her right eye and land on her shoulder. *No more. You're done.* Her silent words were strong, but they did no good.

"I think I'll fix that," he said. In the darkness, one of the man's hands moved from her leg.

She heard the sound of a small knife unfolding and popping into place. A slight amount of pressure on her left wrist.

"I think maybe just a few of these bindings can go away, don't you think? Give you a little *wiggle* room."

The pressure increased, more and more, and Julie waited anxiously for the binding to snap. The zip ties were the thick, industrial kind, but even they would give way to the knife eventually. She was considering the plan he'd given her — wait until he had 'freed' her a bit, then complain that it wasn't enough. She would sit dead-still, unmoving.

If he wanted her to squirm, she would wait until he had taken more of the zip ties off.

Finally, with a *snap*, the zip tie on her left wrist popped off and fell to the hardwood floor. There was still a tie near her elbow, and the two on her other arm.

"There we go," Morrison said. "How's that? Maybe the other side, too? Free those pretty little hands?"

She waited, hoping he would follow through.

He came to her right arm, one of his hands still pressed tight against the top of her thigh. The pressure on her wrist started, and the invisible knife began its work. A few seconds ticked by — Morrison was obviously drawing it out as long as possible, savoring the moment.

She heard a *clicking* sound and waited for the pressure on her right wrist to be released, but it never was.

Instead, the entire hall was suddenly bathed in a brilliant white. The lights on the gym's ceiling had been turned on, and Julie was now blinking to keep the flash of white *out* of her eyes. It took a moment for them to adjust, but when they did Julie finally saw her attacker.

Morrison was shirtless, wearing long black cargo pants, and the same black boots she'd seen on him earlier.

He seemed dazed as well, staring over her head toward the doorway.

"B — boss," he said. "I'm sorry. I was just having a word with our little lady, here."

Footsteps on the wood.

A man's hand landed on her shoulder, and she jumped.

"Looks like one of your ties fell off, Ms. Richardson. Morrison, would you mind?"

Morrison reached out and Julie saw that he held another zip tie. He placed it around her freed wrist, once again binding it to the chair. When he'd finished, he stood up, looking over Julie's shoulder at his boss.

"Morrison, out."

Morrison nodded, then briskly walked away.

The Hawk never stepped in front of Julie. He simply waited there until Morrison was out of the room, then turned on a heel and followed his subordinate out.

Just before he left the room, however, he flicked off the lights once more, returning Julie to her pitch-black hell.

# FIFTY-SIX

THE FLIGHT TO BROWNING, MONTANA, was uneventful. They landed late, the sun already starting to set over the backdrop of the Rocky Mountains. Ben felt the presence of the men who'd gone before them as he looked out over the desolate plains. This area of the country had never been developed further than a few outpost-style cities and towns. Specifically, the area they'd landed in, including the city, was the location of the Blackfeet Indian Reservation, and Derrick had to pull a few strings to get clearance for their plane to land on reservation property, under the auspices of a 'research trip.'

Ben had thought about Julie the entire flight, and the dread and fear he felt for her only added to the anxiety that came with flying. He hated planes — the feeling of not being in control — and Julie was the only person he'd ever met who had been able to quell those fears slightly. She would hold his hand, even as he crushed it between a white-knuckled grip, as they took off and landed.

And she hadn't been there to help him this time. He felt shame for feeling as though *he* needed *her*, knowing that she was likely feeling far worse than he. A simple fear of flying was nothing compared to what she was going through, but it had done nothing to calm his nerves.

They drove away from the mountains, Joshua at the wheel of the rented SUV that Mr. E had ordered and had sent to the small municipal airport to coincide with their arrival. Ben sat in the back, his legs cramped against the seat in front of him, but as it was far better than traveling via plane, he didn't complain. It was a thirty minute drive to the site of the northernmost camp of the Lewis and Clark Expedition, Camp Disappointment.

Roger Derrick sat in the front passenger seat, and Reggie sat next to Ben behind Joshua. Ben had eaten a snack from a vending machine in the airport, but their flight, being a last-minute exchange their benefactor had set up, hadn't been ready for food service. He hoped they'd find something upon landing, but knowing a bit about the backcountry of Montana from his time as a park ranger at Yellowstone, he knew they were hours away from a cheeseburger.

He did his best to quell his hunger, but about fifteen minutes into their drive his stomach squirmed loudly.

"Hungry, big guy?" Reggie asked.

"Always."

"We're stopping over in a little town that's supposed to be right on the trail, right Joshua?"

Joshua nodded from the driver's seat, but Derrick answered. "Yeah, dang tank wasn't even full when we got it. I thought that was a rule? Anyway, yeah, we're stopping pretty soon in a town that's hardly on the map, but it's right next to Camp Disappointment. About 200 people, and not so much as a visitor's center for the trail."

"That's what we're looking for," Reggie said. "Any place with a visitor's center is going to be picked clean of treasures. Something like this — remote, out in the middle of nowhere — that's where we'll find this thing."

"I really just want to find a McDonald's," Ben said, shifting in the seat.

"Hey buddy," Reggie said, "you're in a car with three *expert* survivalists. All of us have been trained to live off the land. We can pull over any time and I'll show you which bugs and plants to eat."

Ben glared at him. "I'll wait for the McDonald's, but thanks."

The town they were headed for appeared in Ben's view a few minutes later, and he immediately knew Derrick was right. The town was hardly worthy of the title, as the only buildings in sight were a gas station that, from here, seemed to be completely devoid of human life and a tiny shack that had the word *bar* painted across the top of it, and it looked even more desolate than the station.

Regardless, Joshua pulled into the gas station and stopped to check his phone's GPS.

"I hope this really is the place," Reggie said. "If not, we're halfway to nowhere and the fastest way back isn't fast at all."

"Daris' group will be looking for the treasure as well," Derrick said. "But you're right. If it's not here, they'll get ahead of us."

*And if they get it,* Ben thought, *Julie dies.*

He shook the thought out of his mind and tried to focus again on the hunger. At least the hunger was mostly controllable.

"I'm going to fill up, but if you guys want to figure out where Lewis' camp *actually* was, we can try to save time."

"You really think it's here?" Reggie asked. "I know Camp Disappointment was the northernmost point on their trail, but why would Lewis hide something there? From what I read, the camp today is nothing more than a fenced-in historic marker, with campgrounds around it."

"Which should make it even easier to find something," Derrick said, "since it's not remarkable in any other way."

"Besides," Joshua said, leaning into the car's open window, "the first clue just tells us that it's on the Marias River. 23 something. Camp Disappointment is on one of the tributaries of the river, but it's likely that Lewis was there when he wrote that first entry."

"So we find the camp, look for some sort of '23,' or walk 23 miles in some direction... or 23 paces? Which direction? 23 degrees? Seriously, if that's the only clue we've got, we're hosed."

"Could be much simpler than that," Ben said. Joshua had finished filling the tank and he re-entered the SUV and turned the key.

Reggie stared at him, and Derrick swiveled around in his seat to see him.

"I mean, Lewis was a smart guy and all, but he never comes across as an intellectual, you know? Not a simpleton, but certainly no puzzle-making genius."

"So?"

"So, I wonder if the answer is really just as simple as it seems. We thought 'Mar 23' is a date, and it's not. Or, at least the 'Mar' part's not. But maybe the '23' *is* still a date."

"A date... for what?"

"A date for when they arrived at camp, or when Lewis hid the treasure. Derrick, your grandmother said they were at Camp Disappointment from the 20th to the 26th of July, 1806, right?"

Derrick nodded. "Yeah, something like that. Which would put them right where we need them on the 23rd of July."

"Exactly," Ben said as Joshua began driving away from the tiny gas station. "So far it all makes sense. But that's just one clue, and there's no telling if it's right or not. Derrick, you got that journal handy? Maybe we can start on the next one or two?"

"Starting to feel like a treasure hunter, Ben?" Joshua asked.

"No. I'm hungry. And when I'm hungry, it helps to take my mind off the hunger by doing something else."

"Fair enough," he said. "Well, stay hungry. There's a lot to do."

# FIFTY-SEVEN

THE AREA OF THE COUNTRY Reggie was now standing in was sacred, in a way. It had been occupied for hundreds — possibly thousands — of years, by Native Americans. Meriwether Lewis had stood on this spot, looking at the vast expanse of the Rocky Mountains to the left and right, as far as the eye could see.

*What was he thinking?* Reggie wondered. *What was he concerned about?*

Camp Disappointment, the northernmost tip of the entire expedition, had been named out of frustration. The Missouri River watershed did not, in fact, extend north to the 50th Parallel, meaning the land Jefferson had purchased was not vastly larger than they'd hoped. Before turning back south to meet up once again with Clark and the rest of the men, Lewis' small outfit camped here, 'disappointed.'

*Or was he? Was there something else to be disappointed about? Or was there nothing at all to be disappointed about, and Lewis was just being coy?*

Reggie had a background in history, even having taught as a part-time professor in Brazil for some time. He loved the story of how the world's people interacted, and why. The lessons hidden within it all. He hadn't spent any time studying the Lewis and Clark expedition, but he was in full-fledged historian mode now. He wanted to learn it all, to discover their secrets and reasons for doing what they did so many years ago.

But there was a more pressing matter, and he knew that, too. He sighed. Julie was gone, taken from their group by the man he had known long ago, the man his subordinates had called The Hawk.

Vicente Garza, a large and imposing figure in the security community, and previously a sergeant in the United States Army. Reggie had known him then, when he himself was working up the ranks as an Army sniper. He'd served at a training camp with him, and had almost been swayed by Garza's promise of freedom — and *great* pay — when he'd left the military to start his company.

Garza hadn't been a bad man, before. Reggie had even admired the man's leadership. His charisma was unparalleled, and many of Reggie's own teammates had talked of leaving to work with Garza.

Then the man disappeared. Simply fell off the map, and those same teammates couldn't figure out what had happened to the man who'd promised them a steady, well-paying job doing what they had been trained for, *outside* of the military.

Reggie hadn't worried about it — people did strange things. Reggie himself had even 'gone off the deep end' once, moving his life and his young wife to Brazil to start a business teaching survival to corporate executives who wanted 'an experience.' He had owned a shooting range, a fallout shelter he'd designed served as their home, and he'd lived there — mostly happily — for years.

And then he'd met Juliette Richardson and Harvey Bennett. He'd crashed into their lives — literally — after they'd been attacked by a mercenary group not unlike the one that had attacked them in Philadelphia.

A group led by none other than Joshua Jefferson. The man had been misled, duped and lied to, and he'd risen to power in the organization his father and brother had been a part of. Joshua's team had been pointed toward Julie and Ben and let loose, and they would have been completely wiped out had it not been for Reggie's stepping in.

When Joshua had defected to the 'good side,' as Reggie liked to say, they had all become friends, eventually creating the Civilian Special Operations team they were now a part of. Joshua got along with everyone well, and he was a solid leader for their merry band of good guys.

Reggie wondered now if Vicente Garza might have a similar story waiting to be written. He wanted to kill the man for what he'd done to Julie, what he'd done to Ben. But there was a part of him — albeit a *small* part of him — that wanted to see if The Hawk was really as bad as his men made him seem.

People did crazy things for money, and Reggie himself had done things he still regretted in the promise of a good paycheck. So he wondered if there was hope for the man? If they caught him, questioned him, allowed him to explain — could his actions be redeemed?

Reggie looked at the other members of his group: Roger Derrick, the FBI agent-turned-treasure hunter who wanted nothing more than to take down Daris Johansson and prevent something he believed in, called 'The Shift.'

Joshua Jefferson, the new friend and ally who'd helped him out of more than a few scrapes.

And finally Harvey Bennett himself, the unassuming park ranger whose resiliency and stubbornness had done the group more favors than any amount of trained guns could.

These men were his team right now, for better or worse. They were it. Good or bad, The Hawk was currently the enemy, the same way Joshua had been their enemy in the Amazon Rainforest. Reggie was a man of his word, and right now his word to Ben was that he would do whatever it took to get Julie back.

And that meant figuring out this mystery.

"Let's see that journal," Ben said.

Reggie turned, snapping out of his meditation. He would have plenty of time after this was all over to explore and study the history he loved so much.

Derrick walked over, holding the journal open in front of Ben. Apparently he wasn't quite ready to simply pass the priceless artifact into someone else's hands.

Derrick and Ben looked at the page he'd opened it to, the page with their first 'clue.' Frowning, neither man spoke.

"Anything else there?" Reggie asked.

"Not since the last time we looked," Ben said. "I just thought I'd be inspired to —"

Reggie waited.

Ben tilted his head sideways.

"What? Find something?"

"I — I think…"

Ben grabbed the journal out of Derrick's hand, who looked at him with an expression halfway between shocked and irate. He stepped closer to Ben, reached out to grab the journal, but Ben swatted his hand away.

"Hang on, I think there's…"

Ben tilted the journal sideways, so the long edge of the page they had been staring at was now parallel to the ground. Ben held the page, letting the journal fall open, its two covers now hanging down below the single page.

The single *fragile* page.

Reggie's heart raced. He knew the invaluable worth of the artifact, and he couldn't help but feel anxiety at Ben's reckless treatment of the book.

Derrick did a worse job trying to hide his emotions.

"Harvey, give me the damn journal," he said, his voice tight. "You're going to rip it in half. You do that and I knock you on your —"

"Look," Ben said, effectively shushing the man. "Right there."

Now holding the page — and the rest of the journal — with one hand, he pointed to the mountains with the other. "See that?" Ben asked.

"What?" Joshua asked. He had stepped to Ben's other side and was trying to understand all the fuss. Reggie, too, was confused, so he walked around the other three men and tried to see what Ben was pointing at from his perspective.

He looked at the page, horizontal to the small mound they were standing on, a ridge that had been named 'Camp Disappointment,' and then he looked up and focused on the range of mountains just in the distance.

And then he saw it.

The mountain range.

And the torn edge of the page.

They lined up, perfectly. Reggie shifted to his right, now standing almost directly behind Ben, and he stood up on his toes and craned his neck to get a better view, more accurate to Ben's own view.

The torn edge was precisely the same shape as that of the range of mountains in front of them. It had been torn purposefully, likely by Lewis himself, to forever match the landscape he'd wanted someone to see.

Someone who might find his treasure.

"It's a map," Derrick said, his voice filled with awe. All Reggie's anxiety, too, had melted away, yet his heart beat even faster.

"It's a *treasure* map," Joshua said. "Ben, you found it. This is the *exact spot* we'd have to be on to see this and have it make sense."

"He's right," Reggie whispered. "We're here."

# FIFTY-EIGHT

BEN'S MOMENTARY FEELING OF PRIDE at having discovered the 'map' within the journal's pages faded quickly. Julie was still gone, they still had a gang of trigger-happy thugs somewhere behind them, and they were running out of time.

"How long's it going to take to get out there?" he asked.

"Where?"

Ben pointed again. He'd handed the journal back to Roger Derrick, who'd inspected it, then placed it carefully into a plastic bag and then into his briefcase once again.

"The mountains. The map is pointing the way, but we still have to get out there. There are more clues, remember?"

"Ah, right," Reggie said. "I was sort of hoping the other ones were just for fun, and this spot was it."

"You're welcome to start digging," Derrick said, "but I think Ben's right. The treasure — if there still is one — is that way."

"Due west, into the mountains. How far, though?" Joshua asked.

Ben looked around at the rest of them. He was on a roll, so he figured he had nothing to lose. "Well, I've been thinking about that, too."

"Yeah?" Reggie asked. "You cracked the next clue?"

"Nope," he said. "Still part of this one. I'd bet you we're supposed to walk along the Marias River, starting from right here, straight up into the mountains."

"But for how long?"

"23 miles," Ben said quickly. "And I'd further bet you that we're standing on a spot exactly 23 miles upstream from where the Marias meets the Missouri."

"In the middle of where the 'three unique Cottonwoods' grow together," Derrick added, a smile on his face.

"Well damn, Ben," Reggie said, matching Derrick's smile. "That's got to be the smartest thing you've ever said."

"That's why I don't talk that much," Ben replied. "But going back to my first question: how long will it take us to walk over there? There aren't any roads, so I don't see any other way up there." He turned to Derrick. "Unless your boss wants to lend us a helicopter."

Derrick frowned. "The day the Bureau just 'hands out' choppers is a day I'd like to see. I had a hard enough time convincing my boss that I needed a larger arsenal of weapons."

"So we walk?"

"No," Joshua said. "There are a few towns up in the mountains. Bit of a circuitous route, but we can drive and get there a lot faster."

"Plus, we won't be 23 miles up in the mountains without a way to get back."

"Works for me," Joshua said. "Let's roll."

# FIFTY-NINE

"OKAY BOSS," MORRISON SAID. "WE'RE ready for you."

The Hawk nodded, stepping away from his perch at the end of the gymnasium. Juliette Richardson sat in the center still, arms and legs bound, her head down.

*She's starting to break*, he thought. *They always start to break.*

Usually it took a scare, or a threat, but sometimes — like in Julie's case — it took something more *psychological.* In her case, it was darkness. Pitch-black darkness for a certain number of hours did the trick, even when everything else had failed.

He never had to touch them, or point a gun at them, or do anything else drastic. These matters were simpler, far simpler than the over-complicated things his men would have had him do.

Morrison, for example, would have ruined every chance they had at extracting information from the woman. His idiocy had nearly derailed The Hawk's plans, but thankfully he had strolled near the gymnasium and heard Morrison's advances.

There was no need for punishment, not yet. Morrison was still a good soldier, and he needed all the good soldiers he could get. The team of recruits he'd sent to retrieve the FBI agent and his friends had failed, at least initially. They had allowed for numerous mistakes, but the small team was now headed toward Montana. The Hawk knew they would make mistakes; he planned for it. Only through mistakes could one learn to succeed. He had no problem with failure, only a problem with failure when there was no disciplinary action taken afterward.

The recruits would be punished, made to understand their failings and what they should have done instead. For that they would grow stronger, and only then could they earn their spot on The Hawk's team. Ravenshadow would be stronger for it, and The Hawk could then charge more for his security.

It was a win-win for them, even if they didn't realize it while they were being punished.

But the discipline could come later. Right now he had a job to do, and that was to get Daris the information she needed.

The Hawk reached the center of the room and looked down at Julie. She was looking at him, under that tussled crop of black hair, looking up at him but not leaning her head back. Her eyes snuck out from her downturned face, only the bottom halves of them visible.

If she hadn't been bound to a chair in the middle of a room surrounded by soldiers, The Hawk would have thought she looked terrifying.

Instead, he knew she was terrified. She was acting, playing the game, and playing it well. She was close to broken, and when she broke she'd give him whatever he wanted.

He motioned for one of the soldiers to bring him the rolling cart Morrison had set up earlier. It rolled over, the glass jars and the box on top of it clinking as they brushed against each other. The man walked it steadily over to Julie's side, and The Hawk watched her reaction.

There was no way she could know what it was, but that didn't matter. She didn't need to. Not knowing would add to her terror, which would allow it to work faster. It would make her break faster.

He strolled over to the cart, slowly, making sure Julie's eyes were following him. He reached down and opened the top of the box that sat in the center of the tiny jars. He opened the lid and extracted one of the syringes lining the inside, and then grabbed one of the jars.

He tipped the jar upside-down and inserted the needle through the lid. Pulling back on the syringe's shaft, he filled the chamber with the silvery, translucent fluid.

Julie's head snapped up.

*Good*, he thought. *She's already starting to break.*

The serum was still in the testing phase, but he'd found that a far smaller dosage was necessary than what Daris' chemists had informed him of. Part of the effect of any drug was a placebo, and it needed to be factored in. Double-blind studies had shown that the placebo effect, in some cases, could be just as strong as the drug itself.

He had factored in the placebo now, knowing that the mere *thought* of injecting an unknown foreign fluid into Julie's arm would cause sheer terror and panic. It would lay the groundwork for the drug to do its *actual* job.

"Juliette," The Hawk said. "I'm going to put this in your arm, and then you're going to tell me everything you know about your team."

She glared at him. "Truth serum? Really? That's science fiction."

"Correct," he said. "But a hit of scopolamine to the neural receptors in the brain, telling it to shut down temporarily and allow voluntary thought to be, for the most part, replaced by *in*voluntary reactions, is *not* science fiction. It's science — and it's in my hand right now."

She tensed, and The Hawk took a bit of pleasure in this. He leaned down and stuck the syringe into Julie's arm. He'd done some quick research online, and though he wasn't a nurse or doctor, he thought he had the basic concept down: find a vein, stick the needle in, and pump slowly.

The bedside manner and precision was for the *real* doctors. He just needed to get the stuff inside her.

She gasped, obviously startled by the painful needle and lackadaisical way The Hawk had done it, but he leaned down further, focusing now on not letting the needle bend. Straight, carefully, and slowly — that was the goal. He pushed the syringe closed, watching the fluid press into her bloodstream.

"Wh — why are you doing this?" Juliette asked.

"It's my job, Juliette," The Hawk said. "And I like my job."

"I don't know anything about —"

She gasped, bucking in her chair and throwing her head back. Her eyes shone white for a moment as they rolled backward in her head, and her mouth stretched open. She rocked a few times, the spasms increasing to an excited intensity then subsiding.

The Hawk waited, knowing this phase was the worst for the patient. This initial intake was the most physically painful phase of the process, but it ended quickly. At such a low dosage there wouldn't be too many side effects, and none would be permanent.

He hoped.

He'd been informed by Daris that her chemists were still trying to understand how the fluid reacted to different blood types, as there were differences. Slight, and largely unnoticeable but for the side effects. They had told The Hawk that they could eventually isolate the active ingredient and focus it, alongside the scopolamine, but that was for a later testing round, after The Hawk's team had delivered what she was looking for.

So Juliette Richardson got to be a test subject of the beta version of the drug. The serum was effective, but he'd had to dilute the potency to ensure there was no cardiac arrest or renal failure. He may need this woman again, so he had to be careful.

Finally Julie's head came back up, and her eyes stopped floating. She blinked a few times, the eyes trying to automatically adjust. Her hands opened and closed, and she rolled her head sideways a couple times, her neck cracking.

The Hawk liked to think the subject was 'resetting,' preparing their minds for his inclusions. The serum worked far better than the smoking method for a controlled, balanced test, yet the effect wouldn't be as pronounced at this low a dosage.

"Juliette," he said.

"I prefer Julie," she answered.

"Of course. My apologies. How do you feel?"

"I feel — I feel okay, I guess. What did you do to me?"

"I injected you with the serum that my boss is developing. It renders the subject 'consciously unconscious.' You are able to respond, and move, but not of your own will."

Julie stared back at him. "That's nice."

"It is nice, Julie. Further, you will have no recollection of this conversation in fifteen minutes when you 'wake up.' There will be a mild-to-severe headache, but aside from that, we don't expect any side effects."

"Great," she said. Her voice was calm, unperturbed, as if she had just been told there was an in-store coupon a clerk had just applied to her grocery bill.

The Hawk loved this part. He couldn't help having a little fun with the subjects.

"Julie," he said. "Who is your fiancé?"

"Harvey Bennett," she said. "Ben."

"Ben, right. But who do you *really* love?"

"I love Ben."

"That's great, Julie. Loyal to the very end. What about Gareth Red?"

"Reggie?" she asked.

"Yes, Reggie. He's a fine-looking man, wouldn't you say? Do you love him?"

"I do," she said, "but in a different way. I always saw him as sort of an older brother."

"Ah, I see," The Hawk said. "Well, let's get into things. Who is Roger Derrick?"

"He's an FBI agent."

"And what does he want?"

"He… he wants to find Daris Johansson, I think."

"You think"

"I mean that's what he told us. I don't have any reason to suspect anything otherwise."

"I see. Why does he want to find Daris Johansson?"

"He wants to stop her. She's trying to find something that's dangerous, at least in her hands."

"Correct."

She looked at him inquisitively, like a mouse looking up to a cat. Unaware of the danger.

Unaware that she was being controlled.

"Julie," The Hawk said, "I'm going to take the ties off of you. Is that okay?"

"Sure," she said. "That's okay."

Morrison walked over and started cutting the zip ties off Julie's arms and legs. The Hawk watched closely, but his man didn't try anything stupid this time. When he'd finished, he picked up the broken ties and walked back behind the cart.

"Thank you, Morrison. Julie, can you move your right arm?"

She lifted up her right arm and waved it once, then set it back down.

"Very good, Julie. Now, that was one of my men, Morrison. How do you feel about Morrison? I believe you had a chance to meet him earlier?"

Julie's face remained expressionless. "I did meet him. I'm going to kill him."

One of the men chuckled in the background, but The Hawk stepped closer to Julie's chair. "Julie, you are not tied down any longer. Do you want to get up and kill Morrison *now*?"

"Yes, I do."

"Okay."

"Okay."

Julie didn't move. She sat in the chair, transfixed, as if the ties were still in place.

"Julie, do you want my knife to kill Morrison?"

"That would work, yes."

"Here, Julie." The Hawk took the last step to Julie's chair and held out a huge combat knife, the razor-sharp blade in his hand with the handle extended out to Julie. "Take the knife, Julie."

She took it. It didn't move. She just held it in her hand, her eyes wide, unmoving.

"Morrison," The Hawk said. "Come here."

Morrison took a few steps forward.

"Closer, Morrison."

He followed the order, and he was now standing directly to Julie's right, his stomach at the woman's shoulder.

"Julie, do you still want to kill Morrison?"

"Yes."

The Hawk waited, watching both his insubordinate soldier and Julie. Neither moved, but Morrison was frozen in fear, not from the drug.

After a minute, The Hawk dismissed Morrison with a wave of his hand.

"Julie, you didn't kill Morrison, even though you wanted to. Is that correct?"

"Yes," she said. "That's correct."

"I see. Julie, we don't have a lot of time before your drug wears off. You'll want to take a nice long nap at that point, and I can't blame you. That means I need to know, *right now*, everything you know about the rest of your team. Can you tell me that?"

"What do you want to know?" Julie asked.

"Let's start with your leader, Joshua Jefferson. Tell me about him."

# SIXTY

THE PHONE CALL CAME TO Reggie's phone, about halfway up a steep mountain pass. Ben was in the back seat, behind their FBI teammate once again, when Reggie slid the phone out of his pocket and looked at the screen.

"Unknown caller," Reggie said. "Probably a telemarketer."

"Let it go to voicemail?" Ben asked.

"Let me answer it," Derrick said. "It's not a telemarketer."

Ben knew he was correct, but he didn't want to think about what it meant. Mr. E, had he been the caller, would have routed the call through a local Alaskan area code. And their current situation in consideration, Ben knew it was far too much of a coincidence for a telemarketer to be calling Reggie's phone right now.

Reggie sighed. He tapped the button on the front of the phone and then another to turn on the speakerphone option. "Gareth Red."

A low, rumbling voice emanated from the tinny speaker. *The Hawk.*

*"Reggie. How are you? How's that gang of misfits?"*

Ben's jaw tightened. He looked from Reggie to Derrick, then to Joshua. Joshua turned to the others and mouthed the words, *need me to pull over?* Derrick shook his head, then spun his index finger in a circle. *Keep him talking.*

Joshua hit the gas, taking advantage of a long straightaway. By Ben's estimate, they were only ten minutes or so from the first of the 'small towns' Joshua had mentioned, and that meant they were only a few minutes from parking and setting out by foot. What they were looking for, they didn't know. But Joshua had marked a few locations on his phone's map, hoping that their search area was relatively close within the two-mile square he'd outlined.

Their technology was better than Lewis' had been, Ben knew, but that meant nothing. Even for an accomplished navigator like Lewis, a small error on his end could mean Ben's group, 200 years later, would be using pinpoint-accurate technology to look entirely in the wrong spot.

It was a gut-check moment for Ben. He knew they'd need luck, timing, and a lot of looking in the right place at the right time. They hadn't even decided if they were looking for a cave, as the clue had initially led them to believe, or something else entirely.

*Was the 'cave' referenced in the clue an* actual *cavern, or was it a metaphor for something else?*

They were looking for a needle in a haystack, but the haystack was the size of a country.

Ben flicked his head back to stare at the phone in Reggie's lap as his friend responded.

"Where the hell is Julie?"

*"She's right here next to me. And she's been telling me all about your little group for the past ten minutes. She'll be unwilling to talk in a minute or so, so I was hoping you would be willing to tell me a little more."*

Ben seethed, his fists clenching. He couldn't keep quiet any longer. "Listen, you little prick," he said, nearly shouting. "You lay a finger on her and — you know what? Screw that. You're already dead."

The deep voice laughed. *"I'm glad you're concerned, Harvey. It means you care. Julie was speaking your praises a moment ago, and you'll be satisfied to hear that she has nothing but wonderful things to say about you."*

Ben closed his eyes, forcing himself to breathe. Derrick was turned almost all the way around in the front seat, his left hand around the other side of the headrest and on Ben's shoulder. "It's okay," he whispered. "It's going to be okay."

*"Anyway, back to the point: Julie was willing — with some urging on our part — to reveal everything she knew about your little band of warriors. The 'CSO?' That's a wonderful idea!"* Garza laughed, louder this time, then came back on the phone. *"She told me about your romp through Antartica not too long ago, and she told us all about your reclusive benefactor. 'Mr. E?' That's really his name? And you don't know anything else about him?"*

"Why is she telling you all of this?" Reggie snapped. "What did you do to her?"

*"Nothing, really. At least nothing that won't wear off soon. She'll be tired, but unaffected. I wanted to test the serum my benefactor has been playing with. There are sometimes a few side effects... of the* permanent

*sort, if the dosage is high enough. But Julie had just enough of it to be willing to cooperate, and no more."*

Ben felt like he was going to lose his mind. He suddenly felt claustrophobic. He wanted to tell Joshua to pull over, to just stop the car and let him out. His fists were white now, yet he still clenched them, opening and closing them over and over again, tighter each time.

*"Let me be frank for a moment, Gareth. And the rest of you. My employer is* very *interested in wrapping up this little adventure as quickly as possible. In order to speed things along, I've sent a few of my recruits your way. They will be meeting up with you in a few minutes, actually. I believe you've already met, back in Philadelphia.*

*"You will cooperate, or you will die. If you give them any grief whatsoever, Ms. Richardson dies. Do I make myself clear?"*

Ben stared straight ahead in the seat. His back was straight, his legs were rigid. He wanted to scream, and yet he couldn't bring himself to even open his mouth to speak.

From somewhere behind the man on the other end of the phone, a woman's voice suddenly yelled.

*Julie.*

*" — we're here, in Philly. In a gym right across from the Ritten —"*

Julie's voice was cut off, and there was a smacking sound and a small yelp.

Ben tensed up even more and he shot his hand out to the side, crushing it against the window. The loud sound made Reggie jump, but Ben's outburst had no effect on The Hawk. With the same calm, practiced voice, he returned to the phone.

*"I hope that proves my seriousness in this matter, Harvey. You have a lot at stake here, son. I hope you won't disappoint me."*

"I'll kill you, you son of a —"

*"Do I make myself clear?"* The Hawk asked again.

Reggie's characteristic smile had faded. He took in a breath, slowly. "Clear, Garza. Clear as glass."

The Hawk hung up, and the phone screen went to black.

# SIXTY-ONE

"HE'S OUT THERE," BEN SAID, nearly shouting. "He's out there, in Philadelphia, right where we were."

"We don't know that, Ben," Derrick said. "Garza said she was drugged, that he gave her some sort of serum."

"She's there," Ben said. "I know she's there."

"What if she is, Ben?" Reggie asked. "I want to find her as much as you do, but we can't just turn around —"

"We can, and we will. Right now."

"Ben, we can't —"

"*Turn around,* Joshua," Ben said. He pulled up against his seatbelt, as if trying to stand. He would tear the thing off its bolts if he had to.

Joshua was still driving, now ascending around another curve in the road. "Ben, I'm sorry, we…"

Ben's nostrils flared. He pulled the seatbelt, fighting against the constraint. "I'm going back."

"No, Ben."

"I am. Try to stop me." Ben flicked the lock on his door and then unbuckled his seatbelt.

"Ben! Stop!" Derrick's voice said. "I agree with you."

Ben was about to push the door open and slide out — he had no idea what he'd do *after* that, but he didn't care about *after* that. He cared about Julie, and he now knew where she was.

*She wouldn't lie to him. She may have been lied to, but as far as she knew, she was being held in Philadelphia, near the Rittenhouse.*

*In a gym.*

It was an odd thing to say, which was why it had stuck in Ben's

227

mind. If she'd have said 'room,' or 'building,' it wouldn't have been helpful — there were thousands of those near the hotel in Philadelphia.

But she'd said 'gym.' Loudly and clearly, just before she'd been struck by one of The Hawk's men. Or The Hawk himself.

Ben looked at Derrick.

"I agree with you, Ben," he said again. "I think she's in Philadelphia, and I think it makes sense to go find her. You find her, you find the men doing this."

"Alone?" Reggie asked.

"No, one of us goes with. We split up, two of us staying here, trying to piece together the next clue, and two of us going back to Philly. It'll take hours to get there, but it could take us just as long here to find the treasure.

For the first time since he'd gotten in the car, Ben felt his mind sliding back to a normal ease. He wasn't 'fine' — far from it — but he was better. He could think clearly.

*This works,* he thought. *Two of us go back to Philly, two of us stay here to find the treasure.*

"What about Garza's goons?" Reggie asked. "He said they're 'going to meet up with us,' remember?"

"They're coming either way," Derrick said. "And Garza's got Julie either way."

"He'll know we're coming for her."

"He already does. He probably started planning for it immediately after he hung up the phone. Julie took a risk blurting that out — however she knew about it — but it's helpful information, and he knows that. He'll be ready."

Joshua nodded along. "He's right. It doesn't change our situation, really. We just got lucky, thanks to Julie, and we need to capitalize on it."

Reggie seemed to be the only one not on board, but he nodded anyway. "I don't like it — it weakens us significantly. But if we play our cards right we can trade them in for a better hand. This way we have two routes to do that — find the treasure before Daris gets it, or find Julie before…"

"Right," Ben said. "And I'm going to find Julie before that."

"Who's going with him, then?" Joshua asked. "Derrick needs to be here, since it's over if The Hawk gets his hands on him. An FBI agent with the journal in his possession is all he needs. And I'm assuming you're not ready to trust us with that book, yet?"

Derrick shook his head. "It's not about trust. I'm staying here in Montana, until I find it."

"So that leaves me or Reggie," Joshua said. "Honestly, I can't justify sending Reggie back — we need him here, to fend off whatever it is Garza's throwing our way. And his knowledge of history could prove more helpful out here."

"So it's me and you, pal," Ben said, directing the statement to Joshua. "Let's make a plan when we get to this town."

"You got it, buddy. We'll get her back. I promise."

# SIXTY-TWO

REGGIE DIDN'T LIKE LEAVING BEN to fend for himself, even though Joshua was there. Joshua Jefferson was a good man, and a capable leader, but he didn't have the friendship with Ben that Reggie had. Reggie had a way of getting through to Ben when no one else — not even Julie — could.

They had a camaraderie, an understanding, a brotherhood that could only be forged in battle. Joshua was a bit more closed off, more personal, so he'd always been just a bit distant from them. Through their shared love of bourbon and their forced partnership in rough situations, Reggie and Ben had become fast friends.

So it had hurt a bit when Ben and Joshua left for Philadelphia, but he knew it was the wise decision. Roger Derrick was every bit as capable a fighter as Ben would have been, and right now Reggie needed fighters.

He could use a few more, but if they had two — armed with 9mm handguns only — that would have to do.

Derrick was driving now, and they were heading straight up a dirt-paved backroad that led into a mountainous valley. The scenery was breathtakingly beautiful, but Reggie was feeling far from romantic considering their situation and his current partner.

They had spoken little, and even then only to share ideas about which direction to move, and when they thought they'd run into the Ravenshadow men once again. After dropping Ben and Joshua off at the town's only car rental facility, they'd booked it farther into the hills, trying to get to the square Joshua had outlined on his phone's map.

Ben and Joshua would ride as fast as possible back to Browning, and then to the airport to catch a commercial flight to Philadelphia. They'd anticipated the entire trip taking three hours if they were lucky, so Reggie and Derrick's job was to keep the Ravenshadow boys busy for that amount of time, until they could coordinate attacks on both sides.

Plans, Reggie knew, were malleable. They changed, often rapidly, and often without the planner's consent. He hoped they would be somewhere in the vicinity of what they'd planned, but he knew it was wishful thinking for their plan to be executed flawlessly.

Derrick knew it too, and he was sure Joshua and Ben did as well. But there was no better plan. Mr. E's wife couldn't meet up with them until at least the next day, and they were running out of daylight hours in this day already.

Unlike Vicente Garza, Reggie didn't have a team of recruits he could simple call into action, anywhere in the country. It was one of the enigmatic characteristics of the man; his charisma and inspirational leadership was large enough that it persuaded glory-seeking young men to join up, ready to do the man's bidding.

Further, Derrick had informed Reggie that the FBI was unable to send support, either. They'd told Derrick that they understood the situation — they didn't — and that they were watching in on them — they weren't. Derrick explained that since this wasn't a 'sanctioned' mission — he had just been tasked with observing and recording Daris' actions — it would take too much bureaucracy and red tape to get things moving in time. Derrick's take on his conversation with his boss was, as he'd told Reggie, a 'typical FBI balking maneuver.' They might recognize that there was danger ahead, but they weren't interested in committing too quickly.

Still, he assured Reggie that the FBI was mobilizing, albeit slowly. They hadn't been prepared for Daris' case to explode like this, and they'd thought Roger Derrick's warnings misguided at best. As much as he'd fought them on it, they would only appropriate more funding if he could prove — in a report — that it was necessary. Derrick suspected whatever would happen would be all over by the time any more of his coworkers got to the party.

Reggie had asked what the policy was on reporting active-shooter situations, and Derrick laughed. He'd told Reggie that they were certainly on alert, but there was no plan in place to handle this specific situation at the moment. They would send a team out to help only if they could find men and women to pull off of other task forces, and that was a long shot at this point.

It didn't sit well with Reggie, knowing that a major acronym organization in his home country, ostensibly created to serve that country, had a hard time sending in backup to one of their own without his 'filing a report.'

But that was their situation, and Reggie needed to be prepared for fighting an army with only two men. He'd done it before, and he had a feeling he'd do it again today.

He made a mental note to 'file his own report' when they returned, demanding that Mr. E not send them out on any more 'discovery missions' without being fully armed and prepared for a battle.

The dirt road ended at a small parking lot, and a wooden sign nearby told Reggie that they were heading into an area of the Lewis and Clark National Forest. Theirs was the only car in the lot.

"That's a good sign," Reggie muttered. They got out of the car and collected their gear — armed 9mm handguns, two each, and enough ammunition to hopefully get them through the next few hours. Derrick also grabbed a pack that he'd stuffed into the trunk. A 'BOB,' or 'Bug-Out Bag,' a pre-packed bag full of survival gear that was meant for 'bugging out' when things hit the fan. Reggie used to sell them at his survival camp in Brazil, and he still maintained a few bags of differing sizes.

He'd been impressed to see Derrick grab it from the safe house, and he'd been dying to pop it open and lust over the contents. As a self-described 'survivalist,' camping and survival gear were like toys to him. He could spend hours in an Army surplus store, even though he often knew more about each item than the proprietor, and most of the gear sold there was so used it was bordering on useless.

"This whole area is National Forest," Derrick said. "Including Glacier National Park. Altogether, there's about 2,000 square miles of open wilderness to explore. So not seeing another person out here probably just means we're looking in the wrong spot."

"Well let's start at the beginning, with the first clue. We found this area Joshua mapped for us, and we're guessing that's the correct quadrant to look in because it's about 23 miles away from where we were, back at Camp Disappointment?"

"Right," Derrick said. "So we're probably close to this 'Cave of Shadows,' but that's not going to make it easy to find."

"Well, Garza's team is heading out here too, apparently, though I'm not sure where they are. But listening to Garza talk about it, it sort of seems like they knew right where to go."

"They could be tracking us," Derrick said.

"How?" Reggie replied. "I know as well as you do they don't have the tech network for that. And any on-person devices we would have... well, would we have seen them yet?"

Reggie felt a moment of unease pass over him. *What if they* had *planted a small tracking device on one of them?*

Derrick shook his head. "No, they didn't. We passed through a TSA-quality security checkpoint at the airport, and they would have pulled me aside and told me about it."

"Or maybe they *wouldn't* have, *because* it's TSA-quality."

"Their scanning system's better than you think," Derrick said.

"My bar's pretty low for those guys, so 'better than I think' just means you're telling me the scanning system's' better than walking between two pieces of aluminum foil."

"Yeah," Derrick said. "It's definitely better than you think."

Even though they'd headed straight through the airport to the runway, they'd gone through a security fast-lane, as it happened to be the quickest route through the airport. Reggie wasn't surprised to hear Derrick tell him the airport would have caught anything like a tracking device on their clothing, but he wouldn't have been surprised either if TSA had simply let them through without even asking about it.

He checked his pockets and the folds of his pants. Nothing. He was clean.

"So how'd they find us?" he asked.

"Maybe they didn't," Derrick said.

"Explain."

"Well, they've got a copy of the journal, right? Daris has people working on cracking the same codes we are, so maybe she's already figured out the second clue, as well."

"And The Hawk assumes we're close to figuring it out, too."

"Which means he's waiting for *us* to find *him*. Or his men, at least."

"Exactly. And he's got Julie, so he knows we're not stopping to regroup or abandon the mission."

"He's set up a trap that we're supposed to walk into. Knowingly." Reggie shook his head. "That does sound like the man I used to know."

Derrick looked at him as they walked. "Yeah, tell me more about that. How'd you meet?"

"Training camp, back in the day. I was hot for some action, and as a hotshot sniper I thought I'd make it known that he needed me for this new security team he was starting up."

"He was active duty?"

"We overlapped for just a few months, so he was already on his way out then, but yeah. Served in Storm and Shield, I think, and probably a few black ops missions as well. Guy seems made for black-level leadership."

"Why do you say that?"

"He's ruthless. Willing to break any rules put in front of him, just to watch his men struggle with them. Kind of guy who puts you through hell just to see how you react to it."

"Like SEALS training?"

"No, like entertainment. The stuff he cooked up for training exercises left a few men severely injured, and I heard rumors that more than one guy died."

"Christ," Derrick said.

"No joke. He's a monster, but no one could ever put their finger on exactly why. Never would be caught red-handed, I suppose, and the kind of grunts that get attracted to his style of leadership seem to be the types who worship him. They think, like he does, it's all necessary."

"Sounds a lot like organized crime," Derrick said. "I'm surprised we haven't heard of Ravenshadow."

"*You* may not have," Reggie answered. "But I'd bet there's a thick file on someone's desk back at your office. Dig around a bit when this is all over, I'll bet you'll find quite a bit on them."

"Will do," Derrick said. "If we can't take them down now, you'd better believe I'll be doing my research."

Reggie and Derrick found a path that led deeper into the forest, the direction they were already heading. He started along it and they walked a half-mile until they came to the tree line, overlooking a deep bowl cut into the valley.

The ridge they were on was steep, but it wouldn't be impossible to traverse if they had to.

"Nice view," Derrick said. "Wish we would've packed a picnic."

Reggie smiled. "I knew I liked you. Glad to see you're lightening up a bit." He turned back to the bowl and strained his eyes to see across it. "Any idea what we're looking for? Little soldiers marching in a line into a cave?"

"That would be convenient."

"This is the square, though, I think. Joshua's coordinates place this bowl right in the center of the grid, so maybe we start at the edges of it, circle our way —"

Reggie stopped, then crouched. Derrick did the same.

"You hear that?"

Derrick waited a few seconds before answering. "You mean the sound of a helicopter?"

As Reggie nodded, he watched the bowl's opposite ridge. Two mountain peaks stood taller than all surrounding area, and between those two peaks, at the rim of the bowl, a tiny black helicopter sailed into view. The rotor wash bounced and echoed off the walls of the bowl, directly into Reggie's ears.

"Well, I think we found what we're looking for."

# SIXTY-THREE

"YOU THINK THEY SAW US?" Derrick asked.

"No way," Reggie answered. "They're coming in hot, heading straight down where that river is. No way they're looking up here."

"Still..." Roger Derrick slid behind a tree, moving carefully and smoothly so as not to attract unwarranted attention in case the men in the chopper were looking their direction. Reggie slid the opposite direction, knowing there was nothing wrong with being a little extra cautious.

"How many are in there?" Derrick said.

"Holds up to eight, maybe nine, as long as they're packing light. My guess is they are — the chopper will park it and wait for them to be done, then extract them back out to civilization. No reason to carry anything extra."

"So they're not staying to camp."

Reggie smiled. "I doubt it."

The chopper landed in the only section of forest Reggie could see, and he was impressed with the pilot's ability to navigate perfectly down through the trees and their extended branches with only a few feet to spare on each side. It wouldn't have been a legal landing anywhere else, but Reggie had a feeling the men that were about to disembark weren't much into abiding by the law.

"Let's follow them," Reggie said.

"Don't you want to wait until they get out, see where they're going?"

Reggie shook his head. "The trees are way too thick. We'll lose them immediately. But if we head down the slope here, follow this rockslide a bit, I think we can keep an eye on them and stay mostly out of sight."

Derrick examined Reggie's plan, then nodded. "Works for me. You ready?"

Reggie checked the magazine again in both guns, then stood up. "Ready."

Reggie led, half sliding down the mountainside into the bowl the helicopter had landed in. He was right; they could see the men — clearly the same soldiers who'd confronted them behind the yogurt shop in Philadelphia — exiting the helicopter and gathering in a small circle near it, beneath the rotors.

Another reason Reggie had wanted to move quickly was that while the chopper was still spinning down, they'd be able to move without being heard. Only a lucky glance in their direction and a glinting of something metallic off the fading sunlight would put Reggie and Derrick at risk of being seen. The cover was perfect — enough to hide behind as they moved down, but not enough that they couldn't still use their height advantage to see down into the bowl and The Hawk's unit.

The men checked their weapons — assault rifles — and then one of them raised a hand and pointed toward the trees.

"They're going away from us," Derrick said. "That's good."

"Yeah, unless we lose them. Come on, let's speed up. The pilot's staying behind, so we'll have to move around the chopper as well. And I'd bet The Hawk sent an extra set of eyes to watch their bird, so the pilot's got a gunner in there, too."

Derrick nodded, but didn't say anything. They had been walking side-by-side, but Derrick fell back a few paces as the route narrowed, walking now directly behind Reggie. Neither man was breathing hard, and Reggie was glad to have a partner who was nearly as in shape as he was.

They reached the bottom of the bowl just as the other group — four men — entered the trees. Reggie began to jog, staying inside the thick forest about ten or fifteen feet and running around the perimeter of the open section to ensure the men in the chopper wouldn't spot them. Derrick kept up, and within another ten minutes they were at the opposite side of the clearing.

"See them?" Derrick asked.

"Nope, but I see their tracks."

Reggie wasn't a great tracker, but he'd learned enough to be useful in situations like this. Besides that, the men hadn't been interested in moving carefully — there were broken sticks about every five feet, and bootprints in the soft forest ground.

They followed along, slowing again to a reasonable pace. The chopper was silent, so Reggie didn't want to take the risk of being heard stomping through the woods.

The soldiers' path was nearly straight, only turning around trees and large boulders. It started back uphill after about a hundred feet, and Reggie and Derrick followed until they heard voices up ahead.

"Right there," Reggie said, pointing. "There's a guy to our right. See him?"

"Yeah," Derrick said. "But he's talking. Who's he talking to?"

The man was relieving himself, talking the whole time. Reggie squinted through the trees, trying to see anyone else that might be near the soldier, but saw nothing.

Finally he saw the tiny transmitter on the man's neck.

"They've got a shortwave radio comm," Reggie said. "He's probably talking to the rest of his team, which could be anywhere at this point."

"They wouldn't have split up much, would they?"

"Probably not," Reggie said. "But let's wait a bit, see if he joins up with them again."

The man zipped his pants back up and turned to leave, still talking. Reggie couldn't make out the man's words, but he thought he caught the word 'shadow.'

"We're looking for a cave, right?" he asked.

"The Cave of Shadows, yeah," Derrick said.

"I think he just said 'shadow.'"

"So they *do* know where it is."

"Seems that way. They're probably expecting us to already be there, or to walk up after they get there, which gives us an advantage."

"It does?"

"It does. We're *not* there already, but they don't know that. So they'll either check it out to see if we are, or they'll split up and leave two guys at the entrance to guard while two others go inside to see."

"Got it. So we need to speed up and make sure we're there right behind them, when they first get there."

"Exactly."

Reggie pushed forward again, satisfied that the man had just been left behind the remainder of his group for a minute. They caught up to him when the hill steepened into a nearly vertical cliff.

Reggie held his hand out to stop Derrick, and the man they were following spun around.

Reggie and Derrick hit the ground, landing on their hands to prevent any noise.

"You think he saw us?" Derrick asked.

"No, but I think he knows we're out here. That's good, though. He's scared. Not sure which direction we're coming from."

"And he thinks there's four of us," Derrick added.

*That's true,* Reggie thought. *They would have no reason to suspect that Ben and Joshua were heading back to Philadelphia right now.*

He calculated, trying to determine if they needed to adjust their plan at all to account for the additional 'phantom' members of their group. They already would have the element of surprise, but Reggie wanted to capitalize on that as much as possible.

"You remember the first fight scene in Patriot?"

"The movie?"

"Yeah, with Mel Gibson."

Derrick made a disgusted face.

"But at least you've seen it. Anyway, remember how he pretends he's more than just one person by running around, staying hidden as much as possible? Even set up weapons in different spots on the trail so he could run to another rifle and fire again quickly?"

"Yeah, I remember how Hollywood made that seem realistic."

Reggie chuckled. "Point is, that's what we're going to do. Since they *expect* four people, I say we run in, guns blazing, but keep moving around in different directions so they never really know how many of us there are."

"Got it."

Derrick paused, then tilted his head toward Reggie. "The Patriot was the *best* example you could think of?"

Reggie shrugged. "What? I liked it."

# SIXTY-FOUR

THERE WAS ANOTHER CLEARING AT the top of the small cliff, and there were enough boulders protruding from its face that scaling the cliff was no big deal. The man Reggie and Derrick were following jumped from one to another until he'd reached the top, and Reggie followed suit.

At the top he waited for Derrick, then poked his head up and over the edge to get a good look. The four men were standing together, all facing away from Reggie.

Facing the mouth of a tiny cave.

*The Cave of Shadows.*

"That's got to be it," Reggie whispered.

"It's way too small," Derrick said. "There's no way a man could —"

One of the men, the one who had been leading them, suddenly ducked and walked into the mouth of the cave. He disappeared from view, then Reggie heard him yell out.

"It's a lot bigger inside," the man said. "I'm standing up. And it looks like it goes on for a while."

The cave was situated on the side of another hill, this one taller and steeper than the one Reggie and Derrick had just climbed. He wondered if Lewis had known about the cave from local Indian tribes or if he had discovered it on his own.

"Look," Derrick said, pointing. "That's why Lewis called it Cave of Shadows."

Reggie watched, at first unsure of what Derrick was talking about. Then, after watching the mouth of the cave for a few seconds and the men standing near it, he saw it.

The shadows created by the trees on either side of the clearing seemed to be fighting. They leaned down, their tips almost touching the sides of the cave's small mouth.

"The shadows are pointing to the cave," Derrick said.

"And I'd bet they look like that most days of the year. Fascinating." Once again Reggie was disappointed that he had no time to explore and examine the unique geological features of this place. Once again he was disappointed that he was here to fight these men, not take a leisurely stroll through the woods.

"I should've been a geologist," he whispered.

The leader returned from the cave, holding a lighted flashlight. He flicked it off and waved for the others to join him.

"It keeps going, like I said," the man said. "And they could be in there, even farther down."

Reggie looked at Derrick and raised an eyebrow.

"Johnny, Evans, you stay out here," the man said. "Kalib, you're with me."

Reggie nodded, silently praising the soldier for his decision to take the largest man in the group with him into the cave. He likely wanted to keep the huge beast of a man near him for protection, but Reggie was just glad he wouldn't have to fight him.

Kalib nodded, a slow, arcing thing that swung his head down almost to his chest and then back up. He gripped his rifle, then followed his leader into the cave.

"Now's our chance," Reggie said. "Remember, invoke your inner Mel Gibson."

Derrick smiled, shaking his head. "You want to lose this fight?"

Reggie chuckled and checked his weapons once more, then prepared to stand up. He slid backwards on his toes, then let his feet fall onto one of the boulders below him. Derrick did the same, preparing for their surprise attack.

Just as the men were about to push off the rock and charge up and over the hill, Reggie looked at his partner.

"Here goes nothing," he said.

Derrick shook his head. "No. Here goes *everything*."

Reggie was reminded once again that to the man next to him, this battle was everything. This mission was everything.

Reggie nodded, and crouched down another few inches, ready to pounce.

And that's when he felt the gun against his back.

# SIXTY-FIVE

"MOVE," THE MAN SAID.

REGGIE dared a glance over his shoulder. The man was wearing a black flight suit and carried a large radio on his belt.

*The pilot.*

It was one of the men from the helicopter — they must have been spotted as they snuck by, and this man had followed them all the way here, waiting until the perfect time to spring into action.

And he had, in Reggie's professional opinion, nailed it.

Neither he nor Derrick had been prepared for an ambush.

*But we can adapt.*

Reggie took stock of the situation. Derrick was to his right, and the two goons on The Hawk's team were still standing in front of the cave, watching their leader and the man named Kalib disappear into the mouth of the cavern.

That meant Reggie and Derrick still might have the advantage. There was only *one* man holding a gun to Reggie's back, and though it might mean a bullet through his spine, giving Derrick an opportunity to attack was now the ultimate goal.

He met Derrick's eyes, then he nodded. *Please understand me,* he thought. *I don't want to have to spell it out for you.*

He wanted Derrick to strike the pilot, to knock him back off the hill, or at least to charge ahead and make it obvious to the pilot that they weren't planning on being easy prey.

He saw Derrick tense up, knowing that the man understood. He breathed out, a sigh, feeling a plan start to take shape.

"Over here, Evans!" the pilot suddenly yelled. "Johnny, give me a hand."

The two men near the cave spun around and saw their pilot standing behind two new faces.

Or rather, faces they hadn't seen since Philadelphia.

"They snuck by the chopper down in the valley. I followed them up here. Rodriguez and Swartz are still back there, guarding the bird."

*Great,* Reggie thought. *There are two more at the chopper.*

That made seven men total, to Reggie's count. Enough room in the chopper with a bit to spare.

Evans and Johnny, the younger recruit whom they'd seen relieving himself earlier, jogged over to their spot just over the edge of the steep hill. Evans held his rifle out, pointed directly at Derrick's gut, while Johnny sneered at Reggie.

Reggie recognized him from the alley in Philadelphia.

"Sup, kid," Reggie said.

"Sup yourself. Get up here, asshole."

"Woah, hey, I didn't do anything to you. Yet."

Johnny's sneer only grew. "The Hawk's going to be *very* excited to see you again, Red. He's been talking about you, telling us all about your little escapades together."

"Well he's full of shit, then," Reggie said, stepping up and over the edge of the cliff and onto solid ground. "We never actually served together."

"That's not what he said," Johnny answered. "He said you were one of us, one of the recruits. Said you washed out."

The memory came back to Reggie in a flash. The kid was right, of course, about wanting to be part of The Hawk's newest endeavor. That had been years ago, and Reggie had never regretted 'washing out' for an instant. He'd seen what this group was about, and what they valued, and he'd wanted none of it.

Derrick shot him a glance.

Reggie shrugged. "I told you I knew the guy, back in the day."

"I'll have to hear that story sometime," Derrick said.

"Yeah," Reggie answered. "You'll have to."

Johnny's abrasive voice cut in. "Get moving. Andrews and Kalib are looking for you in there already, so we need to go tell them what we found."

He stopped, then studied Reggie for a moment. "Shame you couldn't cut it, dude. You'd have been a good soldier, but The Hawk says you couldn't hack it."

"Why don't you and me square off and you'll see exactly what I can and can't hack?" Reggie asked.

Johnny turned around and Evans and the pilot pushed their quarry toward the tiny cave.

"How'd you find this place?" Reggie asked, genuinely intrigued. "You don't strike me as the, uh, *intelligent* type."

Johnny didn't answer. The remainder of the walk was silent, save for the pilot's voice cutting through the dusk air, calling in to his bird their discovery. He explained they were all good, and that they'd be hiking back within the hour.

The pilot sounded authoritative to Reggie, and if he had to guess, he suspected the pilot was one of The Hawk's actual team members, while the rest of these men, including the self-declared leader who'd already entered the cave with Kalib, were recruits.

*The same thing I thought I wanted to be, once*, Reggie thought. He shook his head, shuddering. He'd dodged a bullet then, and he was more glad that he'd 'washed out' of The Hawk's killing squad now than he'd ever been.

Reggie's phone rang. *Crap.* The mercenaries hadn't removed either of their phones, and now they were loudly reminded of that fact.

"Answer it," the pilot said. "Put it on speaker. Tell them nothing about where we are. Got it?"

Reggie nodded. "And if I don't follow your orders?"

The pilot turned his handgun down toward the ground — toward Derrick's feet — and fired.

The shot was loud, louder even than Reggie would have expected, and he heard the shot echo around the round bowl of the canyon.

"There's no one out here to hear you die," the pilot said.

It was true, Reggie knew. This was the no-man's land, the border between Glacier National Park to the west and Indian Reservation. He wasn't sure where exactly they were standing, and they may have been on either side of that line. Either way, unless there was an overzealous park ranger or a lost Blackfeet Indian somewhere nearby, they were as remote as any place Reggie had ever been.

The phone rang again, a fifth time. He pulled it out of his pocket, popped his ears, and answered.

"Hey Ben," he said.

# SIXTY-SIX

"WE FIGURED IT OUT, REGGIE," Ben said from the car he and Joshua were in. Joshua was once again driving, and even though Ben preferred to do the driving most of the time when he was with Julie, he was happy for the reprieve.

He'd planned on sleeping a bit, catching up on news from Mr. E if there was any, and getting his thoughts in order for their plan when they would eventually land in Philadelphia.

"— *what out?*" Reggie's voice crackled through the speaker of the phone. Joshua wasn't sure if he and Ben would have cellular service in the rural backcountry of Montana, and he figured there was no way Reggie and Derrick would have any up in the mountains. The goal was to talk fast, to get as much information to Reggie as possible, knowing that the cellular signal would be horrible.

"The clue, Reggie. We figured out the clue."

Reggie said something unintelligible.

"It's a cave, just like we thought. Probably not very big, though. No searches pull anything up, but we think we found a cross-reference."

Again, something unintelligible.

"Okay, so get this," Ben said. "Mr. E pulled up a database and found a contact at this Blackfeet Indian Reservation, who agreed to do a phone consult. He wasn't too happy to hear that Mr. E already had a team on the ground, but… whatever.

"Anyway, he just called and told us that the Blackfeet have been in this area for centuries, and there are three distinct tribes living here together, just like the Cottonwoods. The first clue was a reference to the second, I think."

Joshua glanced at Ben and raised his eyebrows. *Right,* Ben thought, *running out of time.* He knew the phone's connection on either end could be precariously close to cutting out.

"Sorry. So there's a word that Lewis used in one of his journals — one of the known journals. It's a Blackfeet word, but it was obviously spelled wrong and no one really knew what it was referring to. But when Mr. E asked the guy about the 'Cave of Shadows,' he said he didn't know. But he *did* know this word that Lewis had written. It means 'Shadow' in his native tongue.

"Apparently the Blackfeet Indians weren't completely hostile to Lewis, like history suggests. One of them may have escorted Lewis to the cave. It's in a valley, and they call the valley 'Bowl of Shadows.'"

Ben waited, both wanting to make sure Reggie was still on the other end of the line and wanting to back in the importance of his discovery just a bit. When Mr. E had called them to recap his conversation, he'd assured Ben and Joshua that his contact at the reservation had no idea what they were looking for, and no idea that there was another, more dangerous, team out there looking as well.

They had no interest in upsetting a reservation, a long history of Americans living peacefully in Montana, as it would be a political and media nightmare, even if they did find something in those hills.

Ben was appreciative of this, as was Joshua. The fewer interested parties, the better.

The phone crackled.

"Hello?" Ben asked. "Reggie, can you hear —"

"— her. Find Julie, Ben. Get —"

The signal was lost. The phone died in Ben's hand.

Joshua looked over at Ben. "Think he got the message?"

"No idea. But that was a weird thing to say, right? I already know what we're supposed to do, why remind us again?"

Joshua shrugged. "Beats me. Maybe they're stuck somewhere, don't expect to get out. Or…"

He looked over at Ben.

"You think they ran into Ravenshadow?"

# SIXTY-SEVEN

THE CAVE WAS COOL, AND just like the man had said, it opened up into a surprisingly large cavern once they were inside. Reggie blinked a few times until his eyes adjusted.

Kalib and his leader were there, waiting for them. They each wore a headlamp, and Kalib had either never been taught the etiquette of not shining a light directly into someone's eyes or he assumed he didn't care.

"You wanna drop the light, pal?" Reggie asked.

Kalib glared at him. Or he didn't — Reggie couldn't see his face. The light, however, stayed in his eyes.

"You're the great Gareth Red," the leader said. "My name is Phillip Mance. Welcome to Ravenshadow."

"I'm not in your shitty club, asshat," Reggie said. "And neither is my friend, here."

"Right. Don't worry — I hear you couldn't make it in the first time you tried, so we're not recruiting you once again. But you *are* guests of ours for the time being, so we should get to know each other."

"I'm an open book."

"Thanks, but I'm really interested in that last clue. 'Within the silver lies the gold?' You know anything about that?"

"I know it's a crappy clue," Reggie said. "I thought treasure hunting was going to be a bit more fun."

"So did I," Mance said. "But here we are. What about your FBI pal? Roger Derrick, correct?"

Derrick nodded. "Your guess is as good as mine."

"Is it though? The Hawk tells me you've been spying on Ms.

Johansson for some time. Says you're obsessed with this treasure, even more than she is."

"Well I'm not the one lying on national television and manipulating the media to get my message out there, am I?"

Mance smiled, as if holding back laughter. Reggie felt a bit more relaxed when he saw this. *Apparently they're not as blindly loyal to their benefactor as they are to their boss.*

"She's a nutcase, I'll give you that," Mance said. "But we still have a job to do. She says there's something here. Something we need, and it's our job to find it."

"Well let's look around. I'm sure Meriwether Lewis wouldn't be terribly creative about his final hiding spot."

"We already have *looked around,*" Kalib said. Again with the headlamp.

"Christ, you lug. Get that out of my eyes."

Kalib swung the headlamp down and Reggie felt a brief sense of victory.

"It's not here. There's nothing here. It's just a cave that goes that way —" he pointed behind Kalib "— for about thirty feet. Smashes down to a crawl space toward the end, then nothing. Just stops."

"Any offshoots?" the pilot, still holding his gun against Reggie's back, asked.

Mance shook his head. "Nope, nothing. It's just a crooked tube. Completely empty."

Reggie looked around, now that his eyes — once again — had adjusted. Mance seemed to be telling the truth. There was nothing in sight but curved rock, not even any interesting formations on the floor or ceiling of the cavern. It would make a good shelter for someone traveling over the mountains, but besides that there was nothing remarkable about it.

"Well, you can't go back empty handed," Reggie said. "What's the plan? You think The Hawk's going to just let you into Ravenshadow without Daris' treasure?"

"No," the pilot said. "But we have you. That'll be enough of a prize."

"Will it, though?"

Mance seemed perturbed at this suggestion, frustrated. Reggie was right. They were useless to The Hawk if they didn't deliver, and grabbing a couple rogue treasure hunters wasn't going to do him any good.

Kalib's light bounced around on his head as he did a quick turn, looking around the cavern. Reggie followed the bright beam, watching where it landed on the walls and floor of the cavern. He had to admit, the place did seem completely devoid of anything. Including treasure.

He tracked Kalib's light in a full circle, watching it come back to its previous location, pointing straight —

He stopped. Turned his head slightly.

Then he brought his eyes up to Mance. Had the man seen Reggie? He couldn't be sure.

"Doesn't look like you've got any other choice, then," Reggie said. He turned around to face the pilot and his gun. "Should we all take a little fly? Head back to Philly?"

"Wait," Mance said. Reggie closed his eyes. "You know something. What did you just see?"

He shook his head. "What the hell are talking —" the butt of Kalib's rifle slammed into Reggie's stomach. He fell to the floor, gasping in pain. Kalib had hardly moved, using only the strength in his arms and hands to jam the gun toward Reggie. If he'd been more wound up, or had decided to really get his back into it, Reggie might now have a serious problem.

*I was right not to want to fight this brute,* he thought.

He heaved for a moment, then caught his balance. He stood up, marching up to the taller man. "Do that again, and you're going to find yourself —"

"Enough," Mance said. "Kalib, step back. Let the man talk."

Reggie nodded at Mance.

"Time to start talking, or it's time for us to start shooting. Don't forget your place here, Red. We don't need any prisoners, and we certainly don't need *two.*"

"Right," Reggie said. "Okay, yeah, it's nothing. I just saw something over here." He pointed to his left, next to Kalib's right arm. "On the wall. Frankenstein, you mind?"

Kalib held the light directly in Reggie's eyes for a second, then swung it to his right, pointing it at the wall. The cavern's wall lit up in white light, and Reggie saw it again.

"Looks like a tiny vein of silver," Reggie said. "That's all."

Mance walked over to it. "Yeah, I think it is. 'Within the silver lies the gold.' Evans, bring me that —"

Evans was already in motion, and he now wielded a giant sledgehammer. Reggie had to duck to dodge the swinging hammer as Evans brought it down onto the wall of the cavern.

*Crack!* The hammer broke a large chunk of rock off the wall.

"Stop!" Reggie yelled. "What the *hell* do you think you're going?"

Evans raised the hammer again.

"Seriously," Derrick said. "You think it's *in* the wall?"

"That's the clue, isn't it?" Mance asked. "That's what it says."

"Really?" the pilot asked. "'The treasure is *in* the wall?' I don't remember reading that."

Reggie looked at the pilot. *At least we've got one guy on our side. Sort of.*

The pilot continued. "How would Lewis get it there? *Inside* the wall of the cave? Stick it in a hole in the wall and then plaster it up with more rock?"

Mance stared at the pilot for a long moment, and Kalib and the others looked around at each other.

*Are these idiots really that thick? Or do they not believe him?*

Reggie waited, trying to see the recognition dawning in their eyes. Lewis alone, or even with the help of the other three men he was traveling with, would not have been able to put anything behind a solid wall of rock.

"Yeah," Mance said. "You're right."

"No shit, Sherlock," Reggie said.

Kalib moved toward Reggie again, raising the butt of his rifle, but Mance stepped in. "No," he said. "We might need him. The Hawk wanted us to bring them back, remember?"

Kalib snorted, the giant of a man obviously disgusted. Reggie listened to Mance's words, trying to figure out why they'd struck him as odd.

Then it hit him.

He thought about the helicopter. The bird was rated for no more than 8-9 people, depending on gear, and The Hawk's team alone was seven men.

*Seven men... plus our four.*

Reggie, Derrick, Ben, and Joshua.

*That's too many.*

Reggie's eyes widened a bit as he stared up at Kalib, noticing the man's own eyes growing dark as they slid shut.

In all Reggie's years of training, nothing but experience had taught him his most-prized skill: the ability to anticipate, with near dead-accuracy, what another man was about to do.

Kalib's rifle began moving, toward the man's other hand. He changed his grip on it, so that instead of the club it had been before, it was now, once again, the type of weapon it had been designed to be.

*He's going to shoot Derrick*, Reggie realized.

There wasn't enough room in the chopper for the men, whatever treasure they might find or a small sample of it, *and* the four-man team they were sent out to intercept.

Two of them would have to be killed.

Reggie wasn't sure why, but Mance had told Kalib that The Hawk wanted *him*. Vicente Garza needed him alive.

"Yeah, boss," Kalib said. "But we don't need *him*."

The rifle swung around in a quick arc and came to rest pointed directly at Derrick. He pulled the trigger.

# SIXTY-EIGHT

REGGIE WAS ALREADY IN MOTION, and he reached the huge man just before the explosion. He threw himself directly into his chest, aiming 'for the numbers' just like his high-school football coach had taught him. His forehead struck at the same moment he heard the gunshot.

It was absolutely deafening, and Reggie suddenly realized that an assault rifle firing in a closed, reverberating space such as this might *actually* make him deaf, but it was a fleeting thought. He was still moving forward, Kalib's thick body coming with him. He didn't know if the tackle would be enough to have redirected the gunshot, but he didn't care.

He'd take this man down and *then* figure out what to do next.

The mistake he'd made was that he hadn't been fully aware of his surroundings.

The man behind him, Evans, had casually walked over to Reggie and stuck the end of his rifle into his back. Reggie felt the cold, hard steel barrel and immediately put his hands up.

Kalib shifted, pushing Reggie off him like he was nothing more than an annoying puppy, and stood up. He yanked Reggie's outstretched arm and pulled him to his feet, and Reggie turned around to see what had transpired during his fight with the bear.

All five of the soldiers had their weapons drawn, three of them on Reggie and two of them on Derrick.

Derrick, too, had his hands up.

Reggie looked at the FBI agent and shrugged. "Sorry, man. Did my best."

"It was enough to not get me shot," he said.

"There's still time for that," Mance said. "But not here. We've got plenty of space in the bird for both of you, considering your friends are probably already heading back to Philadelphia right now."

Reggie and Derrick exchanged glances.

"Yeah, The Hawk told us all about it," Mance said. "Said you four would probably split up, but if not, get rid of the baggage." He looked at Derrick. "This guy and your leader, the Jefferson guy."

*Joshua and Derrick*, Reggie thought. *Those are the two 'loose ends,' according to Garza.*

"But he's been working on some interesting tech back in Philly," Mance continued. "I'd bet he could use a few more subjects to test on."

"There's nothing here, Mance," the pilot said. "We're wasting time. Let's get back."

Mance nodded. "Yeah, sounds good. Get these guys back to the chopper. Bird's up in ten."

The pilot rolled his eyes, obviously annoyed with the less-experienced leader's gross misinterpretation at how quickly they'd be able to get back down to the valley and how fast the pilot would be able to spin up the chopper.

Reggie looked once more at the thin, silvery vein that ran along the length of the tiny cavern. He wasn't sure why, but he knew there was more to the story than what the mercenaries believed.

*Not now*, he reminded himself. *We have information we can use, if need be. Not the right time to waste that.*

Derrick was watching Reggie's face, and Reggie nodded to him. The men understood each other, and Reggie was glad Derrick felt the same way. They needed to get back to Philadelphia and try to reach Ben and Joshua before they found Julie.

They were walking into a trap.

# SIXTY-NINE

"WE'RE HERE," BEN SAID INTO the cellphone. "You got any leads?"

Mr. E's voice spoke back through the connection. "*Maybe. There are a lot of buildings large enough to be considered a 'gymnasium,' but without more time to do a cross-referenced between with existing buildings and known addresses, it is going to be questionable whether these four are worth investigating at all.*"

"Of course they're worth investigating," Ben said. "Julie's in one of them."

He knew what his benefactor meant, however. *Julie is in one of them, and if we don't have a* solid *lead, there may not have enough time to search all of them.*

Joshua looked at Ben, his eyes questioning.

Ben nodded. "Four."

Joshua remained stoic, but Ben knew what he was thinking. The exact same thing Ben was thinking.

"We have to narrow it down," Ben said. "Is there anything else you can tell us?"

"*No, unfortunately,*" Mr. E said. "*There is not any more information to go on. However, if there is anything else you can tell* me*, perhaps I can —*"

"No, you know it all already. She just blurted it out, 'we're here, right across from the Rittenhouse.'"

Besides the Rittenhouse Square the hotel sat on, the hotel was the only thing in Philadelphia that carried the name 'Rittenhouse.' There was nothing else Julie could have meant.

They had landed an hour ago, but it had taken that long to get from the airport to the vehicle they'd rented and then through downtown traffic to the Rittenhouse. Joshua and Ben were sitting in the lobby once again, but this time around Ben wasn't admiring any of the charming decor.

He wasn't even looking at the bar. He wanted a drink, but he knew a drink was a reward. It was something to enjoy after a victory, and besides figuring out the clues back in Montana, he hadn't had any victories in quite some time.

"She's got to be close by, Ben," Joshua said.

Ben sighed, then put the phone up to his ear. "Give us an order of most-likely guesses, then," he said. "Top candidate first."

The man on the other end paused, then spoke. "*Okay, I will try. First, there is a white building on the corner of Rittenhouse Square and 18th.*"

Joshua was listening in, his own phone on and opened to an overhead map view of the square. He shook his head. "No, that's not it. There's no view from here. Julie said 'here, right across…' I think she meant she saw the Rittenhouse somehow, like maybe out of a window. There are too many tall buildings blocking anything on that corner."

Ben waited for Mr. E to give them his next option. *'Okay, perhaps the next one is on Locust Street, near 20th.'*

Joshua scrolled around on the map, finding this location. "Could be. Doesn't look like this map's been updated, but there would be a view of the hotel from there. I'll mark it, and we can check it out. Anything else?"

*"The last two are on 19th Street. One at Sansom Street and one on Chestnut."*

"Got it," Ben said. "Stay close; we'll check it out." He was about to hang up, then added, "how's your wife?"

*"She is well. Recovered from her trip to Australia, and she wishes she could join you all now. I have been keeping her abreast of the situation, and she is doing what she can from here."*

Ben nodded. Mrs. E was every bit as enigmatic as her husband, yet the two seemed oddly different for a husband-wife pair. Where Mr. E seemed frail, almost sickly, Mrs. E was a large, confident woman, equally trained in martial arts and weaponry. She had been a valuable asset in Antarctica, and Ben was disappointed she hadn't been able to join them on this excursion. Mr. E couldn't have known, however, what they were getting themselves into, so sending his wife to track down a pawnbroker in Australia had hardly been a strange errand.

She would be tearing her hair out trying to help, Ben knew. Probably fiddling with electronics and communications equipment she didn't understand, getting in the way of the contractors as they tried to finish their project at Ben's cabin. She was more useful in the field, but it was probably too late to send her to Philadelphia — she would arrive the next day, long after the action had ended.

He hoped.

If there was going to be action, he wanted it over quickly, and in his favor. Julie needed him, and he intended to find her and bring justice to the men who'd taken her. There were no exceptions, and there was nothing any of them could say to change his mind. They were all dead men walking.

"You ready?" Joshua asked.

Ben nodded, standing up. He felt for the pistol he wore in his belt, tucked beneath his shirt. He wasn't sure of the hotel's policy on weapons — or the city's in general, but regardless he didn't need to waste time answering questions and digging out his permit. There was enough attention on the area already, with the shooting and 'robbery' that had taken place earlier that day at the yogurt shop.

Even now the streets were blocked in two directions, and traffic and onlookers had piled up where the police and SWAT teams were milling about, lights flashing. He looked out the hotel lobby's windows, seeing the reflections of the bright police lights from around the block.

"Think they'll figure it out?" Ben asked.

"The shooting?" Joshua asked. "Yeah, they usually do. They'll at least figure out it wasn't about robbing a yogurt parlor. But they'll take weeks — maybe months — to get to that conclusion."

"Let's hope the yogurt shop guy doesn't speed things along," Ben said, knowing that the longer the police stayed busy with the shooting, the more time he and Joshua had to find Julie.

"He's in shock," Joshua said. "First thing he'll do when he snaps out of it in a few days is call in his insurance policy. That'll keep him *really* tied up for the next few years."

Ben smiled and nodded as they walked out the front of the hotel, across the street now from Rittenhouse Square. He looked both directions, north and south, and turned right. The city was still very much alive, even though night had fallen over the historic town. The square and the great buildings standing over it were lit, thousands of multi-colored twinkles illuminating the night sky.

"Locust Street, right?" he asked.

"Yes, just past 20th. Let's hustle — it's only getting later."

# SEVENTY

"WE'RE GOING THE WRONG WAY," Ben said, stopping in the middle of the sidewalk."

"Ben, what are you talking about?" Joshua asked. He whirled around, clearly not wanting to slow down. "We're almost there. Locust Street is right up —"

"No," Ben said, shaking his head. "It's not — that's not the place."

"How do you know?"

"Hear me out," he answered. "He said there was one on *Chestnut* Street, right?"

Joshua nodded.

"Chestnut Street is the same street the APS building is on."

"Well, that block anyway."

"Yeah, but it's basically Chestnut Street. And Independence Hall, *and* the Liberty Bell, *and* Old City Hall."

"You sound like Reggie. When did you pick up all the history tidbits?"

"I read the brief."

Joshua's eyebrows rose.

"What? I know how to *read*, Jefferson."

Joshua grinned, just a corner of his mouth lifting up, then it returned to its comfortable place as a single, unreadable line. "So what? All those historic landmarks, but we're looking for a gym."

"No, we're looking for where Julie's being held. She *said* it was a gym, but I'm guessing she hasn't been able explore it much."

"So you think she's being held in a landmark? An historic site?"

"No, not necessarily, but —" Ben started the other direction, walking back up toward the Rittenhouse hotel that sprawled above them on their left. "Let's walk and talk. Or jog. We need to hurry."

"Ben…"

"I'm serious about this. I think I'm on to something, just hear me out."

"Fine," Joshua said, starting to catch up to Ben. "But hurry."

"Daris Johansson hired The Hawk, so it's reasonable to assume that he's working out of her facilities. It's a security company first and foremost, right?"

"Right."

Ben turned the corner and started up West Rittenhouse Square, heading north, retracing the steps they'd just taken fifteen minutes earlier.

"So if he's at *her* facilities, we have to think like *her*. Maybe he told her to give him some space to work, space for his men. But *she's* the one footing the bill. The organization."

"So the American Philosophical Society is probably the owner of the building?"

"*Exactly.* And if I was Daris, and I was as into history and conspiracy theories as she is, I'd probably *love* the significance of putting my facilities on the same street as all those other national landmarks."

Joshua was striding forward next to Ben, now, nodding along. "Hmm," he said. "Makes sense."

"It'll make even more sense when we see it," Ben said.

"You're confident about this."

"It's *right*, Joshua. I'm telling you." Still, Ben pulled out his phone once again and dialed Mr. E's secured line. The man answered in two rings.

*"What have you found?"* Mr. E asked.

"Can you run a search for me?"

*"I still am. Right now I've built up the shortlist to eighteen sites, all buildings that have the characteristics you've requested, and —"*

"Those aren't it," Ben said, interrupting. "It's the one on Chestnut Street."

*"Harvey, are you sure? How do you —"*

"What information on the building can you see?"

*"Well, I… let me see. There is not much, really. Ownership changed hands a few times in the past decade, and — Harvey, these are public records, so I highly doubt —"*

Mr. E's voice cut off.

"You there?" Ben asked.

*"Just a moment. I am pulling up a city zoning map, and superim-posing the Google Map on top, and…"*

"What?" Ben asked. He started to feel excited, his heart rate elevat-ing. *This is it,* he thought. *I know it.*

The Rittenhouse loomed over them to their left, the entrance to the great hotel dwarfed by the building above it, and the Rittenhouse Square sprawled out to their right. Ben and Joshua continued heading due north, following West Rittenhouse Street toward Chestnut.

All around him buildings soared upward into the sky. He had the brief feeling of nostalgia, wondering how the skyline of this great old American city had looked back when horse-drawn carts filled the city streets instead of commuter vehicles and taxicabs. The 'large' buildings would have been minuscule compared to today's architectural behe-moths, but they would have had a beauty to them all their own, their hand-crafted designs each taking on the life of their designers.

He wanted to stop, to close his eyes and just take it in and imagine, but he didn't. Instead, he set his eyes on the target, knowing that any wasted time was time ticking off an invisible clock.

*And when the clock gets to zero…*

*"Okay,"* Mr. E's voice said, puncturing the night air as they walked. Ben involuntarily increased his pace, and Joshua followed suit. *"I have the records here. It appears as though this building sat abandoned for many years, as it was originally a residential home that nows sits on land that is now zoned for commercial. Three years ago it was purchased by a DJ Hold-ings, Inc."*

"Daris Johansson," Joshua said.

*"It must be,"* Mr. E said. *"But there is no proof of that here. The building, however, does seem to have some historical significance, as it was never torn down and never sold for less than a quarter of a million dollars."*

"That doesn't sound like much in this city," Ben said.

*"Well, I am including the entire sales history that has been recorded,"* Mr. E said. *"Starting around the turn of last century."*

Joshua whistled. "Okay, that changes things. This place was worth that much in the *1900's?*"

*"It appears so. Further, the house was immediately re-zoned and then construction permits were taken out upon the purchase. An extensive reno-vation, judging by the number of permits pulled."*

"Get information on those permits," Joshua said.

*"Yes, Mrs. E is already working on that,"* the man said. *"But I do not think it will be necessary."*

"You don't?" Ben asked.

"*No. I am seeing that there was another bid put in to the city for the property, just before DJ Holdings, Inc. closed on it.*"

"Popular place."

"*No, I do not believe the property itself was the reason. The bid put in was for half a million more than the selling price, and it was placed by the APS.*"

Ben looked at Joshua, who was already staring at him, and both men broke into a run.

# SEVENTY-ONE

"THAT'S THE PLACE," JOSHUA WHISPERED. "Set back a bit, off the street."

Both men were crouched down behind a low, crumbling brick wall, peering over the edge at the alleyway that led to the building.

Joshua triple-checked his phone, then nodded. "Yeah, that's it, for sure."

"You see any bad guys?" Ben asked.

"No, but we're not going to from here. If they're guarding the place on the outside, we need to get up the alley and do a perimeter check."

"We don't have time for that," Ben said. "Julie's *in* there, and —"

"We *think* Julie's in there. Don't forget we've got plenty of other places on the map that we're supposed to check."

"She's in there," Ben said again. "Come on."

Ben took off in a jog, running straight up the alley and toward the short, whitish building standing at the end of it. If the place had ever been historically important, it didn't show that now.

The 'house,' as Mr. E had called it, looked nothing like anything Ben would ever want to live in. A row of blacked-out rectangular windows spread along the length of the wall, but the rest of the wall was completely devoid of noticeable features. The plain, boring white-wash had long since faded, and coupled with the dim hue of the nearby streetlight, the wall seemed to be decrepit, yellowed with age.

Ben reached the end of the alleyway and saw that there was another alley — a narrow street, really — that stretched left and right, connecting Chestnut Street to the south with whatever street lay to the north.

Joshua caught up. "Hey man, at least give me a warning when you're going to run like that. We get seen by The Hawk's group and we're dead."

"Fine," Ben said. "Warning."

He darted out again, this time to the right — south — toward Chestnut Street. He heard Joshua groan from somewhere behind him, but the man's footfalls echoed off the old wall and into Ben's ears.

When he reached Chestnut Street, he slowed down and let the adrenaline subside. Though he knew from personal experience that the Ravenshadow men were not afraid to start shooting in public — in broad daylight for that matter — he was standing in the midst of throngs of late-evening tourists and pedestrians. Dogs were being walked on leashes, and families bounded down the great old avenue in both directions.

"This is it," Ben said. "The front of the 'house.'"

The front of the house looked exactly the same as the side, except it was very narrow and had a door on it.

"Kind of an eyesore," Joshua said.

"Yeah, no joke."

The house, unassuming as it was, was certainly large enough to contain a gymnasium. The width of it would have been perfect, and the length was longer even than a typical school basketball gym.

"This could be it," Joshua said.

"This *is* it," Ben responded. "Should we knock?"

Joshua didn't even grant Ben a response. Instead, he continued walking around the facility, just as he'd told Ben they should do.

Ben was growing anxious, feeling strongly that they were wasting time, but he followed behind Joshua anyway. The man *did* know what he was doing, Ben realized. Joshua Jefferson had once been a member of a security team not unlike Ravenshadow. They had met in the Amazon Rainforest, but Ben imagined that Joshua was not unfamiliar with urban reconnaissance either.

Joshua, now out of the prying eyes of the public passersby on Chestnut Street, held his pistol out in front of him, two hands, at the ready. He walked slowly, purposefully, not allowing his steps to be heard by even Ben, walking closely behind.

"Move up to the corner," Joshua whispered. "Let's see if there's a back door."

Ben nodded, knowing Joshua couldn't see him, but walked past his leader and toward the corner of the building. He waited at the edge of it, unsure of what to do next.

It was not often Ben felt out of his element. He enjoyed the outdoors, and nature, and had decided long ago to spend as much time as possible within it. He'd bought the cabin and the land it was on in Alaska, knowing that it would be something he'd hold onto forever, a personal retreat he could always return to to recharge and rejuvenate.

And then Julie came along, and he found himself thrown into a completely different world. It wasn't her fault, but there was an aspect to it all that caused Ben to wonder if it would be different if they'd never met. He wasn't about to give her up, but there were times in their relationship when the tension between loving the woman who'd promised her life to him and his desire to hide away in the cabin forever came to a head.

Now, he was feeling the pressure of being exposed and in an environment he didn't understand and feel comfortable in, and knowing that it was all to get Julie back.

He sucked in a breath, letting it fill his lungs and push his chest out. He needed strength now, especially if they were going in and fighting the Ravenshadow team undermanned.

"See anything?" Joshua whispered.

Ben shook his head. "Not without jumping out there, but I do think there's a door." A single step lay halfway down the alley, adjoined to the back of the building.

"Looks that way."

Ben froze. "This is it, Joshua. I'm positive."

"How can you tell?"

Ben pointed across the alley, at the building *across* from the one they were currently standing behind. He waited for Joshua to follow his outstretched arm, to see what Ben had seen.

About eight feet up, on the corner of the building, sat a mounted surveillance camera.

Pointed directly at them.

# SEVENTY-TWO

JULIE'S ARMS WERE NEARLY BLEEDING where the zip ties had been forced back onto her skin. The second time her hands had been tied was worse than the first — the bonds were much tighter, pulled through a few more clicks than they had before, and the man had even gone to the trouble of finding exactly where the previous zip ties had been and placed the new ones right on top. The deep red lines on her wrists made this an easy thing to do.

She was tired, and at the same time feeling the same way she felt when she overslept. She guess she'd been here almost two days now, or something like that, but she couldn't be sure of how long it really was.

Or what time of day it was. The blacked-out windows offered no information. No sunlight — or moonlight — cast its glow through them, and if not for the blinding lights on the ceiling of the gym that had been on for an hour or so, she would still be in the dark.

Men were milling about, working on tasks she neither understood nor cared to understand. She'd long since given up trying to gather information, no longer believing she could get an edge over The Hawk and his team.

If she was going to make it out of here alive, it would be because of Ben and the rest of the group.

She heard commotion behind her. Suddenly a few men's voices shouted, and a crashing sound — a door, far away — slammed.

She tried to turn her head, but her neck wouldn't lend her the range of motion. Everything felt tight, and even her toes seemed to be disconnected from the rest of her body.

She thought about screaming, but knew it was useless. *What would it accomplish? No one out there is going to be able to get in here unless they take out all of Vicente Garza's men.*

And there were a lot of men.

In the time Julie had been tied to the chair, the one piece of information she *had* been able to gather was that there were between ten and fifteen men. Some looked similar, or they were the same man and she just hadn't recognized them. Some may not have even come into the gym at all, staying somewhere else on the premises. She'd overheard that some of the men weren't really Ravenshadow but recruits hoping to be chosen.

Her team was four, not including herself, and even though she knew Joshua and Reggie were more than capable shots, when bullets started to fly there was no telling what the outcome would be.

It was very likely that any engagement between the forces would end horribly for Julie's side.

*Had they gotten reinforcements somehow?*

Mrs. E was, to her knowledge, staying in Alaska, to help with communications and research, and to provide support for her husband. Derrick, the FBI man, may have been able to call something in, but he'd seemed to be alone the entire time they were together and she had a feeling that sending in a team of agents was a long shot.

The commotion ended, and she sat still, waiting, trying to hear more.

Footsteps.

Multiple people — maybe five?

The gym's door opened behind her, and she tensed up.

*They're coming in here.*

She waited, listening. The footsteps did indeed begin their steady march into the room. Louder with each step. One of the sets seemed to be dragging a bit. Another seemed disjointed, the rhythm of them not matching up with the others.

"Ms. Richardson," a man's voice said. *The Hawk.* "Someone's here to see you."

# SEVENTY-THREE

*THERE SHE IS,* BEN THOUGHT. *She's right there. Sitting in the chair. In the middle of the —*

"Ms. Richardson," the man announced as he stepped into the room. "Someone's here to see you."

"Listen, bastard," Ben growled. "Let her go and I won't —"

A rifle butt smashed into his hip, and felt the searing flare of pain shoot up his right side. The rifle had hit bone, and it was bound to leave a nasty bruise.

But he wasn't dead, and he still had a mission. He shoved sideways, forcing his large frame into the man who had hit him. He caught him off guard, and the soldier flew backwards, into another man he'd entered with.

Another rifle butt crushed his left knee, and he went down. Before he could fall all the way to the floor, however, he felt himself lifted up from behind. He balanced on one foot, allowing the man behind him to help.

Then the man behind him socked his ear with a hard fist, and Ben fell again.

This time, no one offered their help. Joshua was being held tight by three other men, and a fourth was pointing his rifle at his gut.

Ben scowled at the man who'd smacked him, and he lay on the floor, looking up.

"B — Ben? Is that you?" Julie's voice, cracked and strained, reached his ears.

It gave him strength. His knee wasn't broken, and he pulled

himself up. He'd limp for a time, and his hip was going to need a serious bag of ice, but again — he was alive.

*As long as I'm alive.*

He didn't hesitate. As soon as he felt the man's hand on his shoulder once again, he crouched with his good leg and slammed upward and back as hard as he could. The soldier behind him yelped in pain, but his voice in Ben's ears was drowned out by the sound of his nose being crushed.

*And to think, that was only with one leg.*

The man fell, but there were two more on him.

"Enough!" The Hawk yelled. "She'll be here soon, and we need to be ready."

*Daris Johansson,* Ben thought. *That's who he's talking about.*

He looked at Joshua, but the man's expression was unreadable.

*We need a plan. We need* something.

He wondered where Reggie and Derrick were, and if they were having any luck finding the treasure.

"Boss, I have the chopper inbound."

"We have clearance, right?" The Hawk asked.

"Yes sir, it's been clocked and approved. Private chopper, landing for 'emergency refueling' at the hospital next door."

*So* that's *what Daris wanted with this place,* he thought. He wondered what the original 'house' was, and what it had looked like before Daris had torn it apart. She'd replaced it with this monstrosity, and if not for her other crimes, Ben would have still hated her for it.

The 'gym' they were in now wasn't really a gym, but it had some of the same markings. Tall, brick walls on four sides and a wooden floor. It could have easily been a simple warehouse or storage building, but the huge square fluorescent lights on the ceiling gave the entire place very much of a 'gymnasium' feel.

He heard the sound of a helicopter, undoubtedly the same chopper the man in front of Vicente Garza had referenced.

The men seemed to hear it as well, and they all stopped and listened for a moment.

"Won't be long now," The Hawk said. He clapped. "Everyone get to work. I want to be ready when she walks in that door."

Ben bristled. They were staging something in here, that's why Julie was sitting in the middle of the room.

And Ben was supposed to be one of the audience members for this show.

# SEVENTY-FOUR

REGGIE COULDN'T SEE A THING. A thick black covering had been slipped over his head as soon as he was inside the chopper, and it still hadn't been removed. Aside from knowing they were somewhere in Philadelphia, he had no idea where exactly he and Derrick were being taken.

The chopper descended, and before the struts had touched down he was being shoved out an open door, a man on either side of him holding his arms down. He could only assume Derrick was enjoying the same treatment, but he wasn't concerned with the other man at this point.

This whole mission had gone south. A complete failure. He wasn't sure if they could salvage any of it, but he knew if any part of it *could* be salvaged, it was the part about rescuing Julie.

"Stairs," one of the men said, and it was barely enough time before Reggie felt the floor give out, the first of a set of stairs beginning under his feet. He followed them down, the men yanking him back and forth as they jangled around in the stairwell, and he heard Derrick grunt as he slammed up against a wall just behind him.

*Good,* he thought. *At least they're keeping us together.*

The stairs ended and he felt the movement of air outside his hot, stuffy head covering. *We're outside.*

The feeling was short lived, and he was soon thrust into an open door and up another short set of stairs.

He heard people inside, walking and talking. The room felt large, cavernous even. Derrick entered behind him, and Reggie heard the rest of the team that had captured him step up into the room as well.

His covering was violently pulled from his head, and the shock of it caused his head to loll. The bright lights were the next surprise, and he blinked, squeezing his eyes shut tightly. When he opened them, his heart sank.

Julie was there, front and center in the room. The wooden floors and bright lights told him immediately where he was: *this is the gym*, he thought. *This is The Hawk's facility.*

But there was more. Ben and Joshua were here as well.

Ben looked like he'd already been in a fight — and lost — as he was scratched, bruised, and his ear was trickling blood. He was being held by two men who looked both pissed that they'd pulled guard duty and a bit frightened that their loose cannon of a prisoner might explode any second.

*Be afraid*, Reggie thought. *Be very afraid.* He eyed the men holding Ben and then shook his head.

Joshua was also being held, but it was at gunpoint. Two men had rifles pointed at him, and he seemed fine, but visibly distraught.

Reggie knew the feeling. *Yeah, buddy. We failed.*

Vicente Garza's arms spread wide. "Gareth, kind of you to join us! I have to admit, I was not expecting you this early. We thought we were preparing for the arrival of our current benefactor."

"Yeah?" Reggie shot back. "I'm excited to see that b —"

"Knock it off, Red. You and I both know your mouth was far bigger than your skill set. If that wasn't true, you wouldn't be standing right here, right now. Would you?"

Reggie didn't respond. His nostrils flared, his eyes darting back and forth from one man to the next. Far too many to take, and especially without their weapons.

He saw the handguns, two of them, sitting on a crate that had been wheeled in using an industrial forklift. The lift sat in the corner of the room, the crate resting on the forks themselves.

Mance appeared by Reggie's side, then he walked over to the crate and placed his and Derrick's 9mm on the top of it. "This the delivery, boss?"

The Hawk whirled around and glared at Mance. "You will refer to me as 'The Hawk,' or Garza, until you have been officially hired."

Reggie felt the intensity ratchet up in the room. *This is familiar*, he thought. *This is how the man runs his team.* Reggie recognized the sharp, pointed way Garza had dressed the man down, using only a few words. Mance's demeanor immediately changed, suddenly seeming to realize the same thing Reggie already knew.

*You didn't find the treasure, idiot*, Reggie thought.

The Hawk walked over to Mance and the crate and forklift. "Son, I expected you to deliver something to me. *Not* these two men."

"We — we couldn't find it, sir — I mean The Hawk."

Garza stared at Mance. "You failed. Failure in this organization is unacceptable. You will be punished, but I need you and the rest of the recruits until after the presentation is completed."

Mance gulped, the fear in his eyes almost comical to Reggie. *Almost.*

The Hawk waved for two of his men to join him and the three of them —including Mance — began stripping the planks of wood from the sides of the crate. Reggie watched with interest as the package appeared within the shipping crate. One of the men slid the plywood cover off, balancing the four handguns on it and carrying it over to another side of the room.

Reggie watched him place the lid of the crate and the weapons on the floor near a rolling cart. Besides the cart, forklift, and package, there was no furniture in the room.

*And the chair.*

Reggie shuddered as he realized he'd nearly forgotten Julie. He turned to look at her, and was shocked to see that she was already staring at him. She had no interest in Mance and the two soldiers' attempt at freeing the package.

He locked eyes with her.

*Please.*

He knew what she was asking.

*Please help.*

He knew she would be wanting him to not help her, but to help Ben. She would be begging for his life before her own.

He felt his heart tear. He'd loved someone like this once, and it had been the most painful experience of his life.

This, compared to that, was nothing.

The realization dawned on him.

*No matter what happens to me now, it can't be as bad as that.*

Reggie felt the strange thought giving him strength. He let it build inside him to an intensity, a *rage,* that he could use. He'd used this same rage in Antarctica, killing a man with nothing more than his bare hands and the tiny latch on his watch.

He knew now.

Whatever else happened here today, men would die.

# SEVENTY-FIVE

FOR THE FIRST TIME IN nearly two days, they were all here together again. But Julie felt no happiness, no satisfaction. She wasn't excited, and she wasn't joyous at their reunion.

This was *bad,* and it was quickly getting worse. The Hawk had them — all of them — where he wanted them, and she knew, vaguely, how it would play out. She was a guinea pig, and whatever was in that crate was somehow going to be a part of her experiment.

She looked at The Hawk. The rest of his men were busy, scurrying about in the gym, some of them still guarding Julie's team.

Julie herself was unguarded — there was no point in wasting a man on her — and it strangely made her feel even more alone. No one was bothering with her, as if she wasn't even in the room.

As if she were already dead.

The two men and the one called Mance walked over to her carrying the box they'd unpacked from the crate. They set it down about ten feet away from her, letting it fall a few inches to the wooden floor.

"Careful!" Morrison yelled. "Stuff in there's worth more than all three of your miserable lives, combined."

One of the men nodded, but Mance and the other soldier did nothing to acknowledge Morrison's words.

The Hawk was busy setting up three chairs on the side of the room. Julie was going to be a sideshow, an attraction at a private carnival.

*One for The Hawk,* she thought. *Who are the other two chairs for?*

The rest of the men would stand guard, obviously, their massive assault rifles far more than would be necessary to keep her and the other four members of her team in place.

There was a knock at the door behind Julie.

The Hawk straightened up, ordered a few of his men to continue with some task she couldn't hear, and then he turned and marched to the door.

She heard it open, heard the clacking of heels on the hardwood floor.

*It's her.*

Daris Johansson appeared to her right, trailing behind The Hawk. "Welcome, Ms. Johansson," The Hawk said.

"Garza. Thanks for setting this up." She looked at her watch, then over to Julie, then back at Vicente Garza. "I thought we were going to use the FBI guy?"

Julie stiffened, looking over at Roger Derrick, standing near the wall a head taller than the man guarding him. *I'm just a fill-in for the real target. A test run.*

"Ms. Richardson here was, uh, *available*. She's been more than willing to cooperate thus far, and I don't suspect she'll be changing her mind."

Daris nodded. She looked coolly at Julie.

*Bring it, bitch*, Julie thought. *You and me. Right here, right —*

"I can see how Derrick's replacement would be a suitable test subject. She did seem a bit 'on edge' when we first met. She'll do fine."

"Good," The Hawk said, extending his arm down toward the chairs. "Please, take a seat. We're almost ready."

The men seemed to speed up at hearing this, and within another minute the soldiers who weren't guarding Julie's team had all lined up near the wall, next to the forklift and pieces of the crate. Morrison took a seat next to The Hawk, with Johansson sitting on the Raven-shadow leader's opposite side.

The box next to Julie and the rolling cart on the opposite side of her sat unmanned for the moment.

The Hawk stood up, walked over, and turned to face Johansson. "Our chemist's work is complete, and we have been able to extract the scopolamine-like residue from the silver."

Julie's mind raced. *Silver? Extract the chemical?*

She thought back to the very first conversation she and the team had had regarding this mission, back at the cabin. Mr. E had told them about the theft at the pawn shop, then the murder of the old widow. Both had been related to a small vial of some sort of rock, or mineral.

*Silver.*

"My team was unable to locate the remainder of the silver, unfortunately, but as you predicted, Ms. Johansson, we were able to create a suitable alternative to the real thing. The synthetic material, we assure you, will be a perfect replacement."

Johansson shifted in her chair. If she was upset about Ravenshadow's failed attempt to find Meriwether Lewis' treasure, she didn't show it. She watched Garza, tracking his every move.

*She's as sharp as Roger Derrick said she was*, she realized. *She's taking everything in, memorizing every detail.*

*So she can use it later.*

Julie was still spooked with the whole ordeal, but she realized that there was a strong chance that she was *not* going to die here. At least, not from the 'test' of this material. She'd already been injected with a sample of the drug and survived. It had been a painless experience, and though she had no recollection of what she'd done, or told Garza, while under its influence, she felt confident that this test would be no different.

She just needed to bide her time. There was no escaping, not now. Even if she could somehow get her zip ties off, and get to the door, and open it and run out without getting overtaken by the men in the room, Reggie, Derrick, Joshua, and Ben were still in there.

It wasn't worth the risk.

No, Garza might kill her, but it would come after. He wouldn't leave her in the chair in the center of the room. It would be somewhere else, somewhere where the cleanup wouldn't be as messy.

So she waited. She tried to play Daris' game, to take in the information. She didn't have a plan, nor did she think there was any way to make one without having any control, but she watched and observed anyway.

The Hawk reached down to the cart once again, and once again popped open the box sitting on its top. He retrieved another syringe, but instead of reaching down for a jar of fluid next to it, he walked over to the package on the other side of Julie.

"This is just the first batch," The Hawk explained. "We will be ready to ship immediately after our test today, if you still have the buyers."

Daris nodded.

"Wonderful. In that case, my team is also ready to begin production at scale."

The Hawk opened the package and tore away the cardboard from the top. He reached inside and pulled out a jar identical to the ones scattered on the rolling cart. He filled the syringe again, from the top of the jar.

"That won't be necessary," Daris said. "There are still some controls that need to be in place first. We can't have this stuff flooding the market, if it… if it does what you say it does."

The Hawk laughed. "Oh, it does, I assure you. Just wait."

The Hawk walked over to Julie and jammed the needle into her upper arm.

## SEVENTY-SIX

BEN PUSHED FORWARD, TESTING THE soldier's willingness to engage.

It seemed, apparently, the soldier was *more* than willing. He spun out the bottom of the rifle he was holding, the butt of it swinging up into Ben's gut. Then he continued the motion, this time rotating the weapon horizontally on its axis, hammering the side of Ben's head.

Ben went down. He saw stars, two Julie's, and two of everything else.

"You — you —"

The sentence he had formed in his mind failed to come out. The words were there, but his mind refused to participate. He rolled his eyes around, hoping to dislodge any sluggishness in his head.

It didn't work. He still felt dizzy, and now nauseated.

"Try it again, kid," the older man said. The Ravenshadow soldier was shorter than Ben, but he looked to be in his late forties. A stubble-darkened chin shoved out from a chiseled jaw, and Ben could see flecks of gray floating in the facial hair.

Ben stood back up, the man's rifle, now righted, following his every move.

"I really would like to hear this thing go off in here," the man said. "Try it again."

Ben glared at him, his jaw stiffening. He put his hands up, surrendering.

Then he looked over the man's shoulder, toward the center of the room.

*Julie.*

He wanted to call out to her, to see if his words had returned. He opened his mouth and felt the dizziness grow once again.

*Julie.*

She was there, the man called The Hawk standing next to her. He had just shoved a needle into her arm, and he and the woman, Daris Johansson, seemed obsessed with Julie's reaction.

Ben tensed up, also curious about what drug Vicente Garza had put inside her. *What would it do? How long would it last?*

And, most importantly, *what are the side effects?*

Julie's head fell backwards, her eyes open wide. She began to mumble, loudly, and Ben could hear it from his position against the back wall.

The soldier in front of him didn't move, didn't divert his eyes from Ben. *He thinks I'm going to try something again,* Ben thought.

And he realized he just might. Julie needed him, and she needed him *now.*

Whatever 'test' this was would eventually end. And then what? What would The Hawk do with Julie? What would Daris do with her?

He'd seen the way Daris Johansson looked at Julie. Contempt, disgust, hatred. She hated Julie, and she'd hated Julie the moment she'd met her. Ben never understand the cattiness of women, and why they always seemed to be secretly trying to one-up the other, but this was beyond simple hierarchical maneuvering. This was deeper, something Johansson carried with her.

Even now, Daris was leaning forward, literally on the edge of her seat. She had an odd look on her face, a combination of pure, childish curiosity, and fury. Her eyes burned with hate, but her slight smile seemed to imply she was enjoying this.

Julie's head snapped forward again, and she looked right at Ben.

He watched her face, trying to determine if the woman she loved knew who he was in that moment. If she could see him. Her eyes flitted back and forth once, quickly taking in the rest of the room. At this point there was no one behind Julie. She sat in the center of the gymnasium, her back to the opposite doors, and all the Ravenshadow men as well as The Hawk and Daris Johansson were standing or sitting in a wide arc around Julie.

He, Reggie, Joshua, and Derrick were all standing with their backs to the wall in front of Julie, but they each had a soldier, weapon drawn, guarding them.

Julie's face scanned Ben's, but there was no reaction. She was blank, empty.

"Ms. Richardson," The Hawk said. His voice had changed. No longer was he the confident leader, the intimidating figure of power for his men. His voice was calm, almost gentle, and as he addressed Julie Ben wondered if the man's voice was part of the test — perhaps the tone of the man's voice affected Julie in some way.

She turned to look at The Hawk.

"Hello again, Ms. Richardson. I'm glad we could talk in front of the rest of these people. Ms. Richardson, do you see these people?"

The Hawk made a point of drawing a wide half-circle with his open palm, showing Julie the room.

"I do," Julie said.

Ben's heart raced. He hadn't heard Julie's voice since...

*Since before the phone call.*

He'd heard her scream, cry out, beg, but he hadn't heard *her* in so long. Her normal, day-to-day voice.

He was hearing it now.

Whatever was affecting Julie was causing her to be completely collected, at ease. She felt no strife, no pain, and she had no care in the world for the four men — four friends — standing by at gunpoint.

"Good, Ms. Richardson." The Hawk looked over at Daris, who gave him an approving nod. "We are going to move directly into the proceedings."

He walked over to Julie's over side and knelt down. "Ms. Richardson, can you please point to your fiancé?"

Julie's arm lifted up immediately, and she pointed.

At Ben.

He shifted, but so did the soldier in front of him. *Try it,* he thought, remembering the soldier's words.

"Very good. And what about the rest of your team. Can you point to the FBI agent, Roger Derrick?"

She pointed.

"And can you —"

"Cut to the chase, Mr. Garza," Daris' voice suddenly called, breaking into the gym. "I need to know if this drug works, or if we have to go back to the drawing board."

The Hawk seemed annoyed, but he righted himself and stood up. "Of course, Ms. Johansson. I know we are pressed for time."

Garza took a knife from his pocket and began cutting Julie loose from her ties. Ben watched her face, but there was no grimace of pain, no acknowledgement whatsoever that she could even feel the bindings being released.

He then walked over to where Daris and Morrison were sitting on the side of the gym and held out his hand. Morrison reached behind his back and pulled out a handgun, a large 9mm, that he'd had tucked into his belt holster.

Ben swallowed.

The Hawk returned to Julie's side and held out the weapon. "Ms. Richardson, please take this weapon."

Julie reached up and took the weapon.

"Ms. Richardson, you know how to handle this weapon, correct?"

Ben knew she did. It was a Glock, a standard-issue 9mm that could be found all over the world. Easy to use and clean, and easy to break down for storage and transport. Reggie had trained her on it himself, and Ben and Julie would often challenge each other on the small shooting range — a stand of trees behind the cabin — once or twice a week.

She nodded. "I do."

"Good."

The Hawk walked forward a few paces, toward Ben's wall.

"Ms. Richardson, please follow me.

Julie stood up and trailed behind The Hawk. When Garza had reached the side of the gym Ben was standing on, he stopped. He moved sideways over to the soldier standing in front of Joshua, then stopped again. Julie followed, now standing next to Garza.

"Ms. Richardson, who is this man?"

"Joshua Jefferson."

"And do you know him well."

"Reasonably well. We're friends."

"I see. And how long have you know Mr. Jefferson?"

Julie thought for a moment. "Probably six, seven months."

"And do you like this man?"

She nodded. "I like him. He's a good friend, and a good leader."

The Hawk chuckled. He spun his head around and looked at Daris, who was turned in her chair so she could more easily face the proceedings happening at the side of the room. Ben saw her face and noticed the same expression. The combination of rage and satisfaction.

His heart sank.

He knew what was happening. He'd waited too long to make a move, and now —

Reggie, standing next to Ben, caught his attention. The soldiers in front of them were watching their boss and Julie, unable to help themselves. Reggie motioned again, and Ben met eyes with him.

Reggie mouthed something to him, but he couldn't understand.

Reggie repeated it, this time nodding his heard toward Julie.

*Get Julie.*

Ben knew that's what he was trying to say, and yet he couldn't understand. *What is the plan? What are you going to do?*

Reggie shook his head, a frustrated look on his face, then he turned and stood straight again, facing the soldier in front of him.

The Hawk leaned in a bit to make sure Julie could understand him, but Ben could still hear the words he spoke.

"Ms. Richardson, please shoot Joshua Jefferson in the head."

Julie immediately complied, her arm coming up quickly. She aimed, and Ben saw Reggie lurch forward, catching his soldier off guard. Julie was now behind Reggie and the soldier, and Ben couldn't see her or Joshua.

But he heard the gunshot.

# SEVENTY-SEVEN

THE GYM BROKE OUT INTO absolute chaos.

Ben reacted quickly to the gunshot, but the soldier standing in front of him did not. Ben rushed him, taking him to the ground, and he wrestled the rifle from the man's hands.

Before he could get a shot off, the man coughed a spattering of blood and his eyes froze in place, open as he died on the gym floor.

Ben looked up. Reggie was there, suddenly and surprisingly, and had jammed a knife — one he had taken from his *own* soldier's belt — into Ben's soldier's neck.

Then Reggie was gone. A quick burst of assault rifle fire echoed loudly in the gym, but the shots sounded far off. Loud, but not near Ben's location.

He focused on the next threat. Two of the Ravenshadow men were preparing to aim his direction.

He dove down, flat onto the gym's hardwood floor, and tried to smash his large frame down as much as possible. Another burst of gunfire erupted over his head, and a second sounded, one of the rounds landing into the soldier he was hiding behind, the human shield doing its job.

Ben grabbed for the man's rifle and found it close enough to his left hand. He pulled it up, checked it quickly — he had never shot this one before, but the mechanism was familiar enough — and rolled it around and set the barrel of it on the dead soldier's back.

He aimed, fired. Twice. One of the men went down, but the other was still running toward him.

He fired again, and the man fell.

Ben didn't hesitated. *Two down, two already dead*, he thought to himself, counting the men he'd just shot and his and Reggie's soldiers.

The trouble was, he wasn't sure how many soldiers there had been *before* the fight started.

"Ben! The door!"

Reggie's voice cut through the firefight, and he looked up to see Daris and two other Ravenshadow men running toward the exit, the same doors he and Joshua had entered from. He swung his assault rifle around and fired three bursts of three rounds each.

It did the trick. None of the runners were expecting the shots, and the first two bursts took out the nearest man's legs, while the last burst hit Daris in the shoulder. She went to the floor, grabbing at her arm.

The man on the other side of her found himself exposed, in the open, without a weapon ready. Reggie fired from next to Ben, after having picked up his soldier's weapon, and the man went down.

"You good?" Reggie shouted.

"Not now," Ben said. "Where is —"

Then he saw her. She was walking in a circle, dazed, near the chairs where Morrison and Daris had been sitting.

"Julie!" he shouted. "Over here," he yelled. "Walk over here!"

Julie looked at him, still no recognition on her face, but she complied. She began to walk toward Ben.

Ben couldn't see Joshua or Roger Derrick, but he did notice a group of three soldiers running across the gym, aiming for the doors that led into the rest of the building. He considered firing but realized Julie was about to walk into his path.

Two bursts rang out, and one of the soldiers fell. Another burst, and the other two were hit.

*How many left?* Ben thought. *How many more do I have to kill?*

Julie was close now, about halfway to Ben's location. He wanted to run out and grab her, but he knew the risk of being shot — by one side or the other — were astronomically high.

It had only been thirty seconds since the skirmish had begun, and already it was slowing down. Ben could see five men lying on the floor, dead, and he quickly realized they were all Ravenshadow men.

*Come on, Julie. Hurry up.*

Julie was still walking, painfully slow, but she was making progress. He motioned for her to hurry, but she either didn't understand or refused to respond to the hand signal.

Then Morrison was there, behind Julie. Ben didn't see where he'd come from, but he was there, at the side of the gym.

Aiming a pistol at her back.

Ben lifted the rifle again and began to aim.

Morrison looked up from his aim and smiled at Ben, and then fired.

Julie went down.

Ben felt the air escape his lungs. He couldn't breathe. Couldn't shoot, couldn't move. He rolled over, trying to slide forward —

The Hawk was standing over Ben then, also smiling. Like a bird looking at a worm.

Ben twisted around quickly, trying to pull the rifle around fast enough to get a shot off, but —

The Hawk fired his handgun, the same 9mm Julie had used...

Fire shot through Ben's body, all centered around his stomach. Excruciating pain told him everything he needed to know.

Another shot, and this time Ben felt his eyes growing heavy. His thigh was bleeding, profusely, and he could feel every ounce of blood draining away through the two holes in his body.

*No...*

He wanted to cry, to scream. But there were still no words.

He saw Reggie run out of the gym, following a soldier who'd gotten back up and headed for the door. Roger Derrick was still missing. Daris Johansson was lying facedown on the floor, but she was moving, slowly trying to roll onto her side.

But The Hawk and Morrison were still there. Julie was somewhere, too, but Ben couldn't see her. He tried craning his neck around, but any movement whatsoever seemed to cause more pain than the actual gunshot wounds had.

Ben watched, the room dark and fading fast, as The Hawk turned and joined Morrison, then walked toward the exit.

He felt rage, more than he'd ever felt, but it was contradicted by the pain. The searing pain that rendered him immobile.

The Hawk stopped next to Daris. She had successfully rolled over, and he saw her good arm raise up, beckoning for one of her men to help her.

The Hawk didn't hesitate, didn't even speak. He lifted the pistol and aimed.

Then he pulled the trigger, and Daris' arm fell back to the floor, just as Ben's world went dark.

## SEVENTY-EIGHT

REGGIE HUGGED THE TWO WOMEN standing in front of him.

"It's great to see you again, Ms. —"

"You'd better call me Cornelia, my boy," the spunky grandmother said. She smiled, however, and embraced her grandson's new friend.

Roger Derrick smiled as well and reached his hand out to the woman standing next to his grandmother. "Roger Derrick, FBI."

"Mrs. E," the woman said. "Pleasure to meet you. I truly appreciate your help with this matter, and for keeping our team safe."

Reggie looked down at the ground.

"And I'm sorry for your loss," Cornelia said.

Neither Reggie nor Derrick spoke. *What was there to say?* Reggie thought. Their mission had failed, miserably. They hadn't been able to stop Daris, and The Hawk — Garza — had made off with the drug she had been trying to improve. The test had worked — Reggie had seen it with his own eyes, used on Julie. They hadn't needed the Jefferson treasure at all.

Vicente Garza's team was gone, but Reggie knew better than most that a replacement squad was only a phone call and some training away. There would be some time needed for Garza to train them, but time was something they didn't have much of.

The longer they waited, the better equipped Ravenshadow would be to fight back. Reggie needed to find them, and bring their leader to justice, before he could rebuild.

And Joshua…

Reggie felt the wave of emotion. He was a good man, a confident and qualified leader, and he had died in vain.

He could still see the black body bag on the gym floor, the bustling crowd of FBI and local SWAT, as well as streams of Philadelphia police, moving around in the cavernous room. The hardwood floor creaked under the weight of the people, and it bled with the real blood that had been shed by both sides.

There would be a funeral, but since Joshua Jefferson had no living relatives, it would be small. Reggie, Ben, Julie, Mr. and Mrs. E, and Roger Derrick. Possibly a few friends he'd made in Brazil.

Reggie didn't know what religion, if any, Joshua had followed, so their plans for the man's burial and service were a challenge from the beginning. Mr. E was currently working on it, and he'd informed them all that it would be a simple, easy service that honored the man and his work.

But there was *other* work to attend to, and Mr. E had sent his wife to Montana to meet up with Reggie and Roger Derrick, who'd also invited along his grandmother. She wouldn't want to miss this, he'd told Reggie, and Reggie quickly agreed.

They had planned the quick excursion, booked a chartered helicopter to fly them into the same bowl they'd seen the Ravenshadow group land in, and were now standing outside the same small cavern he and Derrick had been led into at gunpoint only two days earlier.

Today, however, they were the only humans in a 20-mile radius. No soldiers, no men trying to kill them, and no hostile helicopter pilots.

"This is it?" Cornelia asked. "I hope you boys are going to carry me inside, ain't no way I'm crawling in there myself."

Derrick laughed. "No, Grandma, we had a scan taken of the entire mountainside. There's a much larger cavern up there." He pointed up the sloping face of the mountain, almost directly west of where they now stood.

"Well then why in the world didn't we land up *there*?" Cornelia asked.

Derrick grabbed her hand and pulled her along, careful to ensure she didn't lose her balance. The old woman was rugged, easily taking on the moderate hike. Still, at the pace she was going, it was going to take a half-hour to get to the top of the rise and find the cavern's entrance.

The GPR scan had indeed revealed a large room inside the mountain, hidden beneath the rock. It appeared to be connected to the smaller cavern they had already explored, and if they were lucky, the hole they'd seen would be wide enough to allow them access by descending into the cavern.

Reggie wanted to explore it, and he'd argued that the vein of silver they'd seen in the cave before might just have been hinting at a larger deposit of silver.

Roger Derrick was happy to oblige, considering his FBI team that had finally showed up had no need for his help at this point. They were hard at work trying to locate The Hawk and Morrison, and Derrick's boss expected him to take some time off and recover for a few weeks.

A spelunking adventure was just the sort of 'time off' he'd needed.

They reached the top of the rise in only fifteen minutes, but they stopped there to allow Cornelia Derrick catch their breath.

"So you were in Australia?" Derrick asked Mrs. E.

She nodded. "A reconnaissance mission, really. Had we known what *you* all would be put through, I never would have flown all the way over there."

"Did you find anything useful, at least?"

"Not really. I tracked down the pawn broker who'd had her shop vandalized, but she was unaware of the widow's murder."

"Did she know what the item was that she bought from the widow?"

"She may have. I do not think she was involved, in the way Daris Johansson was, but simply a close friend of the widow, who felt for the old lady and wanted to make sure she would not go hungry."

"Which explains why she gave her so much money for the artifact," Reggie said.

"And why it got Daris' attention. She must have had The Hawk's team murder the widow."

"I believe that was the case, yes," Mrs. E said. "The widow had ties to the APS, from many years ago, and this item was likely passed down in her family through generations, each of them explaining to the next in line how valuable this little rock was."

"Unlucky," Derrick said. "She had *no idea* how valuable it was. Or that people were willing to kill for it."

"Do we know what it was?" Reggie asked. "Daris seemed to think it was silver, from the Spanish Treasure Fleet of 1715 that shipwrecked."

"It is likely," Mrs. E said, "though we can't be sure. The silver would indeed be valuable, if from just the historic standpoint. The only treasure found from the wreckage, and it was in Meriwether Lewis' possession all along."

"Given to him by Thomas Jefferson."

Reggie reveled in the historical significance of such a discovery, if it were in fact true. But the piece of silver was gone — Daris' team had stolen it, and whether they'd ever see it again was something Reggie wouldn't bet on.

They began moving again, this time unimpeded by any hills or difficult bouldering. The path in front of them was flat, easy to move over, and even Cornelia seemed to be enjoying herself. They walked for another ten minutes until Derrick stopped and pointed.

"Over there," he said. "Look."

Reggie squinted, but couldn't see anything. He waited for Derrick to walk over to the location he'd been pointing at, and only when the large man was standing directly in front of it could he see it.

A hole, in the ground, set up on a slight incline. About three feet wide, and only a foot tall.

"That little sliver?" Cornelia said. "Again, I hope you carry me in there."

"I will, Grandma. But we're going down by rope."

Her eyes grew wide. "I'll tell you what. How about I stay right here, safe on the ground, and play lookout?"

Reggie and Derrick laughed. "Sounds good, Grandma. Don't want you breaking a nail."

"Or losing any of your, uh, *hairpieces,*" Reggie added.

She smiled at him and then sat down right next to the cave. "I can at least hold a rope or something."

Derrick was already rigging up the climbing rope around a tree opposite the cave entrance. He'd brought plenty of gear, and Reggie grabbed a carabiner and began working on his belay line.

"Last time I was climbing was down in Antarctica."

"Yeah?" Derrick asked. "You'll have to tell me about that some time, too."

"You'll have to get me drunk first," Reggie shot back. "And there's not enough bourbon in the world."

Derrick laughed, then tossed a rope to Mrs. E. "Here, why don't you lead? You've missed out on all the good stuff so far."

She grinned, then wrapped the rope around a leg and made a makeshift 'seat' from it. She backed up to the sliver, then laid down on the ground and slid backwards to the hole. She went in feet-first, testing the line as Derrick belayed her.

Reggie guided her progress with a flashlight, and he saw that the floor of the cavern was only ten or twelve feet away. She landed, untied herself, and let Derrick pull the rope up for the next spelunker.

Derrick helped Reggie down next, then followed behind by rappelling into the hole using the secured line and a carabiner. Reggie guided him to the floor, and when he'd finished, the three of them safely in the cave, Mrs. E turned on her own flashlight and spun in a slow circle.

Reggie followed her beam, adding to it his own. The cave was nearly a perfect half-circle, cut out of the mountain by an underground spring-fed river that had dried up long ago. The walls were smooth, and, like the previous cavern they'd explored, there were no stalagmites or stalactites anywhere on the floor or ceiling.

"There," he said, pointing to the right. The cavern narrowed to a crawl space, then finally to a tiny point, nothing but a black hole in the wall. But from this hole a thin strip of silver and quartz emerged, running the length of the wall and up onto the ceiling.

"That little hole is probably all that connects this cavern with the cave we were in," he said. "And that's the little vein of silver we saw. Mostly quartz, I'd guess, but it has some flecks in it."

"Yeah," Derrick said. "No wonder the Ravenshadow crew didn't find anything. There's no way to get here from there."

"You boys — and girl — hurry it up down there!" Cornelia shouted, her voice nearly inaudible from outside the cave. "I'm getting hungry, and I didn't see a Burger King anywhere nearby."

Reggie smiled, then continued following the strip of sparkling rock to the other side of the cave.

"There's nothing in here, either," Derrick said. "But Lewis' crew could have used it for a good shelter."

"Sure," Mrs. E said. "Until it starts raining."

Reggie realized she was right — even though the water would flow downhill, into the first cave, it would be slowed when it hit the narrow hole connecting the two caverns and start filling up this one, like a downstream lake that had been dammed, filling up until the dam was opened.

"Looks like our sliver goes up and then back down over there," Reggie said. "Uphill. And there's another narrow gap, but I think it's tall enough to crawl through at least."

The cavern they were in was more of a fattened crescent shape than a bowl, with tapering ends on the east and west sides. He walked up, toward the western side of the cave, and shined a light into the hole.

"Yeah, definitely opens up again back in there," he said, bouncing the point of his light around on the walls in the room at the other side of the tunnel. "I'm going to push through see if there's —"

He stopped. Backed up a bit, shined his flashlight back where it was a moment ago.

"What's up?" Derrick asked.

"I — I think there's…"

Reggie cut himself short. The flashlight bounced left and right off an object, but he focused on the enlarged shadow it created on the back wall of the next room. He pushed forward on his hands and knees a few more inches, still focusing on the shadow.

Without a doubt, it was an object made by man. The shadow on the wall was of a right angle. The corner of something.

Something that looked like a box.

## SEVENTY-NINE

REGGIE'S HANDS SHOOK AS HE unfastened the clasp on the weathered box. The box itself was in fine condition, as if it had been free of rainfall and spring water the entire time it had been in the cave. But the leather straps that had been tightly fastened around the box were starting to deteriorate, the dried bands nearly pulling apart in some areas.

Reggie could have easily removed the leather straps by simply pulling hard on them, but he was dealing with an antique. An artifact of historic significance, one that would be the talk of the American History community for years.

*The Jefferson Treasure is real,* he thought. *This whole time, Daris was right.*

Meriwether Lewis had brought this box here, the single chest making it through a cross-country trek and halfway back before being brought to rest, until this moment, in this cavern.

And Reggie was going to open it.

He had balked at the request, but Derrick told him it was only appropriate for Reggie to do the honors. He'd lost a good man, a team-mate, two days earlier, and the memory of Joshua Jefferson deserved to be honored in this way. They'd found it, together, and they deserved to open it together.

Still, Roger Derrick couldn't stand completely out of the way. He was right next to Reggie, the taller man crouched down and looking over Reggie's shoulder, a video recording on his phone rolling as Reggie carefully undid the straps.

The first strap fell to the floor, a powdery dust floating up from where it had struck the rock.

"Oops," Reggie said. "I'll have to be more careful with the next one. I'd like to open this thing without damaging any of it, so we can at least get it out to the world the way we found it."

"So we're not going to loot it, then, and steal the treasure for ourselves?" Derrick asked.

Reggie grinned. "Now that you mention it, sure. How about an 80/20 split?"

Derrick winked. "Sure thing — I did do most of the work, so 80% my way is probably fair."

Reggie unfastened the second leather strap from the front of the chest and this time carefully rested the leather band on the floor of the cavern.

"Okay," he said. "Here goes nothing."

Mrs. E was holding the flashlight for Reggie to see, but she pulled out a phone from her pocket as well and began recording.

He lifted the corners of the box, slowly, ensuring that the chest was structurally sound. Satisfied, he pulled up, allowing the hinges on the back to do their job. The lid creaked, then continued upward in Reggie's hands.

He opened it fully and Mrs. E moved the flashlight so they could see.

"My God," Reggie whispered.

Derrick whistled. "Is — is that a human skull?"

Inside the chest, lying in the center of the great box, was a single skull. Worn and faded, the skull seemed to be from a fully grown adult human. It had none of the bleached, clean look of skulls Reggie had seen before, but instead had an almost sullied appearance, as it it had been stripped of its flesh quickly, and thrown into the chest with haste.

Reggie nodded. "Has to be. And look — there's something written on it."

Reggie grabbed Mrs. E's flashlight as they all leaned in for a better look, and sure enough, scrawled on the back side of the cranium, were two words:

*Thine Captain.*

"Thine Captain?" Reggie asked. "What in the world?"

"No idea," Derrick answered, "but look at what it's sitting on."

Reggie only then noticed that the skull was resting on a thin, sinewy sheet, and that neither the skull nor the sheet were on the floor of the chest.

"It's… covering something."

"And I don't think it's just a cover," Reggie said. "Here, hold this guy."

Without hesitation he reached into the chest and pulled out the skull. Derrick gasped, but cradled the skull in his arms like it was a football and he would be tackled at any moment.

"Look at this," Reggie said. He had lifted a corner of the thin strip of leathery paper and shined the light onto the underside of it.

"What — what is it?" Derrick asked.

"It's a map."

"A map?"

"Yeah, it has drawings and markings on the other side of it, in different colors."

Derrick whistled again. "And what's that beneath it? The stuff it's sitting on?"

Reggie grinned a huge smile that overtook his entire face. He plowed a hand down into the stuff beneath the lifted corner of the sheet and pulled out a few of the items.

Small, roundish coins fell through his fingers. Some were more lumpy, as if they had been poured from a different mold, or just molded poorly, while some had straight sides and had a more polygonal shape.

"Coins. Silver and a few gold," Reggie said. He dropped all but one and held it up to his face. "From the Spanish Treasure Fleet."

# EIGHTY

JULIE STOOD OVER BEN'S BED, listening to the sound of the man she loved breathing normally.

*Such a small thing, really,* she thought. *To be enjoying nothing more than the sound of a man's breathing.*

But it *was* no small thing; Ben had been close to perishing from his gunshot wounds. He had lost so much blood, so quickly, that the EMTs that had arrived shortly after the FBI men and women had been ready to declare him dead.

But she wouldn't let them. Neither would Reggie. He was still alive, and he would stay that way. They'd better fix it, or she'd…

She'd passed out after that from her own abdomen wound, and apparently Roger Derrick had caught her before she'd fallen. She woke up in the hospital, three rooms down from Harvey Bennett, a nurse and a doctor standing over her bed. Reggie and Derrick had visited, as well as Mrs. E. Mr. E had even made an appearance on the small TV mounted to the wall above her bed. They'd each recounted the story — the cave with Lewis' treasure, the skull, the map, and the coins.

*Within the silver lies the gold.*

And the gold *did* lie within the silver. Most of the silver coins were, as expected, minted from pure silver, likely from somewhere in South America. But some of the coins weren't coins at all but some sort of powdery substance that had been dried, fired, and stamped into the circular objects that resembled the rest of the coins.

They were fake, but they weren't just intended to be counterfeit coins.

Instead, they were intended to be a method of transport for the plant that Daris' security team had identified: the plant related to the Borrachero found in South America, but this particular strain much more potent — and much more useful as a drug.

Mr. E had the coins sent to a laboratory, which had quickly found the plant's genus and species and sent back a stern warning about the dangers of its unregulated usage. It was an interesting concept, to be sure: hiding a drug within another treasure. But the team knew the real truth:

The Jefferson Treasure was not the real treasure at all.

It was just the map.

Thomas Jefferson had paid Meriwether Lewis to hide the map, to keep a record of its location but not reveal to the world what the second president had possession of. The secret died with him, relegated to a cave in Montana and a very select few people in his line of succession at the American Philosophical Society.

But Lewis wasn't comfortable playing the game. He knew that a weapon of this caliber, of this immense power, was not a secret he was willing to keep. So he had traveled back to Washington, DC to document his knowledge with the powers-that-be of the age.

He had only made it halfway.

Meriwether Lewis, at age thirty five, had been murdered in his sleep in a small inn on the Natchez Trace, because of his knowledge of the Jefferson Treasure. The weight of it made it hard to believe, but Julie knew it was the truth. She had seen what people would do to possess this strange drug, to be able to test it and refine it.

And The Hawk had it. Somewhere out there, he had it, and he was working on it.

Perfecting it.

After three days of recuperating, she'd asked to see her fiancé. They'd resisted, but they had never met stubbornness like hers. They made her a deal: let him wake up a day after the blood transfusion and they'd let her into his room.

Ben, of course, woke up.

She was standing there now, staring down at him, watching and listening to the rising and falling of his chest. A machine beeped on a stand nearby, while a nurse walked in and out, checking metal clipboards and *tsk*ing at some medication or another. Julie ignored the man, focusing instead on Ben.

*I'm here, Ben,* she thought. *And I'm not going anywhere.*

Ben's eyes fluttered, and he groaned. A deep, soft groan.

"Are you whimpering?" she asked, grinning. "Like a wounded bear cub?"

He squinted. "Wh — who are you?"

"Come on, Ben. Don't —"

"Lady, I'm serious. You'd better start explaining yourself before…"

Ben's face melted into a smile, though it appeared painful. He groaned again, then coughed, which caused an even deeper groan.

Julie swatted his arm.

"Hey," he said. "Don't hit me, I'm *really* injured."

"I made sure to hit you on a spot that *wasn't* hurt."

"How do you know I wasn't shot in my arm, too? You were gone half the time, traipsing around with that crooked-nose guy."

"*Traipsing* around?" Julie scoffed. "You don't even know what that *means*."

"It… it's like… you know, moving and… going around and stuff."

Julie cracked up. "You're ridiculous, you know that? Ben, you got shot *twice*."

Ben gave her his best innocent look and tried to shrug. "It was nothing. You got shot, too, and I've been through worse."

"I feel like you say that every time we get done with a mission or adventure or something."

"Maybe every mission or adventure gets worse."

Julie sat back, smiling. She felt like herself once again. The drug had worn off completely, leaving her without a single aftereffect, and the side effects of nausea and headaches had mostly subsided. Ben was back, and they were together. There was nothing else she wanted or needed in that moment.

Except for one thing.

"Well maybe it's time for an even *harder* mission."

He raised an eyebrow at her. "You mean to go figure out what this 'treasure map' thing is that Derrick and Reggie found?"

Julie's jaw dropped. "H — how do you already know about that?"

Ben groaned, louder this time, and the bathroom door behind her opened. She whirled around, her heart racing…

And Reggie stepped out. Followed by Roger Derrick.

"*You!*"

Reggie's huge smile was plastered on his face, and his hands were up, near his head. "I'm sorry, Julie… we just, uh, happened to be in the area, and —"

Derrick's head fell. "It's my fault. We know you wanted to see him first, but I called the hospital. From my office."

Julie knew what that meant. *The FBI called the hospital. No wonder the staff let them in.*

As hard as she tried, she couldn't be mad. "I'm glad three have already caught up a bit," she said. "But next time watch yourself or I'll actually *put* you in the hospital."

Reggie continued grinning, walking over to the chairs at the side of the room, just in front of a large window.

"I like the pink curtains, Ben. You pick those out yourself?"

Ben sniffed, pausing as he searched for the proper words. "No."

Reggie looked back and forth at the three others in the room. "Really, Ben, we need to work on your comebacks. *After* we work on your *defensive* skills."

"Hey, at least I was *in* the action. You two pretty boys got off without a scratch. What were you doing, hiding in the corner?"

"Anyway," Julie said, stepping in, "I was just telling Ben about that *new* mission we need to get started on."

"Oh?" Derrick asked. "My grandmother keeps asking about it, says she wants to be part of it somehow, and —"

"I wasn't talking about *that* mission," Julie said, her smile and eyes turned fully on Ben. "I was talking about something else. Something even better."

Ben's eyes darted from one person to the next, and finally back to Julie.

"I'm talking about our wedding, Ben."

He smiled, just a bit, then looked at Reggie and Derrick. "I told her, each mission gets harder. And she still wants to keep going."

"She's crazy, man," Reggie said. And then he stood and walked over to Ben's side and clasped his hand around his shoulder. "And if you ever mess it up with her I'll beat the crap out of you."

Julie cleared her throat. "Thanks, Reggie. But I assure you, if he does that I won't be needing your help."

# THE PARADISE KEY

Continue the fun! Turn the page for a preview of the next Harvey Bennett thriller, *The Paradise Key!*

The Paradise Key

# PROLOGUE

THE CHILD SAT BETWEEN THE two trees, waiting for death. He knew it would come — his caretaker had told him as much. The two trees were supposed to provide comfort, the feeling of protection.

But they couldn't provide safety.

He would die, just as they all would. It was not a thought that plagued the boy as much as concerned him. He knew about death, as any child of his age did. He understood it, agreed with it. *Everything must die.* The jungle around him, the trees and plants and animals, all of it must go. It was told to him through the stories shared around the fire, and sometimes directly from the older children when they brought him out with the men to hunt.

He was not allowed to speak in those times, but that did not mean he misunderstood. He knew what death was, and he knew it was coming. The two trees offered solace, but not hope. They, too, would die. Not today, maybe many years from now, but they would shrivel up and disappear just like his ancestors — the mothers and fathers of his own mother and father, just as they had. His caretaker, too, would die.

But death was an easy thing to understand when you looked at it from a distance. When it was a story told by an elder around a fire, or a memory described by a hunter after a kill. The child remembered these stories, and they flooded his mind as they came back to him.

He remembered his parents' death, one after the other, struck down by a blow from a neighboring tribe, one even more ruthless than his own. They were gathering food, their only son between them. He was crouching in the brush when they came, not even slowing to search the area. So he had survived, and he had simultaneously learned of death firsthand.

He remembered the feeling. The quick snap of life taken away, not fully recognizing that he would never speak to them again. They were gone, taken brutally and quickly, yet all he could remember was the way his mother had dropped the food she was carrying, spilling it all over the forest floor. The waste of it; he hadn't even reached out to grab it.

He had returned to the village to find it had not been changed in any way. His family and friends worked, played, and slept, as if nothing had happened. No one had known about the attack until he had told them. There was a ceremony, as there always was, and then he was given to a caretaker and life had resumed as normal.

Death was here, and it was coming for him.

He felt it, stronger than he had felt it when it had taken his parents.

Stronger even than the feeling he had when listening to the stories. The forest took everyone, they said, but the taking was always far more brutal when it wasn't the forest doing the work.

He heard the screams. They'd found the village. His home, his caretaker. All of them were there. There were no hunts today, and there were no scouting groups. Everyone would be at the village, preparing the food and clothing. There were three women carrying children, and they would need preparations for their young. Everyone was there, everyone screaming. The men howled with sporadic war chants, not together and organized but scared, knowing.

He crouched closer to the forest floor. He touched the ground, feeling the forest crying out in complaint at the attack. It was all a part of them, a part of *him*. He was old enough to know that now. They were connected, the forest and the trees and the animals and the tribes. Even the tribes they fought, they were connected.

His caretaker had explained it once, in terms of a story that he had forgotten the details of. But he knew the premise: they were all part of the *same* story, part of the *same* world here. Life was far more important than bringing upon the death of others.

So he had run, without thinking and without looking back, when he had first heard the heavy trudging of the feet, crashing through the forest. They were not another tribe, they couldn't be. They were too loud, too big. He was scared, but he was able to push it away and focus on running toward the trees. The trees where the ceremony had taken place, the trees that towered over their small village. He had climbed them once, only to discover that the trees were hardly the tallest around. They poked at the canopy and even scraped it some places, but the inside roof of the canopy itself, he was surprised to learn, was formed by the bottom of even taller trees.

The world was a large place, he had learned that day. It was large, and he was a small part of it. He didn't know how large — his people didn't worry about things like that — but he was always fascinated by the thought of it. The trees he had come to trust loomed over him, reminding him that even when he thought the biggest thing around was staring down at him, there was something even bigger out there, somewhere.

Those bigger things were crashing around, causing the screams and subsequent silencing of his people back in the village. He didn't dare look, for fear of what he might see. Maybe it would be over soon, but what then? Where would he go? The nearest tribe was hostile, and they would jump at the chance to bring death upon him just as the bigger people were bringing now.

So what to do? He waited, crouched and small and shivering in the forest, the two trees offering what little they could — solace and sympathy, which he could feel through the ground. They were telling him that they were there, but that they were sorry they couldn't do more. They were sorry they couldn't help, that they —

One of the bigger people crashed around and came to his spot by the tree. He thought for a moment, hoped, that they wouldn't see him. That he had somehow become a tree, or a bush, or something that didn't seem like it needed death brought upon it.

But they saw him. He knew it when the feet of the thing turned toward him, the shadow of it creeping out and over and around him, consuming him like its owner didn't even need to move to know it had captured him. He sobbed, once, then told himself to be strong. *Death comes upon us all*, he told himself. *Death is not the enemy.*

The feet stepped forward, and he smelled the person. This was certainly not another tribe. The legs were covered, as well as the feet. Some sort of cloth or skin, bunched in places but sturdy, stained with the dirt and mud of trekking through the jungle for days. Splashes of silt on the things covering the feet. Not sandals, but something bigger. Stronger.

The feet moved again, but not toward him. They simply shifted, moving slightly, leaving an ugly streak in the mud. He felt a hand grasping at his hair, which he had kept just long enough to cover his ears. It was black, oily and nice, some of the nicest hair of any of the children his age. He was proud of it.

The person's hand ripped his hair upward, and he yelped in pain. His hair stayed attached to his head, and he stood up with the force of the person's hand. He fought against the hand, but the hand was wrenched around his hair and yanking him up, up.

He cried now, openly. He was a child, and he knew children were allowed to cry. They were encouraged to think about their tears with wisdom, as reactions to a particular feeling. If one could understand the feeling, one could fight against the tears, it was said.

He knew the feeling — pain. Loss. He wanted his caretaker.

He wanted his mother. His father.

He wanted *anyone*.

He looked up, forced to by the hand that was wrapped tightly into his hair. The face was of a man's, but the man's skin was light, not bronzed by the sun but browned by the mud. His eyes sparkled, a light-greenish blue that the boy had never seen before.

He was suddenly scared. The fear gripped him tighter than the hand in his hair, and he sobbed once again. The man stood, frozen. Examining him. Questioning him.

He wanted to speak, to ask why. To understand. The tears kept coming. The man kept staring.

Finally the man released his hand from the boy's hair and reached into a bag he was wearing. It was also made of skin, some sort of leather that the boy hadn't seen before. The man watched the boy with those sparkling eyes as he fumbled through his bag.

He retrieved something from inside the bag, held it tight in his hand. It was sharp, pointed and clear, like water that had been hardened into a tube shape and placed around a shiny, bright point. He pointed it at the boy, near his left arm.

The boy shook, sobbing.

The man looked down at the boy, smiled. He opened his mouth and spoke words the boy didn't know, didn't understand.

"You will do just fine, boy," the man said. "Just fine, indeed."

# ONE

THE MAN WATCHED HIM THROUGH the glass, his hands and arms pressed up against the pane, like an animal anxiously awaiting for his captor to feed him. The man cocked his head sideways, watching Dr. Joseph Lin as he fumbled around with the gray, metal box in his hands.

Dr. Lin knew what the man wanted. It was what they all wanted. *Freedom.*

The man was docile, tamed through hundreds of cocktails of medications and sedatives, but Dr. Lin couldn't help but feel like the subjects were always watching for a mistake, for an opening. Something they might be able to take advantage of.

He wouldn't fail today. He hadn't failed yet, and he wouldn't now. The task was simple, mindless even, but then again that was why it was easy to fail when performing it. The mundane tasks were the ones to be worried about — a person could go through the motions much more easily with these types of tasks and assignments, and that's where mistakes were made.

It wasn't the large-scale, complicated things he needed to worry about. The multi-layered tasks that required a nuanced understanding of something or a delicate hand were, in a way, easier to perform flawlessly. He was the best in the world at those types of things, which was why he was here in the first place.

It was the *easy* things, the simple and repetitive that he needed to be most careful with. That was how he — a world-renowned scientist — had ended up doing the job of one of the lab assistants; the girl had been careless, she had lapsed and allowed a small oversight to become a large mistake.

And here in the lab, mistakes were unacceptable. The assistant had learned that the hard way, but in this environment there were no second chances. There were no lessons — it was perform or be removed.

Dr. Lin was disappointed with the girl's removal, as she had been a good assistant. But he also understood the reasons behind it. He was calm, centered, not allowing the assistant's removal to affect his work, and for that he was proud. He could do the work of a lowly assistant. He could stoop to that level and get the job done. It would mean a later night for him — his own work sat by idly awaiting his return — but he would finish.

The man brushed up against the glass, an inquisitive look on his face. Dr. Lin watched him for a moment. The man turned his head again, his eyes searching the doctor's face. There would be nothing there for him to read, Dr. Lin knew. Even if Dr. Lin had been the type of man to allow the weakness of emotion to show on his face, this man on the other side of the glass was incapable of recognizing and acknowledging it. That function of his neural programming had been stifled to the point of being useless. The 'empathy gene,' or 'emotional resonance,' the marketing suits upstairs called it. The ability for a human to recognize, acknowledge, and respond to a particular micro-expression.

Dr. Lin opened the metal box. The lid snapped up abruptly, as if it had been fitted for a slightly smaller box, and Dr. Lin peered inside. He reached in and grabbed the first tube that lay on top of the pile. He closed the box, then set it down on the cart that sat next to him. He reached for the syringe on the cart and placed the tube inside the back of the syringe.

The man inside watched him. Waiting. Knowing what was coming but unable to react in any overt way.

Dr. Lin pressed the tube down into the syringe until he felt and heard the slight popping sound that told him the medication's seal had been opened and was ready for injection. He turned to the man behind the glass and held up the medication.

"Time for your medicine, 31-3," he said. His voice was quiet, soft-ened from exhaustion. He'd already been awake for twenty-four hours and he knew his job would continue for at least another ten. He was glad there were no meetings scheduled, no reason to use his voice much.

The man eyed him, not nodding or shaking his head. He stared.

Waited. Knowing. Patient yet unaware of his own patience. Hungry, yet sated. Just... *there.*

Dr. Lin slid open the fist-sized door in the center of the glass, revealing a rectangular hole. The scent from the other side wafted out, a mixture of sweat and feces. He made a face, then recovered. The man did not move. Dr. Lin moved back toward the hole, involuntarily holding his breath. The man nudged toward the rectangular hole, then stopped about three inches from it. He looked up at Dr. Lin, waited for him to nod to continue, then he pushed himself against the glass. The skin of his right arm, just below the shoulder, was pushing through the rectangular hole in the glass now, and Dr. Lin reached down and aimed the point of the needle at the open area of skin.

He leaned forward. Pushed the needle onto the man's skin. The man watched, interested, yet unaware of what was happening. Dr. Lin held his breath, an old habit. *Helps to calm the shaking,* his residency supervisor used to say. *Everyone shakes, even when we don't realize we're shaking.* He poked the skin, watched the man for any reaction. There was none. He drove the needle down, farther into the layer beneath the skin, right before it hit bone.

Dr. Lin continued to watch the man's face with his peripheral vision, another habit yet knowing what he would see. *Nothing.* The man was completely unfazed by the needle, just as he had been every other time. Dr. Lin waited a beat, then began pushing the medication down through the syringe, out the hole in the end of the needle, and into the man's bloodstream.

If there was pain, the man didn't register it. He stared up at Dr. Lin, both men nearly eye to eye, and Dr. Lin moved his gaze to focus directly on the man's face. Still no change. Still no registration of emotion. No registration of anything, really.

But Dr. Lin felt something. He felt the wave of surprise, the bizarre realization of what was happening. Or rather, what *wasn't* happening. The scientific reasons behind it, still unknown to him or anyone else, the hundreds of studies and research papers he'd read and pored over, the talks and presentations he'd heard and seen over twenty years of practicing medicine. His mind raced through these resources but every time it came up blank. Every time there was a disconnect, as if there were something out there he was forgetting that would explain everything.

But there *was* nothing out there. He had checked. They all had. For years, they'd checked and re-checked. They had done the research, the tests, analyzed the results. None of it lined up with what they were seeing here. Dr. Lin was the best in the world at this very thing, and he had been stumped for going on three years. It was a professional slight, and he intended to fix it. He would find the answer, and he would publish it. He would prevail, as he had with every other challenge throughout his distinguished career.

He finished administering the dosage of medication and looked back down to the syringe. He extracted it from the man's upper arm slowly and carefully, just as he had a thousand times with a thousand patients, back when he was merely a practicing physician. It was a learned habit, one he could do in his sleep. But he *didn't* approach the task lightly. Something simple like this, the extraction of an empty syringe following the medicating procedure, seemed like such an easy, simple thing.

But that was how mistakes were made. By assuming one was better than the task they were performing. By taking their expertise for granted. That had happened to his assistant, and now she was no longer with him. So he did not take the task lightly. He extracted the syringe purposefully, rolling it slightly between his thumb and fore-finger to ensure none of the serum would drip. It would also prevent any blood from pooling around the tiny wound.

He focused on the syringe, taking his time. Ensuring there were no mistakes.

That was why he didn't see the man's face. Dr. Lin was focusing on the wrong thing, looking at the wrong area behind the glass. He was gazing intently at the man's shoulder and the syringe he was carefully extracting from it, so he didn't notice at first.

Then something in his subconscious called his attention to it. Screamed at him, as if begging him to look up and take note of the man's face once again. He felt the syringe shake in his grip, faltering a bit. He blinked. Once, twice. Then he looked up and saw the man.

31-3. *Thirty-one dash three* was how they said it. The thirty-first group of subjects they'd been testing, and the first male in the group. Related to all of the other subjects in some way.

Dr. Lin took a step backward, then another. Steady at first, then nearly stumbling. He felt the rolling cart behind him as he backed into it, still unable to take his eyes of the man behind the glass. He stared, knowing the man was staring back at him and within seconds the cameras mounted around the room would analyze the situation and automatically send in an alert. They would see Lin staring, record the infraction, and log it in the security manifest.

But he didn't care.

How could he? What he was seeing right now was simply… unexplainable.

And yet his entire job here was to find just this very thing, and then explain it. It had always been a tall order, but then again no one seemed to believe that this was even possible.

He continued to stare, even as he heard the beeping warning sound alerting him to his mistake. Dr. Lin held his pose, staring straight into the eyes of the man on the other side of the glass, his mouth opening and shutting slowly as he tried to comprehend.

*Why? Why now? And how?*

The man stared back, his eyes as expressionless and as stoic as ever, but it wasn't his *eyes* Dr. Lin was focusing on.

It was the man's mouth, upturned slightly at the sides.

The man behind the glass was smiling.

# TWO

"ANY IDEA WHERE IT'S FROM?" Reggie asked. He was standing near the television, where Mr. E and his wife were onscreen, staring back at him.

Mrs. E shook her head. *'Unfortunately, no. We will get the lab scans back next week, if not sooner. But — and we are no scientists — our initial investigation leads us to believe that the skull is from Central or South America.'*

Mr. E leaned in, his characteristically stoic expression tightening just a bit. He moved as though he had no neck, no ability to shift his head from its fixed spot on his upper body. *'My wife is correct,'* he said, *'but she downplays her knowledge of anthropology.'*

"Well, I'll take her word for it then," Reggie said. "Somewhere in Central or South America. How can you tell?"

Mrs. E looked at something offscreen for a moment. *'Human anatomy, and differences in cranial structure among known regions of the world. I just ran a simple search, really. The results are promising, but, as I said, we are not scientists.'*

Reggie nodded. He was sitting in the makeshift office space he'd added to the corner of a small apartment living room in Anchorage, Alaska. The organization he worked for — Civilian Special Operations — had furnished a one-bedroom apartment in the nearby city while they finished their additions to the full-time operations headquarters. He was excited to see what the cabin-turned-headquarters would look like, and he was even more excited to see the reaction of the cabin's owner.

Harvey Bennett was a close friend of his, but he couldn't imagine a person more resistant to the massive renovation taking place at his home. He'd purchased the cabin a couple years ago, but the CSO had recruited Ben and Reggie, offered Ben enough money that it was stupid to refuse them, and began turning his beloved two-room log home into a modern communications oasis. There would be an entire wing added, with a second story, and enough square footage inside to fit three more of Ben's cabins.

Reggie smiled as he thought about it. Ben would pretend to be upset, complain to him and his fiancee, Julie, about it, but secretly love the new, upgraded space. He would enjoy working there with his friends, and he would enjoy the company.

"So if the lab comes back with the same results, will we be able to narrow it down from there?"

Mr. E nodded. *'Yes, but the lab should be able to do that for us. They have the ability to isolate the specific ancestral geography of the specimen, assuming they have matching samples in their database.'*

"I see," Reggie said. "So it's a waiting game."

They were waiting on the results of laboratory testing on a human skull they discovered two months ago in the Rocky Mountains, near Glacier National Park in Montana. The skull had been found with a map, silver and gold coins, and had been stored in a chest inside a cave. All of it had been very exciting, and Reggie's interest in history and longing for adventure had immediately been piqued.

But from the moment they'd brought the skull in to the lab, Reggie knew it was going to be a 'waiting game.' Wait for the skull to be admitted, wait for a team to begin the analysis, wait for results. He would have been surprised with the slow pace of work if he hadn't been in the Army for years. Government work *always* took forever. The lab itself wasn't a government lab, but it was funded with government money.

He had been anxiously awaiting an update for over a month, and his weekly check-ins with Mr. E hadn't been enough to keep him sated. Now, to hear that they were so close to an answer, yet still without a definitive direction to explore, he was growing more impatient.

*'Unfortunately yes,'* Mr. E said. *'But we are optimistic the laboratory will be able to point us in the right direction.'*

Reggie pushed the chair away from the glass desk. It was a corner desk, two simple slabs of tempered glass on a cheap aluminum frame that he'd picked up used, but he liked the simplicity of it. It didn't interfere with the rest of the room, gently falling into the background of the space unless he wanted to see it. Aside from the desk, the chair, and a couch, there wasn't much else in the room for decor. He had a television, but it was currently being used as his computer monitor, so the couch sat in the center of the living room and stared at the blank off-white wall.

He stood up and stretched. He felt cooped up in here, in his temporary home. He had nowhere to go, and he wasn't one for walking around aimlessly in search of something to do. He hated boredom, feared it like the plague, and sitting in an Anchorage apartment with no one but a computer screen to talk to was starting to wear him down. He had books, but he'd already read them. He had food, and while he liked to cook, he didn't like the temptation — anything he cooked he would eat.

So he was frustrated. He wanted out, wanted something to do. He wanted a mission.

"Come on, E," he said, talking to the opposite wall, knowing the microphone was more than capable of picking up his voice in the otherwise quiet room. "I need to *do* something. Can't I at least get a jump on it? Take a flight to Mexico City or somewhere south of the border?"

There was no response. He waited. Still nothing. He whirled around, expecting to see that the video had temporarily seized. The internet connectivity in the apartment was fast, technically within the realm of what the marketers at the telecommunications companies called 'high-speed,' but compared to what he was used to it was no better than dialup.

Mr. E owned a telecommunications company, a small one in terms of market cap, but through a brilliant career of networking and hobnobbing with the DC crowd, he had built an empire with very little overhead and the cash flow to rival the slickest of Silicon Valley startups.

He looked again at the screen, pulling the two-dimensional people on it into focus. Mr. and Mrs. E stared back at him in stark contrast to one another. Mr. E was thin, graying, almost frail in build and leaning into the camera. Mrs. E. was wider in the shoulders, taller, built like a Russian tank, and smiling a wide, unnatural grin.

He almost laughed. He had seen the woman smile — they had spent some time together in Antarctica and shared pleasantries on numerous occasions after that, but the wide, sheepish grin was *his* trademark, not hers. She didn't wear it well, either — it came across as an odd, forced rhythm, like something she knew she needed to do but not something she really knew *how* to do.

"Wh — why are you smiling?" Reggie asked. He was genuinely confused.

*'We* are *sending you somewhere,'* Mrs. E said. *'So pack your bags.'*

"I never got a chance to *un*pack," he replied.

*'Perfect. Your flight leaves tomorrow morning, first thing. Can you get a ride to the airport?'*

He nodded, pulling out his cellphone and holding it up to the camera. "Kids are using these little computer thingies for all sorts of things, including scheduling rides to the airport and calling people."

If Mr. E got the joke, it wasn't apparent on his face. He sat, motionless, onscreen. Mrs. E somehow found a way to widen her smile. It stretched her cheeks out, making her face look gaunt, like a skeleton that had been forced through the business end of a steamroller.

"Okay," he said. "What's the ruse? Where are you sending me?"

Mrs. E flashed a glance at her husband, who revealed nothing. *Man, that guy can act,* he thought. Mrs. E, gleaning nothing from the man sitting next to her, turned back to the camera and faced Reggie.

*'Cozumel, Mexico,'* she said.

"Cozumel? That's an island, right?"

*'It is. And you need to be there by 3:30pm, local time, tomorrow.'*

He frowned. "Why? I thought we didn't have conclusive data from the lab yet?"

*'We do not,'* she said. *'There has been a development elsewhere, and we would like you to follow up on it.'*

"A development?"

*'A situation, if you will.'*

He walked back to the television screen and computer monitor, pushing the chair out of the way. "What kind of *situation?* And what am I supposed to do in Cozumel?"

Mrs. E told him, all while her husband sat silent next to her.

*No way,* he thought. *There's no way I can do that.*

*He'll kill me.*

# THREE

"DR. LIN," THE MAN SAID again, calling his attention back. "Would you please explain to us your infraction?"

Dr. Lin swallowed. He wasn't good with confrontation. He was a scientist, a doctor, ready to analyze and prescribe and confident in his abilities, but he had never been comfortable with this sort of thing. The board sat around him, three of them in person and four of them digitally filling the screens that curved around one edge of the room.

He watched their expressions, tried to read them. The people on the screens — all calling in from their locations around the world — were most difficult. They seemed to feel his scrutiny, and were working to mask their emotion by staring straight into their cameras. He looked at the man who had spoken, then swallowed again. *This man was incapable of hiding his emotion.*

And right now, the man's emotion was especially easy to read: he was livid.

"*Dr. Lin,*" he said a third time. "Do I need to remind you of the gravity of this —"

"N — no," Dr. Lin stammered. "I apologize, I — I was just collecting my thoughts."

The man's eyebrow rose, but he still looked as though he were frowning. "Well I do hope you've *collected* them all." He made a point of checking his watch, a large flourish of spinning it out and around his wrist while bringing his forearm out in front of his torso. If Dr. Lin hadn't been so terrified, he would have been annoyed.

"Yes," he said. "I have. Again, I am sorry. My deviation was remedied, and it is one that will not be repeated, under any circum —"

"There were to be no deviations under any circumstances *in the first place*, Dr. Lin," the man said. The woman on the screen behind him was nodding.

"Yes, I — that was clear, yes. I apologize."

The man stared.

"It was a surprise to me as well. I was unaware of the applied effect of patient 31-3's latest dosage, and —"

One of the board members listening in on one of the screens, a man Dr. Lin had never met in person, interrupted. "Dr. Lin, would you kindly speak as though you are addressing a group of *non*-medical professionals?" the man's voice was thick with a southern American accent, and he smiled a bit as he said it. Dr. Lin didn't for a moment believe the smile.

"Sorry. Yes, I only meant that I was not aware that the dosage *had* an immediate effect."

"Is it your job to be aware of these things?"

Lin swallowed again. "Yes."

"And why were you not aware?"

"I — I was attempting to ensure..." he stopped, looked at the southern gentleman, then continued. "I was trying to make sure there were no mistakes with the medication."

"So you weren't looking at the subject."

"I was not, no. But the reaction would have taken me by surprise nonetheless, whether or not I was watching the patient's face."

"Subject," the man said, correcting him.

"Yes."

"So you were surprised by the *subject's* reaction? Why?"

Dr. Lin frowned. *Do I really need to spell it out for them?* These were the men and women who had *built* this company. Surely they didn't have time for this.

"It will all be detailed in my report, which I will prepare and —"

"I'm most certain it will," the man said. "But since we were already having a board meeting, and I'm sure we are all most interested in what you discovered, I would ask that you indulge us."

Dr. Lin nodded. "Very well. I was administering a dosage of the medication we have designed specifically for 31-3. It was the fifty-third dosage in a nearly two-year timespan, and it was a routine operation."

"For 'routine operations' such as these, do we not have laboratory assistants?"

"We do," Lin responded. "The woman on duty was recently removed."

The man watched Lin's face. He knew everything already, so this was a game. Cat and mouse, and Lin felt the trap closing around him. "And for what reason was she removed?"

He felt the tension in the room shift, tightening up. The woman and man on the screen to his left leaned in toward their computers. The man to his right, sitting next to Dr. Lin's boss, the man conducting the interrogation, looked up at him anxiously. They didn't know the full story, and Dr. Lin was hoping they would have found out some other way than this.

*Any* other way than this.

"She — there was a discretionary incident."

"Also involving 31-3?"

"Also involving 31-3."

"And what was the outcome of that incident?"

"She was relieved of her duty."

"She was *removed*," the man corrected.

"Yes."

The man looked down. There was a manila folder on the tabletop in front of him, but it was closed. He placed his hands on it, felt its surface, then jerked his head back up and stared at Dr. Lin. His bright, large eyes bored into Lin's, and he could almost feel the pressure, pushing him backwards. This man got high from encounters such as this. He *longed* for them. The dimple on his cheek grew, punctuating the man's thoughts.

"So, Dr. Lin, there was an infraction involving your laboratory assistant, and she was removed. A day later you were administering a dosage of the subject's medication and *you* were found to have instigated a infraction. What, may I ask, was the nature of this deviation?"

Dr. Lin sighed. He knew there was no sense hiding behind it now. They would all find out, so he might as well attempt to control what was said. He shifted on his feet.

"The man smiled."

"The *subject* smiled?"

Dr. Lin nodded. "He did. Just after I had finished. He smiled, directly at me."

"You provoked him."

"I did no such thing," Dr. Lin said. "I administered the dosage, extracted the needle, and I saw him smiling."

The woman onscreen sniffed, moving around in her chair to vie for attention without coming across as rude. The man addressing Dr. Lin stopped and turned, waiting. "Dr. Lin," the woman said. "Is it not *impossible* for these subjects to be able to experience what you are describing?"

"We believed that to be the case, yes," Dr. Lin said. "The dosage has always had the unintended side effect of removing the ability for our subjects to respond to emotional stimuli. Smiling, waving, arching of eyebrows — these are all impossible tasks."

"Yet, 31-3 *smiled* at you."

"Indeed."

The man took over the interrogation once again by clearing his throat. "Dr. Lin, the interest of this meeting with you today is not to discuss the nature of the subject's response — that will come at a later time. Rather, we would like to discuss the nature of the deviation itself."

"I understand, and I will ensure that no more such deviation will —"

"Dr. Lin," the man said. "You are our best researcher. Hired away from one of the world's most premier health institutions. We cannot afford to waste a valuable asset such as yourself."

Dr. Lin bowed his head. "Thank you."

"That said," the man continued, "we cannot afford *any more infractions*. Provoking the subjects, as you wrote early on, will only lead to wildly unpredictable outcomes."

"But I didn't *provoke* —"

The man held up a hand. "We must inform you that any more deviations or infractions by anyone on your team will result in your immediate removal from this facility."

Now he was angry. He had *never* been 'removed.' He had never even been let go. He was the best, the one in demand. He waited for offers to come to *him*, not the other way around. How dare these people stomp on his reputation and his career solely out of retribution for an event they couldn't even *understand*? How dare they assume something had happened one way, when he had specifically told them —

"Dr. Lin? Do you understand?"

Lin's face darkened. He couldn't help it any longer. He was a pawn to these people. A tool to use, abuse, and discard. Like his assistant had been. She had made a mistake, and she knew the consequences. But he wasn't an *assistant*. He was an esteemed practitioner. He wasn't one to make mistakes. He hadn't *made* a mistake when he'd stared back at the man behind the glass. He *knew* what he was doing, and he was *observing* the subject. His patient. They didn't understand that.

And he knew that now. They *couldn't* understand that.

"Yes," he said. "I understand perfectly."

# FOUR

07:34AM. BBC WORLD NEWS.
FOR IMMEDIATE RELEASE.
LIMA, PERU.

*Initial reports seem to indicate the discovery and subsequent disappearance of a previously uncontacted tribe of natives in the Peruvian highlands. Located 300 kilometers north of Cusco, Peru, near the dense Parque Nacional Alto Purus and the closest city of Alerta, the last known location of the mysterious city of natives is known only to those who have traveled to visit it.*

*Dr. Rodney Barrett, esteemed archeologist and professor emeritus of Classical Archeology at King's College, reported in an unpublished journal article that 'there have been signs of habitation in the town, though recent investigation has turned up nary a thing. Quite a puzzling instance, indeed.'*

*Barrett declined to be interviewed, citing jetlag due to his recent jaunt to the jungled region bordering Brazil and the Amazon Rainforest, but the journal article he plans to publish next month indicates evidence that Barrett believes the tribe to have been a docile, localized group of native peoples.*

*'The town is really much more like a small group of huts, still well-maintained, with a few larger structures intended for the larger requirements of civilised life. As an example, the structure we are calling Main No. 1, situated in the central area of the 'town,' is a large, rectangular building crafted from reeds and wood poles, and we believe it to be the central gathering place for ritualistic medical practices as well as meal gatherings.'*

314

*While this reads typical of many such Amazonian settlements both in the Basin and in neighboring countries, Barrett went on in the article to describe a conversation with one of his colleagues at King's College regarding the most unique feature of this find:*

*'The town itself has been abandoned, and from what we can gather, it was abandoned quite recently. It really is a curious thing; the town seems to have simply disappeared. There was smoke from an earlier fire, there were canoes filled with lines and tools and even the recent catch of the day. The main hall was found to have a working smoking pit, filled with the meat of fish and game and well past the point of being done.'*

*Dr. Barrett's archeological team, consisting of eight Peruvian- and Brazilian-born porters, three undergraduate work-study students, and three graduate-level archeology students, have all corroborated Barrett's theory.*

*Said one student of the expedition's final destination: 'It truly is quite strange. There was a town, and every indication that this town had been — quite recently — inhabited insofar as a working town should be, but there was no one around. No human interaction with us, and none on our return trip. Very spooky indeed.'*

*Barrett will make a statement to the department chair and attending guests in a week, though no specific date has been set; further information will be posted online as it is received.*

# FIVE

HARVEY 'BEN' BENNETT LOOKED OUT at the cerulean
waters of the Caribbean. The points of the waves lanced up and down,
miniature pinpricks of lighter blue against the deep blue backdrop of
the ocean. It was never-ending, and yet it was full, loaded with life and
creatures and an entire world he didn't understand.

He'd never been drawn to the ocean. He didn't dislike it, per se,
but it was something he'd never felt a deep desire to be near. He
preferred the woods, the deep scent of pines and earth, the moist air
and cold winters. Ben had thought long and hard about this, about
why a person would be more drawn to the warm, maritime climate of
a beachfront umbrella than a secluded, cold cabin, but he hadn't been
able to reach a believable conclusion. He had to chalk it up to a simple
difference in personality — some people preferred one, while some
people preferred the exact opposite.

And this was the exact opposite of what he preferred. Again, he
didn't necessarily *dislike* it, but he would never have chosen it as a
retreat. He never would have sprung for the multi-thousand-dollar
vacation he currently found himself enjoying.

This all was Julie's idea, something she'd been pushing him toward
for nearly a year. Juliette Richardson was the only person on the planet
he'd ever met who was as stubborn as him, and for some unbelievably
annoying reason, it made him love her even more. She wasn't going to
take no for an answer when she'd made her mind up, and this vacation
was no exception.

She'd begged, pleaded, and argued, and finally had simply started
planning the trip on her own, fully aware of the power she had over

him. She set the dates, knowing he was otherwise unoccupied and completely free, and she set the schedule, knowing his preferences, tastes, and expectations.

For that reason, he had little to complain about. He was watching the ocean of the southern Caribbean pass him by while sitting on a deck chair on something called a 'Lido Deck.' The railing in front of him blocked the view of the water directly below the port side of the ship, but there was enough water in the immediate vicinity that there was plenty to go around in his vision, all the way up to the point where the setting sun met the flat, horizontal line of the horizon.

He was wearing a tight-fitting bathing suit that Julie had picked out for him. Flowers that didn't look like any flowers he'd ever seen in real life, white on a blue background. The blue was a good color, but he was constantly feeling like the suit was too tight, revealing more than it had been designed to cover. His shirt was lying next to the chair, and whenever a person walked near the chair he felt as though he needed to reach down and grab it, cover himself, and apologize for exposing his upper body. Julie seemed to be able to read directly into his struggle and know exactly what he was going through, which she used to her advantage by poking fun and making jokes at his expense.

The worst of it for Ben, however, was the footwear. She'd purchased matching sets of flip-flops, which she'd claimed were a popular type of sandal worn by many people, but he had never in his life of thirty-three years felt like he'd had less on his feet. He would have been more comfortable in socks. At least socks stayed on his feet. She told him the flip-flops would take practice to get used to, and his argument against that line of reasoning had been that any time of footwear that required 'practice to get used to' was better off staying in the suitcase.

The flip-flops were currently hanging loosely off his feet, the space between his first and second toes the only thing holding them onto his body. They had started to form to his feet, and he was trying desperately to change his mind about how comfortable they had become.

"What are you thinking about?" Julie asked from the lounge chair next to him.

He looked over, taking an extra few seconds to enjoy the *other* view. He had been enjoying himself on the trip so far, contrary to what he'd initially expected. The food was amazing, the entertainment had lived up to expectations, and the overall feeling of relaxation had somehow snuck up on him and set in, against his desire to push it away. But the best part of the trip, hands down, was the view.

Not the view of the ocean, but the view on deck.

Specifically of his fiancee, and her choice of garments for this trip.

Julie was currently wearing a bikini emblazoned with the

Australian flag, the blues and reds and whites all working together to form an image less enticing than the image of the person it was intended to cover.

He shifted in his chair, not taking his eyes off her.

"Ben," she said, "I'm up here."

He smiled, a goofy open-mouthed grin. "Sorry. I — I really like that swimsuit."

"You like *all* of my swimsuits."

He nodded. *Nothing I can say to that.*

"Did you hear me?" she asked.

"About your swimsuits?"

"About what you're thinking," she said.

He laughed. "I was thinking about your swimsuits," he said.

She smiled back from behind large, oval-shaped sunglasses. "Well, *besides* that. What's on your mind?"

He shrugged, looking once again at the endless expanse of blue. "I don't know. Nothing, really. Just enjoying it all."

"Are you?"

He rolled to his side. "What do you mean? Do I not seem like I'm enjoying it here?"

Julie nodded. "You do, but you're also… contemplative. You're not usually lost in your own thoughts."

He stopped and thought for a moment. She was right. *But what am I thinking?* He was confused about it as well. He was sitting on the deck of a massive cruise ship, luxurious and designed exclusively for his comfort and entertainment, with the woman of his dreams, and he wasn't able to feel completely satisfied.

"I… I just feel like there's something else."

"Something else?"

He frowned. "I mean like there's something missing."

It was Julie's turn to laugh. "Ben, you're in the middle of an ocean on a floating 5-star hotel with free food. What else could there be?"

"I know, I know," he said. "It's not that. This — all of this — is amazing. And you're here. It's not the trip, I guess."

"What is it?"

He looked over at her. "Life?"

"Life?"

"Yeah, I guess."

"Sorry Ben, I'm not sure I understand your meaning."

He sensed a bit of hostility in her voice — a warning shot. *Say what I think you're saying and we're going to have a fight.*

He tried to backpedal. "No, it's not about you at all."

She raised an eyebrow.

"Seriously," he said. "I love you. That hasn't changed. But think about where I was two years ago. We had never met, and I was living in a cabin and chasing bears out of campsites."

Ben had spent the entirety of his adult life as a ranger at Yellowstone National Park. It had been a perfect fit for him, a naturally reclusive and isolated individual. When a terrorist threat forced his hand, he and Juliette Richardson had been pushed together to find out what had happened and clean up the mess.

They had grown close and then fallen in love, and their adventures together had taken them from Yellowstone to the Amazon rainforest, then to Antarctica and a quick tour of United States Midwest. It wasn't a life Ben could have ever imagined, and while he felt proud of his accomplishments over the past year and a half, there was still... something.

"You want to go back to Yellowstone? Keep chasing bears?"

He shrugged. "Sometimes it seems to have some appeal."

"I get that, Ben," Julie said, still laying back while the sun bathed her body. Her head was leaned over, facing Ben, and he could see the outline of her large eyes through the dark ovals of her sunglasses. "But everyone has to grow up."

"Grow up?" he asked. He raised an eyebrow, squinted with his other eye. It was a look she would know well.

"Sorry," she said. "I didn't mean it like that. But still, everyone changes," she said.

"Maybe I don't change."

She smiled. "You certainly change less than anyone I've ever met. And that's what I love about you. But still — don't you agree that it's time to move on from the 'strong silent type?'"

He sat up, looked out at the water, then turned to his fiancee. "I'm sorry," he said. "What's wrong with the 'strong silent type?' and more importantly, why do I *need* to change?"

She shook her head. "You're not getting the point. You don't *need* to change, but that doesn't mean you *won't*. Everyone does, Ben, it's the natural order of things."

"Well what am I supposed to change *into*, then?" he asked.

"I don't know, Ben. But you can't just keep moping all the time. We're supposed to be relaxing. Enjoying ourselves. We're getting married in two months, Ben, and you haven't even thought to ask me how the wedding planning is going."

He was beginning to get a little frustrated. After all, he had been the one to bring this all up in the first place, and now she was making their little spat about something else entirely. He didn't ask about the wedding plans because he didn't *care* — he just wanted to marry her, and he didn't care how it all happened. And besides, she was enjoying it. She loved this sort of thing, so he stayed out of her way.

He sighed, reaching down for his drink. It was something with rum in it, a large cornucopia of at least two different liquors, three different fruit juices, and a lot of ice.

A *lot* of ice.

He stared at the melting pot of booze and fruit juice and mostly ice and sighed again. He felt the frustration growing again as he thought back to his earlier conversation with Julie, which had led to an argument about money. She had wanted these fancy cocktails, but he hadn't been enthused about the nearly twenty-dollar price tag for a bucket of ice with some flavor thrown in. She had argued that they weren't really paying for them anyway, that the drinks — like everything else — were on the company's tab, and that he should forget about it and focus on just relaxing.

"I can't relax," he finally said.

"Yeah, we all know that," she said. "Anyone who's ever met you. We know."

"Well, I wish I could. That's all," he said. He was still sitting up, still rotating the slush around in his drink, waiting for a cruise employee to walk by and ask him for a refill.

"I wish you could, too," Julie said. She laid back down on the lounge chair and stared straight up into the sun. It was just past noon, and the deck was hopping with just about every passenger on the boat. Kids splashed and yelled in one of the three pools, while adults and teens vied for a spot in one of the four hot tubs situated around the perimeter of the deck.

And there were two more decks similar to this one, one at the front of the ship and one near the stern, both up one level. He had been amazed at the size of the place when they'd first embarked, and the novelty hadn't yet worn off. Julie had caught him more than once staring up at light fixtures and the elaborate ceiling decorations with his mouth hanging open.

"This isn't about you, is it?" Julie asked.

He looked over at her. She wasn't looking back at him, but he shook his head anyway. "No, I guess it's not."

"Well you'd better figure out what you're going to do about it, Ben," she said. "We're on a boat in the middle of the ocean. You can't change anything here."

He stood up, stretched, and left his fiancée basking in the sun as he went to find a drink refill.

# SIX

HE BALANCED THE DRINK ON the edge of the counter with one hand as he waited for the bartender to give him the check. The thing was inside of a real pineapple, full of rum and juice and all sorts of sweet things. An extra-long toothpick poked through two slices of orange, a banana, and a maraschino cherry before plunging into the wide, open top of the pineapple.

*Ridiculous*, he thought.

Ben had only wanted a Rum Runner, a tiki drink made with rum and banana and usually a type of liqueur like blackberry. It was sweet, fruity, and felt summery, and he liked them. But the drink he was holding now seemed more like the centerpiece at a tropical wedding than a drink. The straw even spun a loop once, and he knew he would be throwing away the cute purple umbrella lodged into the side of the thing long before he brought the drink up to his mouth.

He signed for the drink, turned back to the side of the ship he and Julie had been lounging on, and stopped.

*What the...*

Julie was talking to a man. Her head was thrown back, her knees touching one another as she laughed at whatever it was the man had said.

The man was out of sight, his head blocked by the floor of the deck right above them, so Ben took a few larger strides and came out from underneath the balcony. He felt a pang of jealousy as Julie laughed, wondering who in the world she was —

*No.*

He shook his head, still holding his pineapple.

*It can't be.*

"Reggie?" he asked.

Reggie turned around and beamed. "Ben, welcome back! How are you?" He walked over and extended his hand. "Nice pineapple, by the way."

Ben nodded. "Thanks."

They shook hands, but Ben wasn't trying to hide his emotion. His expression was one of confusion and annoyance, and Reggie apparently could tell. He brought his hands up, backing up a step. "Easy there, buddy," Reggie said. "I didn't come to crash your little date. E sent me."

"So you *did* come to crash my date," Ben said. "Reggie, why are you here?"

Reggie's smile grew. "We have a job."

Ben looked down at Julie, who hadn't moved from the lounge chair. Her laugh had shrunk to a smile, small and light on her petite face. She shrugged.

"What job?"

"We can talk about it — "

"We can talk about it *now*, Reggie," Ben said. "Because we're on *vacation.* And we're not leaving until I've had about forty of these ridiculous pineapple things." He held up the cocktail and swirled it around in his hand. He caught Julie's eye as he stood face-to-face with his friend and coworker. Only right now, at this moment, he didn't feel friendly *or* interested in working.

Reggie just smiled, the gigantic grin on his face almost contradicting the man's eyes. If Ben didn't know him any better he would have assumed that Reggie was faking it, wearing the smile for his sake.

"How did you get here?" Ben asked.

Reggie shrugged. "I walked on. Just went right through the security wall like it wasn't there."

"Really?" Julie asked.

"They're looking for booze, really," he said. "Let's be honest. They're rent-a-cops at best, working minimum wage for the cruise line. They don't care who comes aboard."

Ben squinted into the light, directly at Reggie. "How'd you *really* get here?"

Reggie's smile waned a few notches. "Fine. Got me. I had Mrs. E arrange it. Through the transit authority, couple calls in to the Mexican tourism board, I'm sure. Still though, wasn't really that difficult."

"You just get here?"

Reggie shook his head. "No, I stayed in Cozumel while you were coming in, then I got on the ship that evening. Been holed up belowdecks with a nice crew member named Suarez. Doesn't really speak much English, or at least he wasn't interested in speaking with me."

"Why'd you wait to come find us?" Julie asked.

"You're enjoying yourselves. I didn't want to ruin that."

"Thanks," Ben said, his face belying the sarcasm. "Definitely haven't ruined our vacation."

"What am I supposed to do?" Reggie asked. "Mr. E said it was urgent."

Ben sighed. He took another glance out at the water, at the receding sunlight as the orange orb floated downward, casting its glow out to the far reaches of their world. He wanted to sit here and watch it, like he'd done every other night of their trip, but he knew that was all over. Even though there was no chance he'd agree to whatever scheme Reggie and Mr. E had cooked up, he wouldn't be able to shake it from his mind. It would affect him, and Julie would pick up on that. She could read him like a book, so there was no sense trying to hide his feelings. He was curious, concerned, interested, angry. All of those things, all at once. Reggie had crashed their almost perfect vacation and given it a death sentence, and there was nothing he could do about that now.

"Okay, Reggie," Julie said. "Ben's not going to drop it, and neither am I. Want to grab a drink."

Reggie's mouth grew by another two inches. His smile was contagious, but Ben's internal monologue fought against the charisma of his friend. *One drink,* he told himself. *One drink, hear him out, then back to cruising. Back to my vacation.*

He deserved it, and Julie deserved it as well.

*One drink.*

# SEVEN

THREE DRINKS LATER AND BEN was starting to feel it. Rum, then whiskey, then some sort of cocktail Reggie had explained was Brazilian in nature, complete with a type of liquor called cachaca, a sort of Brazilian rum.

Reggie had lived in Brazil for a few years, running a survival training camp for corporate executives who really just needed a way to feel important once again. He'd explained to Ben and Julie that he'd enjoyed the information, the practice, but hated the clientele. They were all soft, mentally and physically. When Ben's and Reggie's paths had crossed under unfortunate circumstances, they had struck up a fantastic friendship and had been nearly inseparable ever since.

But now, in the dingy, smoky lounge Reggie had chosen for their 'one drink,' Ben felt as though he wished he and Reggie had never met. Here was a man so focused on his job, so aligned with his mission, that he would stow away on a cruise ship to interrupt the vacation of his so-called friends. Ben was frustrated that he had to waste the time hearing his pitch, but he was also frustrated that he *wanted* to hear it.

"Whatever it is," Ben started, "we're not doing it."

"Easy, Ben," Reggie said. "We just got our drinks."

Julie rolled her eyes. "We just got our *third* drink."

They had spent the last hour catching up — while it was difficult to admit that Ben was glad to see his friend, he *was* glad to catch up with him. He liked Reggie. He just knew there was more going on under the surface. There was a *reason* he'd crashed their vacation.

Reggie held up his hands in mock surrender. "Fine, fine. You got me. Drinks are on me, by the way."

"We know," Ben said. "Why are you here?"

Reggie looked at his watch, a ridiculously oversized military-issue thing that Ben had seen him use as a weapon before. "Right now," Reggie said, "we're heading north-ish. Right? Toward Florida?"

"That's where the cruise ends, yeah."

"Mr. E wants us to take a look at something down there."

"Florida?"

"Off the coast of Florida."

"So the Keys?"

Reggie shook his head. "Other side. East of Florida."

Julie frowned. "Like The Bahamas?"

"Farther north, actually."

"Out in the middle of the ocean?" Julie asked. "Seems like that's a bad place to put anything, right out there where it's prone to get hit with hurricanes."

"It is, in my opinion. But that's where we're heading."

"That's where *you're* heading."

Reggie grinned. "I know you're not wanting to get involved, Ben," Reggie said. "But we need your help. *Both* of you."

"We're on vacation. We already covered this."

"We did. But you haven't heard what it *is,* yet."

Ben crossed his arms. The bartender, a man who looked to be about ninety years old, took it as a slight and backed away slowly from the edge of the bar. "Don't need to know what it is. I'm here with my *wife,* Reggie."

"Fiancée," Reggie said. "You got another two months."

Ben glared at the man sitting next to him. "Make your case, and make it quick. We have dinner at eight o'clock." Reggie's eyes widened, but before he could say anything, Ben jumped in. "And *no,* you're not invited."

"Okay, okay. Here's the deal. Mr. E wants us to check up on something in the area. Like I said, off the coast of Florida, about forty miles east of Palm Beach, and twenty north of The Bahamas."

"What sort of thing are we 'checking up on?'"

"It's a park."

"A *park?*"

"Yeah, like a nature park or something."

"A *nature park* in the middle of the ocean?" Julie asked. She grabbed at her glass, a vodka cranberry made with vanilla vodka, a new concoction she'd recently discovered.

"A nature park off the coast of Florida, yes," Reggie said. "I don't really know much more about it than that. But we've got a week-long pass."

"If you don't know any more about it, why does E need us there?"

Reggie shrugged. "I never asked." Ben eyed him, not believing his friend.

"If you had to guess?" Julie asked.

"If I had to guess, I would guess that he needs us there because he's our *boss*, and he *told us to*."

Ben motioned to stand up, gripping the leather arms of the chair and pushing himself upward. Julie's and Reggie's heads snapped over at him. "Ben…" Julie said.

"No. I'm done here," Ben said. He sniffed. The bartender looked over and Ben gave the man a quick nod.

Reggie stood up next, reaching for Ben's shoulder.

"Listen, buddy," he said. "I don't know what this is about. But I know it wouldn't even be on the radar unless Mr. E thought it was important. Crucial, even."

Ben crossed his arms over his chest as Julie rose to her feet. "Don't lie to me, Reggie."

"Ben," Julie said again.

Ben waited. Watched Reggie's face. It hardened, softened again, then he looked down and grinned. "Okay, fine. I know *a little* about what this is about. Not the end game, not even the real 'why' behind it, but I know the motive of sending us there."

"And what's that?" he asked.

"The security team at the park. They were just hired, contracted by the park's employment department."

"And?"

"And it's a company called Ravenshadow."

### 

Want to continue the story? Find The Paradise Key here!

# AFTERWORD

If you liked this book (or even if you hated it…) write a review or rate it. You might not think it makes a difference, but it does.

Besides *actual* currency (money), the currency of today's writing world is *reviews*. Reviews, good or bad, tell other people that an author is worth reading.

As an "indie" author, I need all the help I can get. I'm hoping that since you made it this far into my book, you have some sort of opinion on it.

Would you mind sharing that opinion? It only takes a second.

Nick Thacker
Colorado Springs, CO

# ALSO BY NICK THACKER

**Mason Dixon Thrillers**

*Mark for Blood* (Mason Dixon Thrillers, Book 1)
*Death Mark* (Mason Dixon Thrillers, Book 2)

**Harvey Bennett Thrillers**

*The Enigma Strain* (Harvey Bennett Thrillers, Book 1)
*The Amazon Code* (Harvey Bennett Thrillers, Book 2)
*The Ice Chasm* (Harvey Bennett Thrillers, Book 3)
*The Jefferson Legacy* (Harvey Bennett Thrillers, Book 4)
*The Paradise Key* (Harvey Bennett Thrillers, Book 5)
*The Aryan Agenda* (Harvey Bennett Thrillers, Book 6)
*Harvey Bennett Thrillers - Books 1-3*

**Gareth Red Thrillers**

*Seeing Red* (Gareth Red Thrillers, Book 1)
*Chasing Red* (Gareth Red Thrillers, Book 2)

**Relics**

*Relics: One*
*Relics: Two*
*Relics: Three*
*Relics: Omnibus*

**The Lucid**

*The Lucid: Episode One* (written with Kevin Tumlinson)
*The Lucid: Episode Two* (written with Kevin Tumlinson)
*The Lucid: Episode Three* (written with Kevin Tumlinson

∼

## Standalone Thrillers

*The Atlantis Stone* (previously published as *The Golden Crystal*)
*The Depths*
*The Atlantis Deception* (A.G. Riddle's *The Origins Mystery* series)
*Killer Thrillers* (3 Action-Adventure Thrillers)

∼

## Short Stories

*I, Sergeant*
*Instinct*
*The Gray Picture of Dorian*
*Uncanny Divide*

∼

## Nonfiction:

*Welcome Home: The Author's Guide to Building A Marketing Home Base*
*Expert Blogging: Building A Blog for Readers*
*The Dead-Simple Guide to Guest Posts*
*The Dead-Simple Guide to Amazing Headlines*
*The Dead-Simple Guide to Pillar Content*

# ABOUT THE AUTHOR

Nick Thacker is an author from Texas who lives in a cabin on a mountain in Colorado, because Colorado has mountains, microbreweries, and fantastic weather. In his free time, he enjoys reading, brewing beer (and whiskey), skiing, golfing, and hanging out with his beautiful wife, tortoise, two dogs, and two daughters.

In addition to his fiction work, Nick is the author of several nonfiction books on marketing, publishing, writing, and building online platforms. Find out more at www.WriteHacked.com.

*For more information, visit Nick online:*
www.nickthacker.com
nick@nickthacker.com

Made in the USA
San Bernardino, CA
09 February 2020